The
CABLE DENNING
MYSTERY
SERIES

by
James P. Alsphert

James P. Alsphert
presents

I
DESTROYER
OF
WORLDS!

A
Cable Denning
Mystery

BOOK
13

Published 2019 by Movies of the Mind

Printed in the United States of America

First printing, 2019

ISBN-13: 978-1-64056-011-6

MOVIES OF THE MIND
www.moviesofthemind.net

CONTENTS

CONTENTS continued

PROLOGUE

I Wake Up Screaming

The snake tightened around my neck as I struggled for air. If I jumped from the tower, it would mean both of us would die. But with my arms tied behind my back and a gag over my mouth suspended over a hundred feet in the air, what choice would I have? But the large yellowish reptile's grip was getting tighter around my throat and I could feel my mouth go dry. His unblinking orange eyes stared at me as if he were going to ask me the question, "Shall we go together, buster, or is it gonna be just you?" Then I saw it. The bulky, dull-metal *gadget* suspended from powerful cables that held it in place—it was ominous looking—that thing that was being hoisted up to meet the snake and me. Workmen mulled around far below us in the darkness with only a few battery lights to illuminate the gawky piece of giant metal that resembled a deep-sea diver's helmet.

Finally, the world's first atomic bomb was poised to explode and change the world forever. Somewhere in the back of my mind I knew it was all a nightmare brought about by the resurgence of *Datura* from my strange trip to Kathmandu over a decade ago. But when you're dreamin' it, and you're in the middle of horror, it seems real enough to give you the night sweats. The python had tightened its grip around my neck so that I could barely breathe at all. I staggered to the precipice of the square hole in the middle of the tower where the gadget swayed in the night desert breezes. I tried to yell for help but the snake's vice-grip prevented me from

1

doing so. Losing all self-directed thought, I fell forward and down, hitting my head on the bomb gadget. Suddenly a blinding light scattered my atoms into a trillion particles of light and dust, but I could see—see into the heart of the explosion! Blues, reds, greens, yellows and whites all inter-mixed and I went flying up with the mushroom cloud, higher and higher until the earth was but a big greenish blue ball reflecting sunlight. I had no form. Only consciousness allowed me to be guided as I continued to float out into space, further and further from the planet earth.

The next thing I knew I was on a sandy reddish planet. I was walking toward what could have been a 21st century version of Grand Central Station in New York City. But it, like the rest of the terrain, was all but dead, gasping its last, filled with holes and bitten by the sand and wind for so many eons that it stood...looking like a hunk of Swiss cheese in the cold, red desert. Suddenly I realized I was on *Mars*. Then I saw it. It was neither animal nor vegetable yet was somehow animated. It floated along with the winds of Mars like a jellyfish on the ocean tides of Earth. But it wasn't a real animate object, for at the far end of the sand's horizon I saw the figure of a man walking slowly toward me. He had on a northeasterner's fishing cape and a bright yellow cap— and had the damn 'jellyfish' on a string, like a kite. "Howdy day, mister, howdy day!" he said. "My *trollippe* here has a mind of her own, just like a woman, eh?" he laughed. Then he looked at me with wise old eyes. "You're wonderin' what in tarnation you might be doin' here on this planet? So am I, frankly, lad. But of course, you came from here a long time ago. This is sorta like home to ya. It was *that* planet, down over yonder, we emigrated to because we fouled this one up pretty bad, son...but, as you see, I've come back home to play on what's left of our little cold planet. Soon it will be completely lifeless, a complete nothing...just a little rock in a big empty space of stardust."

Suddenly I felt sick and I had to run, I had to tell the earth people that the same thing was gonna happen to them if they continued to pursue the insane lifestyle they were presently pursuing! I wanted to talk to the man with the 'trollippe' but I had to go...flee from this place and tell the earth people, shout it out to the earthlings, yell it out loud and strong—*don't do it!!*

I woke up screaming. My bed was wet with perspiration and my skin felt like I'd just taken a warm shower but forgot to dry off. I sat up in my bed still blubbering about telling the people of the earth what the assholes were up to, to prevent them from destroying this blue-green gem of a planet! But no one heard me. I was alone. I lit up a cigarette and leaned back into my pillow. Yeah, even if my voice could be heard all over the dear ol' earth right now, it'd do no good. They wouldn't listen. And maybe nobody cared anyhow. Maybe a whole species of people, like planets, have a destiny, too. Here we are on this little tiny patch of time within the Infinite—and it seemed true that many species or beings that had once dwelled upon this world had come and gone, leaving very little trace of ever having existed at all. Yeah, maybe our homo-centric outlook was a blessing. Who in the hell wants to face extinction from ever having been at all?

3

Chapter 1

THE LONE WOMAN
OF SAN NICOLAS ISLAND

Dead Giveaway

In 1945 rumors were that a fandangled new thing called *'television'* would infiltrate every home in America before the end of the century. Germany's *Telefunken* and Britain's *Electrical Music Industries* were the first kids on the block with the new toy. Later the most significant component became what is known as an *iconoscope*, and RCA in America adopted it for little 12" yellowish screens. Soon a vast sea of television antennas stretched from New York City to Los Angeles, from Miami to Seattle. Hell, I wouldn't own one. Radio was food for the imagination. A movie wasn't, really. All the sights and sounds were done for you. No thanks, I'd rather stick to 'old time' radio and let my imagination create the 'movie of my mind.' But one thing television would do...it would further homogenize nations. Take the good ol' U.S.A. Every "public opinion" money could buy would be seen on television. In 1931 Aldous Huxley talked about how "Big Brother is watching you" in *Brave New World* and George Orwell bringing the next step into place with his authoritarian work, *'Animal Farm'*. *"All animals are equal, but some animals are more equal than others."* Increasingly, it would become a corporate-run world with the military heads sitting around with their boots on the tables, drinking daiquiris and hanging out in the background 'just in case.' But I don't know, maybe the people get what they deserve. Maybe Orwell was right, people are parasites. A lot of people are really stupid, me included. So, maybe when the pablum is measured out and served in fun doses, nobody minds, but falls asleep with a bottle of beer, a babe and that ubiquitous glow in the dark living room. Maybe that's the new and future standard of human living.

But in 1945, *radio* was still the peoples' choice. There was a quiz show called something like *"King For a Day"*. The gist of the quiz show was three couples, man and wife teams, were invited to appear as guest contestants. A level of questions were asked and if the wife knew the answer but the husband didn't, she could tell the moderator and the moderator could whisper it to the audience, but the poor sap on the hot seat remained in the dark. She was allowed to give her husband *one clue.* That was it. So he either knew the answer or didn't. If he got it, he qualified for the *Living Getaway* and they would win some great trip to a luxury resort. If, on the other hand, hubby didn't get the correct answer from wifey's clue, then he goes to the Mystery Box to take his chances on *Dead Giveaway*, where things just might not be what they seem.

What no one could've known at the time, was that murder was also on the agenda this particular evening. I wouldn't know it until much later. But what was cooking up in the rafters of the *NBC Theatre* was anything but a happy vacation to Canada. And in the end, this booby prize would indeed prove to be a *dead giveaway!*

Private Dicks in Strange Places

It was Thursday, February 22, 1945. It was George Washington's birthday. He was born on that date in 1732. I remember that because my safe deposit box at the bank has that number on it. Christmas and New Year's Day came and went like the cool wind that swept through the canyons of Griffith Park that winter. After that terrible nightmare, I got up and stretched. I knew I needed to walk off the bad taste it left in my psyche. I guess my awareness of Albert Einstein's fears regarding the creation of a super-bomb haunted my conscious-ness and so I dreamt it out. Ever since that crap I took while in Kathmandu many years before now, I'd had lu-cid and sometimes terrible prescient nightmares about things that were about to happen. So I didn't discount dreaming about being on top of a tower in the middle of the desert with a snake around my neck while the plan-et's first atomic bomb hung over the precipice like a harbinger of doom, death and destruction.

The garbage man came on Thursday mornings and the roar of his engine echoed through the alley in back as I made my way down the stairs to the street. I decid-ed to walk down to Hollywood Boulevard. I wanted to stop by the Broadway Department Store on the corner of Hollywood and Vine to buy a couple of pairs of socks. My old ones were so damned full of holes, even *I* finally considered them unwearable. One thing about bein' a bachelor, with no woman around to see to things like that, a guy has to buy more socks! Fortune smiled and they were having a sale. Hell, at twenty cents a pair, maybe I'd get three pairs.

After I tucked my new socks into my trench coat pocket, I started up the boulevard toward Highland Avenue. From there I turned right and walked up Highland to the Hollywood Bowl. The morning was sunny but cool as I made my way to the greenery that surrounded the area. I walked all the way to the front row center and sat down, looking up at the big shell shaped amphitheatre that the *Allied Architects* had created—never considered as acoustically good as the originals designed by Lloyd Wright, son of Frank Lloyd Wright. I remember in 1929 when this shell went into place, moved on rails by huge trucks. Now there it stood in 1945, looking out at the world of faces who might never know its history. I was listening in my mind's ear to the instruments and voices that had played the Bowl when I noticed a rather heated argument going on over to my right near a hedge by the entrance to the seating area. I thought I even recognized one of the people. It was Dennis Hoyle, a private dick whose office was also in Hollywood. He was pretty honest I thought, a little cheesy in dress and manners, but okay. At least he was a lot better than some of the other private investigators I'd met and dealt with through the years. The other person was a young woman who had the look of an Eskimo and was quite animated with her hands.

Dennis Hoyle saw me sitting in the front row and started toward me. Oh, crap, I thought, there goes my peace! "Hey, Denning!" Hoyle called out to me. The little Eskimo lady followed. "What's goin' on? Waiting for the next performance here or what?"

"Hello Dennis...naw, just gettin' some fresh air," I said.

He came and sat next to me, took his hat off and wiped his brow. "How do you tell someone it's a stupid wild goose chase—hell, tryin' to find someone who probably doesn't even exist anymore."

"Yeah? We do that a lot. What's it about?" I inquired.

The young chubby woman spoke up. "It's about my mother—I know she's out there somewhere! My father left her and stole me when I was barely walking."

"Out *where* somewhere, lady?" I asked.

"San Nicolas..."

"I'm not familiar with that town—here in Southern California?"

"No, San Nicolas Island, mister, off the coast of Ventura..."

"See what I mean?" Dennis Hoyle said. "She's thinkin' I'm gonna take a boat out there and find her lost momma on some damned lost island."

"Lost island?"

"Oh, Mr. Hoyle—I told you me and my sister can go there! It's only about an hour from Ventura in the ocean," the young lady said.

Then he got up. "Good to see ya, Denning...hope business is good." Then he gestured toward the young woman. "Here...I *will* her to you..." He turned, leaving us both together and I may have detected a slight bounce in his step and a little chuckle as he walked away.

"He is a mean man—and he did not believe me, I think," she said.

"What's your name?" I asked.

"Chauga Lowe...I am *Nicolenes* native."

"Hiya, Chauga, I'm Cable Denning." I extended my hand. "Good to meet you." I motioned for her to sit beside me. I lit up a Lucky Strike. "So suppose you tell me your story, missy. Everyone has a story, ya know."

"You are a much nicer man than Mr. Hoyle...he was very irritable with me...he didn't even want to help..."

"Well, he's probably got an ulcer or something. I wouldn't worry about it. So tell me, Chauga..."

"I was born on San Nicolas Island. But I do not know all of what there is to tell. My father was a whaler, my mother a native-born *Nicolenes.* I was two years old when my father came back to the island and stole me away from my mother. That is all I know. Now, I wish to find my mother..."

"So...where's your Dad?"

"He died years ago in San Francisco. I live with my step-sister and her Eskimo mother and father in South Los Angeles now."

"I see. So how many people are on San Nicolas Island?"

"I do not know. But surely, others will know who my mother is."

"Yeah, we can hope so, huh?"

"I can pay you," she said eagerly. "My father left me some money to live. I am going to go to upper school soon. Will you help me find my mother, Mr.—Mr.—"

"—yeah...Cable, just call me that, okay?"

"Okay..."

"Well, let me see...if we can do it in a day...two at the most. I get twenty-five dollars a day plus expenses, which means—aww, hell, just give me twenty a day and we'll call it even, okay?"

"So you will help me find my mother?"

"Yeah, little lady, I guess I will at that. We'll have to hire a small boat as well, maybe out of Ventura or wherever you said. I haven't had a sea voyage for a long time. So that's another expense." I was thinking the last time I did was with the dying Adora Moreno on a skiff headed for Santa Catalina Island. In fact, she died on the ferryboat heading back. That was a dark day in the memory of Cable Denning, private investigator. It still smarts, so I try not to think about it.

Island In the Endless Sea

It was Saturday, February 24th. Sometimes we forget. Those of us who spend most of our lives as land-locked voyagers on a starship called Earth simply don't know. We forget the vast expanse of sea just off the coast of California that extends clear to the Orient, over 6,500 miles away.

Upon checking a map, I realized San Nicolas Island was almost opposite Malibu. Thus from that point we hired a skipper named Earl Jones and basically what he owned was a large fishing boat with two large engines and one big screw. He told us San Nicolas was about 60 miles out there in the choppy seas, but don't tell my stomach that! It didn't seem to affect Chauga in the same way, but about two hours later we pulled into what must've been a small whaling port at one time. It was on the east side of the island, away from the wind and bad weather. San Nicolas Island proved to be a disappointment to me. It was windswept and barren for the most part, like a huge whale's carcass had risen out of the sea and remained frozen in time. All three of us went ashore and we left the captain to look out over the sea toward Southern California while Chauga and I journeyed inland.

But Chauga was like an anxious schoolgirl, ready to join the Easter egg hunt. Hell, we didn't even know if her mother was still alive. "Cable, where would you look first?" she asked me.

"I don't know. I guess we should try to put ourselves in your mother's position. On this piece of rock, it's anyone's guess." Then I thought. "If it was me, either I'd look for someplace where fresh water could be obtained and second, food. Now...let me see...that could mean a place near the cliffs over there. That's where water might flow down to the sea—what little there is of it here—and maybe your Mom learned to eat herbs and catch fish?"

"I guess that sounds like a good place to start, huh? You're so smart. I'm glad I hired you instead of that stubborn Mr. Hoyle."

"Well, thanks for the vote of confidence, kid, but I'm just as uncertain as you are. I'm just playing a hunch, that's all."

So we looked for signs of a human being. Finally, about a half-hour walk from the harbor, we picked up what looked like some human footprints in the sand. We followed them down a narrow cliff to the beach below. There bending over at the tide line was a short little woman dressed in blue-black cormorant feathers. Chauga was beyond herself and ran toward her mother, but the older woman became fearful and ran away. I tried to follow, but booze and cigarettes had once again hampered my forward motion and I stopped. But soon

12

Chauga shouted at her mother that she was her daughter and at some point the older woman stopped and turned to look at the approaching younger native girl. In a sudden burst of recognition, the two women embraced in the mid-afternoon sun, there on the beach on the island of San Nicolas.

I could tell the older gal was a little leery of men. We learned later through sand writing that a whaler had seduced her and gotten her pregnant. Then about two years later he returned, claimed the child as his own and stole her while the mother slept. Now at last, mother and daughter were re-united. The older woman, who later became known as *Juana Maria*, smiled at her daughter with a strange all but toothless mouth. Her teeth were ground down to the gums through her eating habits, I guessed. Then in a burst of joy the older gal began to move up and down in a rhythmic dance. "*Toki, toki!*" she exclaimed. And then she began to sing with both light and deep chant-like sounds. I felt like I was suddenly thrust back two hundred years and was listening to an ancient language, now all but forgotten.

When we got back to our sea transportation, the Captain was amazed we found the woman and her very few possessions. Chauga was ecstatic and mother and daughter touched and held hands the entirety of the journey home. It came as a shock to me when I learned some weeks later that Juana Maria had died of dysentery just seven weeks into her new life on the mainland. Maybe it was her time. I never saw Chauga again, but I'll never forget that boat ride and the *Lone Woman of San Nicolas Island.*

I had no sooner gotten back from my San Nicolas Island adventure than the phone started ringing. "Yeah, Cable Denning here..."

"Denning, it's me, Lester Keith...ya got a minute? By the way, where the hell you been? I've been tryin' to get you on the phone all last night and today."

"Oh, well, I was about seventy miles off the coast of California having a picnic on San Nicolas Island," I said with tongue-in-cheek.

"Where? Never heard of it! You were probably whoring around with some dame, knowing you."

"Uh—what can I do for you, Lieutenant?"

"There's gonna be a murder and I want you to intervene."

I was a bit taken aback. "Say that again? Me? Oh, big word, Lieutenant, 'intervene'—I thought you were just a dumb cop with a limited vocabulary in this scenario."

"Shut up, big shot, and listen. Someone's about to get killed on a luxury liner down at the harbor—unless we stop it, Denning."

"I'm—I'm not exactly clear what this has to do with me, Lester. Isn't this police business? What've I got, a Dick Tracy secret code ring or something?"

"Very funny. No, but it's German spy crap and I know you've had a lotta experience with German spies—both in and outta the bedroom."

I chuckled. "Okay, touché! So whatta ya want me to do?"

"I'm not sure. The ship's about a third regular passengers, the rest are wounded G.I. returning from combat. Two spies I know of, one Erwin Sigler, the other a Kraut known as Franz Stigler."

"What is this, some circus act? Sigler and Stigler?" I cracked.

Lester Keith did not appreciate it. "How in the hell should I know? They're Krauts, okay? The names all sound alike, anyway. The boat docks tonight about midnight or so. I'll pay you outta my slush fund for such situations. Twenty bucks a day..."

"Twenty bucks a day! Hell, Lester, I get more from a regular client where all I have to do is shoot a Kodak picture and show up in court."

"Okay, twenty-five. It's the S. S. America. Can you meet me at the docks? There's a contact man—a guy named Emil Leichen. It seems he's got something they want..."

"When?"

"Tonight, Denning, I told you *tonight*—whatsa matter, got salt water in your ears?"

"Yeah...I'm tryin' to remember what night it is..."

"It's Sunday night, private detective, Sunday night—does that happen to ring a bell with you?"

"Yeah, okay...I'll—I'll be there...see you then."

"Okay, thanks, Denning. Pier A, Berth 157—be there about 11:30...I'll fill you in." We hung up.

But when it rains it pours and no sooner had I put the phone receiver down than it rang again. "Yeah, this better not be you again, Lester, because if it is, I ain't comin' on account of I've spent most of my time on the phone with you and haven't even got my pants on yet!" I exclaimed over the phone.

15

There was a pause. "Is this Cable Denning's office—and are you a private investigator?" The voice at the other end was strong but feminine and possessed a certain sophisticated charm.

"Oh...uh...sorry, lady, I just got off the phone with a wiry police inspector I know...seems like someone's getting murdered tonight and he wants me there pronto—or at least before midnight."

"You're allowing someone to get murdered?" she asked.

"No, ma'am, it's different than that, but we don't know where to look—you know, the old needle in the haystack trick—so we might be too late when we get there. It's like life, ma'am...everything is in the...*timing.*"

"I see..." she said. She took a deep breath. "Well, that was one way to start off a relationship—"

"—oh? I didn't know we had one?"

"Had what?"

"A relationship."

"Oh, I was speaking of a possible business association."

I was being smart-ass and I knew it. "Yeah, about that...I *am* a private detective. So what can I do for you, lady?"

"Well, it's rather hard to explain...but I'll try..."

"That's usually best. By the way, my name *is* Cable Denning."

"Alright...yes, Mr. Denning. So, you see my husband is also a singer and—"

"—wait a minute here—I didn't know that *you* were a singer...I'm tryin' to take down notes..."

16

"I'm sorry—yes, I'm an operatic singer—so is my husband. But he is from the old country and much better known. I'm American born—"

"—excuse me, ma'am, but do you have a name or do I call you 'female singer' all night here?" I said a little impatiently. Some dames couldn't tell you if they were comin' or goin'!

"I'm—I'm *Nadia Skorkowsky,* Mr. Denning. You may have heard of my husband, *Anton Heidler*. He's a baritone with the *New York City Opera.* A new company, not to be confused with the Metropolitan Opera. I am currently 'second-string' soprano, but I'm working my way up. We're only a year or so old...affordable prices for the common man and woman—at least that's what Mayor La Guardia said. And an opportunity for American singers and composers"

"Sorry, lady, but I'm not an opera person. Can't understand a word they say! So I never heard of you *or* your husband."

"That doesn't matter, Mr. Denning. What I've really called about is that I suspect Anton is in a lot of trouble. So...I probably have to talk to you in person to explain things—plus it's possible they may be listening in."

"*'They'?*"

"Yes, a horrible group called the *Lichter Grabstätte.*" I knew I had heard that name before way back when. But where, how and in what context? Whatever it was, it wasn't good.

"Yeah, so I guess you'd better come see me." I checked my calendar. "How about Tuesday...say...two in the afternoon?"

"Tuesday? Please, Mr. Denning, I don't think I've impressed upon you the urgency of the situation."

"Alright. How late are you up?"

"All night tonight. Anton is still gone and won't be back until—well, that's just it, I don't know when!"

Then I was thinking I'd heard those names before. "Nadia and Anton—yeah, the radio quiz show, right? Your husband missed by one lousy answer. That was you, wasn't it?"

"Yes, Mr. Denning. Indeed, that was us..."

"Well, I'm good at voices. I remember your voice in particular. It was musical. Of course that's not saying your husband's voice ain't deep and resonant—it is. But I'm kind of tuned to female voices since I spend a fair amount of my recreational time frequenting nightclubs where pretty sexy babes in sequined dresses sing the Great American Songbook."

"You do? How intriguing! Perhaps I may accompany you sometime? Anton has an aversion to slumming. But personally I love it...deep caves, sultry nights with smoke and a dull spotlight with a candle on every little table tucked into a cozy corner somewhere. And the music...*Why Do I Love You?* is one of my favorites—oh, and then there's the sensuous *Can 't Help Lovin' That Man of Mine.*" She started singing a few bars. The lady could sing!

I was taken by this personable gal. "Sure, kid! You just let me know when you wanna come."

"Well, first things first, Mr. Denning...we must find Anton...he's supposed to sign a contract for the *Baron Scarpia* in Puccini's *Tosca.*"

"Okay...I'll tell ya what, Madame Skorkowsky, I'm just about to go out on a job. It might be all night. So, can you stay by the phone from six or seven in the morning on, okay? The best I can do."

"Okay, Mr. Denning—and thank you...I'll be waiting." We hung up.

The Looming Fog

It was about 11:45 p.m. when Lieutenant Lester Keith and I met at the Los Angeles Harbor in San Pedro. Except for the giant ocean liner looming in the fog and slowly approaching the dock and the foghorn in the distance, it was rather quiet. "So tell me, Lester, what's this thing all about—I mean besides murder—and who's gettin' killed?"

"Right down your alley, Denning...weird things that go bump in the night coupled with state secrets being smuggled outta this country, directly into the Führer's anxious little hands, so I hear. I don't know yet who the victim is gonna be. Maybe more than one...hang tight."

"Hmmm...I see...*that* kind of murder, eh?"

"Yeah, that kind of murder. The F.B.I. boys are here, too, but they're stupid, inept and keeping incognito."

"Oh, *inept*—another big word..."

"Shut up..."

"So whatta ya want me to do, Lester, sing a song as the passengers come down the gangplank?"

"Very funny—you know, Denning, you irritate me something awful sometimes—and this minute is one of them. Just shut up so you can hear what I have to say, okay?"

"*Okay...*" I said, shutting down. It was quite a sight to see a 26-ton piece of mega-steel sally up to the port dock and quietly ease into a berth with a little help from a tugboat.

"As I told you on the phone about a third of the passengers are civilians, right? The remaining nine hundred passengers are wounded soldiers returning from combat in the South Pacific. For some reason, the government doesn't want anyone to know about these men who will be brought to secret hospitals somewhere here in the states.

"Doesn't that strike you as rather strange, Inspector?" I asked.

"Don't confuse me anymore than I already am. That's not our business, mister. Now, I have an exchequer pass for you to go aboard with the Port Authority before people begin to disembark. I'm gonna stay at the bottom of the ramp while you search out a guy who—" He took a small photo out of his coat pocket and handed it to me. "—who looks like this." It was a photo of a pretty portly but handsome man. "He has several names, I've been told. The one we're lookin' for is *Emil Leichen*. As I understand it, he's the guy who's gonna pass off certain top secret information to either a guy named *Erwin Sigler* or some other German spy called *Franz Stigler*. Now you think you got that, Denning?"

"Yeah, Lester, I got it. So this Leichen fellow is supposed to meet up with either Sigler or Stigler—are you sure it ain't Abbott and Costello or Laurel and Hardy?" I quipped.

"Very funny, Denning. Now...get going...over there...you see that little office? That's where you'll find the Port Inspector. I'll stay here."

"Okay." Under the streetlamp, I looked at the Emil Leichen's photo again. I turned it over. In pencil and barely visible were the initials *A.H.* I wondered if that stood for *'always handy'* and we were chumps barking up the wrong tree. Ya never know. Okay, 'Mr. Private Dick'—time to get serious.

The fog was soupy and I could feel something strange going on around me. I knocked on the Port Inspector's office door. No one responded. The door was unlocked so I entered. But I didn't have to look too far. There slumped over his desk was the now-deceased Port authority! I drew my .38 and quickly checked the bathroom and storage room in the little office. Of course the killer wouldn't stick around. With my gun drawn I stepped outside and looked around. Just up the street Jack Dragna's headquarters were located. I walked toward them, but just then dozens of white busses drove up and the place became a mess of attendants, military personnel and officials who ran around making themselves important. I walked over to the waiting Lt. Lester Keith.

"The Port Authority guy bought the farm, Lester, he is no more."

"What?!! You mean they bumped him off within the last fifteen minutes or so? I wonder why—"

"—is that when you last spoke to him? Maybe he knew something he wasn't supposed to. Or they wanted to block anyone else from boarding."

"Yep. Shit...without a pass you can't go on board."
Keith's eyebrows raised and his forehead furled.

"Well, we can look out for a stubby little guy with a black overcoat and lots of nice black hair, right?"

"Yeah... Emil Leichen. If we spot him, we can keep an eye out for anyone approaching him... ...that's about all we can do."

"What do these other two guys look like, anyway—Sigler and Stigler?"

"How in the hell should I know? It wasn't even the F.B.I. who gave me Emil Leichen's photo."

"No? Who did, then?"

"I ain't sure...my desk officer told me a nice looking woman came in and handed him a small envelope addressed to me."

"Hmmm...'nice looking woman'? That's it? So you don't even know if it's a bum steer or not?"

"Yeah, but it's better than mum-mouth from the Feds."

"So, the question remains—how am I gonna get aboard ship?"

Just then the white busses began to load their cargo. I quickly discovered why the government wanted to keep it all quiet. These were the men who were nearly blown to bits on some remote South Pacific island, fighting the Japanese in a steaming green jungle. Some were nearly torn to shreds by machine gun fire or shrapnel, or afflicted with some horrible jungle disease, which they had little or no ability to fight. Others were blinded, or maimed in a thousand different ways. Many U.S. casualties, I later learned, were accidently caused by our own military maneuvers. Right hand not know what the left hand was doing? One wonders how that stuff can happen! If it was me...if I was wounded as bad as some of the guys I saw passing by Lt. Keith and me, why bother keeping me alive? What kind of life might these poor nearly dead guys have—even if they survived? Regular professions, girls, wives, lovers, friends, or any kind of normal life, would be denied them.

"Just go, Denning...now!" the feisty policeman said.

So I did. I took matters into my own hands and began walking counter to the flow of the medics, soldiers and other personnel. The stench of rotting and infected flesh was terrible and the newly arrived attendants were appalled at the way the wounded soldiers looked. So was I. Somehow I got through the mulling crowds and made my way upstairs to the civilian part of the ship. The place was crawling with military police and I encountered a large group of people awaiting deportment off the S.S. America. I talked with a civilian who had an official look about him and was holding a manifest list of passengers. I asked him about Emil Leichen and he told me he'd be in line, just look. But I spotted Leichen's cabin number #16 on the manifest and made my way along until there were no more people and no more noise except in the distance. There was #16...I knocked on the door.

Kiss of An Alien

There was no answer, so I drew my .38 and slowly opened the unlocked door. It was semi-dark in the room and I fumbled for a light switch. When I finally found one, a fluctuating dim bulb went on above me on the ceiling. But I didn't need much more light to see a body on the floor. It was a portly man with no signs of violence around him. But what was strange was that he had no pants on! I got on my knees to check his pulse. He had none. I turned him over to see the face. Yep, as I suspected, it was Emil Leichen alright! So I started talking to myself aloud. I figured Stigler and Sigler got what they wanted and flew the coop. "Now...who in the hell got here first and why? Who did it...*who in the hell did it*...?!" I mumbled to myself.

"I did," a female voice answered from out of the shadows.

I stood up. I was facing a beautiful young woman with a black dull-leather outfit and artificially colored red, green and blue hair. She also sported shiny red high heel shoes and glowing orange-red fingernails! "Well, hello...don't tell me, you're the new hostess they hired for all new arrivals," I said, trying to throw her off balance with a glib response.

"Hardly," she answered, her voice kind of seductively phony-sweet. "It was my job. So I did it."

"I see. So let me get this straight...you killed this man *for what*?"

"Because he came aboard to hand off vital information to the Germans about the *neutron arrester.*"

"*Neutron arrester?* Last time I heard, it was *atomic* secrets—"

"—more or less the same thing, mister. Too bad I can't let you live, though. You seem like you might be fun to play with."

I ignored her statement. "So, if you don't mind, what side do you work for?"

"Oh...confused, are you...little mortal man?" she said with a sense of power and conviction. "They said it would be like this. You might say I'm an interested 'third party'." Then she slowly swayed her way over to me. "You see, mister, I'm very, very good...when I like someone...and I like you—"

"—yeah, like you liked that dead guy on the floor!" I declaimed. "Thanks but no thanks, sister."

"You'll like it. Ah, my kisses are so...sweet...earthling man. Why don't you give me a try before I simply—*disappear* into thin air, as you would say?" she cooed.

"Ah, so you're not a local, eh? I should've guessed. I thought you were gonna kill me."

She looked at her glowing fingernails. "Not necessarily. I do...make...exceptions. I think you may be one. You think I'm appealing, don't you? Males get clouded with sexual dreams, Mr.—"

"—Denning—Cable Denning..."

"I am known as Abbey Allison—here. But my real name is Zitzy."

"I'm not so sure I'm pleased to meet you, whoever in the hell you are." I glanced at the body on the floor. "What about him?" I bent over and started rifling through his pockets. I found a New York City Opera ticket stub for the opera *La Traviata* by Giuseppe Verdi. Again, someone had penciled the same initials I'd seen on the back of his photo. *A.H*...New York City Opera ticket...of course! Emil Leichen was none other than *Anton Heidler*, Nadia Skorkowsky's singing husband! Now I was wondering how I'd break the news to her that her dearly departed hubby was a Nazi spy. That is, unless she knew more than she led me to believe. Through sleight of hand I shoved the ticket up my sleeve and rose to face Abbey Allison. "So...are you gonna kill me or not? How do you think you're getting off this ship without being noticed? You don't exactly blend with the crowd. Or how 'bout I turn you in for the murder of one Emil Leichen aka Anton Heidler?

She giggled a naughty giggle. "I think I'll keep you around to play with later. Hmmm...I wonder...words against words, Cable Denning. My kiss is traceless. No human mortal can or will find anything that might implicate me. And as for me? I will walk out with the rest of the impatient passengers out there awaiting their turn to disembark—or, perhaps I'll just simply 'evaporate' before your very eyes." She said no more and turned to go.

Poison kisses? So that's how she did it. That's why no signs of violence. "One more thing—where will you be staying?—just in case I get the urge to question you further—and privately?"

"Privately? Does that mean have sex with you, Cable Denning? I think not. Thanks all the same for the offer." Then she disappeared out the door. I eventually found a steward and reported the dead man in Room #16. I gave him my information and said I'd be outside at the end of gangplank with Lt. Lester Keith of the Los Angeles Police Department. He escorted me out of the ship's inner bowels and then down the ramp to make certain I was on the level. He asked Lester Keith for his identification.

"Goddamn it, Denning, what'd you do now?" Lt. Keith grumbled as he withdrew his badge and identification.

26

"Our contact is as dead as a dodo bird, Lester. That's number two—wanna wager on three?"

"Ya know, Denning, I just don't like you tonight. Go home and let *real* police personnel iron out this mess!" he admonished me.

"Swell with me—just remember it was you who asked me to come down here to this hodgepodge, a sacrosanct bunch of deceit and lies—not you personally, Lieutenant—but all the rest of these trappings."

"Shut up and go home...good night, 'private detective'..."

I was looking at the stretchers and broken bodies going by. "Doesn't that mean anything to you, Lester—that blown up carnage all in the name of war games?"

"It disgusts me, Denning, but what the hell am I gonna do about it? I don't make rules, I just obey them and go home when my day is done." And so Lester Keith left me in the fog. But I doubt if he was goin' home.

My little alien assassin had disappeared. Lester Keith didn't ask me if I saw who did it, so I didn't mention her. Instead, I implicated Stigler and Sigler. They were the German spies that got me messed up in this affair in the first place. Besides, can ya hear the reply if I told anyone that a gorgeous humanoid alien babe had iced Heidler? Ha! Instead, I hightailed it to the nearest phone booth and dialed the phone number I'd scribbled down earlier in the evening. "Hello?" she answered.

"Miss Nadia Skorkowsky? Cable Denning here. I think we need to talk," I said, keeping my cool.

"Oh, yes, indeed...indeed, Mr. Denning. Are you able to come up—come up to my place?"

"Well, that depends on where 'your place' is, lady."

"Beverly Hills...451 South Rodeo Drive, near the corner of Virginia Place. It—it's the fifth house down from the corner. It's one of the few houses that isn't in the Spanish style.

"Yeah, I can do that. I'm still down at the docks, Miss Skorkowsky. It'll take me a little while to get up there, okay?"

"Yes...okay...thank you...it sounds as if you found out something. I will be happy to hear what you have to say..."

We hung up and I drove toward Beverly Hills. All the time I was thinking about the angles that could be possible in this case. Was it coincidence that Emil Leichen aka Anton Heidler was Nadia Skorkowsky's husband and happened to show up dead on the S.S. America? Or did she call me earlier that evening to somehow get me involved with her husband? None of it made sense.

Nadia Skorkowsky

I drove into the driveway at 451 South Rodeo Drive in Beverly Hills. The place was dark except for a porch light. I parked, went up to the door and rang the doorbell. I guess the best way to describe the lady in question was that among other virtues, Nadia Skorkowsky was a real looker! The doll had it in spades—beauty and sophistication. She had long, wavy dark hair with dark-brown eyes and stood about maybe five-feet-five or so. She was wearing a kind of flamingo colored night robe that she filled out on top just fine, and wore pearl slippers.

28

We both stared at each other. I suppose she wasn't expecting a tall, handsome and rugged looking detective either...I smiled at the thought.

"Mr.—Mr. Denning?" she finally asked. "I'm—I'm sorry—please come in..."

The joint was a palace, all the way from Persian rugs to a huge Chinese style chandelier in gold, red and crystal that hung from the middle of the ceiling. "Nice place ya have here," I understated.

She was still staring at me. And I was also probably gawking at her. "Thank you...can I—can I offer you something to drink?"

"Yeah, if ya got any fine English gin...or honeyed whiskey in a snifter of hot water?"

"Both of them—hmmm...let me guess what you might feel like tonight. How about the whiskey?" she suggested gently.

She guessed it right. "Yeah, that'd be fine, thanks. It was a little cool and foggy down at the docks..." I said that, fishing for a response. I got one.

"The—the docks? You mean Los Angeles Harbor?" she said as she walked toward a nice wet bar.

"Yeah, how'd ya know?"

"Oh...I didn't...I just guessed...you did say docks." She excused herself to make up the drinks at the fancy little bar with black wood and a large mirror with Chinese etchings on the sides of it. Soon she returned with drinks-in-hand. She was so lovely and moved like a swan, her neck long but in proportion with the rest of her body. "Well, then...here's to a successful association, Mr. Denning," she said as she clicked glasses with me.

We toasted. I took a sip of the whiskey, then poured the contents of the snifter into the rest of it. "Ya know, when I see beautiful women, I always wonder what their mothers looked like. Was your mother as stunning as you are, Miss Skorkowsky?"

"Stunning? Well, thank you for that, but hardly. I use a lot of makeup. My mother was a Serbian aristocrat. Proud, beautiful, well mannered, married to a man she loved and who loved her. She was lucky. A lot of women married for station and had terrible marriages."

"Yeah, so I've heard—what's that movie with Greta Garbo ?"

"*Camille*. Being theatrical, the right clothes, hairdo and makeup can do wonders, you know."

"Maybe. But I've got this feeling you'd even look great with no clothes on and *no* makeup."

She blushed but wasn't offended by my frankness. "Now you're flirting, Mr. Denning..."

"Maybe a little. But I ain't far off, lady. I've seen a lotta pretty dames in my time."

She checked me out from stem to stern. "I'll bet you have..."

"Uh...I've gotta get something off my chest, Mrs.—"

"—if you don't mind, Nadia will be fine, Mr. Denning. Yes, you did sound like you found out something. What is it?"

"Okay...Nadia...yes, I *do* have something to tell you."

"Yes—pertaining to my husband?"

"I'm afraid I'm gonna have to call him your *late* husband...I found a dead man that matched your husband's description pretty good in Cabin #16 of the S.S. America down at the docks."

She wasn't as distraught as I expected. "How would you know that it was Anton, Mr. Denning—I did not describe my husband to you over the phone?"

I reached into my pocket and took out the photo, then the opera ticket. She seemed genuinely disturbed when she saw them. "Now as I got it from Lt. Keith down at Central Division, some good lookin' babe brings in the photo downtown and says this guy is a man named *Emil Leichen*, but not your dear Anton Heidler. This other item, which you may recognize, is from the New York City Opera, Nadia...a ticket for Verdi's *La Traviata.* By any chance, Miss Skorkowsky, were you that woman who walked into the station with the photograph of your late husband for whatever reasons—or am I barking up the wrong tree here?"

She stared at me, in disbelief and half a dozen other thoughts. Then she glanced down at the ticket. But her voice wasn't sad or distressed, but rather matter of fact. "No, Mr. Denning, I was not that woman—why would I betray my own husband?" She took the ticket from my hand. "Yes...Anton and I attended the opera that night—was it a dark suit coat he was wearing?"

"Yep, complete with tie and shirt—but he had no pants on. Any clues why that might've been the case?"

She seemed confused as she tilted her head and looked headlong into my eyes as if she wanted to see right through to the truth. "No pants? Are you sure?"

"Yeah, I know a bare ass when I see one, lady. He may have been changing at the moment he was killed. That's possible."

"Are you now suggesting another woman? I was certain that I was as much as Anton would need...perhaps more. Do you think there was another...another woman?" she asked me so sexily I felt like taking a cold shower. "I guess I'm just going to have to see the body to prove it to myself, Mr. Denning. And *if* my husband was killed, how was he killed?" she inquired again, her voice firming up a bit.

"Far as I can figure, by a *kiss*. There was another babe in attendance, if you must know. She was a dish. She told me her name was *Abbey Allison*, also known as *'Zitzy'*, and admitted killing the guy with a kiss. Either of those names ring a bell?"

She snickered. "Truly? A kiss? You'll have to forgive me, Mr. Denning—but how can a man be killed by a kiss?"

"No doubt you've heard of 'the kiss of death,' Miss Skorkowsky—well, I think this gal was the real thing. I suspect she's an alien creature of some sort because she referred to me as an earthling man. She said she came to prevent your husband from completing his mission—so his contacts wouldn't be a happy group of Boy Scouts exchanging valuable information to the Nazis. It had to do with some thing called a *neutron arrestor*. And, oh, one other thing, you can bet there was a lotta dough-re-me involved, speaking of singing."

She suddenly stood up and appeared indignant. Those beautiful dark eyes flashed and her voice was excited. I knew she liked me. "Mr. Denning, I think you'd better go. I don't know what your game is, but the more you talk, the more absurd your conversation is. First, you expect me to believe that my husband has been killed...second, by an extra-terrestrial female's kiss over a thing called a *'neutron arrester'*? Please, sir...be kind to yourself, I was hoping better of you." Then she softened a bit and said like an afterthought, "That said, however, you *are* handsome."

"Handsome, eh? No more? What about intelligent, perceptive?" I fished. "Yep, that's exactly what I expected you to believe, Nadia...what I just told you. It's what I saw—but you ain't buyin' my story, are ya?" I asked putting my hat on.

"Not...in the least," she insisted. She moved like a woman in control. I watched her body posture, the way she smiled with those marvelous cheekbones bringing out an irresistible charm, the way she held her whiskey glass. "As I said, I was hoping better from you—and of course your rather tactless blurting out about the possible death of Anton—pure theatrics and way below my standards."

I licked my lips and cleared my throat. "Well, I'm sorry I disappointed you. A few things don't add up in my book about you, either, sister—like our phone conversation earlier—things like the tone of your voice was panic a few hours ago, real concern at the very least, not to mention the good ol' *Lichter Grabstätte* boys and girls. By the way, was there something you wanted to tell me about your *'missing' husband*'...before I depart your fair environs here in Beverly Hills?"

"Well, now, none of that matters if he's dead, does it, Mr. Denning?"

"Maybe...maybe not...I've been in this business a long time...dig around a few layers and well, sometimes you get surprised. I've discovered the darker the nights are the bigger the city gets and the more lies are told." I held my ground. "Yeah, kind of like the time you and Mr. Heidler were on the radio quiz show I heard."

"Are you insinuating I'm lying to you, Mr. Denning?" she said indignantly.

"One can't be too sure during these war years, Madam Skorkowsky—especially if spies are involved. But I remembered your time on the radio show—you and your husband. How honest is that show, anyhow...or was that full of spies, too?"

"Pretty honest, I'd say. I'd forgotten you heard that program. Anton and I had a lot of fun doing that contest. So, do you recall the question Anton didn't know the answer to?"

"Yeah, *'the king was in his **what** counting out his money'*, right? Your husband said the king was in his *parlor* when the real answer was *'counting-house'.*"

"Yes, a *dead giveaway*, to my mind..." she retorted.

"What did you say?"

"I said a *dead giveaway*. That was what Anton got when he didn't answer the question correctly. I thought the clue was pretty clear myself. According to the rhyme, the *Queen* was the one in the parlor." Now the lady was relaxed, and suddenly not so worried about her husband, I thought. Dames, who can figure them?

"Yeah, *dead giveaway*, that's what I thought you said."

"Is there something wrong with that?"

"Not exactly, Miss Skorkowsky. But, you see, there were other goings on during your and Anton's time on the show. I read the police report. A stagehand was sure someone had been killed in the rafters above the theatre. But no dead man—sorry—just your nice, cozy little

34

husband, some thirty odd feet above the stage on the gangplanks. Yet the stagehand insisted he saw a dead guy on the planks up there. He went to fetch some help, but by the time he got back with a couple of guys, it was dear ol' hubby all alive and well again that greeted everyone way up there in the rafters!"

She flashed her eyes away, apprehensively. "It was a misunderstanding. Anton always wanted to know what it was like above the stage. So he just lay down on the walkway up there and I guess—"

"—the stagehand saw him in that prostrate position, hmmmm?"

"Yes, Mr. Denning, that's all there was to it."

"A grown man in a radio show contest finds the time to lie down on a dirty bunch of boards high in the air and check out the scenery? He's not afraid to get his suit dirty?" I checked out her eyes. They still averted my own. "Okay, that's all there was to it. But on a final note, you don't seem all that bothered by the news of your husband's death. You seemed more concerned on the phone when you said you didn't know when or if he'd be coming home. And now? So...maybe now ya know, lady...why did you bother calling me in the first place?"

She ignored my question and turned away to look above the fireplace mantle. A large portrait of her in this most lovely deep red 19th century dress hung on the wall. "That...is me some years back. I was playing *Tosca* a lot then. When life rushes you through its paces and rips you open, you have to maintain yourself—and your decorum. I remember the honest words Tosca speaks when she's in confrontation with the villainous *Scarpia*. '*Vissi d'arte, vissi d'more*', which means 'I lived for art, I lived for love...it goes on to say some rather puzzling things next, however. "I never did harm to a living soul, yet *with a secret hand I relieved as many misfortunes as I knew of.*" Then she looked away from the portrait to me. "Of course I kill Scarpia in the play, the terrible politician and would-be seducer."

"And...? Maybe your husband?" I goaded her on.

"Certainly not! There is no '*and*', Mr. Denning. That's the whole story, except Floria Tosca commits suicide when she discovers that Scarpia did not plan a mock execution for her lover, Mario Cavaradossi, but real bullets killed him on top of the rampart."

"Ah, of course, operatically melodramatic..." I chuckled.

"Art copies life, Mr. Denning." She led me to the front door. She still carried herself proud, sophisticated, still looked at me with those intense lovely eyes of hers. "I'm sorry, I guess our association wasn't meant to be. Life's funny that way...isn't it?"

"I guess ya don't always get dealt the winning hand—but thanks for the drink—and *you.*"

"Me?"

"Yeah, I liked you from the first minute I saw you and have spent our time together drinking you in, lady. You've got something—well, something good in you beside cosmetic beauty, Nadia Skorkowsky."

"Now that's a come-on line if I ever heard it, but thanks all the same. What do I owe you?" she spoke, still guarded.

"Maybe a nice forgiving kiss?" I kidded her. I had to admit she was a luscious piece of cream pie. She had the kind of full, moist lips ya just wanted to kiss again and again until—well, until it led to something else and then you could do that thing *and* kiss her at the same time.

"Good-bye, Mr. Denning, I'll send you a check." she said in an iced-up voice. So in the end, it wasn't the niceness that got me, but the quick brush-off. I sensed Nadia Skorkowsky knew something she didn't want me to know.

The Walnut House

It had been morning for a while by the time I got home, but daylight came all too soon with the phone ringing and Ida Latney answering and in her tactful, gentle way, fielding my calls. The most noteworthy call of the late morning was from a *Dr. Apothican*, wanting to interview me personally before hiring me for an *Lf case,* lost-and-found. I agreed. He said price was not an issue and the sooner he sees me, the better. So I agreed to see him much later that afternoon.

On the other side of the barren desert-like terrain—except for oil rigs—called *"Signal Hill"*, I found the *Walnut House Asylum.* At the entrance, on an old discolored brass plate was written: *"Walnut House Asylum For the Criminally Insane".* The place looked like a mansion from a horror movie and I was almost afraid to park my car for fear some insane idiot would steal it! And talking about spooky, a steely old nurse greeted me after I pounded on the door for about three minutes. Her eyes squinted as she came to the door. "Sir...? We are short-staffed at the moment. You are the private detective?"

"Yep, that's me, lady, I'm supposed to be talking to your director, one honorable *Dr. Addison Apothican.* You do know him?" I quipped, seeing the lady had been drinking. Her eyes were blurry and her nose a little red and bulbous. Maybe that accounted for the squinting earlier.

"I am no lady...just Nurse Diesel...this way, please..." She led me down a dark high-ceilinged hallway and finally at its end we entered a black-walnut door marked *'DIRECTOR'.* We were greeted by a lively small man with a well-trimmed moustache and dark, probing eyes. He came over and shook my hand and dismissed the inebriated Nurse Diesel. I observed he gave her a strange and curious look.

"Your head nurse is a few sheets to the wind, doctor," I informed this nervous little man with a deep resonant voice.

"Yes, yes, these days it is difficult to find well-qualified people—and Nurse Diesel has been with me for—for over twenty years now. I allow her to...to imbibe in order for her to tolerate the task at hand." He gestured with four fingers on his right hand. "Please, sit opposite me here..." He spoke slowly, deliberately.

I sat and settled in with my hat in my lap. "So, you mentioned on the phone you were unsettled about something out here, but it was too confidential to tell me on the phone and too discretionary to call the police, right?"

"Yes, sir, this is correct. Frankly, Mr. Denning, I'm concerned," said the slight man. He possessed a fine crop of silvery white hair and it was combed back slick. "So whatever I say to you, please, is on the Q.T. and not to be discussed with any other person—living or dead..." He chuckled. "If...you get my drift..." He definitely had that Boris Karloffian smile and hint of British in his voice. But he was personable enough, I thought.

"So...? I asked, waiting for the punch line.

"So?"

"Just exactly *what* are you concerned about, Doctor.?"

"Oh, that...yes, of course—why I called you."

"Yeah." I took out a Lucky Strike and was about to light it when the Director stopped me.

"Please, sir, it's my wife's condition—asthma, you know...I'm afraid she just couldn't take the nicotinic acid in the air, sir."

"Your wife? She works here too?" I asked, putting away my cigarette and fidgeting with my fedora as I sat across from the good doctor. I was beginning to wonder if it was a family business or not or even if the doc was one of the patients!

"Truthfully, no, but she does pop in unexpectedly now and then. She'll believe I have been smoking again and blame me lamentably for the traces of that damnable weed she will smell in the air."

"I see. So...anyway...why did you call me?"

"Oh, yes, that is...also lamentable. You see our most ferocious, diabolical and unpredictable criminal-minded 'guest' has escaped. *Dr. Theodore Watson.* Even though *'Watty'* always beats me at chess and is truly a criminal minded insane son-of-a-bitching bastard with no scruples whatsoever, I'm a bit fond of him. You see, he killed my wife one marvelous day some years back."

Now I *was* beginning to feel that the doc was the one who belonged behind the nut case cage! "But I thought you told me your wife comes in once in a while to—"

"—well, she does, but from the other side of things, Mr. Denning." Then he lowered his voice in a sinister fashion. "She visits...from the *other side*." He sighed. "I keep her memory dear—and am also reminded to maintain my discipline against all tobacco products. I tried chewing, but it does not do the same for me. It gave me an ulcer."

What the hell had I gotten myself tangled up with now. "I see, sorry to hear that. So what can I do for you, doctor?"

He got up and started for the door. "Will you accompany me? I have something I need to discuss with someone...who...who might be 'in the know', so to speak..."

"Me? In the know? I can't guarantee ya that. I'm just a private dick with a need to pay for the roof over my head. So 'in the know' might depend on the subject matter, Dr.—Dr. uh—"

"—Apothican," he answered

We descended an ancient elevator to a lower floor where yet another world of insanity greeted me. The stench was terrible and the cool, damp atmosphere was stifling. We went about half way down a hall and entered a cell about the size of my bedroom at the office. Immediately the doc went over to a cot and pointed at some scattered papers. "Please take a look at these. They are of great concern to me, along with Dr. Watson's escape." I took up some of the papers and began to look at them. The more I looked the more amazed and

40

apprehensive I became. The eerie drawings were of an oil derrick looking thing with a bunch of computations written all around it. But it was the third sheet that scared the shit outta me. It was a drawing of an explosion consuming the atmosphere of the entire earth and with red wax crayon. Dr. Watson had drawn an expanding red color that represented the flames from the blast. "What—what, uh, did Dr. Watson do before he was incarcerated here?"

"He was a physicist working for the government somewhere...I know not the location...about three or four years ago. Suddenly the heretofore competent doctor went berserk and killed eleven of his cohorts, burning all of their eyes out with a hot soldering iron, except for one female..."

"Yeah...?" I asked still looking at the third drawing.

"She was only forty and quite attractive, I understand. He kidnapped her and held her in a secret basement, being illicit and dallying with her until he decided to burn her also, in a similar way. Then the poor insane man attempted to solder her eyes together with a strand of silver and solder. He attempted the same with the woman's breasts—but failed at that also." His voice darkened. "At some point she must have died a most terrifying and ghastly death—the laboratory report was more vague than absolute, sir."

"I see." I shuddered inside that such an apparently intelligent and okay guy would go nuts and do what he did. Unless...unless some other unknown powers were at work I didn't see in the moment? "Well, I'm gonna ask you something, doc. What was going on in his insane little nightmare down here that would make him draw all these calculations and things? Did he have reference books to help him? Newspapers, periodicals or radio?"

"No, sir, he did not have access to any of those items. He was entirely isolated, on his own. He told me he—well, he preferred *The Solace* and hated humans. He referred to solace itself as *The Solace*, as if it were a sacred place he could go whenever the mood struck him. I was puzzled, but when he killed and partially consumed his male attendant, Oliver Platter, I knew something had to be done then."

"Yeah, I'd say so," I commented dryly.

"But what to do?"

"And Mr. Platter's remains—what'd ya do with them?"

"Well, to be perfectly honest, Mr. Denning, Nurse Diesel and I buried the bones out back. There truly was not much left. When I asked Dr. Watson why he did such a heinous thing, he laughed at me and said he was 'hungry for hate' and did it as a symbol of humanity's end." He stopped and looked around the disheveled room. "I'm afraid that's not much of an explanation now, is it?"

"Oh, I don't know...I've heard worse. You do know what these drawings and computations refer to?"

"I haven't the foggiest, sir, I assure you. Mumbo jumbo to me."

"Have you heard about the research that's been going on for a thing called the *atomic bomb*? That drawing in red looks sort of how I would imagine it. Watson must've somehow 'fore-glimpsed' the bomb and its corresponding mathematics—and how things could go if such a monstrous thing was released to the world, Dr. Apothican."

"My...no—I have not heard of such a device. It does sound...forbidding, doesn't it? Is it to be used as a bomb to stop the war or what?"

"Why do you say that?"

"Well, Dr. Watson was speaking in different languages and one day he was speaking German and Nurse Diesel, who *is* of German descent, understood what Dr. Watson was saying. It seems he was speaking about a huge explosion that would ultimately end the slaughter on the Pacific islands. Perhaps even in Europe and stop Hitler and Mussolini. We are in a terrible war, you know."

I thought for a minute. "How and when did this maniac escape?"

"About a week ago...he seemed to have squeezed his way through a very small shower room window and away he went, lickety-split, naked as a jaybird, to environs unknown!"

"And you put out no warnings or alerts to the authorities?"

"No, sir, I didn't want to 'rill the waters' here at our peaceful *Walnut House*, you know."

I thought...*peaceful?* That's rich. "This guy's dangerous! We gotta find him, and pronto!"

"Well...I was hoping that would be *your* department, detective."

I took a deep breath. "Okay, doc, here's how I figure it. Sometimes insanity lends itself well to extra-ordinary lucidity and ability to tap into other dimensions and dreams. I think your Dr. Watson went berserk at some point, to be sure, but with it he also gained an ability to

tap into a universal 'line' of dreams or communica-
tions—or call it intuitions—that just could be true."

"My dear man, what genius! Yes, of course! Like my
dear wife who comes from time to time to visit!"

"Yeah, sort of like that. I'm not so worried about the
drawings, but this sick son of a bitch must be captured
and either incarcerated a lot more safely than he is
here—or eliminated. Perhaps we can trace him through
the drawings. May I have them to study?"

"Yes…by all means, sir. I somehow see you are a man
of integrity and pledged to duty of justice for all.
Please…do not tell a soul what I told you today. My career of nigh well over forty years would be bankrupt,
sir—I'd say…as dead as the dodo bird!"

Part of me left Dr. Apothican in disbelief. The other
part was shuddering to think what diabolical energy
was now loosed upon the world.

<u>Love Never Has to Say It's Sorry</u>

It was late by the time I got back to my office, exhausted. Ida had already gone home. I lit up a cigarette
and poured myself more than a little gin. Then I began
sifting through the sketches and notations made by a
madman. The guy must've been a channel of some
sort—or clairvoyant. As I read about what Watson considered to be the world of *nuclear fission*, I learned that
a substance called *plutonium* does not occur naturally
on earth and has to be made from a native radioactive
substance called *uranium*. Watson maintained it wasn't
easy, but doable. Once you have the plutonium, he indi-
cated, making a bomb was child's play. His sketches re-

veal a regular looking bomb with a 'bullet implementer' that hit the plutonium, and upon impact—bam! Within miles of the explosion, all would be covered with a blinding light and everything destroyed. That was scary.

I was playing with a pencil thinking when the phone rang. "Yeah, Cable Denning here..."

"Mr. Denning...this is Nadia—Nadia Skorkowsky—I called to apologize to you...Anton *is* dead and Abbey Allison killed him, just as you said. I went to the county coroner's today and—and saw for myself. How may I make amends to you, Mr. Denning, and hire you to handle this most bizarre case?"

"Good evening, Miss Skorkowsky—hire me? I'm still not sure it *was* your husband on that floor, lady. It might've been a plant, a look-alike. And why aren't you more upset? No matter what dead guy was on that ship, your late husband is gone, more than likely forever. Doesn't that bother you?"

"Of course it does. And that's why I want to hire you."

"For what? I thought you wanted me to find your missing husband. I did. He was dead. You identified him. It's over...kaput. Again, unless it wasn't him."

"Now...please, Mr. Denning, this isn't about Anton. I wish to you find Abbey Allison and bring her to justice."

"That's police work, doll. Finding someone is my business. *Justice* belongs to another branch of humanity, for better or worse. But since you said it so sweetly that you want me to find Abbey Allison...realizing your husband's killer's real name was not as you suggest—cut out all the pretend bullshit...and you can call me Cable."

There was a short pause. Hearing her voice raised my temperature in a mighty positive way. I couldn't figure why I was so magnetized to this woman. "Yes, of course, I will tell you everything I know. Can you come see me—tonight?"

"I don't know—I've already been to your place and it wasn't so hot an experience—how about you showing your good faith and running on over here to Hollywood?"

"I—I guess that can be arranged," she said a little icily. "Exactly where are you located?"

"It's in the phone book you got my number from, Miss Skorkowsky."

"So when can I come?"

"How about now?"

"Okay...give me about a half-hour?"

"A half-hour—any later and I penalize all my attractive female clients with that kiss I was talking about two nights ago."

"I'll be punctual, Mr. Denning—"

"—*Cable*, remember? That's one of the rules."

"Yes, Cable, I will remember."

The Black Cat

I don't know why, but I was as excited and nervous as a crawdad on a hot grill awaiting Nadia Skorkowsky. And when she did enter my office, she was ten minutes late and looked like a movie star! When she walked into the office, she was wearing a wonderful dark blue and white large polka-dotted dress buttoned up to the top button, navy heels, a matching purse and a hat that matched the dress, with a blue net veil. She was also wearing a very fine fur coat. She looked sleek and her more than ample curves brought my pulse rate up a bit. Her hair was dark and raven-like and shone naturally. I got up to greet her. "Good evening, lady, I'm glad you found my second story office this time of night. Some people don't. You were ten minutes late, by the way."

"Oh? Am I therefore penalized?" she said as I helped her off with her coat.

"Later..." I said with tongue-in-cheek.

"What happens to those people who can't find you at night?"

"Oh, I'm not sure—they probably die out there in the alley or somethin'," I kidded her.

"Goodness!" she exclaimed. "Maybe that explains the black cat out on your landing, checking everyone out as they approach your door?"

"Black cat?" I had no recollection of ever seeing a black cat around or one ever being in the building. Ever. "Uh...where, exactly?"

"As I said, out on your landing. Go see for yourself."

I did so. I peeked down the hallway, down the stairs. Nothing. "Are you sure?" I said as I re-entered the office. "I saw nothing."

"It's certainly not my imagination, Mr. Denning—"

"—Cable, we promised, no unnecessary formality, okay?"

"Oh, yes...Cable...perhaps the cat went downstairs?"

"Yeah, maybe." I examined the lady standing before me. "You look lovely tonight," I said, taking in that luscious doll.

"Thank you." She looked around the office. "You've—you've had your business in this location long?"

"Yeah, a few years, I guess you could say. The ghosts may have been here longer. You know how that goes." She smiled. "When I quit the police force about 1929 I bought my P.I. license and found this location. Been here ever since."

"I see." She took a deep breath and that wonderful chest of hers expanded. "So...?"

"So?"

She looked at me with scrutinizing eyes, but I also knew it was a woman's way of deciding whether she wanted to get closer to this man—or not. "So at least I'm not shooing you out my door..."

"You can't, it's my joint this time," I chuckled.

"I'm sorry...again...it was very hard to believe considering all the odd things that have been going on. I told you my husband is dead—or, as you suggested, someone who was *purported* to be my husband, is dead. Like you, I'm beginning to think the man who died might not have been my husband Anton Heidler, Mr.—uh, Cable..."

I raised my eyebrows. "Oh? What brought you to that moment of brilliance?" I kidded her.

"I think you were right about something else. Do you recall telling me you thought there was something fishy about Anton going up into the rafters of the little theatre where the radio quiz show was held?"

"Yep—in fact, I can tell you exactly what happened," I said, giving myself the chance to impress the lady with my knowledge of police work and human beings. "I think it went this way: Your husband legitimately told you he wanted to go up into the catwalk and check out what things looked like in the theatre's rigging. I'm not certain exactly how they did it, but somehow a certain party or parties found a way to literally duplicate your husband. Then, when he goes up, someone abducts or murders the real Anton Heidler and does a switcheroo. The 'thing' or man lying on the planks when the stage-hand fellow found him and went for help—yeah, him...well, that was the duplicate. I think the dead man I found was named *Emil Leichen.* Dollars to donuts from that evening on your husband's behavior was ever so slightly different than you remembered, right?"

She seemed amazed and her eyes misted. "Yes, it was about that time when my husband—or whoever or whatever he was—began to behave strangely. Anton and I were having marital problems to begin with and at first I discounted his aloofness. But he went over-board. He never touched me again. He began to sleep out on the sofa, I never saw him without clothes on and he said he developed throat problems and had to stop singing for a while and go to some new doctor, a Dr. Pritchard downtown somewhere. Although his speaking voice seemed like Anton's, he had no singing voice— and that alarmed me, but again I more or less put it aside, for the moment, anyway. I'm sure you can understand my actions early on."

"To be sure, Nadia...to be sure...I do. What doesn't add up to me is *exactly how they did it and the timing.* And, of course, *why?* For example, how was the killer going to know, *one,* that Anton was going exploring up on the catwalk? And *two,* how and when did they get the new body up into the rafters, and as you say, the old body down without someone noticing?"

As once before at her house, Nadia's eyes averted mine, as if she had to lie but preferred not to. "The whole thing is puzzling, isn't it? I'll know for certain tomorrow. I must go down to the morgue one more time and identify something on his body. Anton had a little chunk missing from his right elbow. If that's not the case, then I'll know whoever is down there is *not my husband.*"

"Would you like me to come?"

"Oh...I wouldn't think that as necessary, Cable. Only if you have the time to spend—"

"—I don't think you know who you're dealin' with here, Nadia. If it's the *Lichter Grabstätte* and if they're clever enough to pull a switcheroo on you so you can't recognize your own husband right off, can you imagine what else they might be capable of doing?"

She shuddered. "Ooo! That gives me goose bumps just thinking about who I might have been living with for the past few weeks or months—"

"—yeah, I'd think about that, lady. Anton Heidler had been missing a lot longer than you knew, and Emil Leichen was the likely substitute. In the meantime, I think I'll check out this Dr. Pritchard..."

Just then my office door opened and in walked Abbey Allison, a.k.a. 'Zitzy.' She was holding a .45 colt in her hand. "I don't think that is a good idea, Mr. Denning." Now I figured the black cat's presence on the landing.

"Well! Somehow I thought I hadn't seen the last of you." I said that, kicking back in my chair.

"Smart thinking, mister." Then she looked Nadia over. "And you? You're dumber than I thought." She came around to face the lady. "You thought the dummy I kissed to death was really your husband?"

"I—I suspected differently...did you kill Anton?" a very composed Nadia asked. That surprised me.

"You know better...ladies don't tell, toots!" Abbey Allison retorted. "Humans are so stupid. But for your information, no, I did not destroy the mortal existence of your dearly precious Anton. Dr. Pritchard hired someone to kill Anton Heidler in order to clear the way for the synthetic constructed human-like robot, Emil Leichen."

"So where did Emil Leichen come from?" I asked.

"A fake, a composite, a mock up human, Mr. Denning. You see, Dr. Pritchard had to find a creature capable of being transmogrified into a clone of Anton Heidler using Heidler's DNA helix code. But none of that matters because both of you are going to be used for exactly the same purposes as he was. Things run in threes, you know. Up with the hands, gang!" she commanded us.

I drew the .32 out of my desk drawer and aimed it at Abbey Allison. "Not so fast, lady— you can't haul us off that easy! Do you really think you can kill both of us before I get off a shot?" I threatened. "Think again!"

She thought fast. "So? You can wound me, but you can't kill me, Denning. I'm the winner here. You see, before I even go down, I can lunge at your nice little opera singer here and kiss her firmly on the mouth and she'll be dead in—oh....say, five minutes, tops!"

"Try it!" I warned her. As soon as she saw I meant business and wasn't backing down, she softened a little. "Well, perhaps that *is* a bit crude—and destroy one of our cargo as well. Hmmm...what to do?"

"May I make a suggestion?" Nadia's voice trembled.

"You? Yeah, why not?"

"I think this whole thing is a bad idea." Then Nadia stood up. Her bravery surprised me! "I hate this man, this so-called detective—I think we can both take him in to Dr. Pritchard—and then you may release me for helping you. I am one of you, you know."

"No, I didn't know. Prove it, lady," Abbey Allison demanded.

I sat in disbelief as the sophisticated and demure Nadia approached the unsuspecting Abbey. "I'm waiting..."

I noticed Nadia had her shoes off. Suddenly with kicks to the gut and then the chest, Nadia instantly felled Abbey Allison to the floor! She was out cold. Then Nadia stepped on her throat. "That's how we subdue bad people in dark alleys, Cable," Nadia said a little excited and smiling.

"I don't believe it!" I said, putting my weapon down on the desk. "You're telling me you k.o.'d this raunchy babe with your feet? Where'd you learn to do that?"

"Oh, women have their ways as well, you know. It's called *Kikku*, Cable, a form of martial arts and a certain defense form for women."

"Yeah, I know what it is—I've just never seen a babe do it. And, oh, by the way, what's with '*I hate this man, this so-called detective*' stuff?"

She chuckled. "Well, I had to think of something to get her off guard. Like you, she wouldn't have suspected me to possess a martial arts posture."

"No, I guess not." I looked down at the floor. "Well, what now? I suppose we gotta dump the broad somewhere safe so she won't accost us anymore—at least for a while."

"And Dr. Pritchard?" she asked intently.

"Yeah, and him, too. I'll check him out tomorrow."

"May I go with you?"

"It ain't gonna be a family picnic, Nadia. This guy and his organization—which I suspect is that *Lichter Grabstätte*—are dangerous and probably lethal once they target you for whatever diabolical purposes they have in mind. And...if they're associated with the Oculus, we're in even deeper shit."

She smiled a wonderful sexy smile at me. "We all have to go some time, Cable...how about it? I need a little adventure in my life."

"You may be asking for a hell of a lot more adventure than you bargained for, missy. I don't know. Maybe you can be used as a beard or something..."

"A what?"

"A beard—you know, a cover, like you go into the office as a new patient and check things out and I pick a lock and go into the rear of the joint." Damn, I wanted this woman so much I could taste it! She put her foot up on my client's chair to readjust her hose and I got a glimpse of some pretty good leg. And ya know, I'm not so sure she didn't do it on purpose. "So...how's your, uh, sex life?" I blurted out, unable to contain my desire any longer.

She looked at me curiously and I didn't know what to expect. "My...my sex life? Aren't you rather nosy, Mr. Denning?" she asked in a pert but somehow naughty tone of voice.

"C'mon, Nadia, we're not school kids here, let's not pretend we're not attracted to each other. I can feel it from you just as much as you can feel it from me. How soon we forget—your place, remember? Do you recall staring at me with no uncertain interest when we first met—or was that my imagination?"

"Yes, I do. Admittedly, I was taken with you the minute you walked in my door. But ha! Sex life? Pretty dismal, I'd say—until you came along, mister. Anton never was much of a lover and this other guy or creature or whatever he was—was zero! So that's my sex history for the past five years or so...like I said, dismal..."

"So how would you like to spice it up a few notches?"

"Are you a candidate?"

"You bet—and twice on Sundays."

She laughed a wonderful laugh. "Well, I'll warn you ahead of time—I'm thirty-two, I refuse to use contraception because I would want nothing between us—I'm Catholic—and I suppose I could get pregnant. So...I guess that's an honest explanation of my romantic inclinations, not to mention my intentions with you, mister."

"That says a lot. So you're Catholic, eh?"

"Yes—and no. I'm not practicing at the moment. I think God—"

"—when do you wanna get started?" I suggested jokingly.

"I'm not that kind of girl, Cable. I need to let things take place naturally and take one day at a time. You know, dancing and dining, a few smooches in the car or in the park, a quiet evening on my sofa listening to my recording of *Traviata*...let us *breathe in* our love making first. I'm afraid I'm a little old fashioned. Do you think you can live with that? I realize men are anxious. It's their nature to want to be impulsive, immediate."

"Yep, that it is, lass. But if the bounty at the other end is worth it, I don't think a guy would mind too much. Especially someone like me who's probably been around the block a few more times than you. I'm in a hurry—but I ain't, if you get my drift. In fact, I'm not adverse to a little romancin' as part of the—the act of lovemaking. Shall we give it a spin—on or off the dance floor?"

She straightened out her skirt and put her shoes back on. Then she looked up into my eyes. "Yes, Cable, I'd like that very much. At least we can give it a try. Just take your time, please. I'm more fragile than I look. Plus, I'm—I'm out of practice."

"You do know I'm a bum compared to you, don't ya? I smoke, drink, chase skirts and I was raised in the ghetto in Boyle Heights, came up the hard way...became a cop and when I couldn't stand the corruption in the police force, I quit and here I am...a private dick."

She chuckled. "A what? Didn't you pull that one on me once before?"

"A private dick...I catch 'em all with that one. It means a private detective—it's got a lot of history to it."

"Oh...Uh huh." Then she came around to my side of the desk. "May I—may I touch your face?" she asked.

55

"My face?"

"Yes, my grandmother was a wonderful person. You'd have loved her. She said if one takes their left hand, palm open, and gently brushes the right cheek of your dearly intended, you will receive a definite yes or no. So…may I try it with you?"

"Sure, why not?" I answered, becoming very still.

She carefully reached her hand toward me and I could feel the electricity of her body connect with my cheek as her hand slightly touched my right cheek for a few seconds. "You may do the same with me, if you wish," she said. "I think I got a definite 'yes'."

"Okay." I did the same with her and before I even touched her, her body jerked and a shiver went through her. It was a definite "yes" as far as I was concerned. "How'd that feel? What's the verdict?"

I knew in that minute she wanted to take me into her arms and kiss me down to my shoes. But she didn't. She took a deep breath and then let it out slowly. "I had a baby once, Cable. She lived to be but six days old. She died on the seventh. I was almost eighteen then and unmarried. My parents separated me from the father of the child forever. Perhaps I should have married that man, Cable. But I didn't. And I never saw him again. You see, my singing career was utmost in the minds of my civic and culturally minded parents. So I became an operatic singer."

"Are you sorry?" I asked, listening intently to the lady.

"I was for years. Now I'm not so sure. Raising a child in uncertain times is risky, I think. Different people are designed to be different things in this world. Now I don't think I was designed to be a mother. And it's almost too late. So I just want *love*, Cable, wonderful, plain, simple uncomplicated *love*."

I laughed. "There ain't no such thing, Nadia. There's always a rotten apple somewhere in the barrel. Even if ya got the *best* together, someone or something steps in between sooner or later. It's like everything's got a time to be born, a time to live—and a time to...well, I don't *expect* anymore. I just live in the time we're allowed, here, now..."

She leaned forward and kissed my nose. "Well, then—how about dinner and dancing soon? I'd like to start the time we've got!"

I laughed lightly. "How *much* time is that, babe?"

"As long as it takes to get each other out of our systems—you know, what we seem to need from each other, I guess."

"And after that?"

"I'm not sure, what do you think?"

"I don't know. Every couple's different. Some are highly charged and burn out like shooting stars. Others do a slow extinction route until one day you wake up next to that someone and there's nothing there anymore. But you pretend, you fake it, you make believe the same love still lives there between you. Nobody made it happen, and maybe nobody made it go away, it's just the way of things, that's all."

"And you don't think that's a rather pessimistic way of looking at things? For God's sake, Cable, what if things just get better and continue to grow positively, day after day, month after month, year after year?"

"Well, then, I'd say that's kinda rare, lady—and if it's us, we're kinda lucky. I'm not sayin' it doesn't happen—it's just probably something that gets pulled from the bottom of the deck."

"And us, Cable? Would we be dealt from the bottom of the deck?"

"I dunno. Let's do that dining and dancing first, and see..." I chuckled.

Chapter 2

DANCE OF THE UNHOLY TRINITY

Nadia Skorkowsky and I dumped Abbey Allison's body in an alleyway down by the Santa Monica pier. As soon as she came to, I'm sure she would turn into either a black cat or disappear into her own dimensional ethers. Or—. It's the *or* that concerned me, if she decided to seek revenge. When we got back we parted company with the promise to spend some time together dining and dancing the next Friday evening. Of course, then I didn't know I was about to embark on a very bizarre adventure in the hot, white sands of New Mexico and our romantic liaison and Dr. Pritchard would have to wait.

It was Tuesday, March 6, 1945. Truthfully, I didn't know if I could wait a few days to let things cool off between Nadia and myself before having that dinner and dancing date. Yep, I had restless balls for that lady and after all, we'd very likely end up in an all-night wrestling match under the covers of her nice plush bed in Beverly Hills. She was right, I wanted to push things and so I reconsidered...thought it best to take my time with this lovely woman of class and breeding. Then the phone rang. "Yeah, Cable Denning here..."

"Signor Denning?" a pleasant feminine voice spoke with a slight Italian accent. "You do not know me, but I am-a the niece of Enrico Fermi. *Bess Spitz,* a Jewish lady who said she met-a you, suggested I call you. I am called

Gianna Sacchetti—my madre is called Maria. My poor papa has died in the war in *Italia*." I had heard of Enrico Fermi...one of the scientists Einstein talked about who was working on the atomic bomb out on the desert.

"Yeah, I remember meeting Bess Spitz. Sacchetti you say, huh? If I recall correctly, she said you were involved in some movement to stop the bomb from being made. War is hell and I'm sorry you lost your Dad, ma'am. What can I do for you?"

"Somehow we need to stop my Uncle Enrico, signor Denning. We are all so worried, that those men under Oppenheimer will—will end the world if allowed to do so! Oppenheimer, he is *diavolo*—a devil against God!"

"Well, those are pretty strong words and grandiose plans, Miss Sacchetti. Even if I agreed to help you with this thing, your uncle would be surrounded by military guards and is probably housed behind barbed wire and a concrete bunker of some sort even as we speak."

"But I know Dr. Oppenheimer and my uncle will be in Alamogordo to see the tower during the next few days."

"The tower?"

"Yes, it is from where the bomb will be exploded."

I played a little dumb. "Oh, yeah, I've heard of that tower thing."

"There will be *twelve terrible men*—Miss Spitz refers to them as the *Disciples of Doom*. Please, signor Denning, come and help me talk those stupido men out of doing what they wish to do!"

"I don't know, signorina. People can get killed that way. It's tricky stuff. And if we get caught, they either

60

kill us on the spot or lock us up and throw away the key."

"How important to you...signore...is the future of this beautiful earth we live on?"

"Mighty important, lady." I took out a Lucky Strike and lit it. "Okay, suppose I participate in this insane thing with you, how do we get a hold of your Uncle Enrico?"

"Help me get to the tower. He and Oppenheimer and a military man named General Groves will be there for certain, I believe."

"You *believe?* And don't know?"

"No, I do know...we have sources, signor Denning..."

I took a deep breath and let it out. "Okay...for you and for my friend Albert Einstein—we'll give it a go, I guess."

"Oh, grazie, signor Denning! But I have no money to pay you with."

"This ain't about money, honey—it's the principle of the damn thing. Just get me back in time—if we're still alive, that is. By the way, you sound young—how old are you?"

"I am becoming twenty in November. How old are you?"

"Old enough to be your father, kid. So...where are you now and what do you look like so I can recognize you when we meet up?"

"I am *Italiano*, Mr. Denning—small, dark haired, a little bend in my nose—I'm afraid I am not very pretty. Are you handsome?"

"Naw, kinda old and balding with false teeth—but a good smile!" I lied to make her feel better about herself.

"Oh, then you have aged much lately?"

"Why do you say that?"

"I have a photograph of you. You are middle-aged, tall and handsome with your fedora and fog coat. In *Italia* the ladies would call you *caldo maschio*—very sexy man, Mr. Denning."

"Oh...well maybe not all of that is true, but I do have a good smile!"

She laughed. "Oh...so...is your office near Western Avenue and Franklin?"

"Yep, not too far."

"I visit with a friend on Los Feliz. I come pick you up five o'clock in the morning Friday?"

"Five in the morning! I can't even see to go to the bathroom that time of the morning. How about a little later?"

"I am sorry, but we must leave early. That is because we cannot drive to New Mexico. It will take us one day each way to travel that way. My family has an Italian friend who is truly *pazzo*, but he a good airplane pilot. Basto Granacci will fly us to New Mexico. There we will meet an automobile and drive to a special location, okay?"

"Yeah, sure...fine...I hope you don't mind if I sleep a lot on the plane."

"Oh, no, signore, as long as you are with me when we speak to my Uncle Enrico and Dr. Oppenheimer."

The Death Tower

As soon as I'd hung up talking to Gianna Sacchetti I dialed Nadia's number. "Yes, hello?" that wonderful warm female voice spoke.

"It's—it's me, Nadia. Say, much to my disappointment I need to go out of town for a few days on a job. How about the following Friday for our dancing and dining date?"

I knew she was intuitive. "It's like you said, isn't it, Cable? You live a risk-filled life almost every day—and it's true every time you go out I may never see you again?"

"Yeah, babe, that's exactly what I told you. So...do you still wanna be with me?"

"What is it you say, 'every day and twice on Sundays'?"

"Yeah, sort of...I think I said that to you," I chuckled.

"Yes, Cable, yes...for however long I have you, I want you."

"You're sure of that now?"

"Yes. Risks, danger and all...I've thought about it. And if I don't leap now with someone like you, I might never do it."

"Okay, babe, I'll be back in three or four days tops—I'll call you the minute I get in."

"Promise? I don't know, Cable—suddenly I've gotten stupid—all I do is walk around in my big house here thinking about you. Do you think I'm crazy to take this step?"

"Yep," I kidded her. "Looney as a tune, kid!" I said.

"All the more reason I'll do it! Please be safe and don't even tell me where you're going or what you're going to do. I could say 'be careful,' but I won't. Goodbye, Cable..." We hung up and I felt relieved that Nadia Skorkowsky was still willing to be with an old gumshoe waiting out his turn in line for the hatchet man's visit.

Then I called Ida to tell her I was off on another adventure from which I might or might not return. She was concerned, of course, but also very intuitive. She told me she saw me returning in a few days a little worse for the wear but intact. I thanked her for the good omen and told her I'd take her out for dinner and dancing again soon. That always cheered her up. I think she knew there was a good chance we might end up in her nice cozy little bed—together. Especially if we were drinking.

As promised, Gianna Sacchetti picked me up around five on Friday morning and we drove out to a valley airstrip. Gianna was no beauty by any stretch of the imagination. But she boasted a swell feminine body with all the curves in the right places. She had thin lips and dark hair with a little red in it. Her eyes were a light brown and she probably stood about five-feet four. Her crazy pilot and family friend Basto Granacci really *was* crazy! I could tell we were in for an interesting journey. I slept a goodly part of it.

The airplane ride went fast and we flew into a small landing strip out in the middle of nowhere. We were greeted with a 1940 4-door Chevrolet Master Deluxe by two men and a woman. We journeyed to a whistle stop named *Socorro* that boasted a gas station, a mechanic's garage and a small cantina. But I soon learned it was a front. At the rear of the cantina was a trapdoor covered with a large hemp carpet. Folks removed the carpet, opened the hatch and we descended down some solid wooden stairs into comfortable looking underground living quarters. There were several people in it. "Water is the thing in this land," an older, distinguished man greeted me. "And the heat." He got up and shook my hand. "I'm Walter Damrosch, sir."

"Please to meet you—all of you," I said. "I wasn't aware there would be quite so many of you here—"

"—Gianna was forbidden to tell any more than she had to. Getting you here was quite an accomplishment—eh, Gianna?" The young woman smiled. Then Damrosch got serious. "A drink, Mr. Denning?"

"Yeah, don't mind if I do—gin and tonic if ya have it."

Soon I was sitting with a gin with warm tonic. Damrosch checked me out carefully. "I can tell...you're as hard as they make 'em when you need to be. That's good. You'll need that on this assignment."

"Assignment? I didn't know I was working for anybody," I said.

He ignored my comment. Then he took a big breath and sipped on a whiskey sour. "So, Mr. Denning, why are you here? Thank you, by the way, for volunteering your time and expertise." I couldn't but keep from looking at a doll of a blonde sitting on a small sofa with another man. Damrosch was sharp and caught it. "Let me introduce you. This pretty blonde lady is not a movie star, Mr. Denning, but Dr. Lana LaMarr. She does have a glamorous name, doesn't she? She studies the effects of gamma radiation on organic life forms." She nodded to me and Damrosch moved on. "This tall drink of water is Grey Whitling, anthropologist, Harry Neumann, molecular biologist and radiation expert—and last but not least, Dr. Lawrence Andover, who has two equal roles, that of psychologist and studying the effects of atomically generated explosions at variant degrees of temperature and locale. We are not able to access the laboratory yet, but soon, we are most hopeful. There—I think I said what I was supposed to!"

I took out my cigarettes and started to light up when Damrosch stopped me, saying we must not pollute the converted cellar's atmosphere. I thought it odd, but left it at that. "Well," I said, addressing everyone in the room. "I can tell ya one thing for sure, folks, no matter how you slice it, you're gonna have a hell of time preventing the momentum of the powers that be from wreaking havoc on this planet. Even my friend Albert Einstein confided in me just a couple of weeks ago that the government of the United States has pretty much found itself in an arms race between Hitler, Stalin, Hirohito and God knows who else, maybe even the little Italian pig, Mussolini."

"We require a distinctive formulary," Damrosch commented. "A contiguous way to stop these madmen. Think of it, Mr. Denning," he said as his eyes glanced up toward the ceiling and beyond. "There...standing in the night...a black tower of death...almost complete, nearly one-hundred feet in the air, awaiting the most deadly weapon the world has ever known!" The others nodded their approval and Damrosch continued. "*You*...you, Mr. Denning, must meet in the dark of night with an operative from the laboratory where the despot Oppenheimer holds court. I understand it is a lascivious den of debauchery. Dr. Fermi will be brought to you when you and Gianna have waited in the appointed place."

"So, if I may ask, what are the chances of us getting out of this thing alive—or un-captured?" I asked.

"About fifty-fifty," he answered.

I didn't like those odds, especially just when my life was going so well and I had a Friday night date with a dish named Nadia Skorkowsky. "So when do we start?" I asked, looking around at the faces of my six compatriots. None of them seemed regular human being types. In fact, my intuitive gyroscope kept me thinking about how I felt when I first knew Joe Lorena was an alien personage, a *Sens Parafactor*. That's how I was beginning to feel about these folks, except for Gianna, that is. But what the hell was I saying? I was a half-breed myself.

"Tonight," the good-looking Miss LaMarr spoke up. "You, Gianna and myself will travel to the sight of the tower. It's about an hour's drive from here, but the road to it cannot be used because of military personnel. So we must walk a mile or two from an approach point northeast of the site."

"Don't you think all of this is a hell of a lotta work for a dubious outcome, folks?" I inquired.

"How much is the earth worth, Mr. Denning?" the slender Dr. Whitling spoke up. "Especially the human race..."

"You really wanna know my position on the subject? I think the human race stinks. You're seein' it now—all men really know how to do is breed and destroy! We're in a bloody war to please political agendas and make the fat cats richer! The earth herself, nature and most of what goes with it? That's different, yeah, I think we gotta do what we can to preserve it."

"However you personally think, Mr. Denning, the fact remains, all living things are faced with permanent destruction. You see, sir, nature never repeats herself— once a species is extinct, that's it, I'm afraid," Damrosch reminded us.

"Yeah, I kinda knew that but didn't, if ya know what I mean. So...? How do we stop those insane idiots from pulling the atomic trigger—grab 'em by the short hairs and make 'em cry 'uncle'?"

Miss LaMarr snickered. "Precisely, Mr. Denning. Humans were supposed to be the natural caretakers of the earth. But they have failed on every count, as we see it. Now all creatures that we were sent to preserve are threatened!" she declaimed.

"'Sent to preserve'?" I asked, confirming my suspicions. "You mean you guys ain't from this local galactic neighborhood or dimension?"

They all blinked their eyes at the same time and looked at me. "Fundamental, Mr. Denning, fundamental. We knew you knew, or else we could not have asked you along," Damrosch explained.

"Well, I'm not so sure it's a privilege, folks— especially if I don't make it out alive. Remember, I'm the *human mortal* here..."

"One-half the human, Mr. Denning," Damrosch corrected me.

Entering Evil

It was early Friday morning, March 9, 1945. Gianna, Lana LaMarr and myself were let off somewhere in the middle of a desert. We were told we would be crossing into the *Jornada del Muerto*—Journey of Death—and so we walked for about an hour along cool sands. Gianna was silent, but Miss LaMarr and I chatted quite a bit about the predicament we were faced with. "Oppenheimer believes he is the one to destroy this world, I think," she informed me. "He is a subscriber to the *Bhagavad-Gita* and the ancient Sanskrit languages that speak of such a doom coming upon the world," Lana said with no uncertainty. "That is how the name 'Trinity Project' came to be, Mr. Denning. *Brahma, the Creator, Vishnu the Preserver and Shiva the Destroyer.*"

I chuckled. "Why is the destroyer a female?"

"Shiva is a *male* energy," she answered me.

"Oh...with the 'a' ending, I just thought—"

"—no, sir, it is the male of your kind that are the destroyers. The females try and preserve life. How well do you know your Eastern history, philosophy and religion, Mr. Denning?"

"Not very well, I'm afraid, Miss LaMarr. Sorry, but I'm kinda of like an ignorant gumshoe who got sucked into this very weird and dangerous mission—for no pay, I might add."

"We are all grateful to you. But I do wonder about your role in all of this. What help can you possibly be in the long run?"

"I donno. I'm here, ain't I?" I countered, a little miffed.

69

We walked over a rise and suddenly we all stopped dead in our tracks. There in a pale moonlight stood the black outline of a tower. "There...there is the suspender of death...where the bomb shall reside before it explodes!" she whispered. Gianna gasped but said nothing.

We walked down a hillside toward the tower of death. But we didn't get too far. When we reached the bottom, suddenly five uniformed soldiers with drawn rifles stopped us. Immediately Gianna told them who she was and who we were and that we were here to speak to her Uncle Enrico and Oppenheimer. The soldiers checked out my I.D. and soon we were led to a tent about fifty yards from the test site. We were asked to wait outside. Soon a smallish man dressed in a suit with very little black hair stepped out. "Piccina mio!" he cried out upon seeing Gianna. "What do you do here?" he asked as he hugged his little relative. Then he looked at Lana and me. *"Cosa sta succedendo,* Gianna?" he asked.

"Oh, Uncle Enrico, Mama is sick to death with this war thing—and now worries what she sees in her prophesies shall come true. Please, *zio*, you must listen!"

"Gianna—I am a *dottore di scienza*, Gianna, I cannot be emotional about my work. You should not have come here!"

Just then another head poked out from the tent door. "What's going on here?" a tall, very thin man with a pipe in his mouth spoke. He also wore a suit, tie and a very wide-brimmed street hat on his head. A Colonel Trumbel, the head military representative, informed the man that we had been found coming down the hill toward the tower. "Oh..." Then he glanced at Gianna and us. "Fermi? Do you know these people?"

"Yes, signor Doctor Oppenheimer...this young-a lady is-a my niece, my sister's daughter. I do not know these two others," Fermi replied.

"What are they doing *here*?" the tall man asked.

"I do not know how they knew where we were or what we are doing." Then Fermi gestured toward the tall thin one. "This is Dr. Oppenheimer," he said as he gestured in the man's direction. "He's in charge of the programma here."

Oppenheimer seemed then to speak to Fermi, but was looking at us. "Do they know they cannot remain here? And what is it they want?"

"*Scuse*, signore—I am Gianna Sacchetti and we are here for you to stop the explosion. Many people are frightened and feel—"

"—you'd better leave now, young lady," Oppenheimer interrupted. He turned to the military man. "Colonel, will you please have them debriefed and driven back to town—or wherever they came from?"

Time was running out and we saw no contact person. Maybe he chickened out or something went wrong. "If you don't mind, sir," I said, a little put out at this man's arrogance and air of superiority. "These people have a voice and a will to express to you something that's pretty damn important to the whole world. Are you listening? You are at least in part responsible for unleashing the forces of the universe on an innocent planet."

He checked me out. "And just who are you?"

"Me? Hell, I'm just another nobody hanging around to see if you're really gonna do it."

"Oh, I assure you, Mr.—Mr.—"

"—Denning, Cable Denning—"

"—Mr. Denning, we *are* going to do it. But then again, I have never been interested in politics or economics. I do not possess a radio or telephone of my own and learned of the stock market crash some days after the fact. Some say *I am become Death, the killer of worlds*...and how do you know, Mr. Denning—the inhumanity and disaster that is modern warfare may be halted because of these efforts we now make."

"I doubt it," I answered. "If man hasn't found a way to stop war in ten thousand years, what makes you think he will now?"

"By virtue of the *magnitude*, sir, the sheer size of what we project to be catastrophic for all within miles of the blast site—no, it will be a paradigm changer for all time in this world of ours," Oppenheimer firmly opined.

Lana LaMarr had been studying Oppenheimer's face and expressions, I noted. "But what of all the biodiversity, Dr. Oppenheimer? I am also a scientist—I see what could happen to upset the balances in nature herself. With the scenario you paint, it's almost as if human kind were an anomaly, separate and distinct from nature."

The tall man smiled. "Maybe our so-called 'human kind *is* a misfit, an anomaly, young woman. What is it you research or study, if I may ask?"

"The effects of gamma radiation on naturally occurring organic life forms, doctor," Lana answered.

"Of course some things will be more affected than others, no doubt," he commented, turning his words over slowly. "But scientists are not delinquents, ma'am—" He checked out her fine face and body. "Why is it with your glamour, you did not go to Hollywood or the like?"

I wondered if Oppenheimer was aware there were aliens among us. Of course there was always the possibility *he* was one! But even if Lana LaMarr was a non-terrestrial at least in part, she was dogged about raking Oppenheimer over the coals. "Because I care for things that are real, Dr. Oppenheimer. I may respect your background, but I cannot accept nor respect you and your colleagues for assuming that because a handful of bureaucrats, military madmen and unthinking scientists would release this horror upon the world without due consideration for the long term effect on organic life, that all will be well in the future."

"Well spoken," Oppenheimer replied. "I have thought of these things. They will call me the *father of the atomic bomb,* not Einstein or Fermi here. But all of that is a question yet to be answered." Then he ordered Colonel Trumbel again. "Perhaps these people should be driven away from danger now, if you will." Then he turned to us. "Tomorrow morning at about 10 a.m., 200 tons of TNT with 1,000 curries of radioactive substance shall be detonated here. You are violating a government testing ground simply by being here. I'm sorry—good-bye now." He went back into his tent. Fermi hugged his niece and followed.

We were led away by Colonel Trumbel to a small building with very thick walls. I noticed over in another area many men were piling boxes up onto a twenty or thirty foot wooden platform. Trumbel then left the three of us in the small building—locked in! "I think we are supposed to go home now," Gianna stated. "I was sad my Uncle Enrico was so...so—"

"—unresponsive? Yeah, I kinda got that message, too, Gianna," I said, looking at Lana. "What do you think?" I asked her.

"I don't think they will let us go, Cable," she said. "By virtue of being here we have seen too much, at least perhaps from their viewpoints. I also feel something else is up very soon. Perhaps they will detonate the atomic test immediately after the explosives they are loading up onto that platform out there are in place," the intelligent lady remarked.

Two hours later Colonel Trumbel returned with two soldiers. He had trouble looking us in the eye. "I must ask you to follow me."

"Where to?" I asked. He didn't answer.

We were led straight toward the huge pile of what I now recognized as TNT explosives. The workmen had gone. The two soldiers then bound our wrists. We were led up the wooden stairs to where the stockpile of explosives were awaiting detonation and tied to three of the four 4x 4 corner posts. Trumbel had his men leave and then finally faced us. "Regrettably, United States Government policy for violating a highly classified site such as the Trinity location here is death by firing squad. But my men say they cannot shoot innocent civilian Americans. So...I have thought of a better solution. As I told you, about 10:00 tomorrow morning this entire stockpile will explode. Your bodies will be shredded and then incinerated instantly—with no discernible trace."

The three of us shuddered. "I thought Dr. Oppenheimer commanded you to take us home, buddy," I commented, licking my dry lips. I was beginning to feel dehydrated...or was it nerves?

"Dr. Oppenheimer is a busy man, unable to make all decisions clearly. You heard him. He said I was to *'debrief'* you. Well, this is my way of doing just that. I answer only to General Groves and the President of the United States, sir. I'm sure the preoccupied scientists would not even know you were here—and then—well, *gone...*"

The two women looked helpless as they struggled to undo the ropes now binding them to the posts. "I'm sorry to have to do this. Good luck." The Colonel said no more and descended the stairs.

Good luck? What an asshole!

Countdown

I knew all too well the dawn would be coming soon, and with it the possible doom of one inconsequential human and two alien hybrids. The good Colonel Trumbel had left two MP's below us just in case someone might wanna come rescue us. How thoughtful of him. I was looking up at the ominous black girder tower over to my left. It must have risen at least a hundred feet. That horrid thing, that *death tower* would be the vehicle of doom for the human race, so it had been said. Maybe it was true, maybe it wasn't. I always remembered what Escadero had told me about the necessity of both polarities, good and bad, light and dark, destruction and healing, birth and death.

I shouted over to Lana LaMarr. "Are you still wondering what possible use I might be to this excursion?"

"Yes, I am," she responded indignantly. "Or you, young niece, for talking us into such a stupid, unproductive trap!"

"I did not know. I thought we could speak to Uncle Enrico and Dr. Oppenheimer and they would listen. I truly thought they would respond—at least to our pleas and hear us out!"

"Ya don't know the military mind, Gianna," I said. "We have to remember, this is a *military project* and the scientists are but means to an end—in this case perhaps *our* end as well!"

Neither of the females answered and time went on. Dawn came warm and without a breeze. By nine o'clock or so all three of us were dripping wet, thirsty and beginning the first stages of sunstroke. I began to sweat that certain kind of 'secondary' sweat that apprehension breeds as it neared ten a.m. About that time we heard three whistles blow and all personnel departed the area. So there we were, alone without a soul who really knew where we were. Ten fifteen. Still no blast. We were still here. Then out of the desert sands surrounding us emerged a large greenish membrane of some sort. It was like a huge, thin bubble. But just as soon as it hit the outside air, it turned invisible. The women shrieked while I simply observed. Before we knew it, we felt a wafting of cooler air and an invisible voice was talking to me. Then something cool but solid pushed my head hard against the 4 x 4 I was tied to. "Owww!" I exclaimed as I felt darts of pain enter my skull.

"They will soon return—when they discover I gimmicked the explosion timers. We must hurry," a dark, but pleasant voice spoke. "How am I doing?"

"How are you doing *what?*" I asked, my head throbbing.

"Sounding like you..."

"Not so hot—your voice is too low..."

"Oh? I need to work on that!"

"Who and what in the hell *are* you?"

"Shhh! For now let's get you out of here before the soldiers and scientists come to see what went wrong."

In three minutes we were off the platform running toward the hillside we originally had descended from. The voice and the bubble had vanished just as quickly as it had appeared. But we didn't have time to think about it. We stumbled and fell our way back to our starting point. And just three or four miles from point zero we heard the loudest explosion in our lives and fire and smoke arose to the south. That would've been us... dust and ash and smoke is all that would've been left of us!

Much to our deepest thanks, Damrosch and another figure I couldn't make out greeted us with the car as we arrived at the debarkation point. We got in and sped away quickly as the gathering smoke drifted toward us. We were given water immediately. I looked around for the second passenger up front. I saw no one. "Quite an explosion, I assure you," Damrosch spoke. "But not the bomb...correct?"

"No, not the bomb. Say, didn't I see a figure next to you when you drove up?" I inquired.

"You may have…" came the tentative answer.

"May have? I know you guys are non-terrestrials, but—"

"—in time, Mr. Denning, all in good time…was that explosion simply dynamite?"

"Yeah, and it could've been us up there in that radio-active smoke," I said. "They put some other crap in the mix to check out the effect on the atmosphere, I think." Gianna was shaking and we gave her a blanket while Lana and I were okay, if a bit unsteady. "I believe in miracles, Damrosch—some bloke came in a green bubble that turned invisible, freed us and disappeared."

"Not quite, I'm afraid, Mr. Denning—I mean, that he disappeared entirely," Damrosch said, his voice a little cold on its edges. "You see, we had to strike a bargain—with—with—"

"—with *me*," the same invisible voice who had rescued us spoke up. "Do not flatter yourself, I did not rescue you for your ignorance, but for what peculiarities you possess and your *knowledge*, Mr. Denning."

I nodded my head in the affirmative. Yep, from the frying pan into the fire alright! I turned to Lana. "See? Now you're beginning to see my worth, young woman—I just saved your pretty little ass," I asserted.

"Yes, Mr. Denning, but more than likely at the expense of your own…ass, that is," she responded, as if she knew who it was who might be conversing with us from the perspective of an invisible being.

"Let's not hope *that*," I said. "Okay, Mr. Invisible, I suppose I should thank you for saving our lives, whoever you are, but I can see it comes with a price. You, Cronus-Gor, Zott, Anon and the other Oculus heads just seem to enjoy masquerading around invisibly or highly transformed."

"Perhaps it's 'fashionable' for superior beings..." the invisible one spoke again, his voice relaxed. " You are welcome...but you're also correct about there being a price to pay, Mr. Denning. As I said, I saved you not for your limited little human self, but for your 'other qualities' and your, shall we say, other dimensional knowledge."

"So...for my knowledge? What pray tell might that be this splendid Sunday afternoon?" I said with a hint of sarcasm.

"As Mr. Damrosch said, all in good time...you and I shall have a private, one-to-one talk when we return to Los Angeles."

I knew deep down everyone wants *something*. I hoped to hell it wasn't what I thought it was. But a sinking feeling made me believe this strange new force in my life would be one in a line of many to invade my private and meager existence and hunt me until either I fessed up what he wanted—or I'd be dead. Either choice wasn't a good one.

By the time we got back to the little whistle stop, the invisible one had left us. I never saw the other people again. The group I'd met in the desert went their own way, and Gianna, Basto Granacci the pilot and myself flew back to L.A. Where the mysterious, invisible stranger went or how he traveled I can't say, but I was certain I'd hear from him again—soon. After having experienced Colonel Trumbel, I was convinced that Fermi and Oppenheimer had no knowledge of our peril. Life for them would go on until the appointed hour when the world would change, and one huge fireball and thunderous repercussion would seal the door of the past behind the human race.

Erond Mantis Spiricus

It was Tuesday, March the 13th. After I got back and checked in with Ida—who was mighty relieved that I was sort of alive and well—I had only one thing in mind. I called Nadia Skorkowsky. "Nadia—it's me Cable...hello there..."

"You said you'd call right back! That was yesterday—I've been on pins and needles ever since! I hope this isn't a preview of—"

"—hey, wait a minute, lady—I haven't spoken to you since before I left. Are you sure you haven't got your wires—or your boyfriends—crossed up here?"

"Please, Cable, you don't have to make excuses—"

"—I'm a dependable guy, Nadia. You need to know that. And I definitely did *not* talk to you yesterday!"

There was a short pause. "It doesn't matter, darling. Please...I can't wait—can you come over to my place—like now?"

I smiled. "Oh, yeah, I can...but I do have one question. What is it I said yesterday if indeed I called you?"

I began to smell a rat and it was in that pile of wood on the platform beneath the black tower where I first smelled him. "In fact, you were very—very vulgar, in a way, and highly suggestive. But I guess you missed me—"

"—I swear, Nadia, I didn't talk to you yesterday. I've got a feeling someone else is tapping in on my frequency or something. Did it sound like my voice?"

"Yes, of course. I'd recognize your voice anywhere, Cable."

I thought for a few seconds. "Okay, babe, I'm comin' over—have the honeyed whiskey and the hot water ready!"

"How long, Cable? I've been wanting you all weekend. I'm—I'm all built up inside. That's why I was so upset."

"How about six? Ida's already gone home and all I have to do is clean up a bit and come knockin' at your door."

"Yes, please, hurry, darling..." We hung up. I began to put two and two together. First I get freed from exploding into smithereens by an invisible guy or creature, then he shows up in the car with some not so great news—and now I get the feeling he's tryin' to horn in on my newly found treasure of a girlfriend.

Life is such an irony, and even if you don't intend it, ya go around with two left feet a lotta the time. I wanted everything to be smooth and wonderful between Nadia and me. I wanted to glide into this love affair with both feet forward, one left and one right, and let us enjoy each other to the maximum. But already somebody had thrown a monkey wrench into the works and somehow I had the feeling it had something to do with this weird entity that came up out of the desert earth, rescued three hapless humans—and starting with practicing my voice, was *now* wanting to take over my girl—or maybe even my life!

I rang the doorbell at 451 Rodeo Drive. My stately and sexy woman stood before me in that most revealing flamingo robe—only this time there was a lot less under it! Her thick, wavy dark hair fell to her shoulders and those brown eyes of hers glowed like warm coals that a woman displays when she knows she's falling in love. "Cable..." she said as she grabbed my hand and took me to her. We embraced and kissed passionately at the transom and my hands were all over her marvelous body. Before we knew it, we were in her spacious bedroom wrestling on the floor. When I went to lift her up to the bed she objected. "No, *here*, darling—here where I can feel you thrust into me without any more cushion—than—than my t'other end!" she sighed out of breath. I said nothing, but as quick as a wink I had my pants down and lifted her thin flamingo gown up to her belly and beheld her glowing white skin and dark warm mound. I was erect and ready for this lady and I was now truly appreciating Escadero's "enyouthening" treat he'd given me for helping them. That was a hell of a fine trade off!

By the time I had Nadia's gown completely off and was sucking on her nipples, I was thrusting her big time into the carpet until she yelled and squealed with ecstasy. She climaxed like a knockout punch from Joe Louis and the ripples went traveling up my groin into my gut until I, too, released into Nadia Skorkowsky.

The immediate post-orgasm was filled with tender kisses and sweet nothings exchanged between the two of us. Finally we got up and slipped under the covers of her large, wonderful double bed. She was playing with my lips and nose. "You...you never got your honeyed whiskey and hot water...are you sorry?" she teased.

"Are you kidding? But I do have one question, if you don't mind."

"Yes...?"

"What happened to the dining and dancing part? You know, the one where you said you like to take it slow and easy so it can last?"

"Well, Cable, I guess we can't always predict things. I was so excited thinking about you all weekend—I—I just couldn't wait."

"So does that mean we won't last very long, then?"

She laughed softly. "No...it means I'll want you a lot without all the trimmings."

Finally about three in the morning we got up and had toast and strawberry jam, topped off with those drinks we'd never had earlier. "I do have a question about that phone call—the one that you thought was me? Now, I want you to answer as if I were the detective and you the client, okay?"

"Okay," she cooed, smiling at me. I knew she was giddy with lovemaking.

"So this voice on the telephone you thought was me—can you tell me what I said?"

"Yes, pretty much. You said you wanted my—my—uh, my womanhood down there so bad you could taste it—and that you *would* taste it! Then you suggested you wanted me to take your—your penis into my mouth and suck it until it was so big that you'd split me wide open when you finally entered me—but only after you'd 'licked me out' so that I was open enough for you to—to—well, you get the idea, Cable...after all, you said it. Were you drinking?"

I thought for a minute. "I said all that, did I?" I reflected. Whoever was doing this trick could read my mind because what was true was that those thoughts had certainly gone through my brain.

"I thought it crude, frankly. But that was before I had you tonight. Now you can say anything, as long as you take me *there*—to that place we went earlier."

"I may have thought those things, Nadia, but I would never had said them to you quite like that. I may be a ghetto rat, but I think I have enough class not to say those things, especially to a lady like you. No, babe, it's more my style to simply be quiet and *do* those things."

She was so giddy. "I'm very, very glad...you did, mister. Are you ready for a second round, since you're the boxing type of guy?"

And so we did spend a wonderful night of naughty but nice sexual ecstasy together. Nadia wanted me to hang my hat in her hallway, but I knew sooner or later the complications of my professional life would get in the way, and then the honeymoon would be over. "Well, thanks for the wonderful night, Nadia," I said as I went for the door that day.

She smiled at me and proclaimed, "The pleasure...was all mine, Cable, thank *you*. Oh, I'm going to be doing Puccini's *Tosca* as a try out for the east coast at the Summer Opera series here in town. I'll be in rehearsal for a few weeks. But please don't make yourself scarce, okay?"

When I dragged in about noon, I could sense Ida knew where I had been or at least what I'd been doing. So I thought. To her credit, she said nothing. She simply sat at her desk, smiling, motionless. Wait a minute! Ida Latney was dead still! I went up to her and waved my hand in front of her staring periwinkle eyes. Nothing! I felt her pulse. She was still respirating but without motion. Desperately I looked around the room for a clue.

"*I* am your clue. Incidentally, your secretary is overworked, Mr. Denning, so I put her at rest for a little while," a familiar, invisible voice resonated through the room. "As promised, we meet again."

"You...where in the hell *are* you—no, *better* question—*who* in the hell are you, buster? You must be the son-of-a-bitch who almost messed me up with my new babe calling her and trying to impersonate me!" I was still pissed at that.

"Ah, how imperfect the human ear...that in her anxiousness to hear your voice and be with you she didn't know the difference. What does that tell you?"

"It tells me you're a meddlesome son-of-a-bitch, even if you did save my life and the lives of two other people out there in that damned desert. I suppose you have a name?" I said as I went behind my desk and sat, glancing at the morning mail. "And why me?"

"You do recall my pushing your head against that timber when I rescued you? Well, that was so that my nice smooth head extracting everything you ever retained in that brain of yours. If you were but a common mortal ape-man, I wouldn't be interested. But you're part *Sens Parafactor*—your father's lineage." There was a silence. "Name...let me see...translated into your language that must mean my name is *Erond Mantis Spiricus.* That's more or less a bastardized Latin. You may call me just plain ol' *Erond.*"

"So...whatta ya look like?"

"I'm not so sure you'd enjoy that, Denning. I'm a bit *oddly constructed* compared to your species. You see, I came up out of the ranks of the insect world here on your planet, a kind of cross between what you would call a *praying mantis* and a well-armored, handsome creature called the *potato bug.*" I remembered both of those insects from growing up in my Mom's nice little back yard garden. "In other words, I'm not humanoid or even close. The sight of me may even revolt you."

"I see. Well, since you can do just about everything else, how about transforming yourself into a much more likeable form—ya know, something with two arms, two legs, a body, face and head?"

There was another long silence. "Well...I suppose I could do that. Male or female? You call it, as your ape people gamblers say."

"Definitely male...I've had enough female for a while..."

I began to smell something like slightly burning wire in the office. I quickly glanced at Ida. She looked so eerily silent, like a dime store mannequin with that slight smile on her lips and those blue eyes staring into nothingness. "Ta dah!" Erond announced as a little human figure with an elfin's outfit and a white beard appeared in front of me. "Here I am! I thought I liked *Happy* best of all." He was wearing buckskin shoes, powder-blue britches, a dark-brown suede vest, a bright-red shirt and yellow sack hat. Just like the character in 1937's Walt Disney movie!

It was strange talking to a familiar dwarf whose voice was dark and masculine. "One more question. Since you seem like an okay kind of guy, why did you really impersonate my voice on the phone to Nadia Skorkowsky? I gotta know who else you contacted in this way—"

"—no one...that was my first experiment using your vibrations. Your head is filled with erotic sugarplums, Denning—I will not do it again. I realize now we must let the dramas of ape people play themselves out. Same with the primitive, radioactive polluting bomb your government plans to detonate within a few months."

"Do you know exactly when that will happen?"

"Of course. If you can read the past, why can't you read the future? Begun in 1939, it shall culminate 'successfully' on July 16th this year. Why the niece had problems with her Uncle Enrico Fermi is because it was he who went to the military first to talk about fissionable material used for warfare. And, about two weeks after the successful test bomb, on August the 3rd, a bomb will be dropped on a small Japanese island, Hiroshima and three days later on Nagasaki, a sister island. For all intents and purposes, that will end the war."

I was thinking fast. Damn! So soon...why couldn't they wait to figure out the long-term repercussions? And to drop a bomb on innocent people going about their everyday lives! "Damn, Erond, you do know just about everything, don't you?"

"Everything? Ha! I know just enough to get by, Denning...nothing less, not much more..."

"Ya know, sometimes I get so tired of living—or just existing. Ever want to end it all instead of repeating life over and over?"

"Well, that's because I'm my true self and you're not."

"Whatta ya mean?"

"It's their doing, the *Vuaxnee*, a group of aliens who visited your planet many, many thousands of your years ago. They were exploiters, travelers looking for riches on rich planets. At the time, this planet was one of those. Lots of gold, silver, diamonds, other precious stones, plus zinc, copper and other pure metals. So they came to take. That's where you got it from."

"Who...me?"

"I pity you in a way, Denning. You were first a mixed human with Vuaxnee tinkering, then you were further mixed with your father's blood who was a different kind of alien, very similar to *Sens Parafactors*."

"I've heard some of this story before. But why would somebody do that? Didn't they know the repercussions?"

"Know? Or not care, perhaps, even if they did know."

"Are you making a monkey outta me or what here?"

"You *are* nothing but altered apes, as the Vuaxnee selfishly opposed all co-operative laws of nature, and gave your kind a superior mind, intellect and the ability to mimic your progenitors—*of themselves*. You were an emergency experiment. The extraterrestrial visitors needed slaves to mine and work the thousands of details necessary to bring the earth operation to its highest success. But the Vuaxnee were too few. So they picked from the anthropoids that already existed on the

Earth and began some gene splicing. Ultimately, they created a misfit, miscreant creature from the populations of apes. It was a mismatched, botched job, with the poor altered creature not knowing whether it was slave or master, god or bedeviled thing—or both. But it got the work done!

"The Vuaxnee completed their exploitation of the minerals, gold, precious stones and ores in a few thousand years. But what to do with all the altered species? There simply was 'no room at the Inn' for the Vuaxnee to take back home to Indiana, so to speak! Ah—cause a flood and drown the poor bastards! For you see, these most capable beings created an even, balmy temperature throughout the earth by suspending a *water veil atmosphere*. Release it and the entirety of the planet would flood and everyone would drown...or so they thought.

But the genus to which the ape species belonged was fecund to begin with—and since the Vuaxnee made biological changes to increase their numbers by upping the estrus cycle rhythm of the female from annually to a moon cycle of thirty days—and since so many died in trying to please their masters—you pitiful lost creatures began to multiply like the Sorcerer's Apprentice's broomstick! Even those who survived the flood—still were without identity. So those of you who could not persuade the rest through force or with politics, created a creature-religion of frightening symbols and gargoyles, magic and so-called miracles. Either through armies, politics or religion, *fear* was the ruling factor. In other words, Denning, you are what I call a *Neither* and were abandoned to live out forever the curse that you

89

did not create. Your species will perish in this manner. But it is better that way."

I almost choked on my cigarette. "Uh....okay. So suppose most of what you say is true—what about all the great gurus or mystics and Jesus? Hell, even *I* feel the Christ love from time to time. Ever go into a quiet church when no one else is around? There's something so comforting, real, embracing about it. I don't know, it's hard to explain."

"It's a big lonely, empty sky up there. You apes needed something to hold on to during the dark nights of fear. It takes centuries, even millennia, for beautiful legends and mythologies to grow in maturation, and then one day, the thought, focus, concentration, music, action, love, intuition and acceptance come true for those who truly accept and *believe*. Belief is very powerful, and here's the crux of the matter: *the highest and best part of the self that can be, is manifest in such a personified being. We are 'he', and 'he' is us and we are each other.* That's why any 'god' worth its while is always the highest, grandest, most powerful, omniscient, omnipresent, caring, loving, fulfilling entity there is. God is the Universal Manager of Creation. Make a thought known to the cosmos and it shall be delivered to you. The Vuaxnee knew this about you. In fact, they feared one day you would evolve to be equal or superior to them. That was the price they would pay for altering your genus. That is your legacy from the Vuaxnee—that you can have spiritual perception."

Somehow what Erond Mantis Spiricus was saying didn't lay heavy on me. If anything, it had the opposite effect—it lightened my earth-load and it seemed to allow a light to shine through those dark clouds. "If you know all this, why are you such a mischief-maker and why do you stir up and unsettle people?"

"Like all advanced beings—advanced of *your* species, of course— we become bored and enjoy the game, Denning. It's always been just that simple. Stupid, ignorant and expendable races like yours are fair game. The game's fun!" he laughed.

My need to know overcame my irritation at that. "So a question, Erond. Supposing all that you say is true, then what do you do with it? How does one live?" I inquired sincerely.

"*Let it go*...all of it...just...let it go..."

"And how does one survive, I mean, earn a living, etcetera?"

"If you don't know that answer, Cable Denning, then you know nothing about how the cosmos works. It's easy, really. *Place an order, let it go* and the desire shall be manifest."

"That easy, eh?"

"Yep. It's the ape-man that complicates everything."

"Yet I seem to have complicated something for *you*. What is it you want from me?"

"Ah, the moment of truth, eh, Denning?"

"Yeah, something like that..."

"Ha! You do know there is vast difference between what you call 'want' and actual *need*. So it is, that I 'need' a certain knowledge from you. If...you can deliver post haste, then you will be rid of me—"

"Talking of post haste, I think you'd better release my secretary from that spell. Her periwinkle stare is getting to me."

The dwarf smiled mischievously. "Well, she's help-less—and attractive. You could do just about anything if you wished with her at the moment and she might not know the difference."

"You know, Erond, you *are* without shame! No won-der you talked to Nadia that way. But all the same, I kinda like my women to know the difference, Erond. You potato bug people need to learn a thing or two."

So he went over to where Ida sat in her chair and touched her left forefinger. Immediately Ida Latney sprang back to life. "Oh!" she said, staring at the little man—then me.

"It's alright, Ida. This here is *Happy*—Walt Disney just happened to let him out of his cartoon for the day."

"Wha—what happened?" my befuddled secretary sputtered. "I...I don't understand, Mr. Denning. But I feel dizzy."

"Perhaps you should lie down for a while," Erond said. "I put you into a trance state and things—well, they accumulate in the body."

"You did? I don't remember seeing you before." Then Ida looked at me and I winked. "Okay...yes...I think I should. I also feel a little nausea." I hoped it wasn't what I thought it might be. She started for the bath-room.

"Okay, Ida, why don't you lie down on the bed while I finish up here with Mr. Spiricus, okay?"

"Okay..." I escorted the woozy Ida back to my bed-room. "But I still have work to do, Cable," she informed me.

"It's okay, take a break. Lie down and I'll check in on you later."

"Yes, okay...thanks, Mr. Denning. What did that strange little man do to me? I didn't even see him come in."

"That's because he entered invisibly, Ida. I'll explain later."

I left her with a puzzled look on her face and returned to the office.

"No repercussions, right? She means a lot to me, Erond."

"Oh, no, of course not—in no time at all, she'll be—how is it you say—right as rain?"

"Yeah, something like that. Now, how about answering—"

Sophia Legende

Just then the office door opened and in walked a gorgeous blonde young goddess. She reminded me of a taller version of Veronica Lake and wore a pleated silk skirt with a fine white blouse...light-pink lipstick and cute little dangly earrings. "Oh! Mr. Denning?" She did a double-take on the diminutive Erond. "I'm sorry to have disturbed you and—and your client—"

I felt saved by the bell. "—no, no, it's okay, ma'am. My Walt Disney friend here was just leaving..." I said nodding my head vigorously in Erond's direction. I guess he got it because he scooted off his seat.

"Oh! Of course, Denning, we will be in touch in the next day or two—and perhaps you can answer that burning question I will ask you—and I fervently hope you have the right answer?"

"I'll give it my best, Erond," I said, getting up, taking his little hand and walking toward the girl at the same time. I smiled at her. "You know how it goes, lady, someone comes...someone goes...this is Erond."

"Hello..." the dwarf declared.

"Uh...yes, hello," she answered in a medium toned feminine voice.

I let Erond out the door but before he reached the stairway he had disappeared. I came back into the office and closed the door after me. "I hope I wasn't intruding, Mr. Denning. I do have urgent business to—to negotiate with you though..."

"*Negotiate*, Miss—Miss--?"

"*Sophia Legende* is what they call me. My real name is Sophia Price, but my business demands a—a somewhat more *show bizzy* kind of name."

I looked the babe over. She was stacked with I'd say about 42-24-36 or thereabouts. "I see. So...are you?"

"Am I what?"

"A legend?"

"I—I don't know. I'm just a pretty girl with a job".

"Dare I ask what it is you do?"

She flushed a little in the face. "Well, if I told you, you might not take me on as a client—and that would be—difficult for me right now."

"Well, Miss Legende, there is such a thing as *agent-client confidence*, ya know. It might help us get off on the right foot, if you know what I mean. You see, I'm an angle man and a straight-shooter at the same time. You'll never know when I see something that's pertinent to your case in the nature of your employment if you tell me what you *do*."

She looked around the room with light blue-green eyes. Her long hair reminded me of a blonde Rita Hayworth in some movie I saw a year or two back. She saw me looking at her. "All men look at me as if I were edible, Mr. Denning. As you do, I see."

"Actually I was looking at the Rita Hayworth hairdo—you know, the long in the back, the high, wavy up front look? But now that you mention it, what would you expect? Men are men and women are women , Miss Legende. If I didn't look at you with a tasty look in my eye, you'd think something was wrong with you—*or* me, right? It's always that way with women, I've found—you're damned if you do, and you're damned if ya don't! So what's it gonna be—let me ogle you politely to my heart's content or wear a blindfold?"

She laughed and had a wonderful smile. "Yes—you're right—I'm sorry, I'm just so used to so many men coming on to me with—"

"—that's one thing you won't have to worry about with me. I just met a great gal and I think I'm gonna keep her." Nadia Skorkowsky's wonderful naked body came to mind and I was right, I wouldn't have traded her for the present dish in my office.

"Oh...well, that's nice...I'm always happy to hear when two people find each other in the world and you think it might work out."

"Yeah. Now suppose you tell me what the word 'negotiate' was doing first thing in our conversation? And what's your story, Miss Legende, everyone has a story. What's yours?"

She looked into my eyes for the trust she hoped she'd find. "Well, negotiate...because I don't have a lot of money. My story? Well, let me be simple. First of all I'm bisexual. But I don't do it with men per se…"

"Per se?" I asked, all the more curious.

"I—I—uh—I—I, uh—oh, this is embarrassing for me, Mr. Denning! Can't we skip that part and move on to the crisis at hand?"

"Oh, I suppose we could, but then, as I said, I wouldn't have the angles, doll, and angles can make the difference, you know."

"They can?"

"Yep…in fact, many an angle has broken a case…"

She took a deep breath and those marvelous breasts of hers heaved out and up. "Okay, I suppose it won't hurt. But you promise it's our secret—uh, as you said, an agent and client confidence?"

"Well, you have to remember, you haven't hired me yet. I have to agree to take the job, and that indeed it does not jeopardize my health, if ya know what I mean."

"Oh. That could complicate matters, could it?"

"It could, lady, but I promise I will not share your plight or professional disposition with anyone else, okay?"

"Okay…so…" She took on an angelic radiance to her face and a slight smile fell across her lips. "My first love is my music. I'm a big band singer. But I'm having trouble making ends meet, if you know what I mean? So…I do…I do 'other things' to compensate…"

"Okay, so far I'm with you. Mind if I smoke since you're a singer?"

"No, Mr. Denning. I'm in the stuff all the time. You know the nightclubs—the stench of tobacco, alcohol and God knows what else!"

"Oh, yeah, I know what you mean. So, getting on with it, what are these 'other things' you might be talking about?"

Again she took in that mighty breath with the same result. "Well, suppose you knew a very nice California girl who was very talented, okay?"

"Okay, go on..."

"Well, in her hometown she was a singing sensation, a smash wherever she went! Men and women loved her. But maybe she was too pretty. Her mother was a beauty queen, her father a champion weight lifter, her brother a deadbeat nothing. But her father got tired of the mother and abused the daughter sexually. At first with just touching and playing, and then sooner or later as my mother drank herself to death avoiding the situation, it led to other things—if you know what I mean. I told him I'd tell the authorities. He told me he'd kill me if I did. So I ran away from home. But I didn't want men anymore, Mr. Denning. Or my family. I found women so much more understanding. So I prefer females—I think Freud calls it 'homosexual'."

"Yes, Miss Legende," I said comforting her. "I've heard this story before—it's okay. You are safe here with me."

That seemed to relax her. "I realized men had most of the money in this country. But I didn't wish to have sexual intercourse with them. So instead, I became a different kind of professional prostitute, if you will. I would please men by taking off my top and fondling them and then sucking them off. There, I said it!" she exclaimed, slamming her palm to her chest. The woman

97

seemed like she had just gotten a lot off her abundant bosom, but by the looks of it, there was still a lot left!

"Yes, Miss Legende. You said it. And it's okay. Thanks for trusting me. Now...to the crisis...after all, that's the reason you're really here, isn't it?"

"Yes." Her eyes began to mist. "Once...not long ago, I—I did a favor for a negro gangster here in town who paid me a thousand dollars for—for, well, you know what. Now he wants to me to service all his negro friends and clientele at *Zoot Mimby's Club,* an underground joint downtown on South Central Avenue."

"Hmmm...I see...and you're saying you don't wish to do this?"

"No, that's correct. I wouldn't have done it in the first place, but the money allowed me to purchase a decent wardrobe for the stage, you know, a couple of nice gowns, shoes, makeup, some jewelry..."

"And so you want me to have a talk with this 'client' of yours whom you wish you'd never serviced. You do realize I have no authority to straight-arm the man. He paid you and you did what you did. After all, you know what they say about the oldest profession..."

"Yes, regrettably, Mr. Denning. And there's also something else. Can you help me?"

"Something else? What?"

"Yes. But until I know you better, I cannot speak it. It's too—too horrible for me to think about."

"That bad, eh? Well, I don't know if I can help you, Sophia Legende. The law is a stickler for things like that—citizens telling other citizens what to do without *just cause.* Whether I was with the police department or working privately as I am, it's a rather awkward situation, I'm sure you can appreciate. What's this man's name you want me to talk to?"

"His name is Anthone Demaine. I'm certain he's part of the black man's mafia here in Los Angeles. I understand he's always armed and perhaps a little touchy. I— I would go with that in mind, Mr. Denning." She reached into her purse. She had a small wad of money and peeled me off a $100 dollar bill. "Will that pay for your time, Mr. Denning?"

"Yeah, doll, for my time—but not for my life. If he draws his piece, shoots and asks questions later—well, you can see how awkward *that* might be. Negro men can be testy, especially if they're approached by a white private dick out of his usual territory." She looked surprised, flushing a little. I chuckled. I figured an explanation was in order. "That's short for private detective, lady. So, what is it you want me to say to Mr. Demaine?"

"Simply—well, sort of what I told you. I did the trick for the man as a favor to him since he wanted me so much—but when I told him I don't 'go all the way', he asked me what I was in the business for. I told him I don't do intercourse, but only fellatio. I guess I said too much, because he begged me to service him and he took out ten one-hundred dollar bills and put them on the table where we were having a drink. So I did him. I guess he liked it and before I knew it, I was getting all kinds of phone calls from negro men wanting me to do them."

I was thinking about those webs we weave in this world and how easy it was to get ourselves into deep shit with the wrong people. "I see. Well, as I see it, Miss Legende, it looks like you've gotten yourself in a sticky mess. The best I can do is find the man and talk to him. I'll also tell him to inform his buddies you aren't available to them. Outside of bumping the man off, that's about all I really can do—legally."

Her eyes widened and she seemed frightened. "And if he refuses to stop hounding me along with his 'associates', as he calls them?"

"Then you're in deep doo-doo, lady. I don't know what else to say. But there is one question you haven't answered."

"And what's that, Mr. Denning?"

"You used the word *'negotiate'* when you first came in. What did you mean? You've already given me a hundred bucks."

"Oh...that...well, I was thinking I could do you—you know, a nice private evening alone with me, a drink or two—and then later I'd make you feel very good. That I can promise you."

I studied her lovely face. "Yeah, I'll bet you would make me feel just *grand*, Miss Legende. But it's okay, thanks for the offer, but I think I'll pass, if you don't mind. Nothing personal, you understand."

She seemed a bit disappointed. "Oh...well, in that case, then there's nothing to further negotiate. When can you see Mr. Demaine?"

"For your sake, I'd say the sooner the better, wouldn't you?"

"Yes, Mr. Denning. Thank you for taking a task laden with risk."

"Yeah, 'laden with risk' is right. Don't thank me yet. I gotta check out the weather down at—where did you say Demaine's hangout was?"

"*Zoot Mimby's* is just one of the many negro jazz clubs down on South Central Avenue. It's a walk-down place. Be careful, please, Mr. Denning."

Down deep in my gut a dark place started to settle in. I hated that. Usually when I felt that , there would be something ominous at the other end. I tried to shake it as Sophia Legende talked across the desk to me, but it was roiling around down there like a specter of something shadowy and forbidding. "Yeah, I'll do just that, Miss Legende." I got up as she rose from her seat across from me. She was tall and streamlined, but now that I knew more about her, I felt the beautiful face was a mask that hid harsh and ugly truths about her earlier life. I also wondered what she sounded like as a singer. "You need to give me a phone number where I can reach you, by the way."

CRestview 7069 I'm usually not available after six in the evening and not before ten in the morning." I jotted down the number and escorted her to the door. "I'm sorry, Mr. Denning, that you have to go down there. But if I don't take care of this now, it will haunt me forever—just as it does now—every day since—since—well, you know..."

"Yeah, I know, Miss Legende. I'll be in touch."

She hesitated at the door. "It's funny, isn't it?"

"What's funny?"

"What you just said about 'touch'. A man like you, whom I wouldn't mind touching in the most intimate of ways will probably be the man I will never touch. And the far less desirable ones are always the ones I get."

"It *is* an irony, isn't it, Miss Legende? Well, I'm a wrecked train anyhow—I'm safest at a distance. Yeah,

101

and in a way it's like my own business—and make no mistake, you're in a business—some clients are okay, but most are so-so with the same problems as the one or two or three who came before them."

She smiled a faint smile. "Yes. That's it precisely. A wrecked train, eh?" she echoed my pat line.

"By the way, I think your English and command of vocabulary are swell. You don't happen to be a poet by any chance, do you?"

"No, but I sort of rhyme the words to the music I write. I'm sort of a back lot songwriter. Not all that great, maybe, but fair to middling. I've written a kind of jazz ballad. It's called *'Don't Move Too Fast'*." I don't know. I guess I'm like a poet in a way, you know, writing what I feel from deep inside when I'm lucky enough to access 'there'—wherever that is. My songs are more or less pretty complex, I guess."

"I'd like to hear a song of yours sometime. As I said, let me know where and when you're singing somewhere and I'll come and catch you."

Her eyes misted again. "Will you, Mr. Denning?"

"What's that?"

"Catch me?" Quick as a wink she leaned up and kissed my cheek, then left.

I went back to the reposing Ida. She was snoozing peacefully. I sat at the edge of the bed and thought. *What a hell of a day this had been!* Another question was burning inside me. I couldn't recall exactly when Ida Latney and I had made love last and I wondered if her wooziness wasn't those particular stages of pregnancy. But I'd keep it low profile unless she mentioned it. Suddenly she stirred and opened her eyes when I touched her. "Oh! Cable..." she smiled. "It's so good to see you here watching after me."

"I was a bit concerned. I don't know Erond that well, but I think he's up and up and you won't have any repercussions." I took her hand and felt her wrist pulse. "Hmmm...seems just right to me!" I quipped.

She drew me toward her and placed my hand on her breast. Before I knew it, one soft kiss led to another and we were holding each other so close until we couldn't keep our clothes on anymore. I took Ida in my arms and buried her beneath me, wedging her legs apart as I melded with her by entering that sacred, lubricated womanhood of hers. It was the one thing I wanted to avoid, making love in the back of the office—not to mention unprotected sex! But damn, she felt so young and *good* in my arms and we ran a marathon together until we both burst wide open with carnal ecstasy.

We lay there naked on my messy old bed in silence for a while. "Are you—are you mad at me?" she asked.

"About what, babe?" I asked, smiling beside her.

"You know...about...about doing '*it*' at work?"

"I ain't mad at you, just pissed at myself for being this unthinking cretin as Erond said I was. But it just seemed right. I guess that's the bottom line, don't you think?"

"Yes, Cable, that's the bottom line. I wanted you and I didn't think either. And I feel I'm really fertile right now, too. I know you don't need to hear that, but I was wet before I came to work today thinking about you and hoping something like this would happen. That's always a sign."

I took a deep breath. "I don't wanna think about it now, Ida. We'll—we'll talk about it later, okay?"

"That's what you always say. But we never do."

Chapter 3

ZOOT MIMBY'S AND THE BLOWPIPE MURDERS

It was Friday night, March 16, 1945. She was young and cute as a travel magazine advertisement—and her skin reminded me of pure milk chocolate. Since I hadn't heard from Erond, I decided this was a good night to go out hunting for *Anthone Demaine* and earn the hundred bucks Sophia Legende had paid me. *Zoot Mimby's* was a happening walk-down-into-Hades kind of underground place with incredible music and that lady up there with a very few clothes on singing and moving like a female locomotive on an express train to Paradise added to the excitement of a new place for me. The easel at the entrance displayed a large cardboard cutout of the lady and said her name was *Ayana Javina*, "fresh from Martinique" so it read. What there was of it, her costume was red with small yellow designs. She wore little white slippers, must've stood about five-foot two and had on a very odd neckpiece. It resembled a bunch of symbols that reminded me of a zombie party, you know, black and gold skulls, bones, and other occult looking pieces jangling around her neck. She had a wonderful figure, although not very large-busted, proportionate just the same. There was only one other white man in the joint. I asked the bartender if Anthone Demaine might be in tonight and he pointed with his eyes to a beaded curtain near the rear of the establishment and said nothing. But

105

the entertainment was so delightful, so I sidled up to the bar and ordered some hot buttered rum for a change. I thought I'd get a feel for the place. Surprisingly, Ayana Javina's command of English was swell and she was singing a popular Duke Ellington tune called *Mood Indigo*. Just as she finished, however, some loud drunk negro threw a beer bottle at the bandstand, almost hitting the singer. Then he started up toward her. I knew that meant trouble in a joint like this! I instinctively ran through the throng to stop the guy. The band started up a lively number as I wrestled him to the floor. At once two other black men were pulling the man up and escorting him outside while I dusted myself off and put my fedora back on. Just as I finished our eyes met. She was at the edge of the small stage looking down at me. The throng of noisy men and women went on in their droning voices while the band played. "Thank you, sir!" Ayana Javina's voice rang out toward me.

"You're welcome—I hate drunks who get out of hand!" I shouted back.

"Me, too!" she retorted, smiling at me.

I walked up to her and extended my hand. "I'm Denning, Cable Denning, ma'am. I'm a private detective and just happened to be in here looking for—"

"—*me*?" a voice behind me spoke. I turned to see a fairly tall negro wearing all white, a large white hat and a jacket with a light fur collar. "I thank you, sir," he said in a mellow tone. "I heard what you did for us. I like nervy people. And you happen to fit that description, sir."

"Well, I'm not sure, but if your name is Anthone Demaine then, yes, *you* might fit the description of someone *I'm* looking for."

"Well, it looks like we both win, sir. Please, will you follow me?"

He led me to the back of a fairly large dimly lit room through the beaded curtain. Several very attractive women, both black and white, were hanging out around this very large round blonde table. It was filled with inlaid symbols and designs. "Quite a table you have here," I observed.

"It is *Panamanian Zorro* wood, sir. But its value far exceeds the wood. You'll notice the designs—indicating the magic and sorcery of the Islands in the Caribbean Sea—particularly of the *Taíno* peoples in ancient Martinique of the *Lesser Antilles*. Their magic *was* magic," he concluded, offering me a chair next to him. He seemed quite composed and articulate. "They and subsequent peoples believe in a powerful evil spirit called Maybouya that shamans have to placate with sacrifices to keep the people from harm. But, of course, these are superstitions the natives believe in. The practices of Santeria have moved into the Islands of the Carribbean." Then he leaned toward me and spoke low. "I hope you have no designs on the lovely Miss Ayana Javina, the young lady you came to the rescue of. She is strictly hands-off, and as a matter of fact she must remain virginal territory because she does *psychic tattoo symbols* for the boss. No one...touches her."

I nodded my head, but at that moment I got this inkling this guy was a lot more than he said he was. There was an underlying deviousness about the bloke. He was *very* smooth. "Yeah, I get it. I just couldn't see some idiot accosting her like that."

"Of course, completely commendable, Mr.—Mr.—"

"—Denning, Cable Denning." I took out my P.I. identification and showed it to him. "I'm—uh, I came in to see you on the bequest of a client of mine, one Miss Sophia Legende. Do you happen to know her?"

The negro's eyes became slits. "Yes, she's a hooker under my employ, Mr. Denning. Why is it she sent *you*, if I may ask?"

"Well, far as I can tell, she claims she did you a personal favor of an intimate nature and that seemed to give you the idea that she would accommodate others of your—your—"

"—my skin color? It's alright, go ahead and say it. Miss Legende does seem to categorize us males into color species, doesn't she? You still haven't answered me, however—why did she send you?"

"To ask you to cease and desist making certain sexual demands on her and to keep your own people away from pestering her, if I understand correctly, Mr. Demaine."

Just then there was a ruckus out in the main club area. The band had stopped and a few women shrieked. I wondered what the hell could be next on tonight's agenda!

A couple of men were carrying a body in from outside. They slid the dead man on top of the bar counter. Demaine and I went to check it out. There were a few pretty well but oddly dressed men who had gathered for the occasion. Suddenly Demaine was speaking in a native dialect of some sort to one of the others. He nodded and left. Demaine asked me to stay back while he went in to investigate. No sooner had I turned to go back to the beaded curtain room than I heard a voice in back of me. "You can see, man, this is a complicated place!" she said. It was Ayana Javina.

"Yeah, I guess you could say that. By the way, I really enjoy your singing—and that ain't a line. Anthone Demaine says you're untouchable anyhow, something about you doing ritual stuff or psychically reading for some guy he called 'the boss'?"

I picked up a Caribbean accent from her. "Yes, not only am I especially trained for such a profession as well as my performing, but it was in my mother and grandmother's blood as well. I am from *Martinique*, and the original Taino people are my ancestors. Their lives were filled with mystery, ritual and magic. You do have a name, I am certain of that...you called it out, but I could not understand what you said earlier," she queried.

"Denning, ma'am, *Cable Denning*. I'm a private detective here on a matter of business with Mr. Demaine."

"May I ask what brings a white man into this neighborhood to do a business?"

"As a matter of fact, it's about someone you might know—a Miss Sophia Legende?"

"Oh, yes, she is beautiful. But I—I..." Then she stopped.

"Yes, you were going to tell me something?"

"I can't, Mr. Denning. I've already spoken out of turn. I think I had better go now..."

Just then, Demaine returned to where we stood. I could tell he was uncomfortable with me talking to

Ayana Javina. "It is the second murder within two weeks. I become uncomfortable when people are killed and we are not the responsible party. That man had a blow-dart in his neck. It most likely killed him within thirty seconds or less. His body is still trembling from the poison."

"How do you know that?" I asked.

"The coroner found a very deadly toxin in the blood of the man who was murdered week before last." Then he looked at Ayana and admonished her. "You were told not to fraternize with customers, Ayana. Please go back up onto the stage and sing. Later Mr. M will be here for you. He requires a reading...tonight..."

I could tell Ayana was frustrated, not to mention what a "reading" might be all about, but she did as she was told. "You do keep her pretty tight under lock and key, Mr. Demaine."

"I have to, sir. Ayana is my charge and Mr. M would be most disturbed if anything were to befall her. That includes any kind of male-female association on her part. You do understand."

"Oh, yeah, I do understand. So, mind if we finish our earlier conversation?" I requested.

"No, not at all." He led me back behind the beaded curtain and once again we sat at the large wooden table. He waved his hand and everyone else left. "Now...I am quite put out that that marvelous blonde, white-skinned creature Sophia Legende would actually hire you to dis-suade me from wanting her to—to do...certain things..."

"Yeah, that's her objection. What I didn't know was that Miss Legende happens to work for you? She didn't tell me that part."

"Perhaps there were many things she did not tell you. You most likely saw the white man out there? His name is Jared Rothstein, half rabbi, half gangster. His grandfather was Arnold, the big 1919 fixer of ball games, casinos, liquor, jukeboxes and people's lives."

"So what's Rothstein got to do with Sophia Legende?"

"She's his girl. As much as someone like Sophie can be anyone's girl."

"Oh, she didn't tell me that, either."

"So, I suggest you give the lady her money back, Denning. She's trouble with a capital 'T'."

"Yeah, well maybe I'll do just that. I appreciate your information."

"Don't sweat it, gumshoe. C'mon, let's go out and watch Ayana turn a few notes, eh?"

We walked out into the noisy, crowded club. Ayana had chosen another Duke Ellington song to sing. It was a real tight version of *I'm Beginning to See the Light*, a new song that everyone and his brother was recording and/or performing. Jared Rothstein noticed us and came over. We were introduced, but he wasn't the friendly type. As a matter of fact, he seemed like a creep to me. Whatever Anthone Demaine had told me stuck in my craw like something wasn't all as it seemed. Call it an old gumshoe's seventh sense. You know, like shadows of the real thing? I thought I'd just go along with it for time being. So after Ayana's song, I told Demaine I was sorry to have bothered him and maybe he was right about my giving Sophie Legende's money back to her. I still smelled a rat somewhere in the woodpile, but I'd bide my time until I could figure the whole thing out.

Sophie Legende was too intelligent to be that easily dismissed in my book. Plus she was a singer—so she said—and artistic people are usually pretty honest, upright citizens. Nope, despite the fact that one beautiful woman made herself into a marginal whore to earn money, wasn't the whole story—nope, not by a long stretch. I had a lotta questions swirling around in my head just about now. I had to listen to my gut more. Case in point, I was feeling things about Nadia about now and there was something waiting in the wings that was makin' me mighty nervous. But what was it?

Prelude to Darkness

It was late when I climbed the stairs to my office. But as was the case so damned often, someone was waiting for me. It was about 1:30 a.m. A slight fellow with thick mottled hair was sitting on the floor next to my office door. He started when he saw me. "Oh! I was—huh!—dozing, I'm afraid." He stood up. His eyes were small and intense, his nose bent, a sallow complexion and he had a little tick so that suddenly he would jerk and it would affect his speech pattern.

"It's long after office hours, buddy, whatta ya want?"

"I'm—I'm—huh!—sorry...I think I need to talk to you. You are Mr. Denning?"

"Well, that's what it says on the door. Who the hell are you?" I asked, opening the door. He followed me in.

"My name is *Theodore Watson*—but the good Dr. Apothican nick-named me *'Watty'* and so you may call me that, if you wish. He may—may—huh!—have mentioned—I—I always beat him at chess."

"As a matter of fact, he did tell me that," I answered. Something was wrong. So I would pretend I didn't know too much. And maybe I didn't. "So how's old Apothican these days?" I innocently inquired as I sat in my comfy chair and directed 'Watty' to a chair. But he was wiry and nervous. His eyes darted everywhere.

"When I went back to—huh!—to Walnut House to collect my papers and sketches on nuclear—huh!—physics, Dr. Apothican told me he'd given them to you. That made me angry. So I—I huh!—killed him and ate his heart. He always did have—huh!—a good heart, you know," the man declared plainly.

The last thing you do with a nut case like this is to react with shock. So I just went on. "Oh...he was worried about you, you know. What about Nurse Diesel? She was pretty attached to Dr. Apothican, wasn't she?"

But that didn't register on his brain. "I wish to have my...my papers returned. Do you—huh!—possess them, sir?"

"Yeah, I do. I found them interesting. So you really think nuclear physics is part of the future?"

"Yes sir, I do." I went rifling through a desk drawer and found the papers and handed them to Watson. "I am glad they have not been eaten by you. Then I would have to eat you to regain the content of my papers, you see."

"Oh, yeah, I see, that makes sense...good logic. So what else can I do for you?"

"I've been watching you. You have a—huh!—a beautiful girlfriend. I have always—huh!—envied beautiful people. I do not come from beautiful people."

113

"And if Dr. Apothican was right, you did some not very beautiful things to a lotta people. I've always wondered why, Watson, you of all people, with a genius brain that put all those formulas and proposals together on those papers—why would you kill eleven fellow associates, steal away the most attractive woman and molest her to death?"

He smiled. "I call it the *Numantia syndrome*, at least in part. In Rome—uh, huh!—Roman times there was a woman from the Numantia district of Sumaria named *Mary of Bethezuba* who killed and ate her child. She did—did this—huh!—partly because she saw that the future was not promising and f-f-f—uh, food was scarce."

"Of course," I answered. "Just out of curiosity—why the torture?"

"Why?"

"Yeah, why?...you know, soldering eyes shut with silvery rosin solder is not nice, sexual molestation is bad enough, you name it—"

"—well, to be per—per—huh!—perfectly frank, I think I've been wishing to synthesize—huh!—high technology with the natural world."

"Like soldering eyes shut and other unmentionables?"

"Obsession...obsession, Mr. Denning...one tends to be carried away when one is—is—huh!—given so much freedom to act without other eyes and mouths disciplining, disciplining, disciplining—my—my moth—huh!—mother was always...always disciplining me."

This guy was insane! But I had to stay cool. "Yeah, funny how it so often goes back to the parents, isn't it?

114

Or the genetics—what do you do with the cards you're tossed across the table? Some get luckier than others, eh?" He didn't respond but his light brown eyes followed me as I took out a pack of Lucky Strikes and lit one up. I offered him one and he took it. I lit his cigarette and he seemed to finally relax a little. But he didn't know how to smoke. So he just puffed. "Anyway, when I first talked to the late doctor, Apothican said you were delirious and unpredictable—does that kinda fit you, Dr. Watson?"

"Oh, yes…" He said that in a low, breathy voice, bobbing his head up and down in agreement. "I have—have found myself quite—quite—huh!—mentally dis—huh!—disoriented lately."

"Ever thought about professional help?"

"No! Who can—can know—huh!—can know me, Mr. Denning?"

"I don't know. Who can?" His eyes had a glazed look now and I knew something was malfunctioning in the man's brain.

"No one. I—I work best in the—in the—huh!—in the dark. These papers—most of my ideas came while—while I was—huh!—in complete darkness."

I thought for a minute. I decided to chance it. "Are you aware, Dr. Watson, there are laws against the taking of another's life in this country? You've taken fourteen we know of—including the woman you kidnapped and eventually—*how did she die*, incidentally?"

"Margot…Margot didn't take uh, uh…'kindly' to being in my pres—pres…presence. So I punished her for that."

"Just exactly how did 'Margot' die, if you don't mind..."

"I had never—never—huh!—had s-s-s-sex, Mr. Denning. I told her if—if she was compliant, I would not—huh!—hurt her. But Margot was mean and ill-tempered toward me." His face tightened and his eyes glowed at me like burning coals. "So I—I punished her."

"By...?" I inquired, almost certain it was something I'd regret asking about.

"First I drugged her to—m—m—huh! make her obedient. Then I undressed her. She was barely able to walk, so I—I—huh!—escorted her into the shower upstairs. Then when—when—huh!—when Margot was clean, I took her—uh, huh!—I took her downstairs to the bed I'd prepared for her. I tied her up and made path—pathetic—pathetic attempts to have sex—sexual—huh!—sexual intercourse with her. But I was too nervous perhaps—not—not able to perform uh, adequately."

"So that soured you and so you started workin' her over—you tortured her womanhood because you couldn't get it up—isn't that right, Watson?!" I was pissed and he knew it.

"Yes! Yes!" his voice rose to a high pitch. "I—I attempt—huh!—attempted to seal off her—her eyes so she could not—huh!—see me while I was playing with her down there—but she became worthless—worthless to me. She—she had absolutely no—huh!—response! So I...I experimented with—with huh!—better medicine, better equipment—but the solder would not work on the—huh!—eyes or nipples. I'm—I'm afraid I botched her up a bit...you know. I punished her—her—

116

huh!—vagina by sticking a—a—huh!—very hot large soldering iron right up there as far as it would go. The stench of burning pubic hair and flesh was—was horrible—but I pun...punished her good, didn't I? She upped and d-d-d-huh!—died a few days later."

I sat there incredulous. What diabolical evil must've overtaken this man? I had to take him down. "As I said, Watson, no matter what you did, you gotta pay for it somehow. I think I oughtta take you to visit my friend Lester Keith. Will you come peaceably?"

"Lester Keith? Who's he?"

"He happens to be *Lieutenant* Lester Keith of the homicide division downtown. If we don't put you down, Watson, you'll go on and on like a rabid dog, biting everyone who opposes you or gets in your way!"

"No...I thin—thin—huh!—think not, Mr. Denning. I must be off!"

His eyes widened and he was panicking inside. He got up and backed away. I started after him. But he took an odd looking atomizer from his pocket and sprayed it in my direction. Then he turned tail and ran to the door. I attempted to follow, but the stuff he'd sprayed into the air overcame me and I fainted to the floor! Lights out!

Sounds of the Caribbean

"Mr. Denning, Mr. Denning!" a voice addressed me from down some long, echoing corridor. "Can you hear me?"

Slowly I came around and the first thing I beheld was lovely. I thought I was dreaming. I was in my bed

117

and there above me with a caring smile stood Ayana Javina! "Whoa...what—what happened?"

"I do not know. I found you on the floor. Do *you* know what happened?"

Slowly I started to recollect the visit from the madman Dr. Theodore Watson. "Yeah...I had some bloke here...who...who sprayed some crap...in my face...just as—as he was leaving my-my office..."

"I am sorry. I hope you are not damaged." She got up and went into my bathroom and came back with a warmed washrag. "You are asking why I am here?" She dabbed my face gently.

"Yeah...that did occur to me...but thanks for bein' here. So...why *are* you here?"

"When I read for Mr. M a little later tonight, he told me that Mr. Demaine had thrown you off track by telling you Sophia Legende worked for him and that she was Rothstein's girl and was untouchable and trouble."

"Well...?" I asked, still in a slight haze.

"None of it is true except for the untouchable part. Sophia Legende works for herself primarily, Mr. Denning. She is not dangerous except to someone like Mr. Demaine who cannot have her the way he would like, if you know what I mean."

"How—how did you manage to get away...?" I knew the lady would be in big trouble if she was discovered having this tête-à-tête with a white man in his back-office bedroom!"

"It's 4:30 in the morning, Mr. Denning. I must get back soon. It is the only time I can come. Mr. M keeps a guard on me. But I risked it because you seemed like a nice person and I needed to tell you to stop snooping in regard to Sophia Legende—or they'll kill you!" she sighed. "I would not want that. After all, you're more than just another customer."

"I am?"

"Yes, I always wanted a white man someday. So...perhaps when I am retired from my reading work, we could get together...you know—"

"—I'd be too old then, kid. Shit, I'm too old for you *now!*"

She snickered gently. "Maybe...maybe not. But please, Mr. Denning, stop inquiring about Sophia Legende."

"Why? What possible secret could Sophie have in that blonde little head of hers that would—would cause the Black Mafia to tremble?"

"I beg you, please do not come around the club anymore." She had been sitting on the edge of the bed. She got up, put the washrag back in the bathroom and came back out to look at me in her wonderful coral red dress and dark leather shoes. "I hope you hear me." Then she smiled. "Otherwise, I will have to take you back to meet my Mamma in Martinique with a big tummy out in front of me! Will *she* be surprised!"

"Does that mean we'll be friends?" I tried to laugh but it hurt. Then I got serious. "Who's *Zoot Mimby*, Ayana?"

"The nightclub owner. I don't know. Perhaps he does not exist. I have never asked. The black crime syndicate is very tight and secret here in Los Angeles...many secrets are whispered in the night."

"Yeah, so what else is new? Anyway, thanks for getting me off the floor. How'd you do it?"

"I am strong. Lifting sugar sacks as a child in Martinique. I just dragged you feet first here into your bedroom. Then I kept boosting and pushing you up onto your bed."

"Oh, well, thanks anyhow. I think I like you, kid."

"I like you, too, Mr. Denning. But I must go now. If I do not go I will not remain pure."

"Yeah, I get it—I've heard of stories like that before. Something to do with unadulterated purity of your female person keeps your incoming 'signals' coming in loud and clear for Mr. M, eh?"

"So it is they say. My Mamma still had *her* powers after I was born. I think it is a male possession thing. If some other man has me, then my 'benefactor' will be jealous and have lost his strange bid to keep me pure and that would hurt his ego. At least I guess that's how men think."

"Yeah, pretty close, I guess." I sat up in bed. "So, has Mr. M ever tried to get chummy with you?"

"No. He's strange anyhow. I'm not sure he's all there, if you know what I mean."

"Strange, eh? Who ain't nowadays?"

Then Ayana reached over and took my left hand and held it. She closed her eyes and then placed my palm up to her chest. I was tempted to play with her breasts, but I thought better of it. "Danger...danger, Mr. Denning. Terrible things...some terrible things you will see. You have been to the place...where the blinding white light will happen. Also, a woman with long blonde hair walks in shadow...possibly Sophia. There's also a crazy man...he wants something you possess. He will kill for it. Oh!" she exclaimed as she jerked her body. Then she held her throat. "Someone else you know who cares about you...she is strong, capable...a fine ally—but she is also in danger...threatened to reside in place of darkness. Very dark, deep...little air...rocks, stones I see...Oh! There is death out and about, Mr. Denning...two will die, two will live..." Then she came out of her trance with a jolt of her body. "I must leave you now..."

Ayana Javina hugged me and said no more. She let herself out.

Well, that was one hell of a bucket of crap that lady just heaped onto my life! I lit up a Lucky Strike and leaned against the wall on my bed. Shit! I knew who the crazy man was okay. And the blonde with the long hair had to be Sophia Legende. But *two will die, one will live...?* It sounded like a riddle to me. Who in the hell would that be?! And why, where, when? *What terrible secret could Sophia Legende know that would make the Black Mafia afraid of her—or at the very least, wish to discredit her?*

As per her instructions, I dialed Sophia Legende's phone number about noon the next day. "Yes?" her voice answered. There seemed to be a nervous higher pitch to her tone.

"Miss Legende—Cable Denning here. I think I oughtta return your dough. From the way Anthone Demaine tells it, you work for him and you're some guy named Jared Rothstein's girl. Plus you're dangerous and in deep shit."

There was a pause at the other end of the line. "No, please, Mr. Denning. Keep the money. I—I guess I could expect nothing better out of Anthone Demaine," she said sadly. "None of what he said is true, except may-be—maybe the part that I may be in trouble with his people—"

"—it ain't time to pretend, Miss Legende. You need to be straight with me. I had a visitor very late last night. Her name was Ayana Javina. Do you know her?"

"No, Mr. Denning. I don't know her. But I know *of* her. She's the singer down at that terrible nightclub—why would she risk coming to see you?"

"Yeah, and a hell of singer, too." I toyed with a pencil. "Why did she come to see me? You tell me—to have me hear her sing?"

"You haven't heard *me* yet," she cooed.

"True...I hope to have that privilege soon. But back to Ayana Javina, she wanted to set me straight about *you* and that you are your own profession, or something like that. She's also some kind of psychic reader for a Mr. M. So we need to connect the dots together. One, who is she? Two, who really is Anthone Demaine, who's Mr. M and last but not least, who is *Zoot Mimby*? Or does he exist?"

"I can't say for certain—"

"—c'mon, Miss Legende, the meter's running—tell me why the colored folk down at *Zoot Mimby's* are ei-ther afraid of you or biding their time before they kill you?"

She began to sob over the telephone. "Alright! It's—it's what I know. That day we met I told you there was *something else*. But I can't tell you on the phone!"

Ida glanced across at my frustrated face. "What, then?"

"Can you meet me tonight—around ten—alone—I want you to meet someone…"

"Don't tell me, a rich boyfriend?"

"No, a girl who works with me at—at—well, you know…"

"Yeah, I guess I can do that—where?"

"I work out of a posh place in Beverly Hills. I service a lot of movie people, both male and female. Do you know where the Doheny Mansion is at 905 Loma Vista Drive? It's also called Greystone."

"Yeah, you work there?"

"Yes, the rich and famous have a whole wing dedicated to—to the art of my profession—other than music, that is, Mr. Denning."

"Okay, let me get this straight. 905 Loma Vista Drive at ten tonight, right? How do I get in?"

"Oh—I'm glad you asked. When you arrive, there will be a security person at the gates with the two pillars. Tell him *Dagmar* sent you and you'll be told where to go."

"Okay, Miss Legende, we'll see you tonight."

"Yes, Mr. Denning—and thank you for understanding."

"Hell, I'm not sure I understand anything—yet. But I'm certain you will enlighten me, Miss Legende…" We hung up. I looked across at the fastidiously working Ida Latney. "Well, that's that…"

"That's what?" Ida questioned me. "Late night visitor in the form of a 'pretty little thing'?"

"Yeah, a petite little negro singer from downtown. You'd have liked her. She's real, Ida…"

Ida gave me a cold stare. "Yes, I'm sure she is…"

"Oh, and Sophia Legende—ha! finally finding the cat in her house—*that* will be interesting."

"Is that *that* pretty young thing the one I missed when another one of your clients put me into a trance—and we made love afterward?" she said boldly with a smirk on her face.

"Yeah, that pretty young thing."

"I'm not sure, Cable, but I think I'm late getting my period this month. After all, we did make love when I told you I felt very, very ready for you that afternoon?"

A shiver went through me. "You did tell me that, Ida. How—uh, how much overdue are you?"

"About a week or so…"

"Are you normally very regular?"

"Yes…and no…it does vary. I wouldn't worry about it, Cable. You have enough to think about right now. I—I just wanted you to know."

"Thanks, Ida." I smiled, as if it didn't worry me. "It sure was a wonderful afternoon—and yes, you were incredibly thick and wet that day. Some things a guy never forgets."

"Wanna repeat it?" Ida asked in a demure yet sexy tone of voice.

"Uh…I sure wouldn't mind sometime—but not here…"

"Okay, Cable—but maybe soon? I—I have to tell you I—I miss it."

"Yeah, Ida, so do I…"

The Curse of Greystone Mansion

Greystone Mansion was built in the grand Tudor style with lots of hedges, trees, lanes and driveways. It was dark and few lights were on. The guard at the entrance was stiff but cordial when I mentioned the password "Dagmar" to him. He instructed me to go around to the kitchen entrance, behind the massive grounds of *Greystone Mansion* itself. Purchased and built originally in 1899 for Oliver P. Posey and family. Edward L. Doheny, a gold and oil magnate who was acquainted with Oliver Posey through their mutual mining interests, purchased the mansion in 1901. There was even a Doheny Drive in Beverly Hills. The present estate was given to son Ned for a wedding gift in 1927 and new construction began. I think I was still on the police force when the scandal surrounding Greystone Manor broke out. Shortly after son Ned and family moved in to the newly finished mansion, it seems a guy named Hugh Plunkett, secretary and maybe confidant, turned on and killed his employer Ned Doheny on the evening of February 16, 1929, subsequently killing himself—or possibly the other way around, since it was Ned's weapon that was used. It was never really proven exactly, but Ned was not allowed to be buried in the Catholic cemetery because of a possible suicide. Doheny's wife and five children were on the premises at the time. So, I guess you could say the joint had a curse on it from the get-go. It's funny how things get connected, like blessings and curses, all mixed up with each other. Maybe the mansion was built on some old indian burial ground or the like and *was* really cursed. Who knows?

I found the kitchen entrance and knocked. A very well dressed woman came to the door with a sandwich in one hand. "Yes?"

"Uh. I'm Cable Denning, here to see Miss Sophia Legende?"

"Well, I'm sorry, but no one is allowed upstairs tonight. There's—there's been an accident."

"Accident? Look, lady, I'm a private investigator and Miss Legende's life may be in danger!"

She moved aside and took a bite out of her sandwich. "I'm afraid you're too late. Someone got killed tonight...upstairs. I think it was Sophia—your Miss Legende," she said in a haughty tone of voice.

My heart sank. Though I could imagine someone killing her, it was still a shock. But, yeah, it made sense. Someone else knew I was coming to see her and she was about to spill the beans to me. To that somebody else, it was a death sentence for poor Sophia Legende. "Where's the body?" was my knee-jerk response.

"Like I said, upstairs, but you can't go—Dr. Rueben's orders."

"Stop me!" I barked as I tore through the kitchen to the living room and ran up the stairs. I drew my .38 and started shouting out Sophia's name. "Sophie! Sophie! Miss Legende!"

Suddenly a little white haired man with a nice plump face and lots of thick silvery hair peeked out of a doorway. He was lively and moved quickly. I guessed him to be in his mid-fifties. "Twenty-two vomen here, one moider, and a crazy man! Ayii! That's enough for vahn night!" he complained with a thick Yiddish accent of some kind or other. "Und...vhat do *you* vant calling out like a crazy man?!"

"I had an appointment with Miss Legende, sir—"

"—doctor...Dr. Ephron Rueben. Some...dey call me 'Emergency Room Rueben' but close friends and acquaintances call me plain ol' 'Eps.' So you vahnt I should let you see Miss Legende? Let me show you something else first." He had me follow him down the decorous hallway with fancy pictures, pieces of old furniture and black and white reversed-pyramid tiles on the floor. We entered into a beautifully attired room with a huge bed...made of heavily carved dark wood. A lovely young blonde woman with a soft yellow see-through negligee lay on the bed...dead. "Dis...dis vas *supposed to be* Miss Legende, perpetrated, to the best of mine knowledge, by a *dart* blown from perhaps a reed or the like, Mr.— Mr.—"

I ripped out my I.D. "—Denning, Cable Denning, private investigator."

His silvery eyebrows lifted. "Oh! Vell, dat does change tings a little bit—I am the house physician for all the young tings in this house of *carnal specialty*, shall ve say—and Miss Legende is our star—star, uh, *performer* here, Mr. Denning. She's also sick the least of all the venereally affected vomen here. This lovely young ting's name is Greta Bardini. Such a terrible ting—all of this— as you see, Miss Bardini vas killed in place of Miss Legende. "Please, come this way."

This time he led me down the stairs and out of the house to a back cottage, perhaps the gardener's house in past years. "No one lives here?" I asked.

"Supposed to...but you know how money talks, Mr. Denning—and the owners have—have vacated the premises for the profit of what *else* goes on here, for different climes in New York City, I believe."

"I see," I said as the doctor knocked on the cottage door. An ashen-faced Sophia Legende greeted me. "Mr. Denning! Thank God!" she exclaimed as she grabbed me and held me tight. "I—I didn't know what to think! Poor Greta—she was the girl I told you about—you know, the one who knew—she—she got killed instead of me tonight—I—I wanted to meet you in a more neutral setting than—"

"—such a ting...you know each other," Dr. Rueben said. "I shall be on my vay, but if you please, Mr. Denning, kindly come see me before you go away tonight, ya?"

"Yeah, sure, doc, I'll do that," I said. I closed the door to face the lovely Sophia. She was wearing a white see-through negligee like her dead prostitute sister wore. *What a body!* I thought. I was reminded how men go nuts desiring something like that—cloying and clawing their way to tits and pussy they can't even have!

"Cable, someone *knew*—they knew we'd talked, they knew you were coming and where I entertained my clients—and poor, poor Greta—I asked her to exchange rooms with me because I didn't want to be reminded of—of where I work during—during your visit. Then I heard the screams and Dr. Rueben was on the premises—he...he told me Greta was dead in my room! It should've been me, Cable! He suggested we should meet here in a safe place. But nothing's safe, nothing!"

"Calm yourself, babe!" I bellowed at her. "Now, let's sit down. If the killer's still around and he discovers he shot the wrong babe with a poison dart, he'll be after you—again!" We sat at the tiny little breakfast table with two chairs. "Now...now's the time to tell me the story, kid, all of it!"

She tried to compose herself. But instead she leaned toward me. "May I do something personal?"

"Yeah, I guess, if it don't hurt..."

She leaned those fine breasts over the table and put her lips onto mine real hard and moved them around on my mouth like her life depended on it. When she finally withdrew, she took a deep breath. "There...kissing like that always...always calms me, Cable. You don't mind, do you?"

"No, not at all, whenever you need calming, I'm your guy!" I kidded. Then I drew serious. "Now, no more bullshit, Sophie. What was that famous *'something else'*? Let's hear the whole frickin' tawdry story."

"Yes, okay... You see, Greta Bardini, the girl who was killed tonight—about three months ago, before I had even met Anthone Demaine or ever heard of Zoot Mimby's Club downtown—she—she came to me about having seen something so terrible that it frightened the poor thing half to death. She needed to tell someone. She chose me."

"Okay, so far so good. But why did she choose you—and just exactly what did she see?"

"I suppose she came to me because I appeared more stable than some of the other girls. I'm a bit older, a little more sure of myself, I guess. She had three stunning younger girlfriends who had simply disappeared within the past few weeks. When she called them or tried to contact them, they simply were nowhere to be found. There was a fourth girl, Elizabeth Arden, who'd allowed herself to be taken down to Zoot Mimby's one night for a couple of tricks. One of the tricks was Anthone Demaine. The other customer was a weird guy named *Mr. M* whom Elizabeth serviced as well that night. While she was in the bathroom cleaning up, the window was open to the parking lot behind the club. It was late, she told me. She overheard Anthone Demaine and this Mr. M talking. She turned off the bathroom light and got a stool and elevated herself so she could see. There were five young women she'd never seen before. To her horror she saw they were gagged and their hands were tied. They were also being shot in the neck with a blowpipe by a negro dressed in a black suit, as if it were a sport of his! He was using some kind of fast acting poison, because the girls practically dropped where they were when the poison dart hit them on the neck. She said the executioner was extraordinarily tall and had a skeleton-like, laughing face with big, buggy eyes. As the girls fell to the ground they were picked up quickly and loaded into the rear of a large black hearse—an old one, like out of the 1920's or 30's." I could tell it was difficult for Sophia Legende to tell the story, but so far she was batting a thousand in my book.

"So how did Greta Bardini get involved if it was Elizabeth Arden who'd seen this thing going on?"

"I assume Elizabeth Arden was found out, and she disappeared, too, and so Greta went to find out what happened to her. You see, they were roommates. I guess they were pretty close. She asked me if I'd go to Zoot

Mimby's with her to see if we could trace down Eliza-beth's whereabouts. Needless to say now, that was a huge mistake. It was then that I met Anthone Demaine and ultimately he made his proposition to me shortly thereafter. I think you know the rest." Sophia Legende's lips were dry and she licked them. "So...that's the '*other thing*' I was talking about, Cable." Then her eyes teared. "And now—now Greta's dead!" she sobbed.

I patted her hand. "Okay, Sophie, thanks. I'm not so sure those women were being murdered, however. Does it make sense to you that these guys would be kill-ing off beautiful young women and not making a profit out of them somehow? These guys operate for profit and besides murder, trafficking drugs and more than likely white slavery, maybe there's something we missed. My guess is these young women are being *stunned* by the darts, brought to another location, drugged until they become compliant and then sold off to the highest bidders in the Orient or Arabia or some other exotic location. There they live out a life of en-slaved prostitution." I took out a cigarette and lit it. "It's an old story, Sophie. But...there's something that bites at my butt..."

"God, that's unthinkably horrible!" she cried. Then she managed a half-smile as she looked at me. "What's biting your butt, Cable?" she asked nervously.

"That big tall, skeleton-like dude? That smacks of some kind of Caribbean-type voodoo ritual or the like—doesn't it to you?"

"I don't know, Cable, I have no experience in those worlds—"

"—what if I could infiltrate that group down there at Mimby's somehow and find out just who this Mr. M is and what's *really* going on with those kidnapped young things? Then we'd know..."

"It's scary as hell, but maybe I can help you, Cable...maybe I could go down there—"

"—are you kidding, lady? You're supposed to be dead! I think you oughtta stay that way for a while until this thing blows over. I think it was dark enough in that room of yours where Greta got it, so that maybe the killer couldn't see the difference between she and you. Whatta ya think?"

"I don't know. Maybe you're right." Then she grabbed my wrist tight. "Cable, please don't go back down there—to the club, I mean. Leave those horrible people to their dirty work—tell the police or something—but they'll kill you the next time you're found nosing around down there!"

I took a big drag on my cigarette. "Maybe...maybe not... And the cops? Ha! They don't have the time or manpower to be investigating the Black Mafia more than they already know. I happen to know Lt. Lester Keith for years. Hell, his plate is so full of everyday homicide shit that he's buried in it! This goddamn war has brought more soldiers and sailors into our streets and men go for women, generally—and that means drunk fights—and sometimes murder. Nope, it's gotta be a private investigation..."

"Oh, Cable, I fear for you...I just got to—to meet you. And I like you. It's so magical to have a man in my life who isn't a customer of mine."

"Hey, wait a minute there, gal! What kinda man *who*?

"A legitimate professional man who doesn't want my favors—and above all, is someone companionable, someone I can talk to and have an intelligent conversation with—without him thinking I'm some kind of intellectual slut or the like."

"I kinda like your intellectual side—as long as you keep your clothes on," I kidded her.

"You do—I mean, truthfully?"

"Yep." I found an old clamshell ashtray and ground out my cigarette. "I told you Ayana Javina happened to pop in on me very late a night or two ago. I think we might have an ally in Miss Javina. She knows a lot—and could tell us a lot—"

"—and get killed a lot, just like poor Greta tonight!" Sophia cut in.

"I don't know. I have a feeling the gal can handle herself." I glanced at my watch. "It's getting on to midnight. I'm gonna pop by the doc's for a minute and then see if I can find Ayana Javina—after I check in with Lt. Lester Keith. At least I'll let him know about what I suspect is some major covert white slavery ring. Maybe he knows about it. I don't know."

She looked at me across the table. "When will I see you again?"

"I don't know that, either, kid. I exist in the shadow of danger, Sophia Legende."

She got up and extended her arms to me. I went to her and she embraced me tenderly. "I'm—I'm *very* fond of you, Cable Denning. Please don't get killed—save a Saturday walk in the park for me, will ya?"

"You like walking in the park?"

"Yes...especially with a man I trust." She smiled a naughty smile. "You—you, uh, won't try to seduce me in the bushes now, will you?"

"Depends on the day," I kidded her.

"The day?"

"Yeah, like you can't trust me on Thursdays."

She laughed. "Thursdays? Then what days are safe?"

"Usually the weekend." I put on my fedora and left.

The Death Dart

Dr. Ephron Rueben lived on the premises of Greystone Mansion downstairs. The same lady who'd greeted me when I came into the place directed me to his rooms. I think she was a little put off that I broke the rules and ran upstairs earlier. Rueben was wiry, matter-of-fact but with a sense of humor. He was on the short side, had a slight frame and used his arms a lot when he talked. But he had lots of thick, silvery hair that rose high on his head. I liked the guy. "You should arrive on such an evening, Mr. Investigator. Come in, take a load off." His quarters were austere but the walls were filled with news clips from around the world. "Before you take leave, I vas vondering if you vould help me to carry Miss Bardini's body into the back of my station vagon."

"Yeah, sure. But why not have the county come pick it up?"

"*Everyting*...everyting here at Greystone is confidential—even dead people. Once the police begin to investigate and discover vhat really goes on here—ay! ve'll be out of business!"

"I see. Now, what was it you wanted to see me about?"

He checked out my eyes. "Are you a humorous man, Mr. Denning?"

"I can be...depends on the company and the occasion, I guess."

"So often t'ings get distorted—ya—like vhy a disease should be ascribed to a definite race and not all people. This humor vill perhaps enlighten you: Ruth and Golda vere valking along and Ruth says, 'Ya know, finally, my son is getting married. He's engaged to a vonderful girl—but he tinks she may have a disease called herpes.'

Golda says, 'Do you have any idea vhat this herpes is and can he catch it?'

Ruth is in dreamland. 'I don't know,' she says, 'I'm just so thrilled my son is getting married—about the herpes, I don't know...'

Golda goes home and looks in her medical dictionary. She calls Ruth on the telephone. 'Ruth—I looked it up in my book—you know, that herpes disease you vere talking about?"

'Ya.'

'Vell, it's okay because it's only a disease for gentiles!'"

I chuckled. "So...what's your point, doc?"

"That people assume a general malaise is not for everyone—such as a highly communicable disease. Some appear to be exempt from suffering. And I'm a Jew, I know about suffering—ya!"

"Okay...your point...I've got a busy night ahead."

"Vhat is it...ya can't take a minute out vith patience here? I'm coming to it, I'm coming to it! Ya know, detective, I don't even vanna take your blood pressure—I might die just reading it!"

"Okay, maybe I *am* a little tense—"

"—tense? A little tense? I'd say you are a vinding spring in a coo-coo clock! Relax. And let me inform you as to vhat I tink you're up against, Mr. Denning. Unless I'm mistaking, zat particular death earlier tonight of Miss Bardini indicates a crime ring of some kind is operating here in Los Angeles. Vhat ring I don't know. Who do you know kills people with poison darts except six-year olds who watch Tarzan movies?!" he said, gesticulating with his arms.

"I'm already on to that, doc. It's the Black Mafia operating outta downtown somewhere. But I sense a Caribbean connection. Don't ask me why or how just yet."

"Vhat...? Black Mafia, downtown—Caribbean? Vhat vould they be doing sloshing around in the Caribbean? You know, I'm always disappointed vhen somebody's wrong. And vhat if you are?"

"Then I'm wrong, but that's where I'm going now. To *Zoot Mimby's* downtown—that's the club that at least two now-deceased white girls went to recently. It's also the place Sophia Legende tells me the girls talked about during their short stay here on earth as having some very weird goings on."

"How quaint is your lingo, Mr. Denning. Ya, all of us have a short stay—just some shorter than others. Such a ting that you vould traipse in there as a private investigator. Do zey know you?"

"I'm afraid all too well. I was the guy who Sophia hired to talk to a guy named Anthone Demaine. And that's when I met the girl from Martinique—Ayana Javina."

"Better let me go mit you, zen…"

"*You*!?"

"Ya, vhy not?"

"A white Jewish doctor in a black nightclub by himself after midnight, are you kiddin'? If they don't bump you off for the way you look, then they'll for sure rob you of all your gold and dump your body in San Pedro bay!"

We both looked at each other and laughed. I knew I was gonna like this man. "Now I *really* vant to go! Such a ting that I walk in the joint, order a drink, ask for directions because I'm lost and check tings out. Ya? And you can sneak in the basement and see vhat's going on, eh?"

"Maybe that ain't such a bad idea after all. You be the white decoy upstairs while I explore downstairs. Hey, wait a minute—how'd you know they had a basement?"

"All dose downtown places have basements. It vas the fashion in the teens and twenties vhen a lotta dose buildings vere built—I should know, I vas a poor Jewish boy on *South* Los Angeles Street, Mr. Denning!"

"Just call me Cable…"

"Ya, you burly mensch, just call me 'Eps', okay?"

It was 12:48 a.m. when Dr. Rueben and I parked around the corner from *Zoot Mimby's*. I turned off the engine and looked at Eps. "You sure about this?"

"I don't know. Remember, I have to be back to bury Miss Bardini's body before sunrise."

137

"All you have to do is distract them. Ready?"

"Ya, like a Jew in the middle of Africa—*alone!*" He looked a little hesitant. "Ayi! Vhat have I gotten myself into! My mother always told me never to go outside at night—but here I am!"

"Yeah, doc, and you'd better be sure. Hesitation is one thing you can't afford. Now, if you wanna stay here and stand guard to keep the car from getting stolen—I'll take my chances—"

"—no, Cable...I just have to breathe in a few good breaths...my mother also told me *that!*"

He got out and walked around the corner. While he covered the front of the joint, it was my task to penetrate the basement and see what I could find. The back alley smelled like pee and over-ripe garbage. A bum slept under a piece of army canvas and it was so dark I had trouble seeing any back entrance to *Zoot Mimby's.* There was no basement window, so I'd have to enter through the back door and find the damn thing, hoping to hell I wouldn't get caught. Unfortunately the back door was locked, but with a little picking from a trusty little tool I carried around for just such purposes, I managed to open the door. A rush of hot, noisy air hit me as I entered. Immediately to my left there was another door. I knew that was my destination....*and* it was open. Dimly lit wooden stairs led down to the basement proper. It was essentially a storage room for cases of cheap gallon bottles of wine and beer. There was a narrow red door near the far corner. I put my ear to it. I heard a mumbling of some sort. I tried the knob. It was locked. Again, I got out my trusty little tool and picked away until I could hear the lock give it up. I slowly opened the door. I could sense there was something or someone else in the small room. It was pitch dark and I fumbled around for a light switch...no luck. Finally, a pull string in the middle of the damned room hit me in the face and I yanked it. And there appeared none other than Ayana Javina. She was gagged and tied to a large chair with only her slip on! I didn't say a word but immediately untied her. "Cable! How—how did you know I would be—"

"—shhh! I didn't. I just knew I had to get to the bottom of this thing. Are you okay? Did they hurt you?"

"No...but they found out I'd been to your place and—and Mr. M told Anthone to punish me by deportation back to Martinique. I guess they could have killed me. But I am no longer of use to them. Or they have other intentions for me I do not know of. I was a stupid girl, Cable!" She clasped her arms around me. "Thank you! I am so thirsty and have to go to the bathroom. But there is no toilet down here!"

I chuckled. "Well, let's get you a gallon of cheap wine and when you're good and drunk, you can pee in the bottle!"

"Men can do that, I cannot...!" she said indignantly.

I thought fast. "Okay, let's get you topside. I'll put you out in the alley until I'm through putzing around down here." I grabbed a bottle of beer and we made our way up the stairs. I let her out into the alley.

"Okay, go now...over there..." I suggested.

"And you won't watch?"

"Don't be silly—watch a woman pee?"

She giggled and lifted her slip and bent down to pee across from me. "Thank you... But you don't have to go back down there. Cable—I know the whole thing—I know what they are doing! There is nothing downstairs. They have their twelve young women..."

"Twelve young women?"

"Yes...please, come with me to your car. Let us go from here. If we are caught, they will kill us for certain...on the spot!" We walked briskly around the corner to my car. Eps and I had agreed on about a half hour. It'd been twenty-two minutes by my count. I checked the streets carefully and then helped Ayana curl up in the trunk of my Dodge coupe. I left the trunk door open slightly and then got back into my car. In precisely 33 minutes Dr. Rueben came walking around the corner. He got in. I opened my door get out.

"I come in, you go out—*vhat is dis*—hide and seek?"

I quickly went around, told Ayana we were going and we'd be out of the area in minutes. I closed the trunk and I got back in. "I found one thing, and one thing only, doc—and it made the whole trip worthwhile. Did anyone think it curious that you were in there?"

"I hope not—maybe the blackface helped!" Then he smiled. "Just joking. I don't think any of the big shots were in tonight. A couple of negro men looked at me veird, but dat vas it!" His eyes were curious. "Zo...vhat vas it you found?"

"Good. That means we probably won't be noticed." I smiled. "It's a surprise. But we need a safe place for her."

"Her? Her who?"

"Ayana—remember, the singer I told you about? Well, she came over to see me against all the rules a night or two ago. So I guess they found out and they were about to punish her. She says by sending her back to Martinique. But I don't think so…I think they wanted to find out what she knew and then kill her."

"Mein Gott, Cable! How long have I known you?"

"About three hours or so…"

"And you live like this? I tink *I* need a doctor!" he said, fanning himself. "And vhere is the young voman going to stay? She cannot stay vit you, nor vit me at Greystone. Vait a minute! A great idea I've got!"

"Yeah? Well, better tell me now while we're carrying the precious cargo around in the back of my car that running out of air in the trunk."

"My sister Yisha—she's charming—and very Jew-ish—but as good and dependable as the gold."

"Where does she live?"

"Not far from vhere ve are—almost in the Silver Lake district—near Fountain and Virgil Avenues."

"It's late…you sure?"

"It's okay—Yisha only sleeps when Yahveh comes. Ya, the olden Hebrew God—you know vhen Moses says, *'his God is God'*—ya dat vahn. So when God comes into her house, Yisha sleeps!"

"Oh, okay…"

It was about two in the morning when we pulled up at 1252 N. Virgil Avenue. I got the bedraggled Ayana out of the trunk of my car and we delivered her to the front door. And as it turned out, the doc's sister was a charac-ter and a gem with a heavier accent than her brother. She was about the same size as her brother with frizzy silver hair and wore reading glasses that hung on leath-er strings. She was also a music buff and had a large col-lection of 78 r.p.m. recordings. "If you tink dis collection is big, you shoulda seen his brother's collection—Aram had twenty-five hundred records before he died."

"And what happened to them?" I asked out of curiosity.

"Oy vey! De wife, she gives dem avay to de Annual Jewish Fundraiser at the temple. Broke my heart vhen I hoid of it." Then suddenly sister Yisha was aware of the exotic Ayana. "Ve are needing to get you to a bath and bed, young lady. Vhat do you do?"

"I am a singer—and I am crazy about the Jewish composers—Berlin, Arlen, Mercer, Kern, the Gershwin brothers—"

"—vell, den, ve vill have a vonderful time of it, von't ve?!"

I took Ayana aside and told her I'd come over tomorrow after she'd rested and we could talk. "We have to save those girls, Cable...I feel partly responsible now...we *must* save them!" she said in a committed insistent voice.

"So...where are they gonna be, Ayana?"

"On Martinique—we have to beat the Voodoo King and his dart blowpipe. Slowly he shoots them, a little at a time on the neck until on the day of sacrifice they are only zombies, not alive, not dead! Once a month for twelve moons, it is the *Night of Santeria*—when the young virgins—so they say—are sacrificed, one each month for twelve months. We must save them from the horror of *Maybouya!*"

"Maybouya?" I asked.

"Maybouya...oh, Cable! He's the most fearsome of all the Carib Gods. He requires sacrifice in order not to do evil things to the tribe's people," she exclaimed as she clung to me.

"That bad, eh?" I said in a low voice. "Does that mean you want me to travel to Martinique—with you?"

"Yes...I don't know exactly how, but I am a *remnant* Taíno. We need to penetrate the tribe after we find out when the ritual is being held. But we must act fast!"

"I think we're going as fast as we can for the moment, kid," I said. Then I hugged her and said goodnight.

Chapter 4

NIGHT OF THE MAYBOUYA

After I dropped Dr. Ephron Rueben off at Greystone I came straight home. I needed a drink. I sat behind my desk with my hat cocked back on my head and my trench coat hung on the coat rack like another person was in the room. I took out a Lucky Strike and lit it up. I poured a generous amount of fine English gin into the same ol' glass and saluted myself. "Here's to you, you old sniff-nose, drinking, smoking, womanizing son-of-a-bitch!" I downed the whole glass. The drawer with the bottle of gin was the same drawer that contained Maria Voldt's late, great testament to life and love. I took out the old folder she had left me, filled with poems so brilliantly written that I swore one day I would get someone to publish them so the world might benefit from her poetic genius.

I turned on the radio and sat back down at my desk. I turned on my desk lamp and I thought I saw the words *"Come Visit Me"* written on the inset. I directed the light to the words and looked again...they had disappeared. Maybe it was a message of some sort. Some marvelous music was playing on the radio, a piano concerto I think. Whatever it was it fit perfectly to Maria's words as I declared them out loud to God and the world:

"If you leave behind and cannot find
She who loved you most and best

Do not find me here moldering in the past
But riding the corona of a distant sun—fast
And to the point of every starboard dream
That life whooshed by and left no seam
For you to dive into, my sweetest man
Because I knew you, too, wore footprints
Deeply in the sand—and could not lend me a hand
That would free my kiss from your lips
Nor your groin from my own anxious hips
While I was still earth-young enough to
Have you plunder what was the thunder
Of my heart in loving you. mv

I hadn't realized it until now, but Maria Voldt's world and words would haunt me all of my life. What *if?* I asked myself. What if I had taken her to me and nurtured her in all ways, loved her and supported her in her wonderful poetic ability—would she have lived? Or was I pipe dreaming again that she would be just as endangered here as where she died on that hilltop in Ventura County? Could I have loved her long term? As wonderfully odd as she was, would the two of us have adjusted to being together although we came from two different worlds? As I slugged down my last gin for the night, I realized I'd never know the answer to that question. With or without us, life goes on like a big pavement roller, squashing us all into the asphalt sooner or later.

Before I knew it, it was Tuesday, March 20, 1945 and that morning I informed Ida as much as I could about what was developing. I told her about the death of Greta Bardini via a blow dart and meeting Dr. Ephron

Rueben, the follow up with the frightened Sophia Legende and last night's escapade in finding Ayana Javina in the cellar of the Central Avenue club. I also told her I felt that some bad rituals akin to something like voodoo or some other bad shit might be happening somewhere soon. She recoiled at the idea of the terror some of these dark arts invoked. But being female and having an interest in me personally, I think she was equally concerned about which female might be attracted to me and how would I respond to either Sophia or Ayana. I didn't comment.

Ida and I worked pretty hard on regular cases until about noon. She went off for lunch and I picked up the telephone to call the much neglected Nadia Skorkowsky. "Yes, hello...?"

"Nadia, it's me, Cable—sorry I haven't gotten back to you sooner, but I've been in and out so damned much lately—"

"—I miss you, Cable," she said. That was all. She didn't reproach me for not following through with our wonderful night together.

"That's why I called—I miss you, too, lady," I replied. "So what are the chances for a happy reunion soon?"

"How about tonight? But I must warn you, after I sing a lot I'm very horny and tonight I have rehearsals for Act I with a very handsome Cavarradosi. Can you handle it?" she snickered.

"Oh, I don't know. Maybe you oughtta try me out...whatta ya say?"

"Yes...yes, yes! I'll be back from the theatre about 10:30. How about eleven tonight?"

146

"You got a date, Nadia. See ya then." We hung up. I got out a cigarette and lit up. Yep, there'd be a hot time in the old town tonight!

After Ida left late in the afternoon, I was wondering about whatever happened to Erond Mantis Spiricus, the potato bug creature.

We are each other, he told me that day. If that's so, what is individual identity then? Another thing that bothered me about him is that he claimed by pushing his shiny bald pate against my head on the wooden platform beneath the Death Tower out on the desert at Alamogordo, that he absorbed everything that was in my brain. Did that include what I knew about life? About women? About the *Fen de Fuqin?* I wondered. But it was a moot point. I had no way of contacting Erond.

Before I left for Nadia's that evening, I called Dr. Rueben to see how his sister Yisha and Ayana Javina were getting along. He reported to me that they were having a splendid time listening to the Great American Songbook together and having coffee, tea and cakes throughout the day. I told him I'd check in with Ayana tomorrow. There was a story she had to tell me.

I also called Lt. Lester Keith of the Los Angeles Police Department, Homicide Division. I told him I suspected the Black Mafia headquartered at *Zoot Mimby's Club* and was up to something unsavory. "You know, Denning, you keep nosin' into police business and you're gonna end up dead like one them girls! How many times do I have to tell ya to lay off?! Now, suppose you let me handle this, huh? I'll sniff it out and let you know what I find. All of this Caribbean mumbo-jumbo, though...spare me, private detective! Pull yourself together, Denning, or else I'll haul you in for mental incompetency! Stay away from Mimbo's place—"

"Zoot *Mimby's*, Lester—not Mimbo's. You know where it is?"

There was a momentary silence. "Uh...sure—it's where all the other joints like that are...on South Central. You might narrow it down for me a little.

"It's near the corner at Adams."

"Oh, yeah—it's a walk-down puke place, right?"

"More or less."

"Thanks, and stay away from the frickin' joint, hear?"

"Right, Lieutenant..." We hung up.

The minute I got inside her Rodeo Drive home, Nadia enclosed me in her arms and kissed me until I had to come up for air. "Babe! Whew! Is that what singing does for you?"

"Yes, and thinking about you," she breathed. "Cable, please, let's not talk now—let me take you to my bedroom and—"

"—whoa, Nellie! Without a drink or allowing me to take off my coat and hat?"

"Yes—and no! I need you, Cable—now—please...?"

I followed her into her bedroom. She was wearing only a robe and soon that was on the floor as she began to undress me. Soon we were entwined in each other's bodies and Nadia threw her long shapely legs around me and plunged my manhood deeply into her with no foreplay. We rocked and rolled for over an hour until finally we both cried 'uncle' and lay there on her large bed, exhausted. "Oh, wow!" she exclaimed. "Cable, how

148

can this be—that I couldn't think of anything except you for all these days? You satisfy me so!"

"I'm flattered, babe. What about your music? Didn't you say you're doing '*Tosca*' or something?"

"Yes, but I know that music so well. I'm polishing up the ensemble scenes now. Cross your fingers, I'm hoping to land the New York City Opera production next year if this production goes well. There is supposed to be a scout for the New York company's conductor, Mr. Laszlo Halasz, attending our performance.

"That's great, doll. I'm happy for you. I hope you get it."

"And you? Are you okay? You look a bit strained and those bags under your eyes—have you been getting enough sleep?"

"Uh...probably not. All truth be told, I'm an insomniac and walk the streets late at night, sometimes into the early hours just before dawn."

"I see...not me... I sleep like a baby—except when I'm thinking about you and what we could be doing. Then I get restless."

I chuckled. "How about a drink?"

We went out to her kitchen and sat naked opposite each other. "I'm not usually like this, Cable, sitting here nude, staring at you like a heartsick teenager—and leaking on my nice kitchen chair!"

That made me all the more hot for the babe. "Yeah? Show me..."

I got up and went to her side of the table. She stood up and there indeed was a small blotch of wetness where she was sitting. "See? It's us, darling, you and me combined. Isn't that wonderful?" She sat back down and took a sip from her drink. "So what's been happening for you? I'm not sure I want to hear all of it. But are there some new intrigues in your detective life?"

I downplayed it. "Naw, not really. Now, let me see...nothing much but the Black Mafia, a white slavery ring, two or three dead young women, a Jewish doctor with a sense of humor, a beautiful blonde prostitute who can't stand doing 'it', a light-chocolate Caribbean singer with a mysterious past and a police lieutenant who doesn't believe me most of the time. Not much else except the regular everyday crap, you know."

She looked at me as her mouth dropped open. "You are kidding, aren't you—that's a normal week for you?"

"Some weeks. I wish I *were* kidding."

"Oh, Cable...I didn't know...I mean I really didn't know! How can one man handle all of that without going nuts?"

"Ha! I *am* nuts, doll, or didn't I tell you that part?"

She got up and poured us another drink. Then she stood above me. "Please...will you stand up?"

I did so. "Yeah...?"

She put her arms around me. "Let me see now...I'm 5' 6" and you're about six feet tall, I'm pliant and you're muscular. We fit, Cable, in or out of bed. And speaking of which, I'm pulsing for you right now—again. I can't believe myself! Can we go back to bed—I've missed you so much. I wanna do some catching up." Then she kissed my whole face, ending with my nose. "Is that alright with you, big boy?"

"Yeah, sure, babe, I've missed you, too." She took the open palms of her hands and cupped my balls and penis between them.

"This...gives me a rush, Mr. Private Detective Denning...will you oblige a girl?"

We went back to bed and made love again. Nadia Skorkowsky and I went away for a while, went away to that land of carnal, selfish ecstasy where nothing counted except the moment and the passions that poured out of us like a waterfall of desire and satiation.

The Deadly Mambo

The next day I called Dr. Rueben's sister Yisha and asked to talk with Ayana. When the young woman from Martinique came on the line she sounded very happy to hear my voice. I told her I needed to know everything in detail about what was going on and what was gonna happen to the "twelve women" that had been kidnapped and perhaps already on their way to Martinique. I suggested I pick her up and we go to a more or less public place so she could tell me the scoop in detail. I was certain eyes and ears were everywhere once Demaine and Mr. M discovered Ayana had gotten free of her basement prison.

It was about 8:30 p.m. We found a small bar nearby and settled in a tight little corner. Ayana was a vibrant young woman, smart as a whip and spoke of what she'd learned by overhearing Demaine and Mr. M. talk. "You see, as I already told you last night, the *Maybouya* is an evil spirit that needs these young women to complete a cycle. But no one has ever seen Maybouya." Then she shivered as if someone had walked over her grave. "But...there is a living horror whose name is *Mambo*, a High Priestess. She is a beautiful and terrible *thing*, Ca-

151

ble—and I swear on my name, she is also a large *snake!* She emerges from a huge hand-woven basket as a viper, then by the time her very long snake-body reaches the ground, she has transformed into *Mambo*, a beautiful naked woman who is then clothed in a bright feathered robe by the ritual master. I think he is the strange tall man with the blowpipe. So Mambo invokes Maybouya and tells him she has the sacrifice prepared for him. It is Mambo who leads the young virgins to their deaths over the deep fiery pit of *Mount Pelée!* Oh, Cable, we must save those young women! It may even be too late now! But we must try!"

"Hmmm...Pelée...isn't that a volcano that exploded in the first part of this century? I remember my mother telling me about it."

"Yes, in 1902 the mountain exploded and killed at least 30,000 people. Now it has calmed, but still smolders just below the surface. Near the top there is a hole—what do you call it? I say *colinda* or something like that—"

"—*caldera*—I think that's it."

"Yes! That is it—*caldera*...it is like a boiling pot of molten rock. It is there that Mambo brings the sacrifice to appease Maybouya. If the woman does not jump on her own, Mambo pushes her into the molten lava below. In a way, she is more feared than Maybouya, because he is invisible. It has been told to me by my grandmother that Mambo can take over anyone's body anytime she wishes—if she wishes."

"Now that's scary—not only a shape changer, but capable of inhabiting someone else's body with them still in it—whether they like it or not? Spooky."

152

"Yes." She said that and then reached her hand across the table and took mine. "I know I have not told you, but I am very happy to know you, Cable. Even if you did not decide to come with me to Martinique."

"Well, thanks, Ayana. I'm happy to know you as well. But I can't let you go off on such a perilous journey alone."

"Oh, there are a couple of relatives who would help me. One is my Uncle Kalinga—he hates the sacrifice religion of *Orinoco*."

"How good is your uncle with a gun?"

"Oh, I do not think Uncle Kalinga has ever seen a gun. He lives on the bottom slopes of Mt. Pelée, near Saint-Pierre. But he would help."

I knew in my heart Ayana wouldn't stand a chance coming up against the religious rituals that had frightened and intimidated those ancient peoples for so many generations. So I was resolute. I would go to rescue the girls, at the very least. And who knows, maybe even shake up these lousy rituals and the beliefs in them.

I told the lady I was leaning in the direction of helping her and accompanying her to the Caribbean island of Martinique. I drove Ayana home with dances of sugar plumb fairies in my head thinking how nuts I was to do this thing. Why should I care if a dozen pretty white American women get cooked in a volcano? But I did. That was also Cable Denning.

About 10:00 p.m. I journeyed to Greystone Mansion in Beverly Hills. I thought I'd talk to the venerable Dr. "Eps" about the latest developments. I didn't know why, but I had a feeling his insights would be revealing.

153

"You're going *vhere*?" he asked me, his eyes widening considerably. "I hardly know you—yet vhy do I get the feeling you like committing suicide! And that pretty young *shikse* you vant to follow there? Dey vill cook her, too! No, the three of us vill have to go incognito, I think."

I did a double take. "*Three* of us? Naw, doc, I can't risk you—"

"—vhat's a matter—I'm too old, eh? Is dat it? Vell, let me tell you something, bruiser, I'm as hale and hearty as a thirty year-old! Just ask Rose—she'll tell ya already I'm able to leap tall buildings in one—"

I smirked at him. "—Rose? You rascal, you didn't tell me..."

"Vhy should you have to know everyting?"

"Seriously, what role could you play in this very risky trip, doc?"

"Vell, first of all I can heal...I'm pretty big on that! I am a good navigator so ve von't get lost. And va-va-voom! Vhat else could a fifty-six year old bachelor get into vit lots of pretty Martinique light-chocolate vomen around, eh? Plus I need a vacation...such a ting!"

I laughed out loud. "You rascal, you! I guess it's true what they say, huh?"

"Who says about *what*?"

"*Just because there's snow on the roof doesn't mean there ain't fire in the furnace!* I quoted a post card I saw once in a drug store rack.

"Dat's right! So, ve tree go togeder, ya?" he asked, his eyes trying to figure out what I was thinking.

"Okay...the three of us—but I gotta check in with Ayana to make sure she has no objections," I said extending my hand. He took it. "Deal."

"Ya know, Denning, even though you're too old to be my son, I hope you don't mind if I see you kind of in dat light. I got no children. You're as close as it gets, mine boychik kemfer...and friend."

"Yeah, sure, Eps, if that makes ya happy. Now...when do we leave and how—we gotta figure that out."

He nodded. "Yeah, good idea. Ask the young lady—she got here, didn't she? I imagine ve vill hop, skip und jump from California to Florida? Once there ve can hire a cousin of mine. He owns his own air flight service—*Flying J Travel*—and boy, does he fly around!"

"Flying J Travel? Are you sure he ain't no 'fly-by-night' kinda guy? And why wouldn't we buy a ticket for a regular airline?"

"Oh, no, Cable, ve cannot do dat. It's vartime, have you forgotten? And my cousin Lennie is up and up—he just takes small groups of businessmen around dose islands, kind of like a flying taxi vitout the military knowing about it. Ve may have two or tree ports of call before ve reach Martinique. The lesser Antilles make an arc between Puerto Rico and Trinidad off the coast of Venezuela," he said matter-of-fact.

I got a funny feeling all of a sudden. "Yeah, I, uh, I forgot about the war for a minute. How—how did you know that about the islands? I'm not even sure where the screwin' *'lesser Antilles'* are myself."

"Oh...vell, Cable, I haven't been a dumbkopf all of my life, have you?"

"I don't know, doc, I'm beginning to wonder..."

I wondered if maybe it wasn't so smart to travel on *April Fool's Day*. It was a cool Sunday morning when Ayana, Dr. Rueben and I grabbed the route south to pick

155

up the Dixie Overland Highway in San Diego and em-
barked by automobile for Florida, driving at speeds that
would have threatened the transcontinental record-
breaking feat on this highway done by Colonel Fletcher
in 1926...it turned out to be a grueling non-stop trip and
it took another whole day down Florida's coast to Miami and to locate cousin Leonard Hanner. He was a wiry
little guy with a moustache and dark thinning hair. His
airplane was also a little on the thin side, able to take
only twelve passengers at a time. We were three of
them on a two-motor 1934 Douglas DC-1 that went
maybe 200 miles-per-hour tops. It shook a lot when it
took off from Miami's small *other* airport in the middle
of the night. Military rules were strict at the time and
unauthorized aircraft were not allowed. Somehow we
got to be an exception, pointing up the fact how easy it
was to sneak into the United States if you really wanted
to, by landing in a remote, lesser known air field.

The travel route was from Florida to Nassau in the
Bahamas, on to San Juan, Puerto Rico and then to Martinique, which would be the longest stretch of ocean
beneath us, around eight hundred miles non-stop. As
we approached Martinique on a bright sunny morning
five days after leaving Los Angeles, it looked like a beautiful island paradise from the air. And indeed, it was so.

Lennie Hanner was a fine pilot, as it turned out, and
we settled into a descent on a small landing area near
Fort de France. We said good-bye to Hanner and told
him we needed to contact him by telegram when we
were finished in a few days. His next planned trip to
Martinique was unknown and it was more or less
"catch-as-catch-can" as far as his being able to guaran-

tee us safe passage back to Florida. So much for that. Our next problem was finding or renting an automobile that could take us from Fort de France to Saint Pierre.

From Paradise to Hades

There was a rattletrap bus that took us into *Fort de France* and checked into a box-shaped hotel. The doc and I decided we'd share a room and we paid $3.00 extra for an additional 8' x 10' ft. room and bed for Ayana. The weather in Martinique, we discovered, is what is called *'monsoonal'*—which means tropical by any stretch of the imagination. It was probably about 85 degrees and humid. Ayana had told us about the weather patterns—no cold season, lots and lots and lots of rain with hot days—it didn't seem to bother her.

I knew I had to think like a criminal. Where would they conceal twelve lovely blonde, young American women. hide them? How would they transport them? Who were their contacts? I told Dr. Rueben and Ayana I would sleep for a little while, then hang out in some local taverns, check with trustworthy locals and see if I can find out just what the hell these bad guys did with the girls.

It turns out that was not possible. I couldn't speak French or the local dialects and had to wait for Ayana to catch up on some sleep and then take her with me. It seems the doc had contracted some kind of bug and he was having stomach difficulties and needed to rest. Ayana told me she was not too familiar with the nightlife of *Fort de France* and it would be far better to travel on to *Saint Pierre* and ask around once we arrived at *that* destination. She told me that people and districts were very different in Martinique. Especially the tribal Taíno people. I was completely unprepared. Think about this: white people were less than 5% of the population and their national flag was a deadly white snake on a dark blue background! Suddenly I was reminded of *Mambo*, the terrible goddess who transformed from snake into woman! Oh, yeah, it all fit. Most local citizens spoke French, but the majority of the population was descended from slaves and thus spoke a kind of *Creole* language among themselves. The Taíno had *their* own language as well.

So it was decided we'd see about transportation first thing in the morning and get to *Saint Pierre* however we could. So we slept.

The Winds of Hell

It was late morning...Thursday, April 6, 1945 when we began our most bizarre journey to Mt. Pelée. It was only about 30 miles to a lovely little coastal village called *Belle Fontaine*, just 12 miles from *St. Pierre*. We decided to take a local bus filled with people, fruit, vegetables, chickens and yelling children. Gasoline was very expensive, so they not only jammed the bus to the gills, but it ran only once a day. It took us an hour and a half over a muddy road filled with potholes. But I guess it was worth it, because in a way being in *Belle Fontaine* changed my life. How? Well, we needed to find a guide in the area, someone who could fill us in on the local customs and maybe even the ritual upon the crest of Mt. Pelée. One of the best decisions I ever made, took us to a local school where grades 1 through 8 were being taught in a large building of wood with thatched roofing. I figured a teacher would be just the ticket...right? The women of the island were rather large-hipped and round—except for schoolteacher *Letichia Moreau*. She was tall, slim and strikingly beautiful with great cheekbones and indented cheeks. Her eyes were a misty green. I estimated her to be about five-foot-eight or so and she wore a thin off-white dress and sandals. Her hair was black and long. She didn't have too much upstairs in the bust department, but her nipples stuck out through the thin linen dress. When the three of us addressed her, she was polite and very well spoken in English. "I graduated from Yale University. I wished to be where the coat of arms spoke loudly to me: The Hebrew on the crest translated to *'Lux et Veritas'*, Light and Truth," she trilled with a marvelous smile. "I will be happy to meet with you after class—about four o'clock? Will you come here? Nice to speak real American English again."

"Yeah, sure," I answered. "We just wanna pump some info out of you..."

"Pump? Is that how you say it where you come from?—how quaint."

"Yeah, well, I'm a ghetto rat and those words are part of our East L.A. slang. I'm sure you have slang words here on Martinique."

"Oh, yes," she laughed. "Surely we do."

We went to the only 'café' in town and shared a small table with a pig and a few dogs. But the food was delicious. We had ample servings of a local fish called *Balaou*, served with white beans and a small serving of

159

local fruit. Ayana said it was a staple and she enjoyed being home. But Dr. Ephron Rueben was sullen and quite different than when in the states. Something was bothering him, but I didn't know what. When I inquired, he told me he was still suffering from the effects of the runs he'd had when we first arrived the day before. I wondered.....

About 4:00 p.m. we walked back out to the local school building and found Letichia Moreau. She needed something to eat, she said, and so we got her some food at the same restaurant. The four of us sat around the small wooden table, talking.

"So...if I may ask, do you have a regular degree for teaching or *vhat*,vay out here in nowhere?" the doc asked.

"My master,s degree is in psychology, a branch of which shall be called *behavioral sciences* one day. I also minored in history of the Caribbean islands, especially the Lesser Antilles, Venezuela and surrounding islands. We have a very fascinating mixture of peoples."

"Is it true that I have been used to only one little side of the story?" Ayana spoke up. "The Taíno do not inter-mix much and coming to America was very difficult. A black person is considered very low there."

"Yes," Letichia continued, "it is so, Ayana. I had that experience as well. Your people are now much mixed in with everyone else. But once upon a time, wars were fought to keep them separated." Then the tall, elegant lady looked at all three of us. "So...what brings a pretty native girl, a doctor and a private detective together?"

"Ve got our vires crossed and all got on the wrong airplane!" the doc quipped. "I am kidding you, pretty lady," Then he pointed to Ayana and me. "Deese two vanted to rescue—some—some *stolen vomen* from the United States dat ve tink ended up here, *maybe*. I needed a vacation from being a doctor for prostitutes, so I volunteered—and here I am! You haven't hoid of any kidnapped young blonde vomen, have you?"

Her face grew serious. "No, but I do know white slavery does exist on this island. You see, it is part of a ring that sells young white women to rich black Martinique men—and perhaps for other reasons..."

"For other reasons?" I asked, my ears pricking up.

"Yes, there is still sacrificial black magic and ritual existing on the island, particularly in this area—and Mt. Pelée is the destination for at least one tribe I know of." The three of us looked at each other.

"Is it my ancestors?" Ayana bragged a little. "I am Taíno, you know."

The older woman smiled at Ayana. "I think the whole world is mixed in blood, Ayana. You are light-skinned negroid—more than likely descended from the *Arawak* people who first inhabited the *Orinoco Delta* and eventually spread to these islands in the Lesser Antilles as the *Caribs or Island Arawaks*. They were lovely, intelligent people. They even are attributed to having coined words that were incorporated into the Spanish and English language like *canoe, hammock, hurricane*— and were a very organized people in a land of plenty. After Christopher Columbus came to the Bahamas in 1492...actually not landing here until his fourth trip several years later, the Spaniards ignored our island, having more interests in other areas. Despite Columbus writing glowing descriptions to the crown, of the *natives* and the beauty of their way of life, a return of the Spanish colonists to the Hispaniola and other larger islands caused the demise of the peoples there through slavery, famine and disease. Many, many years later our island became part of the French crown and then French colonists arrived here along with Africans to work the sugar fields. This caused our island to be quite prosperous. However, the Caribs resisted the French expansion, but they were quickly dispatched because of the superior weapons of the French. This is why there is such a strong *creole* influence now in our culture. And there are now those who today are resentful and using the voodoo rituals of *Maybouya* have turned evil and hate the white skinned peoples. That is another reason the rituals have continued with such fervor. And if they have stolen white women for a symbolic victim, then all the more you may understand their choices."

"Hmmm...perhaps a kind of revenge, eh?" I said, checking out those wonderful greenish eyes that belonged to this charming and intelligent woman.

"You might say that, Mr. Denning—"

"—Cable, please call me Cable, Miss Moreau."

"Then you three may call me Letichia...more than I can say for my very obedient and fearful students," she chuckled.

"Fearful?" I asked.

"Oh, you know how some superstitions endure. Many of my students come from *Saint Pierre* and believe there is a huge snake woman called *Mambo* who transforms at the time of the dark moon—that is when the ritual is performed."

"Which brings us to the matter at hand, Letichia. You see, twelve young women were drugged and stolen off our Los Angeles streets by members of the Black Mafia. We believe there was a Martinique tribe member who used a blowpipe to subdue—or kill—anyone who was designated as next in line for a nice little dart to the neck."

"Ve need to speak to people—ya know, people who know something about vhat's going on around here—den ve can go in and rescue the pretty young tings from a horrible fate!"

"There is one doctor here in this community—Dr. Rodriguez, speaks a pretty good Pigeon English with a French accent," Letichia suggested. "Perhaps you may visit with him?"

"Ya! Doc to doc—not always fruitful, but ve can give it a go!"

Then she looked at Ayana. "And you, young woman...have you relatives here?"

"Yes, I have an uncle who lives at the bottom of Mt. Pelée."

The doctor excused himself and while it was still light, decided he was going to pay a visit to Dr. Rodriguez and find out what he could. In the meantime, Letichia suggested a walk on the wonderful beach, so the remaining three of us strolled along a lovely sandy cove with a calm sea washing our bare feet with lukewarm salt water. Ayana said she wanted to walk alone to be with her thoughts, leaving Letichia and me to wander the long stretches of light-colored sand.

There was a nice harmony between the two of us and as I walked and talked with this stately woman, I began to relax inside. "So...you're—you're not married—children?" I asked.

"No...in my most formative female years I attended school. I had an American boyfriend or two, but that was it. Now I'm too old for children. Forty is too old to risk it, do you not think?"

"Hell, I'm forty-five and feel like eighty some days," I complained.

"Perhaps that is because you live such a pressured life, Cable. Here on the island, when the ocean breeze enters your breath, it also enters your spirit."

"What a wonderful thing to say." I was thinking about a discovery I made long ago in Cozumel, Mexico, a little island off the mainland and a certain special young native woman named *Travillia.* I had privately thought for years that before I die I would like to walk the shores of Cozumel with that pretty young thing for companionship. Yep, after it was all said and done, I could hang up the fedora, the trench coat and the gun and eat mango and cocoanut in a hut with no windows and sleep next to a lovely young woman. What's better than that? "Ya know, I've thought that one day...Maybe I'll give all this up and just become a beachcomber," I said.

"I, too, have thought of that. But my life here is gentle compared to yours, Cable. And I would not know how to handle a man anymore. If someone like you became my companion, that is. Forgive me for being presumptuous. I was thinking from my female self. I find you excitingly attractive and it has been a long time for me."

"Ha! Me? Excitingly attractive? Are you sure? Well, let me tell ya, lady, I smoke and drink and chase women, I'm a sex addict, I live on the line between life and death and make weekly visits to the county morgue. I see corruption, religion and politics as the canker sore of human existence, the cancer that eats everyone from the inside out that takes precedence over time, tide, taxes and ice cream! I've seen things that make this tropical paradise here seem like another planet!"

She studied me. "Indeed...this is so? So you have the disease of the desperate societies then. Such compulsions will certainly make you die at an early age, Cable."

"Maybe...but what's the difference? It's what you're living now, I think. I like what I do for the most part, except that some of it is getting to me now and that's why I told you what I just did."

We finally walked back up to the only cafe to search for the doc but he was nowhere to be seen and we figured he got tied up with Dr. Rodriguez. Ayana swept in and out, wandering alone along the water's edge, like she must've done as a child. As dusk settled in we gathered some dry wood and built a small campfire down on the warm sands of *Bellefontaine* beach. "What shall you do when you find these young women?" Letichia asked.

"Salvage as many as we can, contact the authorities and get the girls back to the states."

"You may have trouble extricating them from the Maybouya cult, if indeed that is where they are. There are two things against you to begin with. One, these people believe in *malioyas* which are malevolent spirits that roam among humans and are evil influences. Two, everyone takes hallucinogens before the ceremony upon the hillsides of Mt. Pelée. Thus they are literally 'out of their minds' and become susceptible to those influences, being capable of much violence and distorted thinking when the ceremony begins."

The fire was flickering across her beautiful face as she sat on the sand across from me. "I suppose that's why one day I'll just walk away from it all, Letichia—like now...just walk away...fade into the sky and woodwork of the world, and before I become one with the earth again, I'd like to live a simple life. Would you like to know my secret dream?"

"Yes, Cable, I would..."

"Well, I'd love to just sit around on an old box somewhere and play a beat up old wooden guitar and sing the Great American Song book to my heart's content. Add to that maybe one beautiful woman like you who I could shower with love and lovemaking—at least until we can't anymore."

We both laughed there in the oncoming darkness. "That seems very little to ask of life, Cable," she sighed in a quiet, breathy voice that seemed musical to me. "Or...perhaps not. So few are contented. When you tell me that, I wish we had met sooner. I might have made you a good mate and companion. I can see your comprehension is excellent and you have seen much in your life. It does not hurt to be tall and handsome—and I'm sure, virile."

"Thanks, lady, I appreciate that. Oh, yeah, 'seen much'...that's rather an understatement, but you're right. I've seen more than I want to say. How 'bout you, Letichia Moreau? What is your heart's desire?"

She smiled and looked across at me, the firelight lighting up those greenish orbs of hers. "Perhaps it is changing by the moment," she tittered. "You are making me wish I had a male companion like you, Cable. Intellectual companionship I can take to my bed at night. Would you not say that is a wonderful combination?"

"Yeah, for some, I guess so."

Just then Ayana approached us with a negro dressed in khaki. His voice was deep and resonant. I stood up. "Sir, may I see your identification and passport, please?" His English wasn't too bad.

"I don't have a passport because we flew here during wartime on a private airplane." I handed him my wallet. He checked it out.

"You are policeman in United States of America?" he asked.

"Kind of...I'm a private investigator. In fact, I'm here on a case."

He stepped closer to me to check out my eyes. I would learn later that the natives could tell a lot about people through their eyes. "Who else comes with you beside pretty young woman?"

"There's only Dr. Ephron Rueben, but he went to visit another doc, a man named Dr. Rodriguez?"

"I'm afraid that is not possible, Mr. Denning, sir."

"No? Why not?"

"Because Dr. Rodriguez is dead, sir, hours ago. And there is no Dr. Rueben. He kidnap or you think he murder Dr. Rodriguez?"

I was stumped. I looked over to an alarmed Letichia Moreau. "Mr. Moddo, the doctor was with us until two or three hours ago. He said he was going to visit Dr. Rodriguez to ascertain information about the rituals up on Mt. Pelée," she said.

The tall policeman looked intently at Letichia. "You are school teacher, yes? Do you not teach my Isabella?"

"Yes, I do."

"Then do you swear this man was with you for last few hours?"

"Yes I will." She came over and took my hand. "He is my fiancé." I did a double take.

"Ah..." He said, knowing the score. "How quick islander get to meet United States stranger—and be engaged."

"Yes, it happened rather suddenly, Mr. Moddo," Letichia said. In the meanwhile Ayana was completely puzzled.

"Then, please come with me." The three of us followed Mr. Moddo to town and into an alley. We found a door that read *'Alfredo Rodriguez, Docteur en Médecine'*. We entered and almost immediately we saw the body of the deceased on the floor by his office desk. Moddo bent down and peeled away the dead doctor's shirt collar. "You see this? It is a poison dipped dart...here is—uh...puff on neck."

Now it figured. I hit my head with my palm for not seeing it before. "Shit!" I exclaimed. "I was a patsy. Dr. Rueben was their set-up man. He treated all the young white women that came into Greystone Mansion in Beverly Hills! He selected them out, told the Black Mafia the choice babes, got paid per head for his work and then saw to it that they somehow ended up at *Zoot Mimby's* downtown. And he's here to make sure the job gets done. That means he not only knows we're comin' but who we are and what we're gonna try to do!" I glanced at the tall policeman. "How many local men do you have, Moddo?"

"Nobody go near Mt. Pelée—only foolish tourist go before war! Native not go—ever! That is evil place, now...belong to *Maybouya*! We have no men who will go."

"Not even you?"

"Not even I, sir. I am sorry. White girls will have to die."

"Well, not if I can help it," I said, looking at Ayana and Letichia.

"I looked at a calendar, Cable," Ayana pointed out to us. "The 12th is night of the dark moon. That will be the night of the first sacrifice."

"That means we have less than a week to figure out exactly what we're gonna do and how we're gonna do it."

"I can help, Cable—if you need me, that is. I shall be able to act as your other eyes and guide you in the right direction. That's the least I can do," Letichia said, giving Mr. Moddo a quizzical look.

"Thanks, Letichia—that'd be a big help."

The frustrated local policeman went away, warning us to stay away from Mt. Pelée. I could tell he believed in *Maybouya*, the sacrificial ceremonies and more than likely in the existence of *Mambo*, the female priestess who's supposed turn from snake into a human woman.

Letichia turned to Ayana and me. "Do you have a place to stay?" she inquired.

"I have telephoned my aunt Zebu in Saint Pierre and will stay with her. Cable, will you come with me? There is little room, but you are welcome."

I looked at Letichia. "How far is it to Saint Pierre?" I asked Ayana.

"Ten or twelve kilometers or so," Letichia answered. I could feel she wanted to be with me, and maybe I felt the same. "You may stay with me while you are here."

Somehow I'd formed a nice bond with this tall, slim schoolteacher. "If it's all the same to you, Ayana, I think I'll stay here with Letichia and form some attack plans. Then we'll travel to Saint Pierre—not tomorrow, but the next day—share what we've come up with, and we'll further discuss what our best options are, okay?"

Ayana looked at the both of us. I knew she knew. Call it a woman's intuition or instinct. "Sure...yes...okay, Cable...I have a girlfriend here I will go to see and tomorrow she will take me to Saint Pierre. Can you meet us there?"

"Yeah, sure—just tell me when and where to go..."

"Her mother lives in Saint Pierre. It's next to Bordenne's Souvenir Shop."

"Okay. If you see the doc, tell him we're here, okay? I still can't figure out what happened to him after he visited the dead doctor—"

"—yes, Dr. Rodriguez—me, too, I have wondered..." Ayana replied as she began walking away. "Tomorrow,

Cable..." She said goodnight and disappeared down the dirt road.

Letichia and I walked toward the foothills for about fifteen minutes. The maiden schoolteacher lived in a nice clean little house with four rooms. She made us some herbal tea and within about twenty minutes I was horny as hell for the woman! "What did you put into this tea?" I asked politely.

"Imagination..." She answered quietly, a slight grin on her face.

"*Imagination?* Then I wonder what you were imagining, because I'm—uh...I feel quite randy at the moment, if you know what I mean."

She gave me a great big smile and those pearly white teeth of hers shone in the candlelight of the small kitchen. Her light-black skin shone. "Yes, my mother gave this to my father when she wished to—to make him interested in her for the remainder of the evening. I am feeling the same, Cable...I hope you are not offended by my rather crass way of approaching you romantically."

"Well, let's put it this way—*it's a first!*"

"I knew when we talked at the beach I wanted you. It is very strange. I have not felt desire for any man for—for—well, for a very long time. Now you walk into my classroom and here we are."

"Yeah, life's funny that way, ain't it?"

She giggled. "We have lots of water here. Would you like to bathe with me? Unless you are too bashful," she said coyly.

"Yeah, I guess we could do that. "

We undressed and she looked like a long milky chocolate bar with tits. Her skin was near flawless and her stomach near flat. She had very inviting, slightly protruding lips and she put her hair up not to get it wet. "It's this way, Cable." She led me out of the house into the backyard. There was a large metal tub that reminded me a rancher's cow trough, only larger. "It is crude compared to what you are used to, but it's clean and comfortable."

The water was barely cool as we stepped in and sat beside one another. "Boy, I've had a couple of firsts with you already, lady!" I advanced in a strong voice. "First you drug me to excite me 'romantically', as you put it, and now I'm having a bath with a lovely woman in a cow trough! Back in the states, that's what they are, ya know."

"Oh, dear...maybe it goes with my birth sign. Yes, I'm a Taurus—you know, the bull? Does that mean I should drink the water from the trough or something?" she jested. We both laughed.

I looked up into the star-filled sky. "It's strange, isn't it—I mean, how people can get rid of everyone else just to be alone together. And in some cases, it's almost as if the fates planned it that way, eh?"

"The Fates...yes, incredibly intense ladies...I remember reading of them in college. In fact, I cannot recall their names, but what they represented: *birth, initiation...profession, passion, love, consciousness and death.* Are you familiar with them?"

"Yeah, which one are *we* on tonight?" I asked, knowing the answer.

"Oh, I think we are in *passion*—perhaps her sister, *love* may come one hour or day or year later." She had a strong, yet gentle way about her. "May I touch you, Cable? I haven't touched a man in a very long time—years..."

"Sure, Letichia—I'm touchable..."

She kissed my wet shoulder with her sweet, warm lips. It gave me the shivers. Then quietly she stole up to my ear and kissed around that. After that her long tapered fingers reached into the water for my leg and slowly massaged it up toward my somewhat more private parts. And as she did so, she reached her head around toward my mouth and we kissed. Like her, it was gentle yet strong, warm yet aloof in an indescribable way. Soon we were wrestling in the water and she spread her long legs so I could thrust my hand between them and open her up. But it wasn't necessary. She was already swollen and wet down there. I pinned her against the back of the tank and penetrated her. She gave out with a sensual shriek and we made love in the cow-watering tank.

During the night a thought kept niggling at me: *what happened to Dr. Eps Rueben?* Far as I knew, he went to visit the doctor. Now...was Dr. Rodriguez killed before or after Rueben visited him? And if he knew about the murder, why didn't he contact us and let us know? And above all, *why* was he killed?

We slept wonderfully together and the next morning we both felt refreshed and vibrant, so early in the morning we did it all over again, only this time without the water tank. After a delicious cup of coffee, a hell of a lot better than what I made back in L.A. anyway, we began to discuss our game plan. "You know, I have a very good friend who's a tea leaf reader." Then she laughed. "I promise she won't give you the same tea I gave you last night! Perhaps she may shed some light on our quest to the save the young women. Then we'll go to Saint Pierre and rejoin with Ayana. Okay?"

I laughed. "Ha! That tea's pretty powerful stuff, lady!"

"Today's Friday and I have to go to school. I'll let you off at Maisa's place on the way over. Is it not strange about the doctor you came with? What does your detective sense tell you?"

"What does it tell me? Well, for starters, something strange is going on here, Letichia. But at the moment, I haven't got any proof. I suspect what I told you yesterday—maybe Rueben is in cahoots with the Mt. Pelée group. Who do you know today who kills with a blow-dart?"

She looked out the window. The sky had turned grey and a brisk wind was kinda blowin' things around. "It may rain today..." Then she came up to me and kissed me on the cheek. "I would prefer to stay in bed with you all day. But duty calls. And we must get to my tealeaf reader friend. She cannot speak English very well, but she will understand you and somehow you will understand her. It is how she is."

Under an increasingly dark sky, we walked toward her school, then turned up a ramshackle street with ramshackle buildings, and Letichia led me to the front door of a small hut-like house. A shriveled up old man with no teeth smiled at us and said something in French to her. I guess he must've invited us in because that's what happened. Letichia turned to go, but then ran back to me as the old man disappeared behind a large curtain to announce us to the lady of the house. My lovely tall schoolteacher threw her arms around me. "I cannot believe this is happening to me, Cable!" her voice tumbled out of her. "I am so lucky—and I don't wish to leave you!" She kissed me. "Do you know how to find your way back to my house?"

"Yeah, second star to the right," I answered, smiling at her.

She held me even closer. "Yes! That's how I feel, too. You took me there last night, sir. Maybe again tonight, too?"

"I don't know, it depends on whether or not I'll have had any other takers during the day," I joked.

She looked at me intently, then gave me a big grin. "You know, when I was a little girl I dreamed about a man like you. And he was white-skinned just as you are. Funny, huh?"

"Yeah, babe, funny. I'll see you this evening and if you're not too tired, we're gonna have to discuss a few things about that bunch up on Mt. Pelée and see if we can save the girls."

"I am hoping that Maisa will help. She's quite gifted."

"You said her English wasn't all that great? I'd hate for the whole session to be in French."

"Enough for you to understand, as I said. Simple words." Then she held my face between her long, tapered fingers. "Remember the Moirai... last night? I think passion is already turning into love, Cable. I hope that—that doesn't put a pressure on you."

I nodded slowly. "Well, we are who we are and feel what we feel. I guess I kinda learned that along the way. I'm feeling a lot more—than I imagined too, kid."

"Keep safe, Mr. Denning—and watch out for the storm." She hugged me once again and ran out, leaving me in a semi-lit room that smelled of some kind of tropical flower. There was a fresh bouquet of them on a small table. They were medium-leafed, kind of light purple with lighter edges. Their perfume was subtle and intense at the same time—like Letichia. Or one could imagine it to be much like the aroma of God...interesting thought.

Soon the little old man with no teeth gestured to me to step behind the burlap curtain. I entered a small, smoky room with a little round table in the middle. There was a white dish in the center and two candles, one black, one white. On a small bed lay a very old black woman with thinning white hair and also no teeth. She mumbled something as she held an emblem suspended by a chain around her neck. "Water...there. Hot. *Eau chaude.*" she croaked. I saw a small pan over floor under a primitive fire on the dirt floor. It was boiling water. She then pointed to a shelf above her small bed. "*Il y a un thé, mister.*" I reached for a small sealed jar of large black, green and red dried tea leaves all mixed together. "*Da...*" She pointed to a golden teaspoon by the fire. The window was open, so a lot of the smoke went outdoors. But all the same, it was smoky as hell in that little room. I was wondering why in the hell didn't the lady prepare things herself until I noticed she had no legs! She saw me staring at the absence of her lower limbs but paid no attention. "Pour teaspoon in water." I did so. I would later learn it is an art form of intuition called *Tasseography*—or reading tea leaves. Now we waited while the tea boiled and the gathering storm outside grew in intensity.

"Do you speak much English?" I finally asked to break the silence.

But she did not answer. Instead her eyes were rolled back in her head and all I saw were the whites. After another ten minutes of silence or so, the old lady motioned for me to pour the tea into a large mug also on the shelf above her. I did that as well. The tea steeped for about ten more minutes and then the old woman directed me to pour off the water outside in the dirt and return with no water among the large tea-leaves. Finally I handed her the cup. Her eyes lit up as she studied the cup. She took an index finger and gently rubbed the lip of the mug. Then she slowly descended her finger until she came to the first tealeaf.

"You come at...at a time of *grand mal*—the time of *malioyas*," she said. "You come to—to ruin...*de detruire*..." Then she moved her finger ever so slow downward, in a spiral. "Oh! *Pas de lune...jeudi*...soon—"

"—look, ma'am, while I appreciate what you're doing, if I can't understand it, then it's no good. Can you say it in English, please?"

She broke a slight smile. "I try...Mr. Lover Mon..." She said that seeing something else in the mug. "You, Letichia—ay!" Then her face grew taut and her eyes widened. "You...you come...to destroy *rituel* ...*en Pe-*

lée—go home, mon, go home!" Her voice was now low and guttural sounding. I thought the so-called "tea leaf session" a failure.

I'd taken off my trench coat and fedora and began to put them back on. "So, thanks anyway. Now I wish I drank that tea!" I complained.

"Oh!" she uttered with a hiss. "Saint Pierre—find *Bordenne*—he help...now go!"

I gave her five bucks and left the house, holding onto my hat as I started back toward Letichia's house. The winds had become furious. I got back into the little house just in time, for a deluge of water fell from the sky. It was so torrential that I couldn't see past the open front window! It rained and rained as the wind grew in intensity. I wondered how the coffee, sugar and cotton plantations survived this kind of abuse from nature. It was almost as if the gods were striking against me being here on this lovely gem of an island that had suddenly summoned something black and ugly from the sky.

About 1:30 p.m. the door opened and in walked a soaking wet Letichia. "Cable! Thank God you are well! I was so worried about you!"

"Yeah, me, too—about you, I mean. Here, let's get you out of those sopping wet clothes." We went into a little porch area and I helped her strip. Her beautiful lithe body revealed itself to me there in that dark afternoon. "Do you have this weather often? The storm bring you home early?"

"Yes, it is best to do this for the children." I followed her into the house as she began re-dressing in dry clothes. "No, it is an unseasonable hurricane, I think. I have a basement, but it may flood. I think we should stay in the house for now. We must think of what to do also—if the roads are washed away, we will not be able to get to Saint Pierre. Have you heard from the doctor?"

"No—and no, not a peep. I guess we can chance it to Saint Pierre and meet up with Ayana—but how do we get there?"

"If the storm does not pass soon, we must go before dark. After that, though it is only twelve kilometers to Saint Pierre, it will be so dark we shall not see anything. I have a cousin who has an old vegetable delivery truck. If we paid him a few American dollars, I'm sure he would take us there."

I looked outside. The water was now being driven through the windows of the little house we stood in even though the temperature was mild. "I think we'd better go *now*, lady. Where's he live?"

"At the edge of the village, toward Saint Pierre," she answered, combing her hair out with a very large wooden comb.

We half-walked, half-ran as the wind and rain pushed us around. By the time we reached her cousin's little fruit and vegetable shop, we were both soaked to the bone. His name was Emil and he agreed to take us to Saint Pierre once I slipped him a twenty dollar bill. I knew the storm was ferocious because the canvas overhang was ripped to shreds over Emil's little store. The man had a very old Chevrolet panel truck. We got in and took off in blinding rain.

The main dirt road was wet and muddy as we slid around the coastline like a Walt Disney cartoon of *Night On Bald Mountain*. The only thing I didn't see was the large demon looming out in front of us. But maybe that was coming. I had a feel that it was. But we made good time and it was light enough for us to get into town and be dropped off in front of Bordenne's *Souvenirs* store. *Bordenne!* It was the very guy that old Maisa had spoken of! Maybe tea leaves don't lie. "The one thing your tea-reading friend told me was this guy's name. The rest was just warning me off and telling me to go home," I told Letichia.

"Oh, dear, Cable—Maisa is very accurate. Maybe we shouldn't go through with this terrible undertaking. We could get killed, you know, if we're found out!"

"I don't want you to go with me, Letichia," I insisted. "Maybe you'd better go back home—now, while you still can."

She looked at me while her cousin smiled and looked on. "I'm a woman in love, Cable—and I'll go where my man goes, if he'll have me. No matter where we go...and please don't try and change my mind!" she cautioned me with a resolute firmness. *That* was the last thing I needed to come up right now!

I took a deep breath. "Okay, but remember—I told you I wasn't crazy about sticking around on this planet—but you still have a real meaning, teaching children how to get on in this nutso world of ours. Are you absolutely sure you don't wanna go back with Emil here?"

"Yes...absolutely," she answered, folding her arms together.

We said goodbye to Emil and knocked on the door of the house next to the Bordenne souvenir shop. Ayana answered the door and we were let in immediately. "Cable, Letichia! We are having a hurricane!" she

180

warned us. "Daddy Gareaut says it will be a big one, too!"

"So how long will it last?" I asked.

"I don't know. No one knows. It depends how slow it moves in the sky with the winds from the ocean driving it. I grew up here. Some are pretty bad and last several days."

"We don't have several days. We've gotta find the doc, make plans with you and Letichia and get on with it," I said. "You haven't see Dr. Rueben by any chance?"

"No. I am worried, Cable," Ayana said. "The same men who killed Dr. Rodriguez may have kidnapped Dr. Rueben—or worse!"

"Yeah, I've thought of that. We gotta have a pow-wow—here and now!" I exclaimed.

Both women looked at each other. "*Pow-wow*? What does this mean, Cable?" Letichia inquired innocently.

"It's an old American Indian word for having a war council or the like. It's kinda what we need to do just about now."

"Oh," Letichia answered, more or less understanding.

We met Ayana's girlfriend Bali and her mother Bali Kort. They allowed us to sit at their large wooden dinner table with two candles and we began our "pow-wow" in earnest. Time was ticking away and the storm was growing in intensity outside the door. We had to pull together a game plan. Case in point: find Dr. Rueben, see if we could find out where the kidnapped young women were being held, find a way to steal them back and get us all the hell out of Dodge safe and sound!

"Are you implying you cannot continue without Dr. Rueben?" Letichia asked.

"No...if it comes to it, we proceed regardless. But we need a game plan," I responded, looking over at the drenched but still lovely woman.

"Bali Kort, Bali's mother, said we should connect with Mr. Bordenne next door. He knows all the storage sheds, garages and possible places to hide the women, she said," Ayana piped in. "She might know of a few. But no one will go out into that hurricane, Cable."

"Yeah, let's hope it blows over quick. Maybe Mrs. Kort can introduce me to Mr. Bordenne. While I'm filling him in on the situation, maybe you three women can start a check list of places that might be good candidates, eh?"

"Yes," Letichia agreed.

Bali Kort Leone was short and heavy-set and wore a straw hat in the house. Her somewhat slimmer daughter, Bali, wore a light-pink dress with no underwear and no shoes. The mother and I made a dash for next door and she introduced me to Mr. Bordenne and left to rejoin the other women. Bordenne was a very dark-skin negro, medium built with warm brown eyes and a good smile, even though two or three teeth were missing in the front. "Ah! Da hurricane grows by the minute, mon. I had to help the ladies at the market place clear their tables a little while ago," he told me with one of those Caribbean accents that's part Creole, part French and part some kind of pigeon English.

"Yeah, I can imagine. This is my first hurricane—so you might have to fill me in on some details."

182

"To be sure, mon, but what can I do for you?"

I stood in front of the man explaining what I could about the situation. He was nodding his head as he listened intently. Finally I finished. "So...if you had kidnapped twelve sacrificial female lambs, and you were gonna hide them, keeping in mind it'd have to be something more or less permanent since they use only one sacrifice a month, where would you stow 'em?"

"This terrible, mon! I have heard of such things, but have not seen them. No one goes up the mountain anymore, not since long time now."

"So the voodoo folk have it all to themselves?" I inquired.

"I do not know. I am superstitious man—but I will try help you."

"Thanks for that, Mr. Bordenne."

"You call me *Poola*. That means 'fighter' in American English."

"Okay, Poola, you can call me Cable. Now...do you have any idea where those women might be?"

"There is old closed up boarder's house beyond the town, toward the cliffs. It has leaky roof, mon, but many rooms. It is called *Zambia House*, because after big 'boom' of Mt. Pelée, people moved around. A group from Zambia lived der for years. It was built by crazy Venezuela man in 1906, two years after explosion."

"Why is it you think that's where the young women might be?"

"Because Gaia Lumbuno told me many supplies have been brought to Zambia House of late. Yet no one is supposed to live there."

"Then that's it, Poola! When can we go?"

183

He looked out the window. "Not this night, mon!" he said, looking up to the sky with a shudder. "Often when moon get dark, big storm come in from sea with winds *Obeah* command."

"*Obeah*?"

"An ancient practice. Those practicing Obeah take possession of the shadow and is sorcerer—and makes sacrifice."

"You guys sure have a lot of gods hanging around on this island."

He ignored my statement. "Tomorrow, perhaps, when the water has stopped falling so hard from sky, we will go to Zambia House."

"Yeah, sure...we'll keep an eye on the weather."

I went back next door and found Ayana and Letichia playing an odd game with the other two women. They were playing by candlelight. The light wooden board had 24 pit holes, the twelve on the side contained smooth root beer colored pebbles. "We play *Wari* on *Mancala* board, Mr. Denning," Bali said. "Will you watch?"

The wind howled around the not-too-substantial hut house. "Okay if I smoke?" I asked, looking over at the wonderfully composed Letichia. She sat straight and upright, her still damp clothing showing her nipples through the thin dress.

"Mamma and I smoke Cubano cigars—yes, please do. We will be honored," Bali responded.

I lit up and approached the seated women. Ayana looked up at me. "So...? Did Mr. Bordenne help?"

"Yes, I think he did. He told me an old boarding place called *Zambia House* out by the cliffs...north of here, is suspect number one. No one is supposed to live there, but he heard that a lot of food and supplies have been brought there lately."

Bali Kort had a deep voice. "No go there—much bad magic! Ghost of dead walk the sand there by sea. They do not sleep, for they are cursed!" she admonished.

"Well, cursed or not, with all due respect, we gotta check the damn place out. Time is running short here, ladies..."

Letichia and I slept that night on the floor of the Kort hut. It was as uncomfortable as hell and we simply touched each other however we could during the long, windy and rainy night. I was thinking what an odd thing that is, reaching for someone just to know they're there. Then I thought that's what a baby does. It wants to know the mother is nearby for security. Maybe as adults we never lose that need.

Where the Dead Walk

Fortunately for us, by noon the storm had all but passed and cleanup had already commenced in the village of Saint Pierre. I went next door and asked Poola Bordenne when he could take us out to Zambia House. He told us it would be early in the early evening, although he preferred not to go out there once it was dark. When I asked him why, at first he was somewhat vague. "Things...there be *things* out there, mon, so Poola has heard. You be ready to go before sun sets on ocean?"

"Sure, whatever you say, Poola. See ya then."

It was just about dusk when Letichia, Ayana and I climbed into Poola Bordenne's produce truck. Ayana rode in the back and Letichia and I up front with Bordenne. The one road out to *Zambia House* was thick with mud and strewn with all kinds of debris blown by the winds of the ferocious storm from the day before. Large waves came crashing into the cliffs below us from a roiling sea. "Ah, ocean angry at wind," Poola said.

Soon in our headlights, loomed the lone image of a large mansion-like edifice on the cliffs overlooking the restless sea. We parked around the side, and Bordenne grabbed a flashlight and nothing else. I checked out my .38, helped the women from the truck and headed toward the front of the place. The front door was ajar and we stepped into a dark, spooky room the size of a dance hall. Immediately our eyes caught two candles glowing at the far end against the wall. What looked like an altar had a naked female body on it. We cautiously approached. There on a high table with a long black scarf laid across her belly was a lovely young white woman with blonde hair and wonderful skin. Except for that, she was totally nude. Poola went up to the body and touched her hand gently. "Oh, she is dead, mon."

"Oh, Cable," Letichia said with a tear in her voice. "Who is she? And why would they be killing the women already?"

"It is also a sacrifice, perhaps," Ayana said. "My mother told me when I was little girl. The voodoo people sacrifice a white virgin to prepare, and to thank Maybouya for helping them in the past."

"Wait a minute," I said, taking my hat off and scratching my head. "That doesn't make sense. Didn't we learn that they needed twelve young things to complete their once-a-month cycle? Plus, I doubt if we're alone in this joint. Obviously the roof doesn't leak and it's been fixed up. Someone's here. Anyway, if so, *why* did they kill this girl? Unless there are more, that leaves only eleven." No one cared to answer that question. "And who *is* she? How would any of us like to be someone lying there without one person knowing your name?!" I looked at the others. "That's one of the things that they never tell you about in this world—you can die tomorrow—no, today, *right now*—and nobody will remember you tomorrow. You can be a saint and live a life of serving others or a lady of the night like her, but you get forgotten just the same." I looked over at the lovely young blonde who seemed asleep on the table. Her bare feet were sticking out over the edge, white and lifeless. I lit up a cigarette. "Yeah, that's something that's always griped me. Despite man's decency, despite his good intentions, despite the odds he overcomes—like that poor girl there—we're all forgotten." I lowered my voice and walked over to her body and looked down. "Maybe someone loved her—maybe several some ones. She lived and breathed and laughed and cried and wore pretty clothes and became a whore because she *was* pretty. Is that a price the profession pays? But is it worth dying forgotten?" Then I turned to face all of them. I'd gone crazy. "But evil? Oh, yeah, evil is remembered—the devil is a hero, folks, or didn't you know that? He's remembered because he's still around...he *can't die* so he's always there, lurking in our presence

187

and memory every minute of every goddamned breathing day! There's no promissory note written to guarantee a fun life—some are okay, some get a raw deal. This lady got one of those."

"What is essential—and what is *not* essential?" Out of the darkness a familiar voice arose. "Very good, Mr. Denning. But you had one thing wrong, sir, if I may say so. Louisa—you see, she does have a name—will come back to life, sir, perhaps not life as you know it or she knew it before. She will be of service to the power of the *Santeria* and especially to *Maybouya*."

It was Demaine. "Somehow I expected to find you here, Demaine," I said. "Where are your bodyguards? You're gonna need 'em around me, you worthless piece of sexual reprobate crap!" Demaine bristled but kept his cool demeanor. "And what did ya do with the doc—did you kill him, too?"

"Sometimes I vish it vere true, Cable, but not so—such a ting I knew I vas going to be afraid to tell you—but vhat choice do I have?" It was the voice and body of Dr. Ephron Rueben who now stepped out of the darkness!

"You, too, doc? I was just beginning to like you!"

"Same here, boychik. But business is business—and simply said, that's all this is...business! I'm afraid I vill have to see all of you lovely people—well, *done avay vit*. Ve can't have traces, you know."

"Why, Ephron? No doubt you killed Dr. Rodriguez? Why?"

"Vhat can I say—it vas difficult for me, but he vas getting too nosy!"

"That figures. And these lovely young women...why in the hell would you do something so vile in an already villainous world?"

"*Money*....vhat else? Retirement on Martinique, I hear, is quite delightful—and inexpensive. Too bad you von't be able to join me." He looked at Letichia. "Now dere is something to crow about, Cable! A gem of the islands—such a price she vould summon if she vere just a little younger!" He approached my frozen lady. "Vhat, dear, did you intend to benefit from knowing dis dead man here? Oh...you mean you didn't know, he's been dead for years, but he still exists, breathes, eat, sleeps and makes love? But for all reasonable intents and purposes—dis man is dead! He's such a case of too much, dear miss, simply *too much*. And for all dat effort? Now he shall die for it. You see how easy it is to die for nothing? Oy! Such a pity!"

"Perhaps dead to you, doctor," Letichia returned. "But not to me. And it's men like Cable who cared enough to risk his life to rescue these young women—*without money*, I might add!—and that gives me hope for the world" she scowled at him.

Anthone Demaine now came over and held Letichia's chin with his fingers for a minute. "You *are* comely." Then he stroked her breasts and ran his hand up between her legs. "Nice. We almost decided to make you and Ayana voodoo walkers—zombies—but we have subsequently decided simply to kill you. You see, the caldera we use within the bowels of Mt. Pelée is scalding hot—and the skin will melt from off your bones before you know it. That's the merciful part. You will suffer little. Personally, I like suffering. So I will endeavor to think something up to uh...how shall I say...to 'frustrate' the scenario before we do away with you pleasant and stupid people."

I went for my gun but Demaine did not react. "Okay, you two, hands up and no funny business!" I demanded of them.

But neither of them moved an inch. "Go ahead, Denning, shoot!" Demaine bragged. "You can do me no harm with your bullets. I am impervious to your stupid primitive weapons."

"Uh...vell, I should tell you, Cable, out of respect for de relationship ve almost had—Mr. Demaine is what is known as a *Maybouyan Santero*, a high priest who has been exempted from ordinary death." Then he glanced at the pretty young corpse on the table. "You zee, dis young lady has been chosen to be Mr. Demaine's *I'naru' Apito*, his—his, how shall ve say it—his *forever bride!* She vill be fitted with de a sacred necklace, much like the *Guani'n* worn by chiefs, that will help her during the *Operi'to*, when her presently dead spirit vill ascend to life after life. Such a ting! I vould never have believed it myself had I not witnessed it first hand. Zo...you may shoot Mr. Demaine, or you may put your pistol away, Cable...either vay it vill not save you."

I put my gun away. I needed to stall for time—somehow. "Okay, I believe you. Now what?"

"What is next, happens tomorrow evening, the *Night of the Dark Moon*," Demaine responded in a soft voice. "You see, when there is no visible moon, the dark forces may more easily erupt from the depths of the earth. Before the first maiden is sacrificed, I shall be joined with my pretty blonde lady here in matrimony. The first of

190

the eleven maidens shall be sacrificed thereafter, at midnight. Seems appropriate, doesn't it—something old gets something new? There is a reason only eleven young things remain, for in 11 is found the power to achieve synthesis, from one world to the other, Mr. Denning. Maybouya has taught us the bridge between life and death, you see, sir. In the meantime, you and your three companions shall be our 'guests' and kept safely out of the way—until it is time...for your own 'giving to the cause', just prior to the marriage ritual tomorrow night."

"Why don't ya just do us in right here and now?"

Demaine smiled an evil smile. "*Why*, sir? Because I wish you particularly to witness what it is that moves beyond your mortal awareness into the realm of the supernatural. Then you will see *real* power, Mr. Denning, I assure you."

I decided to control the urge to tell him what I'd seen in my lifetime. "Okay, since we're gonna die anyway, I suppose we should see the show first, eh?"

"Dat's the spirit, my boychik!" Rueben exclaimed. "Life is brief and miserable anyhow—so vhat's de difference—you know, in de long run?"

"Yeah, I guess you're right," I answered pretentiously.

"Cable! How can you be so indifferent?" Ayana moaned. "I'm too young to die—especially this way!"

I knew she wouldn't get it, but I winked at her. I just had this feeling it wasn't our time and when I get that feeling, something always comes up to prevent the intentions of the bad guys from manifesting. But as we were led away I leaned toward Ayana's ear and whispered, "Hang in there, kid, it ain't over until it's over..."

Dark of the Moon

We descended some old rickety wooden stairs and arrived at a large solid door. There was an ape of a black guy standing guard with a huge grin on his face. "Samba Grand...tie their hands," Anthone Demaine instructed the man. He did so. Then the big man opened the door with a large skeleton key and suddenly we were in a room full of young half-dressed pretty young women. "This...will be your company for a few hours, ladies. They will be...uh...leaving tomorrow afternoon." Then Samba Grande secured us to a long steel pipe going along the far wall. "You will be taken out every three hours to—to use the restroom outside. In the morning you will also be given a potion that will make you sleepy. It will be administered a little at a time or else it shall stop your hearts." Demaine gave us a sickly smile and left. Samba Grande locked the door from the other side. There was no electricity and several candles lit the large basement room. The damn place smelled like something between a soothsayer's den and a bordello.

We met the ladies and explained to them we had come to rescue them, but got captured instead. I felt sorry for Mr. Vegetable Man, Poola Bordenne, for he really had no role in this strange turn of events. But all four of us were here and that was that. The girls were sorry to hear we had failed on our mission. They explained that Demaine had picked out a gal named Louisa Martelli for his Santeria bride. They had no knowledge that the young woman had been drugged to death and soon, like a vampire, would rise from the dead and yet still be dead, sort of. I had to admit it was complicated and I never quite understood how it worked biologically.

"So who goes first tomorrow night?" I asked, looking into each of the eleven pretty faces.

"We don't know about tomorrow night," responded a tallish blonde with thick lips and dark blue eyes. "Is that when Louisa gets to be the bride—are we the maids-of-honor, or something?"

I realized the young women hadn't been told the truth. The bastards hadn't told them they were to be sacrificed one at a time into a fiery hell under the cone of Mt. Pelée! "I don't know," I fibbed.

"What will happen to you?" the blonde asked.

"Oh, us? We're gonna be treated to a nice picnic down a caldera on top of Mt. Pelée—up there on the mountain above us. Ain't that sweet?"

Letichia was on my left and Ayana on my right, with Bordenne next to her. "Cable...oh, darling...what shall we do?" Letichia whimpered. "Just when my life had turned into a beautiful dream with you—"

"—let's not talk about it right now, Letichia, okay? I gotta figure a way outta this mess." I turned to the girls. "What have you discovered since you've been here? Tell anything that might be a clue to help us figure a way to escape from this hellhole."

For two weeks prior to our arrival, the girls said, they'd been kept under lock and key except for the bathroom and a shower every other day out in back, one at a time. They were fed healthful, local foods and allowed exercise together daily down where we were.

In a couple of hours, the girls flopped on their thin floor mattresses. The four of us were exhausted as well and I found myself drifting in and out of a nightmarish sleep until Letichia's head would bob over onto my shoulder and wake me up. But morning came too soon and by noon we were already traveling with two other vehicles up a rutted, impossible road half way up Mt. Pelée. Bordenne's vehicle was bringing up the rear with Letichia, Ayana, Bordenne and myself and ritual partakers in the "produce" back end. I noticed his truck was low on gas.

Then we were all climbing on foot up a mountain to the sky. Even though Pelée is only about 4500' ft. from sea level, it was nevertheless a hellish climb. A whole crew was already inside the volcano, I was told. Too damn many years of smoking had cut my breath capacity at least in half. As I struggled along to reach the top, I felt foolish as both Ayana and Letichia had to help me the last thousand feet as loose stones made us slip and slide as we climbed.

At the very top of the volcano there were two caldera holes going down into its core. The larger one had a rope ladder attached to it. They unbound our hands and we all climbed down about fifty feet onto a ledge. Then Samba Grand led us to a large lava tube that wound down further into the depths of the beast. Ten minutes later it began to get hot and all of us were sweating. Then suddenly at the end of the lava tube, we were faced with a most frightening yet extraordinary sight. It was a deep, smoking, molten rock hole, descending about a hundred feet or so, its core glowing orange-yellow in the darkened cavern. Maybe the natives were used to heat, but it was so oppressive I wanted to take all my clothes off and run up the hill into the fresh air! And speaking of clothes off...soon the bride-to-be appeared. It was an eerie experience watching a girl you knew was dead yesterday walk toward the ritual altar the next day. But it was a hideous charade, I felt. She wasn't really alive, just an animated *she creature* somehow resurrected by Demaine. She had no clothes on and her lovely body was all but perfect. I'm certain that's why Demaine chose her for his own. He was both a snake and a wolf in sheep's clothing because I knew full well that after he'd partaken of the young maiden to his heart's content, he'd have her killed and start all over again. He was sexually obsessed. He was a type of man I recognized. I might be a sex addict, but not obsessed—or at least not in that gruesome way.

Somewhere from the deep recesses of the cave, eerie sounds of a slow drum started up. Then appeared the only man-like creature I feared among the whole group of the *Santerias*. He wasn't really a human, I sensed, but may have been at one time. He was also the alleged dart blower, Skeleton Man. Later I would learn his name was *Mr. Mortis*—the famous and mysterious incognito *'Mr. M'*. I soon realized he was the officiating priest of the ceremony. As he took his place at a stone altar, he was a formidable sight towering above everyone. It was frightening to see the whites of his huge eyes as he turned to face us with the orange glow from the fiery pit below at his back. It was like watching King Kong peek into your soul. Those film directors couldn't have created a more effective scene! He began to chant in time with the drum. *"Ma-a-bouya, May-a-bouya, May-a-bouya,"* he chanted and the rest of the pack picked it up and soon the whole cavern was filled with the reciting voices and that damn persistent drum! He raised his long arms slowly up above his head until finally he clapped his hands together and everything stopped.

Then the bride, Louisa Martelli and her bridegroom, Anthone Demaine, were escorted to stand in front of Mr. Skeleton Man. His voice was dark and deep. He would've made a great singer. I should tell him that. I couldn't understand much of the ritual because it was a cross between French and something ancient. Just then I heard a whisper in my ear. "Do not be alarmed, Denning, it is I, *Erond*. Do not speak. Stay still until I give you instructions." I hope nobody saw it, but my face must've suddenly lit up ten shades...all odds changed with the presence of Erond. How in the hell did he find me? Hell, what am I saying?...the same way he found me on that goddamned tower when the atomic bomb was gonna explode.

About half way through the wedding, I heard Erond's voice whisper again. "Now cause agitation, interrupt the ceremony, Cable—now!"

I didn't know what the hell to do, so I yelled out. "Who wants to jump into the pit first?!" Every eye in the cavern was upon me. Before anyone could gain their senses, I ran over and grabbed the hand of the not-quite-wedded bride and dragged her over to the edge of the pit. "Ha! Now, what are ya gonna do, huh? You May-bouya nuts really *are* nuts!" Samba Grand started toward me. "One false move and the girl goes, you overgrown coconut!" Then Erond told me to try to get both Demaine and Mr. M close to the edge of the steaming caldera. I thought fast. "Okay, Mr. M and Mr. Demaine— I've got a deal for you. Let the girls, my three companions and me go and I won't throw her in."

I was beginning to think that the towering Mr. M was not able to speak—or at least not in my language. Then Demaine approached me. "You're being thoughtless—and stupid, if I may say so, Mr. Denning—"

I had to appear to have lost my reason. I was making it up as I went, so of all the nights to do it, this was it. "—no, Demaine, I'm *not* being thoughtless *or* stupid—I grow weary of all this bullshit and I want to kill someone. How's that sound?" The bride-yet-to-be had a wonderful golden neckpiece with a skull on it that Mr. M had placed around her neck during an earlier part of the ritual. I ripped it off her neck. The poor girl was either so dead or so doped up she didn't even notice! But I *did* notice Mr. M grabbed his throat as if my holding the neckpiece was strangling him. I squeezed the gold medallion harder. He winced and wailed from pain. Now I knew I was on to something. "Can't take the pressure, eh, Mr. M? Well, mister...the pressure has only just begun—unless, of course you wish to make a little deal with me so we can strike a bargain here. You let us all go and guarantee us safe passage back to the states, or both the medallion and the girl go into the fiery furnace below."

Finally, the eyes of this tall skeleton of a man, began to widen and he rose up bigger than life itself and those terrible eyes fixed on me. Then he uttered in that low booming voice—"*Vous...êtes...mort!*" his huge voice rocked the cavern. I knew enough to figure what he said was that I was dead!

"Bravo! Know any more good tricks, buddy boy?" I said, trying to provoke him. "We're all dead anyhow. *When* really doesn't matter now, does it? But it looks to me like it's *you who deserves to die!*" I squeezed the medallion really hard. The big man yelled out in pain. Now I knew I had him. "You want more of this? Huh?" I heard Erond urge me again: *"Get them both to the edge..."* "Okay...if you and Demaine will step over here to collect his blushing bride—and this precious voodoo-enchanted neckpiece—*and* guarantee us safe passage back to the United States of America—then it's a deal."

Demaine looked at Mr. M and they both moved cautiously toward me. I backed up closer to the edge of the smoldering precipice. I was continuing to squeeze the pendant at will and Mr. M continued to respond with extreme pain. "Mr. Denning...please, sir, you do not understand the gravity of this situation. If Maybouya becomes irritated, he will send—"

"—Cable! Look—over there!" Letichia shouted to warn me. And sure enough, a large basket that had been sitting by the altar near me began to open and out slithered a humongous snake! But—and I say this incredulously—as it stretched out to its full ten or twelve feet, it began to change into a gorgeous babe! She wore nothing except a shiny black tiara on her equally black hair. Her body was exquisite and beguiling. I don't know why, but I was instantly attracted to her, wanted her on the spot, then and there! Those eyes of hers kept changing color in the moment, depending on what light struck them. At once the congregation was on its bellies droning in unison, over and over and over: *"Mamba! Mamba! Mamba!"* We four abductees looked at each other, not knowing exactly what to do.

"You see? Now you've done it! That's exactly what I was about to say, sir. That is *Mambo*—but you'll notice the local people call her *'Mamba'* because when she's angry, she becomes a violent, merciless female creature!" Demaine stated, his voice noticeably shaking with fear.

"I've known a few women like that," I quipped. I continued to squeeze the medallion in my hand and Mr. M. continued to squirm in pain. I wasn't sure whether or not dear 'Mamba' was sizing up the situation, but she started toward me. As she got within three feet of me, she stopped. Her now yellow eyes glowed at me in the semi-darkness. Her pupils went sideways in long black slits and her body had very small scales all over it. Now I got it. She was after the medallion in my hand. It must've held some strange power because the great Mambo-Mamba got down on her knees before me and bowed her head. She opened the palms of both hands and supplicated by tilting her head up and down slowly, holding her hands out in front of her.

"She is begging you!" Demaine said. "She must have the medallion so the ceremony may continue—or else Maybouya will punish her severely! Have a heart, sir!"

I looked at Demaine in disbelief. *"'Have a heart'?* Is that what I heard you say, Demaine? Well, I don't know if the lady communicates in English or not but tell her *'up hers'* and buzz off, as far as I'm concerned."

The bowed-down worshippers continued to chant, *"Mamba, Mamba, Mamba!"* and I was getting tired of the whole damn thing pretty damned fast! Demaine approached the kneeling she-creature with Mr. M. The tall zombie-like priest gently brought her to her feet and placed the great bird feather robe to hide her comely nakedness. He whispered something in her ear. She froze where she was, and dropping the bird-plume robe to the ground, began to withdraw back into the form of a snake. "Zsha! Zsha!" he bellowed as he lifted his arms toward the congregation. Yeah, *"Zsha! Zsha!"* yourself, I was thinking. Meanwhile, the would-be bride began to come out of her drug-induced coma and started to look around like she didn't know where she was. She looked at her odd wedding clothing. Then she began sobbing. Maybe she hadn't been dead after all! Both Letichia and Ayana went to her rescue and pulled her to the sidelines as the caldera below us began to grow brighter and brighter. By now Mr. M had opened the top of Mambo's circular straw house and the snake that had been a woman but moments before, slithered quietly back into the tall basket. Then the basket just vanished right before our eyes!

"Get those two men on the edge, Cable!" Erond ordered me once again. Then he said something I didn't get at first. "Now, watch this!" Suddenly the entire cavern began to shake—the volcano was beginning to stir again and the smoke and steam blew up from the fiery core below like it was being driven from Hell! People began to panic and run for the lava tube that led upward. For a few minutes pandemonium broke out and I knew whatever was gonna happen to get us out of here had to happen now.

I held my ground and dangled the medallion over the edge of the roiling precipice. I still held tight to the groggy Louisa's hand. "Come and get it, you two—or down it goes!" I shouted.

Demaine seemed frustrated as hell. "You cannot destroy the medallion—throw over the girl, but you have no idea of the significance of that piece. Whoever possesses it could rule the world!" I glanced at the face of the thing. The skull was in the middle of a square that in turn was encased in a square. The writing along the circular edges looked more like Arabic or the like than the local language.

"Yeah, and that's exactly why you're not getting it, Demaine. Assholes like you are self-serving bastards who'll sell their mother's false teeth if it profited you! No, it's going overboard, I'm afraid, mister. Unless you promise to release us and get us all back to the states safe and sound—ya got it, buddy?"

Mr. M started toward me, but Demaine held him back. "Mr. Denning, sir—I beg you to reconsider—you'd be destroying balances needed in the world. Light and darkness are both necessary. Destroy the medallion and you destroy darkness!" Suddenly Skeleton Man broke away from Demaine and started toward me full bore. I didn't think, but let go of the medallion and it fell into the fiery, molten pit a hundred feet or so below. Mr. M was stunned at what I'd done and actually reached for the falling piece, losing his balance and toppled into the damned hole himself without a sound! Demaine turned ashen white.

The walls were continuing to break apart and so I grabbed Louisa's arm and started for the lava tube that led to the surface. I shouted to Letichia, Ayana and Bordenne to run for it. Then I turned to look back at the Black Mafia voodoo man. "The show's over, Demaine. You lose!" I said as I whisked past the still stunned man, following my companions.

Then he drew a revolver. "Stop! I'm still an L.A. street fighter, Denning, like you—and two to one I can kill you and Louisa with two bullets before you get to that tunnel!" he bragged.

"Yeah? Well, maybe you can—and maybe you can't."

"You have no idea what anguish you have caused me this day! How could such a dumb street detective be so smart and careless at the same time?"

"Practice, Demaine, on guys like you." I looked around as the glowing hot fire and smoke began to fill the crumbling cavern. "I suggest we get outta here now, Demaine. I'll tell ya what, kill us here and you'll regret it." I was bluffing...stalling for time, hoping he wouldn't catch on.

"What do you mean?"

"Just what I said. I don't think Maybouya would care to have his sanctuary here filled with violence and bloodshed that he didn't approve."

"You're stalling, Denning—so now you're—" Just as he lowered his gun to fire at Louisa and me, an invisible something whacked the gun out of his hand and booted him toward and over the now-steaming precipice. Erond had saved the day again. I took the half-conscious Louisa in tow and we ran through the lava tube and I boosted her butt up the rope ladder to comparative safety.

Along with the fleeing members of the religious cult, the four of us ran, slipped and fell as fast as we could down the slippery and rock-strewn slopes of Mt. Pelée. Twenty minutes or so later we got to Bordenne's truck. Fortunately, Bordenne had the key to his delivery vehicle and we piled in and careened down that treacherous road as fast as we could. We got to *Zambia House* and collected the girls after I conked out the one remaining guard at the doorway. We crammed the eleven young women plus Louisa, Ayana, Letichia, Bordenne and I into that delivery truck and sped away, barely making it to the outskirts of Saint Pierre before we ran out of fuel. Bordenne and I went afoot and found a farmer who had a large gas tank on his land for God-knows-what. He loaned us a five gallon container. We paid the man and hastened back to pour the gasoline into Bordenne's truck. Then we were off and didn't stop until we were back in the heart of *Fort de France*. It was early morning and we found a park where we all piled out and collapsed onto the grass, exhausted.

Chapter 5

TWO WILL DIE, TWO WILL LIVE

It was Friday, May 18, 1945 when Erond created a space in me to hide out while he possessed my physical body. It felt like he was a psychic vampire, taking from my own psyche the energy I would normally use to make decisions and actions for myself. So that night "we" took a walk down Hollywood Boulevard, the true Boulevard of Broken Dreams. We went into a rowdy bar near the Egyptian Theatre on Hollywood Boulevard. I got this feeling Erond was itching for a grand ol' knock-'em-down-slam-'em-out fistfight. Sure enough, a couple of rough looking sailors stood at the bar and damned if he-me didn't wedge into between the two and order a drink. At first the sailors didn't say much, but when Erond-Cable started demanding that they give him more space, they were not happy about it. Before we knew it, one of the sailors hit us smack on the jaw and down we went. But soon I was up and within minutes fifteen servicemen and locals were breaking up the place until the cops were called. Soon we were hauled down to the Hollywood station and jailed. Erond was having the time of his life.

As it so happened, while my leant-out body sat nursing my cuts and bruises, along comes Lt. Lester Keith of the Homicide Division. "Denning—is that you?"

Erond parodied my voice pretty well. "Yeah, it's me, Denning."

"What the hell did ya do...and what the hell are ya doin' here? I thought you'd be at home sleepin' with your nice secretary—Miss—Miss—ah—what the hell's her name?"

My *guest* didn't answer because he didn't know for sure. "Yeah..." was about all he could muster.

"So what'd ya do?"

"I started a fight with a couple o' sailors—and boy, did that feel great. Now that was *fun!*"

"You what? You been drinkin'? What am I saying? Of course you've been drinking. Damn it, Cable, I oughtta just leave you there for a few years until you cool down."

"But you can't," Erond volunteered my voice.

"No? And why can't I?"

"Because I have to rob a bank tomorrow."

Lester Keith scratched his head. "You know, I'm gonna get you outta this here place, Denning and if you promise to go directly home, go directly to bed and sleep it off I won't press charges on you."

"Okay, thanks," Erond-Cable said.

We took the trolley car and Erond took my body directly to my office. He went to the telephone book I kept on my desk. There he saw Ida Latney's name. He rang her up. "Ida? This is Cable...I wanna come over—you gonna be home?"

"Why, yes, Cable, it's four o'clock in the morning, and besides, where do I ever go on Friday nights except maybe to a movie or I'm with you?"

"Well, I'm gonna take you around the world tonight," he-me said.

"Have you been drinking, Cable? Because if you have, you can just stay home or find someone else to make love to—"

"But it's *you* I want, babe—right here, right now. I'm gonna come over. Where do you live?"

I knew he was cutting the corners pretty risky. "What do you mean where do I live? You know darned well where I live—same place I've always lived—I mean, at least since you've known me."

"I'm on my way, Ida. Good-bye!" We hung up the phone. "Not bad, eh, Cable? Is that sort of like you are? Never mind, you can't talk anyhow. What's Ida's address...? He finally found it in my address book in the center drawer of my desk.

We drove over to Ida's and when we knocked on the door, Ida opened it with a suspicious look on her face. "I don't know if I should let you in, Cable. You're acting really strange and it's almost five o'clock in the morning. After all, I've—"

Before the poor girl could finish, we grabbed her and dragged her off to the bedroom. Ida fought tooth and nail and finally slapped my face—hard. "Cable! You're—you're behaving like some—some animal!" We felt our face. "And you were about to make love to me unprotected!"

"Unprotected?" There were obviously some things the praying mantis-potato bug didn't get. "Yeah, oh, well..."

"What do you mean, 'yeah, oh, well...'? What's going on with you? I think maybe you're on some drug or something. You'd better go home and we'll talk tomorrow, okay? Tomorrow's Saturday. Please call me."

"Yeah, okay..." was about all we could say.

I'm glad I didn't have to sleep, because I didn't. Erond was rehearsing what to say and do for his next twenty-four hour stretch of pleasuring himself. About ten the next morning, he took all the bullets out of my gun and we walked to the nearest Bank of America. I could tell Erond must've watched gangster movies because he was acting just like one. He went up to a nicely dressed teller. "Okay, you dirty rat—up with the hands—and all the dough ya got!"

Erond pulled my gun on the poor, trembling man. "S-s-s-s-sir, I—I don't have very much yet—we just opened—and all I have is—"

"—hand it over, sister!" he continued.

"But I'm a *man*, and I don't think—"

"—you want me to plug you here and now? Huh? Is that what ya want? Because if that's what ya want, you're gonna get it! Here, now—see? Is that clear— you're gonna get a slug right between your eyes, see?"

Just then a very dignified gentleman came up to us. "Sir, what is the meaning of this?"

"What's it look like, buddy? You wanna stop me— huh? Just gimme the money and nobody's gonna get hurt!"

"How—how much would you wish, sir?"

"Twenty-million—that's how much I want!!

The older man flushed and began to fan himself. "Sir, I doubt that all the banks in Los Angeles together have that much money available—in cash!"

We looked the man over and saw lots of petrified people standing around. But I also knew someone had called the cops because we were taking so long and it wouldn't be long before we'd be back in the local hoosegow. "You're stallin'," we said. "The cash or no-body lives to tell the tale!"

Then sirens were heard outside and in rushed five policemen with their *loaded* guns drawn. But upon hearing the sirens, we had put my gun away and were acting quite nonchalantly when the cops burst upon the scene. They arrested us anyhow and before we knew it, we were downtown facing Lt. Lester Keith again. "This time it's almost murder, Denning! Last night you fight sailors and today it's robbing banks. What's your next trick, mister—assassinating a president or somethin'?"

"I wasn't going to hurt anyone," we said. "You saw my gun wasn't even loaded."

"Yeah, but *you're* loaded—now I'm a busy man and I'm gonna talk to you later because I suspect there's something else going on here. Go home and shave or something—and get some sleep—your eyes are bulging like some damn bug!"

I hadn't mentioned it, but Erond—through my eyes, of course—had noted on my appointment book I had written Nadia's name down for tonight, Saturday. "Is this the charming, classical young woman who's very attracted to your pheromones—the one I spoke to ra-ther suggestively over the telephone sometime back?" he asked me.

Don't even think it, buster! I wanted to say. Of course we couldn't communicate verbally and I couldn't an-swer, but I thought: "*Attracted to my pheromones—and not me? You mean men and women go through life be-*

208

lieving it's them that attracts another person—and it's really just the damn chemicals?"

So it was, against my better judgment, that Erond-Cable went over to Nadia's fully expecting a night of romping in the hay with a beautiful young opera diva. We arrived, but I don't think Erond was prepared to accept Nadia on her own terms. She was as horny as hell and the minute we came in the door about 8:30 that night, she knocked us out by wearing a light-blue almost see-through gown. She was statuesque to begin with, so standing there at the doorway in that outfit was quite a marvelous sight. "Hello, big boy," she said in a sexy, sultry voice. "I'm very glad to see you."

I don't think Erond knew how to respond next when she went over to us and put her arms around us and kissed us. *Why is it I can see what she's doing, but I can't feel it?* More than likely it was my body's 'guest's' special ability to *fix* it that way. Damn! I was beginning to regret giving Erond permission to do this asinine thing!

Obviously he'd studied my voice pattern and slang sufficiently to paraphrase me. "Hiya, doll...I really like what you're wearing," we said.

"You do? I wasn't sure. It's all for you, handsome—the outside—*and* what's inside.

But I don't think he was as certain of himself as he thought he'd be. "So whatta ya wanna do?" we asked Nadia a little nervously.

"What do you mean, what do we want to do? I'm almost undressed and in the perfect mood—and you're asking what we should do?"

"I'm thirsty," we said.

"Thirsty? What can I get you, my poor darling?"

"What do I normally drink?" we asked.

"Are you okay, Cable?" She paused and studied my face. "You know you always have either a fine English gin or honeyed whiskey in a snifter of boiling water." She leaned up a bit to smell my breath. "Have you been drinking already? All I can smell is your tobacco breath."

"Just straight whiskey will do tonight, babe," we said. Now Erond was trying to be independent from me. But it wouldn't work with someone who was rather used to me and my habits.

"But you told me you couldn't stand straight bourbon, Cable."

"I did?"

"Yes, you did, unless you were pretending. So what will it be?"

"Something strong," we said.

Nadia didn't say another word, but went over to the bar and after making a small batch of honeyed whiskey, poured us a large jigger. Now it so happens I'd had experience with aliens before and they don't hold their alcohol all that well. So my obedient girl brought the drink to us. "Here you are...and may that cure whatever is ailing you," she said with a faint smile. I knew she suspected something.

Erond-Cable took the glass and drank the whole damn thing straight down in one gulp. Nadia was astonished. "More!" we demanded.

"Cable Denning, for God's sake! Now I *know* something's wrong with you! You've always savored that drink—and never have I seen you drink it without the steaming snifter—let alone in one gulp!"

210

"More!" we insisted.

Nadia shut down and went over and poured an even larger glass of the honeyed whiskey. We drifted over toward the bar. "Here!" She handed the drink to us. Again, Erond's inexperience was leading the way to disaster. He gurgled the entire drink down in two or three gulps. "I'm quickly getting out of the mood, you know. I've never known you to be so short on words. It's—it's almost like someone else is inside you operating your body and my darling Cable has gone away!" she complained.

Now the alcohol was beginning to affect us. Somehow Erond's psyche could not tolerate alcohol in my body. "Bathroom—where is it?"

"What do you mean, 'where is it'? How many times have you used my bathroom, Cable? I'm giving you the benefit of the doubt and surmising you're drunk—it's down the hall to the left, just before my bedroom—remember?"

We grunted something as Erond-Cable made a beeline for the toilet. We started vomiting. We leaned over the bowl like it was a sacred altar as we barfed our way to dizziness. Soon we collapsed on the floor and we fell asleep. I don't think Erond Mantis Spiricus was having a good time. When my body was through with the retching, Erond was physically exhausted and simply not used to a human body. But it did kind of ruin Nadia's night. In fact, she was disgusted with Erond-Cable, thinking of course it was me and that I was too damn drunk to respond. So she sent us home. I felt helpless, not being able to defend myself. Finally about 11:00

p.m., we put on our trench coat and hat and said good-night to Nadia Skorkowsky.

Local Opera Singer Kidnapped

By Monday May 21st the Erond Mantis Spiricus episode in my life faded into the background noise that defined my *living-on-the-edge* existence. But trouble with a capital "T" never fades from my humble human foraging for sustenance, and so when I called Nadia on Sunday to apologize, I think she was having second thoughts about who she thought I might be. Or is it *whom*? Regardless, my plate was full with regular clients, Lt. Lester Keith trying to figure out what to do with me, my figuring how to square it with Nadia without having to tell her the truth about Erond, the prospect of being the main donor in Erond's *breeding factory* in order to get some "fun" into the praying mantis-potato bug race of intelligent creatures, dealing with Ida and her feelings, being vigilant about Zxyphon's next move with me and the Oculus, the pending atomic bomb test explosion, and last but not least, Ayana's psychic prophecy about "two shall die, two shall live." *Who would die? Who would live?* I asked myself. Then there was Sophia Legende and her persistent phone calls that I need to go see her because there had been someone prowling around the grounds of her little cabin in back of the Beverly Hills mansion. Nadia had also reported some odd things around her place. I wondered if there was a connection.

I had planned to see Nadia again on Saturday night. I think she was willing to let bygones be bygones and give me a second chance to behave myself. But on Thursday evening she called and sounded distressed. "Cable! I think someone was in my place tonight. This time while I—while I was taking a bath!" she sputtered in a frightened voice.

"What makes you think so, babe?" I asked.

"As I said, I was in the bath. I thought I heard some floorboards creak at a spot down the hallway where I know they always creak when someone walks on them. Then I thought maybe it was just the house settling after the warm day we had. But...a few pieces of my intimate clothing are missing. One drawer in the bedroom dresser had been partially left open. A nighty, some panties, a brassiere and some of my laundry waiting to be cleaned was taken! I realize it sounds weird, but I don't think I'm that crazy, Cable. What do you think I should do?"

"Why didn't you call me sooner—like when all this allegedly happened?"

"I—I thought I might be jumping to conclusions. So I thought it through, retraced my steps to make sure I myself hadn't done those things."

"And?"

"No, Cable, someone definitely has been here. Will you come stay with me? I may not like you very much at the moment—considering the way you behaved last week—but I trust you and I know you can protect me. And...of course, I'm willing to forgive and forget."

"Thanks, Nadia. Do you want me over tonight?"

"Yes. If you don't mind. At least until I settle down and we can resolve this thing so I don't think I'm making it all up."

"I'd dismiss it a little more easily, except for one thing..."

"And what's that?"

"A gal named Sophia Legende, she was one of Dr. Rueben's patients out at Greystone Mansion. She's been pestering me on the phone because she felt someone was prowling around her place in Beverly Hills as well."

"And you think these incidences are connected?"

"I don't know...could be the only thing in common so far is that you both know me."

"Have you been intimate with Miss Legende?" Nadia probed.

"No, babe, I haven't. Our relationship was professional. She was the link between Rueben and *Zoot Mimby's* club downtown."

"Oh." She said, with a little frost around the edges.

"So—it's about seven o'clock right now. How about if I get out there by ten or so?"

"So long? Can't you make it sooner? Telling me about that other woman has more or less unhinged me."

"Okay, I'll get out there just as soon as I can."

There was a pause. "Cable? I just saw a shadow out by my living room window. Oh...please hurry...now I'm truly frightened!"

"Don't let your imagination run away with you, babe," I said, putting a cigarette between my lips and lighting it. "Keep your doors locked, don't answer your door unless you recognize the voice."

Then a real fear entered her tone. "Unless...unless he's...he's already in the house—Oh, Cable! What if he's hiding—"

"—don't get yourself all worked up, Nadia. I'll be there in a jiffy, okay? Just hang on, kid..."

"Okay, I'll do my best...but please hurry, darling!" Nadia whimpered under her breath. I knew she was running scared.

We hung up and I called Lester Keith. He'd gone home for the night and so I called there. "Yeah? Inspector Keith here," he answered.

"Lester, it's me, Cable. I wanted to ask you—"

"—you've got a lotta nerve calling me at home. It'd better be important. I still haven't figured out what to do with you. I can't keep on protecting you."

"Whatta ya mean? Ain't it your credo *'serve and protect'* as a cop?"

"Yeah, but that don't go for you, wisenheimer! So whatta ya want—it's late and I'm listening to the radio with my wife."

"Have you had a lotta extra calls from reasonably young single females about being stalked lately?"

"Denning! Personally, I just get the ones who've been *killed*—but I know Joe Rensonal across the hall from me at work tells me shit...like there are more and more reports about women bitchin' that some asshole who wanted to screw 'em gets frustrated when he can't and starts scaring the shit outta them. Where do ya start lookin' for reasons why men do these things?"

I thought for a minute. "Hmmm...I guess we gotta find a specific pattern, an m.o. that will eventually nab this nutso idiot."

"Good luck. Now, is that all, Mr. Bank Robber?"

"I tell you I didn't rob any bank, Lieutenant. But if I tell you what really happened, you'll lock me up in the nuthouse for sure!"

"Try me, I'm pretty understanding..."

"Not with this you won't be."

"Just tell me, Denning, or I'm gonna hang up."

"Okay...it...it was a—a strange praying mantis-potato bug creature who wanted the experience of being in a human body. So...so he, he, uh...well, he made a deal with me to inhabit my body for seventy-two hours because he had saved my life on two previous occasions—"

"—Jesus! There you go again, Denning. Yeah, I think you're right... I'm gonna put your ass in the nuthouse and throw away the goddamn key...but not before I ring your fool neck!"

"See? I told you. Lester...you know me...have I ever lied to you?"

"How in the hell would I know?" he growled. "I just know you get yourself into some real strange shit, buddy!

"Well, so my question is this—did you ever run into a stalker who takes dirty laundry along with intimate items from a woman's bedroom dresser drawer?"

"I don't know about the dirty laundry, but sure...a lotta sick men take lingerie items from time to time. I'd say pretty common, in fact."

"But not the dirty laundry?"

"Crap, Denning, how do you know this client's on the level? And besides, you stop messing with it at a certain point, ya know—that bein' when it becomes police business."

"Yeah, Lt. Keith, I know when it becomes police business—after the woman is missing—or dead!"

"One wrong step and I'll kill you myself!" he prattled. "What the hell can I say? We're goddamn busy down here. Yeah, sure, some victims slip between the cracks at the mercy of sex-crazed men. But we catch a lot of 'em too. Go to sleep, Denning, it's late. I gotta get back to the radio and Mrs. Keith. You know how that is..."

"No, I don't, Lester, but I can guess. That's one reason I'm single."

"Goodnight, Denning." He hung up.

On the drive over to Nadia's, I was thinking of Maria Voldt. *"The only time I'm happy is when we are as one, and then time herself evaporates, leaving me no rival for your love."* That was the part that stood out to me from a longer poem in the anthology I inherited after her death. Who *was* Maria Voldt ...really? Was she an angel messenger, reminding me that love is all we ever really have—if we're lucky? And was it really possible to "feel as one" with someone else? I know I've had some marvelous moments with women in my life. Sometimes I believed I truly loved them. But what is love? A woman who puts a ring through your nose when you become her husband? A son who wants nothing to do with you because you weren't much of a Dad? A nightclub singer whose own loneliness makes her accept you on your terms? Or is love what I had for Boots Blake or my mother Florence Denning or my wanderlust sire who desired my mother enough to cross the boundaries of propriety to have her?

By the time I reached Nadia's place, I was feeling unsettled. Some pending doom was descending on me. I knocked on her door but no one answered. She did say right away *tonight*, right? After pounding on the front door unsuccessfully, I went around to the back. That door, too, was locked and so, my old detective instincts cut in and I kicked the door open. "Nadia!" I shouted out. But there was no response. Now red flags went up all over the place. Frantically, I ran through every room of her house and the garage. Her car was still there! Now I suspected foul play to the nth degree. Crap! How could Mr. Big Shot here be so dense and off base about her panic. But who had kidnapped her?—or worse! I checked the drawers and jewelry boxes. Nothing was disturbed. In my business, a stalker who ultimately kidnaps his dearly intended, ups the ante to a crime of passion—maybe even murder! I needed to get the ball rolling and get some publicity out there and let Lt. Keith know about a new missing persons case. I called the newspaper and gave them the data, including my name as a private detective whom Nadia had called just prior to her kidnapping. I called Lester Keith, but he wasn't available. So I got the right department and they told me I'd have to come down and file some papers to get some action started. I hung up the phone.

Who had complimented Nadia recently? Maybe someone at work? Maybe someone she knew. Or maybe it was someone *I know!* A light went on inside of me and I thought of the name Dr. Theodore Watson or "Watty", escaped convict from an institution for the

criminally insane! Quickly, I tried to put the pieces together. First Watty escapes, comes back for his papers
but Dr. Apothican is killed because Watty killed him
when the good doctor told Watty he gave the papers to
me. Big mistake. Watty had something he called *"Numantia Syndrome"*, a mental disorder, its name taken
from a city in Spain where the Roman conqueror Scipio
the Younger laid siege in 133 B.C., and somehow managed to numb the minds of the local inhabitants to be
unaware of the pain and sorrow of others. At least that's
how I remember it. And Watty had it in spades! I ran to
the phone and dialed Greystone Mansion. When I told
the reception person who I was, she said she'd find the
person I requested. Soon a familiar voice came on the
line.

"Cable? Do you have a new development? You must
think me crazy calling you like that—but now some
things are missing from my little cottage in the back of
the mansion—remember the one?"

"Yeah, there is a new development! Listen carefully,
Sophie. I didn't tell you because I didn't consider it important at the time, but someone I know quite well—a
pretty babe like you—has just been kidnapped! I have a
feeling you're next because of your association with
me—don't hang out in that cottage! Can you move back
inside the main building?"

"Kidnapped?! Oh, Lord, Cable! I can't move right
back in—a new girl has my old room. Whatta are we
going to do?"

"I'm not sure. I've got one clue. Let me ask you this,
has any of your dirty laundry been swiped?"

There was a pause. *"My dirty laundry*?! Like what?"

"Lingerie—you know, panties, brassieres, socks, night gowns—any of that intimate kind of apparel?"

"I don't know. I have a hamper in the back. I only send it out once a week. I'll check it and get back to you right away. I'm frightened, Cable! I feel so helpless—like I'm a sitting duck in a shooting gallery or something."

"Okay, okay...I don't wanna lose two of you on the same night! Tell ya what, Sophie—do you, uh...have any clients tonight?"

"No...it's been slow since—well, since Dr. Rueben isn't soliciting for us anymore. But it'll pick up from the downtown guys—you know, the married politicians and the like?"

"Yeah, I know most of 'em. So...I'm gonna come pick you up and for tonight you can stay in back of my office—remember?"

She laughed lightly. "Yes...I remember, Cable..."

"I'll take the couch in the office."

"You don't have to, you know. In the back of my mind I've wondered what you'd feel like—in bed, I mean."

"Well, you probably won't find out, either, Sophie. I've never paid for it in my life and I don't intend to start now."

"What if it's free?"

I hesitated. "Let's not worry about those things right now, okay? We gotta make you safe for the present. I'll be out there in about a half-hour—pack a bag and tell the management you'll be out of commission for a few days, okay?

"Yes, okay, Cable. I do have a singing job Saturday night at *Drisco's Supper Club* down on Wilshire. Will you come to hear me?"

"Yeah, sure enough—if one of us ain't dead, that is."

"Ooo! Don't even say that Cable! It scares me!"

I drove out and picked up the beautiful blonde bombshell named Sophia Legende, whose real surname was Price. She looked and smelled great. I tossed her suitcase in my trunk and off we went to my place. "We'll find you better quarters tomorrow. I just gotta figure out where it's safe and what it'll take to get you there."

"I don't mind staying with you for a few days—I mean, if it's okay."

"Well, I've got Ida my secretary and my clients in and outta there—the place can be Grand Central Station a lotta the time."

"I see. Well, it will do for tonight anyhow," she said and smiled at me. "I'm very grateful, Cable, and I'm sorry about your friend getting kidnapped. Have you reported it to the police?"

"The police? Ha! That's kinda like sending your Mom a fruitcake from Turkey—you never know when she'll get it. Naw, the cops are hands full most of the time."

Sophia Legende had a wonderful laugh and I told her so. She put her head on my shoulder as I drove. "Why is it so often the men like you aren't really available. I know you don't know this, because I never told you. But when you were gone to Martinique, I said a prayer for you every day and night and worried about you, Cable. I just think you're special and I have this feeling you'll never let me know you well enough to get inside."

"Yeah, that's probably true. But it's also because of considerations for your safety, doll. Ya see, lots of women have bought a quick trip to the graveyard because of me in the past fifteen years or so. I'm dangerous, kid, so the sooner we resolve this thing and get you back to your regular job, the better!"

We got to my office and Sophia Legende and I sat and had a gin and a cigarette together. "So, Cable, I know you're very smart—you must've made some connection as to who it is who knows you and is wanting to kidnap your friend and me."

"Not yet, but I'm workin' on it, lady."

"I like that."

"Like what?"

"The way you call me 'lady'. It's pert and tough and—and well, 'homey' at the same time. I know that doesn't make much sense."

"So what *don't* I know about you? You've told me your past, sort of. You told me you had a thirst that no man's kiss could survive, more or less. And you protect yourself as best you can. You rely on your beauty to make a living like a lotta hookers. So what else do I need to know, Sophia Legende?"

"Don't go so fast, Cable," she purred as she took a big drag on her cigarette. "I'm kind of like you, I guess—a wrecked train on the siding. But sometimes I don't think I really want to get back onto the main line again. I've been there. I'm not sure I like it. I remember a romantic poem when I was a young naïve girl. I didn't understand it then. Now I do. *'Forever and ever, the song remains a* game, and who knows why love can't remain the same?' I put those into a song I wrote. Remember the one I told you about—'Don't Move Too Fast'?"

"Oh yeah, vaguely." I wanted to know where the lady was coming from in the deep inside place. "So what are the rest of the words like?"

She began to sing them. *"Don't move too fast, it's already tomorrow, please turn off the light, and fade out all the sorrow...Don't move too fast, please take your time to make me, hmmm.....and maybe pretend that you might have found me, surround me with your dreams. Don't move too fast. I said at the first that I had a thirst no kiss could survive...but you turned it around, what was lost was found and now I'm alive! Don't move too fast, it's later than you think, turn on your glow and hand me that drink before you go...'cause forever and ever the song remains a game...and who's to know why love can't remain the same. Kiss me again...hold me again, and kiss away the pain I came with...light my cigarette, so you won't forget me...but don't go too fast...'* More or less like that, Cable..."

I was very moved. For a moment I had fallen in love with Sophia Legende. Misplaced singer-movie star shuttled to some sideshow as a selective prostitute. "I don't know how commercial the tune is, but I'd say in some musical world it'd be a hit!" I encouraged her.

"But not in this world, right? Is that what you're saying, Cable? It's okay. I'm a big girl. But did you really like it?"

I smiled at her. "You bet I did. I hear songs all the time—new songs, old songs—and the babes who sing 'em down at all the clubs I frequent. In fact, I'm looking forward to hearing you sing on Saturday night."

"That's wonderful, Cable, thank you."

Sophia and I talked until about two in the morning. I showed her my disheveled bedroom and got ready for bed myself. Tomorrow would be a tough day of work with Ida and two new clients. New people are a mixed bag for me. I'm excited to hear their stories—but most of their stories are the same. So then there's a letdown. I suppose that's why I get the adrenaline when I'm chasing bad guys. It's out of the ordinary ken of my everyday business life.

As I tried to get comfortable on the couch, Sophie poked her head around the corner. "Good night, Cable— are you sure you don't want to share your bed with me tonight? I *could* relax you, you know. I'm good at that."

What man in his right mind would've passed that up? But I did. "Thanks, Sophie, but I think it's best just to hang out separately tonight. I got a big day tomorrow as well."

"It's her, isn't it?" she asked me. "The girl who got kidnapped. You really care about her, don't you?"

"Yeah, I—I guess I do, Sophie. If I think about it, it's pretty gruesome—the whole damn thing. I'm trying not to get emotionally involved in the worrying end of it. So I try to think like a detective and figure out the curves and angles. Maybe we'll find the rotten apple that way. It's too bad, ain't it? There's always gotta be a rotten apple in the barrel. That's the thing about life, I guess."

"If you change your mind, Cable, you don't have to knock...just come on in...and slip into bed," she lilted in

224

a soft, sexy voice. I think I would need my head examined!

Nadia made the front page of the newspaper by morning. But not the way she would have wanted it. **"LOCAL OPERA SINGER DISAPPEARS - SUSPECTED KIDNAPPING!"** was what the caption read. Well, it was good to see that they took me seriously. Maybe I had some clout downtown after all. About 9:30 a.m., Ida came through the door. I was still in my clothes, barely awake, sitting on the loveseat checking out the newspaper. "You—you look all wrinkled and terrible—did you sleep there?"

"Good morning to you, too," I growled. "Yeah, there's someone sleeping in my bed. I closed the door, but now I gotta go...uh...use the facility and wash up. I hope I won't wake her up."

"*Her*?" Ida's voice got an edge to it.

"Yeah, Sophia Legende—remember the gal I—I—uh, interviewed and then she hired me to talk to Anthone Demaine down at Zoot Mimby's?"

"Oh, yes, that—that was the day we—we made love on your bed. Do *you* remember *that*?"

"Of course I do, Ida. Why would I forget something like that?"

"Oh...I just wondered." Then she looked toward the bedroom door. "Is Miss Legende going to stay with us for a while?" she asked with a bite of sarcasm.

"Next day or two I'll make other arrangements. Do you recall Nadia Skorkowsky—the opera singer?"

"Yep, the one you've been dating—and sleeping with?"

225

"That one...well, she's disappeared. I think she's been kidnapped. And that's why Sophie's here. Just before Nadia vanished, she told me someone had been in her house stealing lingerie—and dirty laundry. Same thing started happening to Sophie. So I grabbed her before she got kidnapped."

"Oh, dear, Cable!" Ida exclaimed in a low, dramatically breathy voice. "Do you have any idea who did it?"

"Not yet. Only that each woman had a connection with me. So you understand, then?"

"Of course. The lingerie I can understand...but taking someone's dirty laundry?"

"There are sick people out there on the streets, Ida."

"I guess so!" Ida went about her morning duties and I sneaked past the reposing Sophie and got cleaned up. On the way back, Sophie was sitting up in bed stretching, with those tempting breasts sticking out underneath her sheer white nighty.

She yawned and smiled. "Good morning, handsome. I heard voices. Your secretary, no doubt?"

"Yep...Ida...did you sleep okay?" I inquired, feeling a bit awkward.

"Yes, as a matter of fact. I sleep wonderfully in your bed. Thought about you, though. A girl can't help wonder, you know..."

"Yeah, I thought about it, too, Sophie." I pointed to the bathroom. "It's all yours. I'll be out here working if you need something."

About an hour later Sophia Legende stepped out into the office. She was wearing a mint-green skirt and a white blouse and looked refreshed. I'm sure Ida was taken with the beautiful woman who had slept in my bed. "You must be Ida," she said.

Ida stood up and extended her hand across her little desk. Sophie came over and took it. "I hear you're quite the girl."

Ida smiled sheepishly and then looked at me. "Oh! Cable must've told you he considers me indispensible."

"Yes, something like that. I love your skin—it's so fine and fair, no blemishes. Never went through the pimple stage, eh?"

"No...I was lucky, I guess. You're also very lovely," Ida said, checking out Sophia's fine face and body.

"Thank you, Ida. I take good care of myself." Then Sophie looked over at me behind my desk. "That's more than I can say for that lunk over there who's going to kill himself with alcohol and cigarettes."

"And *women*," Ida added the third ingredient to my life style.

"Oh, yes—and women. How could I forget?" She looked over in my direction. "I wonder if *they'll* help kill you, Cable..."

"Very funny. You two need to talk about something else—quietly. I gotta talk to a prospective client."

"Mrs. Overly said to call her about 11:00 a.m.—or she'd call you," Ida instructed me.

"Yeah, thanks, Ida..." Then I looked at both of them. "Ida...would you mind taking Sophie out to breakfast up the street. Here..." I took some money out of my pocket. "Then come directly back, is that clear? If there's more than one kidnapper, one's watching Nadia and the other's keeping an eye on this office and who comes and goes. Especially if someone notices Sophie's not at Greystone Mansion."

Both women looked at each other, their eyes widened. "Really, Cable?" Sophie retorted. "How do you know that?"

"I don't. I'm just taking no chances at this point. Now you two get outta here and let me concentrate on this phone call."

The two women left together, chatting as if they'd known each other for years. Women are good that way, I guess. I think men find it harder. I dialed the phone. "Yeah...Mrs. Overly? This is Cable Denning, Private Detective. I understand you called?"

The voice at the other end was light, sophisticated. "Yes, thank you for being so punctual, Mr. Denning. I feel awkward about calling. I'm not even sure I should be. But I thought if I explained the situation to you, you'd at least be able to shed some light on the subject."

"I'll do my best, Mrs. Overly. I've learned over the years that everyone has a story. So I'm all ears..." I lit up my first cigarette of the day. I took a deep drag and settled back in my comfy chair. "Shoot..."

"Okay, here goes, Mr. Denning. My husband is gone a lot. He's a captain in the United States Army Air Force. There was a War Department production contract negotiation going on at Lockheed and it was necessary for him to be there. He was involved with the development of an airplane called the P-38—a fighter plane. There have been several new models since its conception to correct the limitations discovered throughout these war years and he has been very involved in that."

"Yes, I know the airplane, Mrs. Overly. Dubbed *Lightning*, I think it is. It's been the main thing in the sky for the Army Air Force."

"Yes. Well, anyway, my husband was called away suddenly about three weeks ago to respond to a top-secret project in New Mexico. I think it was to an Army airfield there—in a God-forsaken desert area called *Roswell,* I believe. I haven't heard from him since...except for one time. And that was a note in a woman's handwriting!"

"A woman's handwriting, eh? What did it say?"

"Will be gone indefinitely—Enola needs me. Dick."

"That's it? Not signed 'love, Dick' or anything?"

"That was it, Mr. Denning. My husband and I were not—how shall I say?—not very demonstrative. You see, I was one of those young star-struck girls who married a uniform. He was a handsome man in '38 when I met him. We married the following year."

"I see. Do you know a woman named 'Enola'?"

"Never heard of her. It's strange as well because Dick was not one to waste his time on women—including me. So I'm all the more puzzled."

"What if *Enola* isn't a woman, Mrs. Overly? What if she's an *it?* And your husband's engaged in some military project, where maybe *Enola* is the code word."

"Then what about the female's handwriting?"

"Well, that could be a secretary at the air base writing for him. Maybe he's been injured or incapacitated or something—or even away on a long tour of duty. You know how secretive the military folks are."

"I'm not so sure. Dick could certainly write me or call within three weeks, Mr. Denning. Unless, of course...he's—he's—"

"—not with us anymore? Let's not think that yet. How do you feel I could help you?"

"You're a private detective. I have money. I could afford to send you anywhere to investigate and maybe find him."

"I thought you weren't that close."

"We aren't—but wouldn't you want to know? I'm not getting any younger, you know. I married Dick when I was barely twenty—I'll be thirty in a few years. Then life's pretty much over for a woman."

" Do you have children?"

"Dick wasn't around long enough for me to get pregnant, Mr. Denning. He was a career man. It's like being married to a doctor."

"Yeah, I know the syndrome. Well, I guess I could begin by checking out Lockheed, you know, the factory with the big burlap sack covering it with rubber cars around it? Ha! But I doubt they'd let me in."

"Dick had an apartment near Lockheed, off Vineland Avenue."

"Why didn't you say so?"

"I just did."

"So...give me the address. What about a key?"

"I have an extra. May I go with you?"

"Do you wanna?"

"Yes, if you don't mind. I'd—I'd like to see how Dick lived away from me." What she was really saying was, *'I wonder if there's another female's scent in the place,'* I surmised.

I left a note for Ida and Sophie that I was out on business. I'm sure they would bond closer and that was good, because Ida didn't have many girlfriends. And I didn't really know about Sophie, but I suspected she was more or less a loner of sorts. But who knew?

The twenty-six year old Mavis Overly was as cute as a button with a nice smile and curious disposition. She lived down near the beach in Santa Monica, so we decided to drive separately and meet in Burbank. There was something about her. I would've pegged her for an alien had she not been so down–to-earth in her American speech and manners. She stood about 5' 4" and had an average body with medium long auburn hair and light blue eyes. We got to Dick Overly's apartment about 12:30 and we found Apartment 4-B on the second floor. We entered. It was all too pat. It reminded me of a movie set that had been pre-propped to fool someone into believing that someone had actually lived there. But I wondered.

"I'm gonna look around," I told Mrs. Overly.

"Help yourself. You can call me Mavis, if you like. I wasn't expecting —"

"—expecting what?"

"That you'd be so—well, frankly, so handsome and personable. I think of private detectives as rather droll and preoccupied. You know, drinkers, smokers, womanizers? But I can tell you care. I sense it."

"You can?" Now I was beginning to feel very odd about this woman. What if she was a spy? What if she had killed her husband and this is all a set up? Or even more intriguing, what if she was an *alien* spy doing a good job of covering her tracks?

She looked at me with those blue eyes of hers. "Yes. It's a gift of mine. I can also see you have little or no fear. In your line of work, that's pretty important, isn't it?"

"You're—you're, uh, very perceptive. Yeah, I guess so." I went rummaging around Dick Overly's desk. Tucked away in the corner of the top-right drawer I found a folded sheet of typewriter paper. There were scribbled words in pencil on it. It read: *'Glenn L. Martin...Enola Gay...Roswell Army Air Field...Tuesday May 1st...Col. Paul Tibbets...B-29 being constructed...be there!'* There were enough clues on that paper to write *War and Peace*, I thought. "Oh, Mavis, you might wanna come here a second."

She came over and I showed her the paper. She put her hand on my shoulder tentatively. I could tell she was lonely. Or it was a ploy? "What's it all mean? And who's Enola Gay?" she inquired. "He told me he was going somewhere in New Mexico. So he met with a Colonel—Mr. Tibbets about something. Big deal. It's the woman that bothers me."

I didn't believe her and took a chance. My intuition was working overtime. "Would you mind copying it down, please?"

"Why, we can just take the original."

"But I want you to have a copy and I'll take the original, if you don't mind. Is this your husband's handwriting here?"

"Yes, it looks like it." But aliens don't know everything, and Mavis Overly—or whoever she was—had

232

just slipped up. For as she wrote she matched the handwriting on the damn paper!

"May I see your husband's original note to you?

"What for?"

"Just for clues...ya never know what you discover..."

"I don't have it with me."

"It doesn't exist, does it, Mavis?"

"Why...why would you...say that?" she sputtered.

I took her writing and the original and showed them to her. "This is why, Mavis. You wrote *both* of them. And dollars to donuts you *never* got what you told me on the phone Dickey boy sent you—what was it again? The way it sounded, it was all wrong, lady, plus I'll wager the Enola is a B-29 airplane, not a woman. You also knew that. You'd better come clean, kid, I ain't wasting my time on people who lie. I've done enough of that in my life!"

She flushed. "So...you know..."

"Yeah, I know. It was all a hype-job to get me to believe you. But why? Unless someone like your 'husband' was under duress, he would've never written that note. So, I suggest, you made it up on the spot...whoever you are...to get me here." I looked into her blue eyes. "So just *why* did you get me here?"

She turned and walked away. "I'm sorry, Mr. Denning. I'm a better model than the #420, but we have to get used to humans and the subtle ways they interact."

"Yeah, I'll vote for that, toots!" I bellowed. "Why in the hell do you guys even bother? Why don't you just come out and say it, '*I'm an alien and I don't look like you—but we'd like to communicate better with you,*' or something like that. You're just lucky I've had alien experience, doll, else wise you'd be a lot worse off about now. But you still haven't answered me. What role did you perceive I'd play in your scenario here? Sorry ain't good enough, money or not. I hate being set up for a patsy."

"A patsy?"

"Yeah, a sucker...a number one schmo who you think probably doesn't know the difference between a real human and a transplant."

She cast her head down. "No, you're right. I was clumsy. But I must tell you why, Mr. Denning. You see, my co-operative is also someone I'm in love with. Dick—not his real name obviously—got caught by the military authorities for stealing secrets—and is now being held prisoner and interrogated in that terrible desert place in New Mexico!"

"Aha! Now we learn the truth at least. Love rules out, eh? Well, at least you have some of the traits of a human female, lady creature."

"Please don't call me that. I'm a *being*—just like you're a being."

"Okay, okay...I take it back. We have as much chance of springing your boyfriend as we have of getting a snowball out of hell, Mavis—by the way, what is your real name?"

"*Sirracca*—you may call me that."

"Alright, Sirracca, here's what I suggest. Go home to your leaders and tell them the U.S. is gonna explode a big bomb pretty soon. I'm not exactly sure when. It'll change the world—"

"—that's why we're concerned!" she interrupted. "It will rip a hole in the fabric of your atmosphere and deplete your ozone layers and begin to deteriorate everything on this beautiful planet of yours. Can't you help?!"

I stopped and lit up a cigarette. I walked away, looking out through a window to a lovely little garden below. "I wish I could, Sirracca," I reflected, calming my voice. "I've thought about this thing a lot. Any reasonable person would. But humans aren't reasonable by nature when it comes to an awful lots of things. War is one of them. Look what devastation is happening in Europe right now, the Pacific islands, even the Libyan desert. Crap, what can one little half-cracked gumshoe do with a world gone amuck?"

"Step one...you can help get Dick out of his prison so they won't discover who he is."

"Did you say discover who he is? Do you know how many reptilian aliens are in the armed forces? They *love* this kinda shit! They nailed him for who he is within hours—if they didn't know ahead of time!"

"Really? Oh, that's so terrible! They might kill him, then?"

"If he's of no use to them, yeah, they might." A shiver went through her. She looked into my eyes for help again. But I knew the score.

"How did you detect *me* so fast?" she asked, avoiding the reality.

"That's because half of me is also half of someone like you, doll. My mother unknowingly bred with an alien...but ya know what?"

She half-smiled as she saw me smile. "No, what?"

"I loved him...that wild, adventuresome son-of-a-bitch..."

"Where is he now?"

"Dead, I was told." Then I turned to Sirracca. "Everything dies to get reborn, doesn't it?

"Yes, Mr. Denning." She took a deep breath. "Have you ever been in love—I mean, really loved someone?"

"Yeah, I have. I was in love with a beautiful Mexican gal. We had everything. She...she died from some blood disease a few years back."

"I'm sorry. I sympathize. I would all but perish if they killed *Narro*—that's Dick's real name."

I was getting restless. "I see." She sensed it.

"Well, thank you for doing what you did by coming here. I don't have any money with me—"

"—forget it, kid. We'll even it up another time. I wish you luck."

I left Burbank feeling bad as I glanced back at the burlap covering the factory where war magic was imagined and produced. Once the military's got you, it's hard to get out.

A Night to Remember

As I suspected, Ida and Sophie hit it off and were still chatting when I got back to the office. I delighted in watching them get on so well. I took a shot of gin to relax me when the door opened and in walked a short, heavy-set man and two accomplices. I knew the breed. "Herr Denning?" the short one with the heavy German accent asked.

"Yep—that's me. What can I do for you?"

He looked at the two lovely young women as his henchmen helped him off with his coat and he gave his hat to them. "Vell...I vould prefer to speak...alone vis you...just a few moments..."

I sent the girls out and they said they'd be gone the rest of the day on a shopping spree downtown. I led them out into the hallway, hugged them both and away they went. I sat behind my desk. "Okay, who are you and whatta ya want?"

"Mine name is Oscar Brandt—und I vill pull no punches mit you—as you Americans zay...I am from the *Lichter Grabstätte.*"

"Ah, the Lichter Grabstätte—I imagine you boys and girls are having a pretty bad time of it just about now."

"Ya...ve are preparing to leave zis country. But...first...ve vere vondering...if ve offered you...proper compensation...Herr Denning...vould you be villing to— to perform vahn last task?"

"Why should I? I haven't even done a '*first* task' yet. I don't even like you guys."

"Perhaps a million American dollars—in za bank of your choice?"

I must've reacted positively, because Oscar boy began to smile a little. "A million bucks? What—what would I—I have to do for it?"

"Vell, you must come to za secret laboratory so ve may show you. Und if you agree...zen...you vill be one million dollars richer, Herr Denning. Othervise, peasants like you vill vork all of his life for—for—vhat is it you Americans zay?—'peanuts'.

"And if I don't agree? You know, I'm kind of leery when it comes to German laboratories. I had my memory erased once—my whole identity. So, if I'm not willing, what'll ya do?"

He made a sinister all-knowing grin. "In zat case, ve vill have no choice but to kill you. Because if you agree to come to Lichter Grabstätte headquarters und ze laboratory, you vill have seen—"

"—yeah, I already know the score, Brandt—I'll have seen too much and you're gonna have to kill me...right?"

"Precisely, Herr Denning. Thousands die every day for the Third Reich and der Führer—vhat difference one more life?"

"Well, if it happens to be mine...I care." I knew I needed to stall for time, but I was hoping he'd give me a clue. That's what a good spy does, doesn't he? "Can you give me a hint? Let me see—this is a world war we're engaged in...hmmm...would it have anything to do with the atomic bomb Hitler is desperately trying to perfect first?"

"Ya! How bright! And how exacting, Herr Denning. Ya...you are an intelligent man. I vas told zat you exceed your common man limits. Now I see vhy."

"Don't butter me up too much, you might get disappointed in the end, buster. I told you, I don't like you guys. But then again, I don't much like politicians right here at home, either. Maybe it's a toss-up—I don't know."

He arose and his henchmen helped him on with his coat and gave him his hat. "In certain circles I am considered...uh...shall ve say, 'influential', sir, und hope your answer is yes. I vill give you until next Monday to decide." He got out a card from his fine greenish-brown wallet. "Lovely American alligator from your state of Florida—isn't it nice? You call zis number und ask for *Mr. Johns.* The secretary vill let me know und I vill call you immediately." He began to leave. "I suppose you vill not shake my hand, but it is an honor to have met you, Herr Denning." He offered his hand but he was right, I didn't take it.

"Nothing personal, 'Herr' Brandt, but I'm not crazy about the people you work for."

"Please...make no mistake—Monday, May the 28th. Auf Wiedersehen, zen, Herr Denning." He bowed graciously and left with his goons.

Hours later, while I was smoking and drinking my way into a stupor, Ida called and told me she'd like to have Sophie come stay with her until we found Nadia's kidnapper. I wasn't certain whether the gesture was a token of an oncoming friendship or a way to keep Sophie away from me. But as it turned out, Ida's mother was coming to stay with her for a few days, until Monday—*my* deadline to get back to Oscar Brandt. So, for the time being, would Sophie stay with me until Sunday night? I agreed and an hour later, the blonde with it all entered my office, looking healthy in every way. "Well, what'd you guys do—empty the stores of their merchandise?" I asked her.

Sophia Legende smiled. Then she saw the full ashtray and the booze on my desk. "You *will kill yourself* if you continue like that, Cable—I hope you realize that. Ida's very concerned."

"Yeah, well, what I do with my body is my business," I said, a little tipsy and ornery. "You look a hell of lot better than I do tonight anyway, Miss Legende."

"Thanks, Cable. Are we a little intoxicated already?

I chuckled. "Ha! Intoxicated? Yeah, that's a good word for it. Hell, if you lived the life I do, you'd be drunk morning, noon and night! And...young woman...trying to keep from being intoxicated by your feminine charms, is my challenge of the evening."

"Well, you won't have to worry about it tonight. I—I have to go to work out at the mansion. Would you be kind enough to drive me if I pay you for it?"

"Pay me for it? Look, Sophie, some things are done in pure friendship—no money necessary."

"Thank you. My last client can bring me back. You've been very good to me. I'll never forget you. You don't even remind me of anyone I've ever known."

"That part's good—I think...you, too, Sophie. I wish we'd met in a different lifetime."

She looked at me oddly and cocked her head. "Different lifetime? Do you believe in that? I think I used to. Not so sure anymore..." She started for the bedroom. "By the way, you do know that Ida is crazy in love with you—maybe *obsessed* might be a better word. What are you going to do about it?"

"She told you that or you just guessed?" I inquired.

"No, Ida's a very fine and discreet lady. I gathered from simply the way she spoke of you and some of your hair-raising adventures—and of course, how good you've been to her."

"Oh...I see. What am I gonna do about it? Nothing, I guess. I'm not sure *how* I feel about Ida. I know I like her awful much. But I ain't cut out for what she wants. You know kids and a mortgage?"

"Then let her go, Cable. I can tell...she wants you completely, but she's afraid she'll lose you if she puts too much pressure on you. And I agree, you aren't cut out for the domestic life. There are a lot of fine young men who are."

"That—that's what I've been telling her for years now." I took a big swig of gin. "Yeah, domestic life...I tried that once. It fell apart right there in front of me, it did—yep! Right before my eyes it went 'zip'!"

It was a funny feeling driving Sophia Legende out to her place of business. On one hand I wanted her. On the other, what she was doing with and to other men turned my stomach. I knew I'd better stay away.

Saturday rolled around a lot quicker than I expected. I had promised Sophie I'd go to hear her sing at a class joint named *Bar of Music* on Beverly Boulevard and Fuller. My bedroom looked like a woman's dressing room in a Broadway show house. It was about seven in the evening when Sophie told me she was going to lie down and rest. I told her I had to use the bathroom before she dozed off. When I came out she was sitting up in bed with nothing on except a blanket covering her chest. "Cable, please come here and sit with me...just for a minute."

I did so. "What's the matter—you got the jitters about tonight?"

"No, Cable, I've got the jitters about *you*...all week I've fought it off."

"Why, am I scary? And did you win?" I joked, trying to keep it light.

"You're scary to my heart. Sometimes I won, yes, sometimes no. It's difficult. Maybe it's the proximity, you know, being exposed to you each day, hearing your

241

voice, your laughter, your tough edges, your more sensitive ones—"

"—hey, wait a minute, gal, are we enamored with a phony image of me here or what?" I got up to go. She pulled me back down. "What? You gotta get your rest and then warm up your voice, you know." I could feel the blood rush through my veins.

"Cable...would you hold me while I rest?"

I couldn't hold it in anymore. "Damn it, Sophie, I'm trying not to fall in love with you! How about some help here, okay?"

Her voice was soft, sensual, deliberate. "I think it's too late, Cable. I think I fell in love with you last Tuesday night as you were driving me to work. I looked at you in a certain light as you were talking away. And then I just knew...I was in love with you and didn't know what to do about it. You don't know how many times I wanted to walk out there, wake you up and lead you to this bed."

I was silent for a minute. I reached for her hand and held it. The warmth of our electric currents traveling up and down into each other made us both know in that minute that time was willing to stand still for us, that something we'd call love was knocking at our doors and we both felt we could answer, knowing who the other person was—and it was safe. "Same for me, Sophie, all truth be told. I've been fighting it, too. I—I'm stuck, you know. On the one hand I want you. On the other I don't know how I feel about all the men you see every week and what you do with them—not to mention the margin of your safety in knowing me at all!"

She raised her voice. "—no man's ever been inside me, Cable—except—well, except you-know-who when I was a young girl. But all of a sudden I want *you* inside me—like—like I suddenly grew up and now I'm a grown woman and love makes all the difference! So many men think it's just about sex. But sex without love is just another cookie on the plate. Do you understand what I'm saying, Cable?"

I sat there on the bed in the twilight with the neon sign across the street changing the colors of the room. And here was a beautiful young woman who desired me. Except she was a whore—like I was a male whore in my frolicking days, only I didn't sell it, but just gave it away. "Yeah, I understand, babe. But all that said, it doesn't necessarily mean we should act on it. You have to admit, it's kinda odd making love to a hooker who's—"

"—take me away with you, Cable! Come hear me tonight and then let's run away for a couple of days, okay? I promise you—you don't even know me—but I know you sense me. I can be so good for you—give us a chance, at least to get our feet wet together?"

I smiled at the beautiful naked woman in my bed. Her Rita Hayworth hair with the bangs over her forehead, slightly mused. "Yeah? So what's in it for me?" I jested with a smirk.

"Oh, you'd be surprised...you might even be glad I've had so much—uh, so much *experience*—I will treat you like a prince, Cable—and bring your manhood undreamed of pleasure! I realize women like poor Ida can't compete—"

243

"—oh, crap! Ida! I totally forgot to invite her tonight. I'm sure she'd love to hear you sing—"

"—she can't come anyhow. Her Mom is with her, as you know, but her Dad is coming to pick them up for dinner. I think the parents live in Palm Springs or somewhere out there in the desert. So it's a rare occasion for them, I'd say."

"Oh...well, that takes care of that."

"So? Will you take me away with you?"

"Where would you like to go—*if* we go?"

"By the sea. I love the ocean. The sounds...the smells...there's a poem I learned years ago. *As my eyes search the skies from the edge of the shore, you are here in my arms for a moment or more, then a tear rushes down to the sand and the sea, and it cries, 'come to me, come to me'.*"

"That's haunting, Sophie. I'm glad you like poetry. I'll have to read some Maria Voldt to you."

"Maria Voldt?"

"Yeah, someone I knew years ago—a young Bohemian who lived in the foothills above Ojai, near Ventura. She was connected to something wonderful."

"I love good poetry. It's like good music."

I finally got up from the bed. "You do know, lady, even great intimacy is a temporary fix."

"I'm not sure I know what you mean."

"Everything runs out, Sophie, sooner or later. That's why in the end I'm beholden to nothing—no one. I guess I'm afraid of losing—again. It's happened a lot in my life."

"Then it'll be for just *now*, Cable. You and me running from the world, huh?"

"Yeah, I guess something like that." I glanced down at her. "You know, it'd be awful tempting to strip and be with you right now. But I won't. You know why?"

"No, Cable, why?" she said, her eyes aglow.

"I know it'll sound strange to you. But it's like a beautiful statue looks best untouched. I wanna savor you as long as I can until my lusty animal side takes over and takes you. Then we'll have joined the ranks of millions of other people in the world 'doing it' and eventually coming up empty. And that hurts...sometimes a lot."

"Does it have to be like that? Isn't there some kind of happy medium? I'm not asking for the moon, Cable. Just you when you feel you want me and we can be together—a few hours, a few days, a few years."

"Get some rest, kid. I'll be out in the office sorting out some papers. I also have to make a major decision about Monday."

"Monday?"

"Remember those three guys who were here just before you and Ida left? Well, they are members of the most active German underground in America—a group called the *Lichter Grabstätte*. I've had dealings with them before."

"May I ask what they wanted?"

"Oh, not much, probably just my life. They're getting ready to pull up stakes here in the U.S. But they also wanna take one more stab at controlling things. That's my guess, anyhow."

"And you?" she asked, her eyes now wide open. "What would they want with you?"

"I'm not sure this time. But by Monday evening I've gotta say yeah or nay to one of their schemes."

"So what would prevent you from just politely saying 'no'?"

"That isn't how they play ball, Sophie. They're hardcore players and when the chips are down for them, they'd do just about anything to come up smelling like roses. Plus there's a small matter of a million bucks."

"A million dollars?!" she probed.

"Yeah, seems they're offering me a million bucks if I do what they ask of me. But I wouldn't know what that is until Monday. Probably sell out the nation. If I refuse after I've seen their headquarters, I'm dead meat. If I say no before I check out what it is, there's a fifty-fifty chance I'll survive to my next birthday, at least."

"Oh, Cable!" Sophia Legende opened her arms and the blanket fell down from her chest. Her white, solid large breasts stood out to me like lighthouses on a stormy night. I glided into them and before we knew it, our lips were clenching together like a firing squad was awaiting us. "God, I love you kissing me! When—when is your—your birthday?" she asked nervously kissing me all over my face and neck and ears. It felt great.

"September 13th. I'm too damn old for you," I sighed as I began to peel my clothes off. So there we were, an old gumshoe and a beautiful blonde courtesan about to leap off into an unknown chapter of the he and she world.

"I'll...I'll bet not! I'm just right for you," she declared under her nervous breathing. "You're a Virgo. You're business-like, enjoy the arts, intellectual, sensual only when you want to be. You have great humanity and you serve others unselfishly."

"Ya—ya don't say! Me—philanthropic? Now that's a laugh!"

"I—I want to be with you, Cable...but not here, not this way."

Something unexpected happened then. We both stopped and looked at each other. It was like we were both pros in our respective worlds and whatever wisdoms the sum total taught were now being shown as golden apples to us. "You felt it too, didn't you?" I asked.

"Yes, I don't want to spoil it. Can we wait until we go away?"

"Yeah, let's do that." I put my shirt and pants back on and the beautiful blonde with the long, fluffy hair sank into my bed under the covers and neither of us said another word about it.

It was about 10:00 p.m. when I arrived at the Bar of Music. I hadn't been there before...and found it really unique in that the area where the stage was set up was actually behind the bar! It had two huge grand pianos. Folks were seated either around the bar, which was a large half-circle following around the shape of the stage, or at tables in the main part. The place was crowded and my sexy lady was already up there singing—a dream-like vision. And she really *could* sing. Her voice was like marshmallow with spicy frosting. Funny thing about music. It can transport you in an instant or bore you almost as quick. But this night, I was in for a treat and the buxom babe in a tight-fitting gold lame gown had my undivided attention. And I was daydreaming, transported to a bedroom with her somewhere along the oceanfront in Malibu Beach! My, how odd and curious life can be!

Sophie was singing an up-tempo version of Irving Berlin's *Let's Face the Music and Dance* when I first noticed some babe sitting at a table looking at me. There were two guys with her. She was dressed to kill, too. But it was the tantalizing Miss Legende who had my full attention. Then she launched into a classic...*Dancing In the Dark* and suddenly I was in a cozy little cottage tucked in the woods and Sophie and I were making out by a little fireplace. When she got to the place, '*looking for the light of a new love to brighten up the night, I have you, love, and we can face the music together*', I was a goner. And I felt she was singing that song directly so me. Of course, so did a hundred and fifty other guys in the joint. She got well-deserved applause as she finished the song. Then the small combo started playing and my eyes drifted. Suddenly I heard a voice above me. "Hello, there...may I join you for a moment?" she asked me. It was the same babe who'd been sitting with the two men. They had disappeared. I smelled a rat and had had a few drinks too many. She had a small European accent.

"I dunno. I—I rent out for a hundred bucks an hour, lady," I commented, slurring a bit.

"You're underselling yourself, Mr. Denning," she replied, smiling at me. "May I sit?" She was about five four with a slender figure and dark shortish hair. She wore a well-tailored light-grey suit with smart red high heels.

"Yeah...yeah...sure... So I'm under-rating myself, is that it? How—how much do you think I should get paid, lady?"

"Oh...I don't know...maybe a thousand United States dollars an hour. At least." She sat directly across from me. "I'm supposed to be going home. But I had to speak to you first."

"That—that's nice of you, Miss or Mrs.—"

"—Miss Berger—Adelein Berger..."

"...so...what...what is it you wish to speak to me about, young woman with the pretty smile and bright brown eyes?"

"It's about what I came here for."

"Oh? And what might that be? I hope you're—you're not a cheap chippie—because if you are, I have to tell you I'm full up—"

"—no, Mr. Denning, quite far from that." She was wearing a marvelous silver-blue pearl necklace.

"Then what is it?"

She scooted over in her chair and whispered in my ear. "I am supposed to kill you—if you do not report to *Lichter Grabstätte* punctually day after tomorrow."

That lifted my eyelids. "You what? Why are you telling me this now? I—I kinda suspected it when old grump face showed up at my office a few days ago."

"Ya...Oscar Brandt...I do not like him. He *will* kill you."

"And you won't?" I asked, wondering what her reply might be since she was obviously a spy of some kind.

"Not now. It is a rule, Mr. Denning, we should not come face to face with our victims prior to shooting them—or whatever is decided to eliminate them with.

249

And I have contacted you on my own vermission—volursion—"

"—*volition*, Adelein—that means motivated by your own—your own private will. And just why would you tell me this?"

"Because I've been tailing you for some time and I report to Herr Brandt. I think you're an interesting man. And probably a good one. Besides, my work is almost over here. In January I lost both my brother and my uncle in the *Ardennes* battle with the Americans. I've had enough of war also. If I spare your life, I was wondering if you will put in a good word for me where it counts. I would like to become an American citizen. Can a German spy become an American citizen?"

"I don't know, Adelein. Most of the time they're shot. But I don't know—don't know enough about your character or anything. Would you make a good...good citizen?"

"I took out enough time to want to know who you are—"

"--are we huddling from the cold—or are you two just being friendly?" Sophia Legende's voice broke up the conversation. I looked up.

"Hiya, babe, this is Miss Berger who was supposed to—to kill me—but now wants a favor," I said, my drunken brain getting worse by the minute.

"Well, now, isn't that grand? All that in a friendly meeting." Sophie gave a half-smile. "What *kind* of favor? Like the kind I give, maybe? How do you do, Miss Berger. I'm Sophia Legende."

"I am pleased to meet you, Miss Legende. I wish I could sing like you sing. I'm afraid I have this light, breathy croak for a singing voice. That's about it."

We all laughed. "No, Sophie, Adelein here wants to become a U.S. citizen and disavow her allegiance to Hitler and the Gestapo—and in the bargain—I—I don't get killed."

Sophie's eyebrows raised. "Oh, so you're one of those. I always wondered what it might be like to be a female spy. Is it fun?"

"Not much," Adelein answered. "Men are pigs and sexually active twenty-four hours a day! That's all they think about, if you ask me."

"It's true, some of them. There are...are good men too, like Cable here." Then Sophie looked at me. "I've got to work tonight—can you take me out the ranch?"

"Yeah, I guess so."

"Thanks, Cable." Just then, but not really to my surprise, Oscar Brandt and his two henchmen walked in. They were in a hurry. Brandt spotted Adelein. The pretty spy kissed me quickly on the cheek and ran for the back end of the nightspot. The three men followed. "What's that all about, you think?"

"Oh, I think they'll either pump her for...for answers...or pump her full of lead—or both."

"Why don't they just pump her? I would. That's too bad—I think just pumping is more fun, don't you?" I didn't answer that question because I recalled Sophie mentioning that she was bisexual and that didn't sit too well with me, especially since she had made it clear she wanted to be with me as a male.

"You're sounding excellent, kid, I like the sultry, breathiness —quiet...desperate...looking like a million on the outside but hurting on the inside. It shows, you know."

"Thanks, Cable. It does? 'Quiet and desperate', eh?"

"Yep. It makes for a good entertainer. Suffering makes the best nightclub singers in the world, I'll wager... "

"Aren't you going to try and save the young lady those guys went after?"

"Nope. She's on her own. Birds of a feather, Sophie. Besides, I'm in enough deep shit with the Lichter Grabstätte—that German organization I told you about—so I think I'll leave the sleeping lion lay."

"Cable...do you think we could run away for a day...I'm not working tomorrow. Just twenty four hours in a beach hut together?"

"Yeah, why—why not?"

"I'll have Senator McMahon—err—my client—bring me home. Probably about 3 or 4 in the morning. I know I'll wake you, but I will be quiet and get some sleep. Then we can start early?"

"Sure, babe." I took both of her hands. "Thanks...thanks for the music tonight, lady. I—I think you're a hell of singer, you know that?"

"Really? I know you've heard a lot of them. And I don't practice nearly as much as I should. Be I guess between what I wear and what I sound like, the boss here likes me."

"So do I, Sophie....so do I. And so do all these other people around us. Notice the admiring looks? Those are for you, hon—you deserve them..."

She looked in the direction from which our little German spy exited. "Have you heard from Miss Skorkowsky—I don't know why, but I think about her."

"Yeah, so do I. I'm lost. I don't know where to start looking, but I'm trying to put pieces together as we speak. I need a few more clues. Detective work is like putting together a jigsaw puzzle. Sometimes it's just a few pieces, sometimes it's massive, with a lot of little pieces."

"I know you miss her. And you just barely got started?"

"Yep."

"I'm sorry, Cable, I hope you find her." She turned to leave and went back up to the bandstand, her lovely blonde hair waving behind her. Suddenly I was in a land of love and rainbows, a warm hearth and Sophia Legende the day after Christmas morning by my side. *Long Ago and Far Away* paralyzed me because Sophia Legende's sincerity reached out to me like an invisible specter on a beautiful night. *'Long ago and far away, I dreamed a dream and now that dream is here beside me...long the skies were overcast, but now the clouds are passed, you're here at last! Chills run up and down my spine, Alladin's lamp is mine, the dream I dreamed I dreamed was not denied me...just one look and then I knew...that all I longed for long ago was you'* caved me in until even through my half-drunken stupor I could only see that lovely vision of a woman reaching out for me up there on the stage.

One Night With You

Suddenly it was Sunday, May 27, 1945. By 10:30 a.m. we were driving toward the ocean. I'd never seen Sophia Legende so happy. Her marvelous light blue-green eyes were alive with enjoyment and anticipation. I knew in my heart she was feeling these stolen hours were just for *her*, a private moment in eternity where no one could reach us, and the silent joy of our companionship would be enough for her. And ya know? It was.

A few miles up the coast from Malibu we found a place with a few rustic, but charming cabins about a mile inland down a bumpy road. We got into Cabin #4 and decided to take a walk to the beach to get some fresh air and divest ourselves of the effects of city-life. We found a group of rocks where a marvelous sea cave stood, jagged and worn by the surf for millions of years. The sky was clear blue and the wind almost non-existent. But ya know, it was just like life. On the horizon loomed a giant bank of fog that was making its way in toward us. So we enjoyed frolicking in the surf for a few minutes, but the water was cold and Sophie wore only a pleated skirt and a white blouse with no brassiere underneath. Later I learned she didn't have on any panties, either! Ah—a fun-loving woman was Sophie Legende!

The fog came rolling in about 2:00 p.m. with a chilling breeze behind it and so we made our way back to our little cabin. There was a small fireplace and some wood out back. So I lit the old brick thing up and soon the chill began to leave. We'd purchased a little wine, bread and cheese that we sat and ate before the fire. I saw a little girl now and then in Sophie's eyes, as if the wonder and mystery of the moment was a brand new adventure for her.

"Oh, Cable, even if we don't do anything except this—I'm completely happy!" She leaned over and kissed my cheek. "It's you, Mr. Denning, that makes all this possible, you know."

"I aim to please, Miss Legende," I said lightly as we clinked glasses containing the wine. "I want you to have a good time, Sophie, and forget all the crap you go through every week. Be a child again. That's what I do when I go roaming up at Bronson Park."

She looked at me with such a sweetness I don't think I'll ever forget it. "No wonder women fall in love with you, Cable. You just *fit* so many of a woman's ideals. You're good at heart, what you do professionally is to be admired, you're tall and dark and handsome, you're very sexy—and you're here with *me!*"

"Ah, but you forget the risks a woman takes knowing me. She's gotta jump through a few hoops as well, lady. I'm dangerous to be around in more ways than one, Sophie, and to be involved with me romantically is tantamount to fighting a battle against a raging tide in a typhoon."

She smiled as she took a long drink. "All that, huh? Well, truth be known, I don't care. I just want you, Cable. Now. I don't even know why or maybe none of that matters, but here we are—and I want you to make love to me—I mean, *really* make love!"

I took a deep breath and thought of Nadia momentarily. "You sure of that, now? I'm content just to hang out with you—even though you're so desirable that if I thought about it—"

"—I have a lot...to offer...Cable...don't think about all that other stuff, please? Just us, here and now."

"Okay. Do you like poetry?"

"I love poetry—you know I do—especially if it's good."

"I think this is one of her best..." I went over to my coat got out a carefully rolled sheet of paper. Then I sat down beside Sophie. She locked her arm in mine as I began to read:

> *"We were migratory, like the birds that circle*
> *To land, I was circling around you to alight*
> *In the hand of your embrace to keep me*
> *Safe from the world that grates at my fate*
> *Each day. My aching heart makes me say:*
> *You, of all men, came to harness me*
> *Tether my rope on the slope of life*
> *Even though I knew so soon you would be*
> gone
> *And, like an old song half-remembered, I'd sing*
> *It in my silent repose because I chose to love you."*
> mv

Sophie's eyes were watering as she wiped the tears. "Oh, my, Cable—I—I didn't expect that. Is this that lady you spoke of?"

"Yeah, Maria Voldt—poetess extraordinaire."

"Who is she?"

"Doesn't matter, really—she's dead now. It was a case of city-bred man meets country girl who had the

256

soul of a mistress of words and a closeness to nature. We had a very brief love affair when I was hiding out in the mountains above Ojai some years ago. The bad guys traced me, and killed her to get back at me. So, you see, I carry a few other monkeys on my back, Sophie—not the least of which is the guilt that I was the reason a few people died violent deaths."

"Oh, Cable, I'm sorry—I know it pains you. I sense she was in love with you. Is that why you drink and smoke and womanize so much?"

"Who knows? To try and forget? I'm not so sure. Maybe because a part of me doesn't care all that much for me anymore."

She nibbled at my ear. "*I* care for you, mister. Can that be enough for right now?" She took my hand and placed it on her breasts. "I've been wanting to do this for a long time. Oh..." she sighed as she closed her eyes. "I'm tingling down there for you, Cable. Please, draw those shades and let's go to bed."

With the cold fog meandering outside and a warm fireplace crackling away, I stripped. But the professional Sophie retained a sheer white nighty as she slipped under the covers. "I can see I'm gonna have to earn my way to you, eh?" I joked.

"Yes, indeedy, Mr. Cready!" she commented wryly. "You'll have to nuzzle your way into me. Just don't move too fast. I'm afraid I'll blink, and it'll already be tomorrow." As I scooted in beside her and she saw my half-erect male member, she smiled. "Cable...can you turn on your glow and take me away?"

"I don't know. Let's find out. But...I am concerned about your current status of female vulnerability. Can you get pregnant? I hate to use anything, but if I—"

"—no, Cable, I want nothing between us. I'm 29 years old, so I guess I could conceive. But as I've told you, I've had no activity inside me for at least fifteen years. In fact, if I conceived your child, I would love it! I've always wanted a child of my own. Please, don't hold back, when you take me, hold me tight—you won't break me!" she tittered.

"You know, Sophie, somehow I believe that about you. So...where would you like me to begin, lady?" I asked with a grin.

"Where do you usually begin?" she countered.

"With this..." I slowly bent over to her lips and kissed her gently. She responded by wrapping that long blonde hair around our heads as she kissed me back. Soon she placed my hand on her womanhood and I began to massage it. She began to tremble and soon sat up, all but ripped her nighty off and dug into me like a weasel going after a groundhog! I moved down her body and put my mouth to that slit below her mound. She sighed and moaned and was so wet that my tongue almost weighted down from the thickness of it. She couldn't stand it anymore, so she reached for my arms and brought me up to her mouth once more, while at the same moment my fully erect manhood penetrated that lovely, very warm wetness and she went into near convulsions with the pleasure of it! She let out with a passionate cry. Then we spun away into that land of passion and ecstasy that desire evokes and we were lost in each other.

Two hours later we lay spent and naked upon the bed. The fire had dwindled to hot coals in the fireplace, but desire continued to make us cling to one another. Why do some people evoke this closeness out of us more than others? "Did you know that you're a phantom bird?" I finally broke the silence.

"A phantom bird?" she laughed, those green-blue eyes alive with fulfillment and happiness.

"Yeah, once I knew a man named Jedediah Penn who had a brother. The brother's wife painted this incredible picture of a woman turning into a bird and she called it *Woman Is a Phantom Bird*—she's present, but elusive, and above all, no one can possess her."

"That is true, I believe. I wish men would get that. You can have us, but not without respecting our terms of engagement, so to speak. What do you think?"

I loved this aspect about Sophia Legende. She was intelligent as hell and capable of going from love making to deep philosophical discussion. "Well, my experience tells me not all women know who they are or what they want. Plus females in general are subservient to men in most societies. Child bearing, food preparation and doing the wash. Ain't that about it for most women except your kind of woman?"

"Maybe," she laughed. Then she felt my crotch. "Oh! We're so wet, Cable! Did you spurt a lot into me?"

"Yep. How did it feel?"

"Cable...it's—it's, uh, hard to describe...it felt so wonderful...for the first time in my life, believe it or not, I feel like a genuine, bona fide woman!"

"That's great, babe—I'm so glad I made you feel like that."

"What about you? Were you satisfied with my—my special favors? You do know it's taken me years to refine some of those skills."

I laughed. "Well, you know, Sophie, I'm just kinda plain and simple. I love great raw sex with a hot babe. That's about it."

"Well, whatever it was—I loved it," she chortled. "Do we ever get a rematch?"

We both got sad for a moment. "I don't know, Sophie. I may not even be alive come Monday night. I still haven't made up my mind as to what I'm gonna do about Oscar Brandt and the Lichter Grabstätte."

"Oh, dear God, Cable—what—what are your alternatives?"

"In a way, it's kinda like marriage...I'm damned if I do and damned if I don't! Either way, things will change around like a chess game board when two pros are playing for keeps."

In the early evening we went out for a simple but nice dinner at a newly opened restaurant a few miles down the Roosevelt Highway, called *The Sea Lion Restaurant*. It used to be the Las Flores Inn until last year. Wasn't any wonder why they chose that for the new name...you could hear a lotta seals barking nearby. I called Ida and told her I would be outta town tomorrow and not to come in. She said she might drop in during the afternoon and had I seen Sophie. I lied that I hadn't because I didn't wanna hurt her—but suspected she'd be in tomorrow after she got through with her work at the mansion. You know how women can be about other women when they like you. Hell, men can be even worse!

That night Sophie and I made love four more times. We bonded like Adam and Eve in the Garden of Paradise and slept wrapped around each other like two kittens in a warm box.

All the way home the next morning I was thinking about what Ayana had said about "two will live, two will die". I needed to know before the bodies started piling up. We packed up Sophie's things and I drove her over to Ida's place. "I suppose I shouldn't say anything about our stolen night to Ida?" she asked me.

"Uh...well, I'd prefer it if you didn't. You know how secretaries are."

"I know how *women* are, Cable. You can't fool me. I know she's not only crazy about you, but that you've had her."

"Well, yeah, we slipped up a couple of times."

"I won't mention it again."

I patted her on her knee. "Thanks. How are you feeling, babe?"

"How am I feeling? Full of you and wishing it could go on forever. But I'm worried about you, Cable—*what are you going to do*?!"

"Well, Sophia Legende, I've never been one to skirt around a situation. I usually face the lion in his lair. Tonight I'm gonna make that call and tell 'em I'm gonna be there to see the laboratory and ask what could I do that's worth a million bucks beside sell out my country."

"And then after that—you—you're dead, right?" Sophie flustered.

"Maybe...maybe not. I've gotten outta worse scrapes."

"You have?"

"Yep."

We pulled up to Ida's place. Sophie looked at me with that one blonde bang over her right eye and those beautiful orbs glistening at me. Her lips were moist and inviting. "I want to kiss you, Cable. But I want to kiss you 'hello', not goodbye. Will you see me again? Now that I've got an itch for you—you know where."

I chuckled. "If I'm alive and kickin', yes...yes, Sophie Legende. Yeah, babe, I'd enjoy seeing you again...very much, indeed. Please just be considerate for Ida's feelings, that's all I ask."

"Of course, I'm very fond of Ida. She's a good woman."

I escorted Sophie to Ida's front door. Ida smiled and welcomed us. I stayed only long enough to ask Ida if she was coming in later and she said maybe not since she was pretty caught up and would probably spend the rest of the day getting Sophie acquainted with her new surroundings—and maybe the two of them would go shopping—or something. It was the 'or something' that always bothered me. What *do* childless women talk about when they're together? If it ain't men and lost loves, then is it the kind of makeup they wear, clothes they love, movies, movie stars or things purchased at a store—what else could it be?

Chapter 6

STRASSENEUZUNG (Crossroads)

It was Monday night. About 5:30, late that afternoon, I called the number Oscar Brandt had given me and those damn Germans had me blindfolded and in the back of a limo in no time. I rode for about thirty minutes and I could smell freshly baked bread in the air close by. Soon we were in a building and before they removed the blindfold, it felt like we descended in an elevator. I was brought immediately into the presence of Oscar Brandt. He was alone in a dimly lit office with a large table with maps, designs and diagrams strewn about. "Ah, Herr Denning..." he said as he greeted me. "I am glad you have decided to...to see tings our vay!"

"Hello, Brandt. Yeah, looks like either my love for money or desire to preserve my life came into play—so here I am. I told myself earlier, there's nothing like facing the lion in his lair."

"Ya, und your predecessors at the Oculus...told me about your lack of...*fear*...Herr Denning. To be commended...so today ve have two categories of subject matter to discuss." He led me to the large table. "Vahn has to do vis zat lovely blonde lady you vere vis over za night. Vhat I am going to say may disturb you, but zat is not my concern. Spoken frankly, ve have near-perfected an alteration of ze *dna factor* so ve may 'modify' a human being. As you might postulate, finding volunteers is not easy." Then he spoke very slowly. "Especially...*half-alien ones.* Ve want you to impregnate Miss Legende, und zen ve vant to extract her forming fetus und—und, vell, shall ve say, 'toy' vis it a bit to create a new human being, sird generation, fully utilizing your extra-terrestrial genetic strand code."

"Third generation?"

"Ya. Ze first two vere very unstable—nine, actually *monstrosities*, Herr Denning. Ve have come a long vay since zen."

"You know, Brandt, that's one of the reasons I hate people like you. You don't give a damn about individual considerations, let alone feelings. Everything's in a test tube for your kind of despicable creature, ain't it?"

"Vell, your vitriol is noted, Herr Denning, but after all, ve must advance ze human race beyond its current archaic und stupid state of existence, vould you not zay?"

"On that point I might agree with you. But then again, I'm not crazy about the human race, either, let alone demented individuals like you and *your* kind."

He studied my face. "You mean zat, don't you? Are you a German-hater or a born pessimist? Or have you zeen too much already?"

"I think I've seen too much. It kinda spoils the appetite to wanna keep goin'. What keeps people like you alive, if you don't mind my asking?"

"*Determination*...ya, dat's it—determination to honor ze Führer's vishes. Ve are a determined people. Ya...zat keeps me alive, Herr Denning, and experimenting vis vhat ve vill call za *ever-new*."

"Okay, so while I'm trying to digest this first proposition you leveled at me so I can ask you appropriate questions, what's the second—I can't wait..."

He chuckled more or less under his breath. "Vell, it is simple. Ve transform you into a twin of President Franklin Delano Roosefelt und call a meeting of his most important atomic people—zen you ask to see all za plans—ze latest! You photograph zem und present zem to me. Zen...you may live a life of luxury in a country of your choice."

I couldn't believe these guys! "Oh, is that all? You guys must be desperate! And if I said yes for a million bucks, just how would you implement the plan—*and pay me*, by the way?"

"Oh, *implement*...big vord for ze little man. Again, simple: ve now have za means to duplicate from vahn cell an entire human being...*gut gemacht, nein*? Za real Mr. President vill be put to sleep temporarily—und zen—zip! you take over und a few days later you, Herr Denning, are a million dollars richer!" Then he reflected. "Paying you...vell, ve could send it to you special delivery—or deposit it in a bank or repository of your choice."

"Tax free, I assume?" I jested.

"Very funny—naturlich! So vhat do you zay?"

I was thinking of Erond and his proposition about breeding with the females of his praying mantis-potato bug genus. "I think I like the first deal the best. Does it pay a million bucks, too?"

The plump little man laughed. "You have to be joking! How can I compensate you za same?! Zey are very different—vahn a serious und potential life-threatening undertaking—vhile za ozer is fun!"

"Maybe, maybe not—it ain't always fun, ya know..."

"Ya? Is zat so? I vould not have imagined!"

"Try it sometime, buddy." I was thinking fast. I was also missing Nadia. "If you've been following me so damned much, then do you Krauts know about where Nadia Skorkowsky might have disappeared to? I'll make a deal with you—I'll do the breeding program for free if you find Miss Skorkowsky."

"Nadia Skorkowsky? Ah, ze opera zinger—ya. I know nuzzing about it. But...I *am* disappointed in you. Somehow I sought you might be...vell, bluntly stated, a little more adventuresome, Herr Denning. 'Free' means nuzzing to us." He took a deep breath. "Zo...you must see zis Sophia Legende *very soon* or za deal is—is *off!*" Brandt warned.

"And what if she refuses? Some women are sensitive about things like having their embryos taken away for scientific purposes."

His eyes narrowed to slits. "She cannot refuse you...after all, she is *in love*—is zat not so? But as soon as she is pregnant—ve vill come to put her to sleep, und zen steal away za teeny, veeny embryo. She von't know." Then his eyes widened with visions of grandeur. "Und zen some new species vill be born unto za vorld, Denning, *a new species*—somezing so diametrical-ly...*'different'*...und opposed to ze ignorant Slavic brains zat now populate our little planet."

But I was only listening off and on while Brandt bragged on. I was thinking about FDR. "So how long does it take to 'grow' a new American president, Brandt?"

He was still in his dream. "Oh...perhaps two months, give or take."

"How about inhabiting his present body by setting FDR's consciousness aside for someone else's?"

Now I had his attention. "You...can do zat?"

"Not me, but someone I know can. He doesn't need the money but he might be your man, so to speak." I was thinking the praying mantis-potato bug manifesting in front of chubby little Brandt. "He will have a price, but it won't be money. Something else you guys might have."

"Ya? Now I *am* intrigued, Herr Denning. Vhen can ve meet...dis magic man and me?"

"I don't know. I'll see if I can get a hold of him."

Then he got stern and curious. "Zo...just how do you know all dis sings? zat knowledge is not common information for a 'gumshoe detective'—is zat how you say it?"

"Ya—errr...yeah. Now, look—I'm starting to sound like you." He smiled just enough to notice. "But no, not common at all. It just so happens that he wanted to inhabit my body for 72 hours. He didn't quite make that. But at least 48 hours is probably your top bet." I took out a cigarette.

"Please...Herr Denning...do not smoke in mein office. It is not good to inhale eefen ze used smoke—und cigarettes vill shorten your life."

I put it away. "Yeah, okay...sure."

"Vhat is dis man's name?" he interrogated me.

I cleared my throat. "Well, Brandt, the good news for you is that he *isn't a man*—but I'm sure both Lichter Grabstätte and the Oculus are familiar with visitors from other star systems and dimensions."

"Ya...to be sure...so...zis being is zen an extraterrestrial?"

267

"You might say that. He's a cross between a praying mantis and what we know as a potato bug, the cricket family. He's highly advanced and I would urge you not to mess with him in a negative way."

"Ya...I zee vhat you mean...my, my but you are curious sort of man. I do know our records indicate you are, however, only one-half human male. Ze other half is comprised of those silly well-wishers, ze *Sens Parafactors.* Zey vant to help, I suppose, in zer own vay—but it is tedious vhat zey do. Gene splicing to *integrate* instead of *change* zis dismal species here on earth. Der Führer vishes only zat, you know. To change ze degrading mixed blood, to eliminate ze culls, so it vere, und create a new *super race of beings!* Heil, Hitler!" he declaimed.

I walked toward the other side of the room. "Ya know, Brandt, truth be known, I don't *know* what the truth is. When I was young, I thought I did. It's like never reaching the end, never quite attaining what you set out to accomplish." Then I turned to him. "Even you and your Führer—don't you know this cannot be? Don't you know the reptilians will defeat you with lies and numbers too many to conquer? Even *if* Hitler is right and Jews are corrupt and Slavic peasants stupid and mad scientists gone crazy with the atomic bomb and politicians feathering their own nests—the *real world goes on*, Brandt, some overseeing eye watches us and decrees what shall be in the end. One day even the reptilians will lose and someone else will take their place, for better or for worse. It's just the way it is."

"Vell, vell! Such a discourse! You are very articulate, Herr Denning. So...vhat is ze potato bug's name, if you don't mind?" he insisted.

268

"*Erond Mantis Spiricus.* You'd like him…"

"Sounds like a Roman soldier to me. Und now, you are certain zis creature inhabited your body for—for vhat?"

"He wanted to screw my girlfriend with my body but his desire."

"Oh…zat casts a strange light on za situation. Did it vork?"

"Nope. His psyche couldn't take the energy after a while."

"Ya…I zee…vell, goes to show ve are all different now, aren't ve?"

"Yeah, Brandt, we're all different…"

The Voice of My Heart

The minute I got out of the secret headquarters for Lichter Grabstätte and they removed my blindfold, I knew I couldn't go home. I had to go somewhere for a late night drink, somewhere where music and gaiety reigned and I could somehow feel real again.

So I drove down to Misty Sheridan's old haunt, the *La Monica Ballroom.* I didn't know if she would still be singing there, because it was going through a lot of changes the last time I was there. But it was Monday night late and the joint was dark. So I cruised along Santa Monica Boulevard until I saw a place I'd never ventured into before. It was called *The Orange Note*, a small club whose neon sign displayed an orange with a musical note stem on it. I got out of the car and put a Lucky Strike to my lips. I was about to light up when I felt a sudden pain in my chest and my left arm began to go

269

numb. It hurt so damn much that I fell against my little Dodge coup and held on to the rider's side door handle. Slowly I made my way into the car and sat in the rider's seat where there was more room. I tried to breathe deep but the pain persisted. So this is what it was like, when the Grim Reaper gave the warning signs. Finally my smoking, drinking and general way of life had caught up with me. Well, I figured, 45 years ain't so bad. Crap, I didn't even acknowledge my birthday this year. Neither did anyone else. So, what the hell, maybe this was it. *'Cable Denning Dies Behind the Wheel'.* It coulda said that. But there's another knowing deep inside, the one that told me it wasn't my turn—*yet.* After about twenty minutes the pains subsided and I got out and thought maybe that drink would do me some good. But I'd keep the smokes out of my mouth for the rest of the night.

A small combo was playing. There were only a few scattered souls sitting around. I went up to the bar and ordered a hot whiskey in a snifter. Soon the bartender delivered and I felt much better after the first sip of the hot alcohol. There was a nicely dressed middle-aged woman sitting next to me looking at me through the bar mirror. "You're—you're pretty handsome, mister, but you're pale as hell—like you just seen a ghost or something," she pronounced with a decidedly British accent.

"I just did—*mine.* I think I just had a heart attack outside," I answered.

"You—you don't say. Well, that's how my husband died, ya know. He just said he didn't feel too hot, got a tight chest and died on the sofa listening to Edgar Bergen and Charlie McCarthy on the radio."

"Sorry to hear that." The lady was pretty drunk but not objectionable. "You must miss him." Just then the combo began to play a swinging version of *The Way You Look Tonight* and memories flooded my brain like a fresh new tide in from Malibu.

"Naw, not much...you see, we weren't that close. I'm—I'm not so sure I even loved the bloke. He worked, came home, listened to the radio, went to bed, got up and went to work. Fourteen years of that. My best—best years, mister. My name's Lynne, by the way." She extended her hand, I took it. It was warm.

"I'm Cable, pleased to meet you, Lynne."

"Do you want me to take you to a doctor—I mean, for your heart?"

"No, thanks, I'm okay. I'm kind of a fatalist, I guess. When my time comes, it comes and that's it."

"You men are—are all—all alike," she stammered. "You're slaves to habit—habit kills, ya know. If it's the wrong kinda habit, that is."

"So what brings *you* in on a quiet Monday night?" I asked her. She was actually quite pretty with wisps of silver in her light-brown hair. She was wearing a decently low-cut black dress with a fine but odd silver neckpiece with a strange emblem suspended from it.

"Oh, me? I guess I get lonely looking out of my—my kitchen window all the time. I don't like shopping. I don't like housework."

"What *do* you like?"

"Archeology and handsome men like you. But take a look, Cable, I'm forty-five now. Nobody wants a once-attractive forty-five year old woman anymore. I'm—I'm a has-been in our society. Especially if you have a German last name. My last name is Fromme."

"I think you're still very attractive, Lynne. Everyone's someone."

"Or *was* someone. I—I think at some point we—we probably cease being counted in the world...someone cuts us loose and we drift until—well, until we die. That's—that's it, don't you think?"

"Yeah, it could be. Would you like to dance?"

She looked at me incredulously. "You—you wanna dance with a broken down old broad who's half-drunk?"

"Yep. Come on! By the way, don't they have a singer in this joint? What's a band without a singer?"

She put her drink on the bar and took my hand and we went out into the crowded little dance floor. "To be sure they do. She's a real knockout, too—*Alana Charity*. But she only comes in Wednesday through Saturday nights. Don't fall in love with her, though. Her boyfriend's a big time mobster here in town." Then she moved in close and whispered into my ear. "Thank you, Cable, this is the first time I've danced in a public place in years. By the way, I'm forty-five, too..."

"You already said that. You're welcome, Lynne. You don't look that old, though."

"You see, forty-five's different for a man," she returned. "Women grow old to men after thirty, thirty-five these days. Men want hot young stuff, don't you think?" She looked up at me and smiled. "But you wanted to dance with me instead of that pretty young thing looking at you from that table of young things—over there."

272

I glanced at a platinum blonde who, dollars to donuts, was a German spy from the good ol' Lichter Grabstätte.

"I'm used to it," I answered. "I'm here with you now. I kinda like it. You're also a good dancer. How'd you learn?"

"Lawrence never liked to dance, so I would go out to a day-club and dance downtown. That—that was a life-saver. I—I would've left Lawrence, but I had no income of my own." She laughed to herself. "So I was the domestic slave and he was—he was the—the bread winner." Then she looked up into my eyes. "What about you? Your fedora, your trench coat when you came in. Are you secret service or a policeman?"

"Nope, just a plain ol' private dick."

She double-checked me, her eyes widening in humorous curiosity, her mouth in an anticipating smile.

I knew what she was thinking. "You know, private eye, detective—the guy who becomes a voyeur, taking Kodak pictures through windows of cheating husbands, wives, lovers and the like."

"Oh…" She smiled. "Well, it could have meant something else."

"By the way, that—that attractive dangly thing on your necklace. What exactly is it?"

"I'm glad you like it. It's a *Minoan Phestos disc*—I think this is the most singularly important find during my archeological days. No one knows its exact language, nor how old it is. Personally? I think it's a map of the visible star systems and how wonderfully vast this universe is."

"It attracts me for some reason," I said, studying her breasts at the same time.

"Know what I think?"

"What do you think?"

"That it's our true native language from another star system. I found that so many times some races of people were just so advanced and technological they just didn't fit the time slots they were allotted by history—they couldn't have evolved the way Darwin said—I mean, from this planet. Sounds crazy, huh?"

I smiled inside. "Oh, I don't know. I've seen some pretty strange things in my life. Yeah, I can see that as possible. It's an old planet."

"Sounds like you're at least open, Cable. I like that. In fact, I think I like you a lot. I'm glad we met."

"Me, too, Lynne, me too…"

I left *The Orange Note* and Lynne Fromme that night thinking that my life had changed. It wasn't any better or any worse, just different. At any time I could drop dead from a heart attack and no one would hardly know the difference. Maybe Ida or Sophie or even Lt. Keith might miss me, but I wouldn't make a dent in the inexorable ride the human world was taking toward its own doom. I felt once the atomic bomb exploded, that would be the beginning of the end. Somehow through the years life would be degraded an inch at a time until one day whether through population explosion or atomic explosion as a result of stupid arms races to see who can kill the most of who—one day—the human race would mostly perish. Lamentably, along with it would go nature and the beautiful world of spontaneous creation that would go on evolving ad infinitum. But the Mother herself, good ol' planet Earth, would outlive us all. She might limp for a while, but she'd continue on. The problem had always been humans. And if remnants build themselves up again in numbers and invention, then it would begin all over again. And then the big out-breath would begin to exploit her riches all over again until one day, maybe a million years or less from now, she would be depleted and sustain a lot fewer numbers. Maybe we'd all be aborigines eking out a living honestly from the soil. Yep, the more I looked at it, the more I felt humans were a failed experiment.

Now, to get back to the office and face some facts. Cases in point, what happened to Nadia Skorkowsky? When is the bomb gonna go off in Alamogordo? Can I outwit the pompous and sharp German minds in the Lichter Grabstätte? And would Sophia Legende *catch* when we made love regularly and could her embryo be taken without her knowing about it? And how could we keep it from hurting Ida? It looked like my workweek was cut out for me.

End Part I

I, DESTROYER OF WORLDS

PART II

CONTENTS

Chapter 7

HOLD BACK THE TIME, MY LOVE

It was Wednesday, June 6, 1945. A year ago today allied forces came storming onto the beaches of Normandy in France. Well over 9,000 Americans died that D-Day morning. The amphibious landing included about 160,000 men, 5,000 ships and more than 11,000 airplanes. It was the beginning of the end for Hitler. Between that invasion and getting his ass kicked in Russia, the handwriting was on the wall. Why didn't smart men like Oscar Brandt see that? Or by now did the Germans have their heads in the sand too deep?

Ida sat at her desk typing away. I wanted to ask her how she and Sophie were getting along, but I refrained because I didn't want to show any egg on my face that I desired Sophie so damn much I could taste it and she could tell. And, I had to get to work on this getting Sophie to conceive thing. Oscar Brandt and I settled on ten thousand bucks for the delivery, plus a promise he'd never ask me again. Nothing was mentioned about my personal safety afterward. And talking about breeding, I hadn't heard from Erond Mantis Spiricus on that subject. Personally, I hoped he forgot about it. But I doubt it. But niggling at me beneath all of it was what the hell happened to Nadia Skorkowsky? Where was she? Where could I begin to look? What similar cases were there that mimicked her kidnapping?

Adeline and Cable Jr. were coming out to visit on Friday the 8th and would stay in Mom's old place at the end of Vine Street in the Hollywood Hills. The place had been locked up and will probably need a cleaning. My son would be 12 years old this month! What did he look like? I'd only seen him a handful of times during all these years. I don't think he liked me. Well, what the hell, who could blame him? But what would he want to know about his Dad? Or his Mom? The whole thing unsettled me. I wouldn't know how to handle the kid. What to say, what to do—hell, I was hardly a good model for a growing young American boy. Every once in a while I thought of his mother and when she and Nan might be back in this world. *What a nutso life I've lived!* I said to myself that morning. I knew one thing for sure. I was never cut out to be the *'good ol' Dad'* type of guy. When I picked them up at the train station I'd have to look decent, shaved and make sure I don't drink too much that day. And ever since what I thought to be a heart attack, I'd cut down on my smoking a little. At least for now.

The phone rang. "Yeah, Cable Denning here."

"Denning, this is Lester Keith. Just checking up on you. Have you recovered from your amnesia of drunken brawls and robbing banks?"

"I told you what happened there, Lester. C'mon—how many years have you known me?"

"Too damned many. But for now, I'm givin' you the benefit of the doubt because I need your services."

"What, again? How come you're always nice to me when you need me—but most of the time you treat me like shit?"

"Oh, just call it fatherly love, Denning."

282

"Yeah, so what can I do for you?"

"Well, I got this strange case I'm workin' on, see? And it don't quite add up in my book."

"Exactly what doesn't add up?"

"Well, to be perfectly frank, I may be goin' nuts myself. You see, I got this Dr. Pritchard locked upstairs in the clink for the murder of three people who existed yesterday, but don't exist no more, as of this morning! Now I know you've had experience along those lines, Denning. So I want you to come down to the morgue with me and see what the three supposedly dead people left behind them when they disappeared."

I smiled to myself. "Yeah? Welcome to life down hardball alley, Lieutenant. It's these little occurrences that remind you now and then that I haven't been hallucinating these past years. Okay, swell. What time shall I meet you?"

"Well, how about 7:30 p.m. at the morgue?"

"Yeah, okay."

"One other thing. Have you ever heard of a mobster named *Nick Milano*? He's got his ass in the middle of this thing."

"Nope. Can't say I have. What's he got to do with this case?"

"I'm not sure, but I think someone set him up to make it look like he killed the two guys and one woman that ended up on the slabs at the coroner's office."

"If you have 'no body of evidence', as I recall you saying, Lester, then you've got nothing to hold him on, right?"

"Wrong. Wait until you see what I've seen with some secret service schmuck looking over my shoulder."

"But you don't think he did it?"

"I know Milano—it ain't his style. He's a smooth operator. You know the type...rich, handsome, slick so it ain't easy to pin anything on 'im and make it stick—oh, and hangs around pretty babes like you do."

"Oh, a kind of gangster version of Cable Denning, huh?"

"Let's put it this way—even so—when you see what you'll see, you'll realize Milano *couldn't have done it!*"

"Now you've got my curiosity piqued. See you tonight..." We hung up and I sensed I was going to see something really strange downtown.

Just as I was about to address Ida about something, the phone rang again. "Yeah, Cable Denning here," I voiced in my usual gruff manner.

"Is Ida there? If she is, pretend I'm someone else." It was Sophie. "I'm going berserk wanting you, Cable. I don't even like my work anymore. I just want you. Oh, and speaking of which, can you take me to work tonight—maybe about 9:30 or so?"

"Yes, Mrs. Lorenzo," I said, making up a name. "I guess I could do that. Tell me what address you live at."

"Don't come to Ida's. I'll tell her I'm taking the streetcar out to Beverly Hills, okay? I'll wait at the corner. I need you, Cable..."

"Yeah, okay, Mrs. Lorenzo. I'll see you around 9:30." I hung up.

Three For the Price of One

The City Morgue was always a depressing place to visit. Not just because it was stuffed with stiffs, but because of its drab, lifeless look. Frank A. Nance had just retired the end of last month from the Los Angeles Coroner's office and was succeeded by Ben H. Brown. I didn't know much about Brown. I got there about 7:45 and Lt. Lester Keith was inside waiting. "Can't tell time, Denning? I've been waiting around for you in this damn place for over twenty minutes."

"You oughtta feel at home here, Lester."

"Very funny. So, soon as I gather up Dr. Sarino, we'll get down to business." We walked to a little office down the hall and found a Filipino man with a very gentle disposition. But he had a worried look on his face. He led us downstairs to a locked room. Inside there were eight gurney drawers all tagged with different colors. The doctor opened one. There was the very fresh-looking corpse of a fine looking gentleman who had a small pink scar over his right eye. I don't know why that stood out to me, but it did. Maybe because it was pink. Then the doc opened a second drawer next to it. I was astounded. An exact duplicate of the other fellow presented itself. Dr. Sarino did the same with a third drawer and out slid an *exact duplicate of the first two men!*

"The Secret Service men have asked me not to show this again—to anyone. So this will be your last look. They are taking the bodies with them somewhere," Sarino said.

"Yeah, and I'll bet I know why. Gee, they so pretty," I said. "Three for the prince of one."

"Funny man. Cut out the joking at a time like—this is serious shit we're dealin' with here."

"You don't know the half of it, Lieutenant. It's like unidentified flying objects these days—no one wants to

285

talk about them. So, they'll sweep it all under a rug and that'll be that."

"How do you know that?" Lt. Keith challenged me.

"C'mon, Lieutenant, you've seen it a hundred times. That's how they keep secrets from you and me."

"Thanks, Dr. Sarino," Keith said. We left the building. "I think you're full of bullshit most of the time, Denning. Wanna grab a quick cup of coffee and I'll try to forget some of the things you say, okay?"

"Yeah, why not?" I said, knowing I had a busy night ahead of me. We found a little place near Broadway and Aliso streets. It was busy, so we found a small table at the end of the counter. "So whatta ya really think, Cable?" the policeman asked me.

"You called me 'Cable'—does this mean were going steady?"

"Shut up and listen! This ain't no piddley little nothing, buster. This is big time, ya know! I saw it in the faces of the Federal men. They were runnin' scared when they saw those three bodies. But what I can't figure is the link between them and Nick Milano. That was his likeness. I got some mug shots downtown and that's him alright. He's hard to trace down, but he has a singing girlfriend who works at a little jazz club on Santa Monica Boulevard toward the beach, *The Orange Note,* I think it's called. Her name is Alana something or other."

How strange it was that I should've happened to stumble upon that club just nights ago! "Yeah, *Charity*. Her name's Alana Charity."

"That sounds about right. How did you know?"

"Well, I was on my way to the La Monica Ballroom last Monday night, but it was closed. I wanted a drink, so I spotted the *Orange Note* just down the street."

"Now ain't that a coincidence? Anyway, I'd do it myself, but Milano knows me. Maybe you could go in and pump the babe for where he might be. I can't just let this thing rest, Denning. It's eatin' at me. I've let too many of these anomalies whiz past me, pretending they don't exist—but now I'm beginning to see they do. Maybe you were right after all, the goddamn world is infested with aliens!"

"Well, maybe not infested, but at least somewhat 'populated' by beings that look like us but aren't really us. And who knows, maybe it's us, Lester." I took out a cigarette, then decided not to smoke. Keith noted it. "So, I'll pop over there later tonight."

"Thanks, Denning. Let me know as soon as you find anything. I can't let this one slip by. I just might not sleep at night knowin' the world is, as you say, 'populated' by extra-terrestrial *things.*"

"Yeah, but we're things to *them.* What's the difference?"

"Plenty. We were here first. If we don't nab these bastards, they'll take over everything—even I can see that!"

"Maybe they already have, Lester. Ever think of that?"

"No, and I don't wanna think about that. One day at a time, mister." He paid for our coffee and we parted.

I had a little time to kill before I picked up Sophie, so I decided to take a famous Cable Denning walk along another Boulevard of Broken Dreams—downtown Los

Angeles...1945 at 8:45 p.m. A overly painted prostitute who'd seen better days, a WWI veteran selling leaded pencils at a street corner, sailors, marines and army men popping in and out of the myriad of cheap bars and nightclubs, a newspaper boy calling out in the night, a cop talking to a shoe shine boy, smells coming up out of the grating in the gutter... a cross between sewerage and won-ton soup...a fire truck screaming through the night—these were the sights and sounds I knew, as if I were voyeur into a thriving, pulsing nighttime exist-ence. But there were the quiet ones, too, those that hid in the darkness of an alley way, lost and forgotten, eking out a day to day survival amid the debris.

As she promised, Sophia Legende was on the street corner when I drove up in my little Dodge coupe. She looked wonderful in a light grey skirt and a white blouse, unbuttoned at the top just enough. She got in and she leaned over to kiss me. "Hello, Mr. Denning. I'm happy to see you!"

I kissed her. "Hello, babe." I resented taking her out to the mansion because I knew other men would kiss and fondle and paw her all night. "You sparkle tonight. Where to?" I kidded her.

"Forever with you, Cable...just forever...it doesn't really matter where—as long as I'm with you." She looked at me in the darkness as headlights came and went, lighting our faces. "I know...you don't have to tell me, I hate it, too..."

"Hate what?"

"That I have to share my body with any other man. But you do know, I'm not letting any other man in—where you go, honey. You do know that, don't you?"

"Yep, I guess I do. Yeah, and I guess I think about it, maybe more than I should. But that's what you do. So? What am I supposed to do about it?"

"Well, you can make me a legal part of your life and let me stay home make bread and pasta, fix you a drink when you come home." Then she looked out her side window. "But neither of us is the marrying kind, are we? But I have thought about it, lots."

"Yeah, it's funny, huh? Ya wanna possess something good once you have it—and in wanting it so bad ya ruin it, right?"

"Something like that, I suppose. Yet...one wonders." She scooted over very close to me. "So...how was your day?"

"Oh, more or less the usual." I thought it best to keep Oscar Brandt's agreement with me a secret for the moment. "The Lichter Grabstätte wants to transform me into FDR so I can have access to atomic secrets for them. Lt. Keith called me and when I met him at the coroner's joint, he showed me three dead triplets of a gangster who's not dead."

"What?!!" she exclaimed. "Oh, Cable, you have the strangest things happen to you! So will they kill you if you don't deliver—and how are they going to transform you into FDR? And who's the gangster?"

"Will they kill me? Sooner or later, probably. I don't know exactly how they do it. But Brandt said they could. The crook's name is a big time operator known as Nick Milano. I never met him, but Keith seems to know a little about him. I don't understand much of that situation, either. The Fed boys are coming to 'dispose of' the bodies'. And that's my world, babe—over and out. How about yours?"

"Women in love become obsessed with thinking about the object of their affection. So I thought about you most of the day. You know, painting scenarios that I felt might work for both of us...but if I move too fast, I might lose you anyhow. No woman's ever had enough glue to have you stick, has she?"

"No, not really. It's spokes on a bicycle wheel for me—each spoke a different female personality who helps to balance out my fretful life. I don't know, Sophie, but I think maybe we shouldn't go any further than we are now. It's not that I don't want you—Lord knows I do—but you're gonna get hurt or killed if you hang out with me too much longer."

"So what? Desire is a funny thing, Cable, it tends to make obstacles become less important. Are you saying you don't want to see me anymore?"

"In a way, I wish I *could* say that to you. But I can't. There's something that draws me to you like a bee to honey, *honey*," I laughed. "So what the hell am I gonna do?"

"Love me...that's all I ask from you...just love me..."

I dropped Sophia Legende off at Greystone Mansion and headed off to Santa Monica to catch *Alana Charity* at the *Orange Note*. It was about 10:00 p.m. and the club was half full, and for a Wednesday night, I guess that wasn't bad. The doll of a singer was a redhead about five-four or so with a petite, wild body. She sang like a slinky fox, almost curling her tongue around the microphone. She had a pretty good voice too, along with everything else. She was warbling a Richard Rodgers' tune called *Lover* in a very sensuous way. No wonder the likes of Nick Milano was bedding this broad. She had a subtle, appealing way about her and as I sidled up to the bar and ordered a drink, I was sure I saw Lt. Lester Keith in the shadows at the far end of the bar. I don't think he wanted to speak to me. I really think he was just making sure I was present and accounted for.

I needed to get to Nick Milano, so I went to work. When the lady was finished with her set of songs, I went up and tossed a few bucks in her tip jar upon the stage. "Thanks, Miss Charity, and please do—give it to your favorite charity." I laughed.

She didn't say anything at first but looked at me, more or less puzzled. I figured if I start makin' time with the lady, it might stimulate a little excitement in the joint and I'd get led to Mr. Milano. "*I'm* my favorite charity, mister," the gal responded in a rather high speaking voice that reminded me of a New York telephone operator.

"You're also *cute*, lady. I don't care where you spend it, but let's see a little less costume and a little more tits and legs!" I remarked, checking out the faces in the dark. "Do you put out after hours?" I thought that might offend her.

Just then a humongous man approached and stood in back of me. But I think Alana Charity was put out. "You're way out of turn, mister. No, I don't put out after hours and I think you'd better scram or you'll get trouble. I think you've already attracted it. This is a decent

291

establishment and there ain't no sellin' of extra goods, if ya know what I mean?"

"Oh? Sorry about that. You just had that Boyle Heights look on your face, lady—"

Suddenly she lit up and her eyes widened. "—are you from Boyle Heights? Me, too, mister. What street?"

"Marietta, off East 7th street for a while," I answered.

"Damn, I lived only a few blocks away—off Whittier." She rushed down the three stairs from the bandstand and came right up to me with her hand extended. "I am happy to meet a man from my neighborhood—most of us didn't make it out." We shook hands. "I'm really Bettina Krause—but they know me as Alana Charity. You can call me that. But at heart, I'm still a Boyle Heights girl."

"Good to meet you. I like your singing. My name is Denning, Cable Denning. This is my second time here. The first was a Monday and you weren't here breathing all those wonderful vowels into the jazz tunes."

"Thanks, Cable," she tried out my name on her tongue. "I'm gonna zow 'em with my next song. Will you stay for it?"

"Yeah, sure, what is it?"

"It's called *Little Girl Blue*—but I don't feel blue tonight. In fact, I feel great!" I noticed she was a bit hyper and wondered if her dear boyfriend had been supplying her with a little something.

"No, I'm not familiar with that tune. But I'll stay." It's really funny in a way, but it's so much easier to talk to someone from your own neighborhood. I didn't have to carefully select my words.

I walked back to the bar and soon, as I was hoping, that mean ol' bouncer followed me. "We don't allow flirtin' with the hired help, buddy. So, I'm askin' ya kinda nice and pretty-like...cease and desist or else I'll have to boot ya out of here."

"Yeah? Well, fuck you! That young thing up there is so damned cute—and I like cute," I persisted. About that time Lt. Lester Keith left hurriedly without acknowledging me. I'm sure he thought I'd flipped my lid. "I think I will flirt with her a bit after her next song—you don't mind now, do ya?"

"But me and the lady *do* mind, buster. Now you're using foul language in this here nice establishment—and the boss wouldn't like it." He stepped on my right shoe and ground his heel into it.

I looked down. "Now, was that nice?" I took a flying swing at the bloke and he hit the deck in no time flat. People began moving away from the fracas and the band played fast and hard. Then another guy arrived, and they dragged me off somewhere behind the stage into a little room. There the original bouncer hit me hard in the gut, then tied me up.

"We gotta wait for the boss to say it's okay for you to go home. You got some kinda punch, buddy."

"Yeah? Well, so do you! I don't like to be messed with, 'buddy'. Unless you're a cop with good cause, you're violating my rights as a citizen," I maintained. "Are you a cop?"

He didn't respond, but left me tied up in the tiny broom closet. What was nice about it, though, was that it had no roof and Alana Charity's version of *Little Girl Blue* came in loud and clear.

About an hour later the big boy bouncer came in with my trench coat and fedora and untied me. He led me out into the cool night air, in front. "Now, buddy, don't come back!"

"But I wanted to meet your boss and compliment him on the fine establishment he has here," I said, still trying to find a way to Milano.

"You must be nuts, because I ain't gonna grant that little wish of yours on account of the boss ain't here anyhow. Blow, buddy!"

He disappeared back inside the Orange Note and I went around to the back of the joint. What was I looking for? Just as I was about to go, a big Cadillac drove into a marked spot in the alleyway. And sure enough, out came Nick Milano with two henchmen. This was my chance. I'd left my gun and holster in my car, so I had no defense except to fly by the seat of my pants. As they saw me approach, right away the goons drew their weapons. "Mr. Milano? I'd like to talk to you—just a couple of minutes, if you don't mind?"

Nick Milano told his men to frisk me but hold down. "Are you a cop? If you are, you're wastin' your time, pal," Milano spoke. He had a nice resonant baritone with a little east coast in it. "I told 'em all I know and Pritchard's the one you want anyway."

"No, I'm a private investigator. Don't worry, Milano, it's not about you or your nice drugged up girlfriend— it's about what I saw at the county morgue early tonight."

Suddenly his face paled. "Yeah? Well, you'd better come into my office." They led me into the back door of the Orange Note and up a flight of stairs to a nice office overlooking the parking lot. He then dismissed his goons and told them to wait just outside the door. "I ain't the boss here, but I own the joint." He looked at me curiously, trying to figure me. "How did you come to know Alana Charity, mister?"

"Oh, you must mean Bettina Krause. We grew up in the same neighborhood. I'm from Boyle Heights."

His face relaxed. "Ya don't say...well, that makes things different. I was raised in Sewer City, too."

"Yeah? Well, then you know who I am—at least inside..."

"I learned ya never know who somebody is, even when they're dead and buried. What's your name?"

"Denning, Cable Denning."

"Denning, eh? Didn't someone write a book about you a long time ago? Something about sex and vampires and the like?"

"Yeah, *Death On the River*—but that was quite a while ago."

"I recognized some of the old Los Angeles River in that book. The gal who wrote it—was she a moll of yours?"

"Not really...just a fine writer and poet..."

"Oh...well, now to business. So what did ya see down at the morgue that brought you all the way out here?"

"Three *more* of you, all nice and dead in that special filing cabinet they have there for stiffs."

"Yeah, I seem to be showing up all over the place. How do *you* figure in on this thing?"

"I don't—at least I hope I don't. Lt. Lester Keith of Homicide invited me down to the local friendly morgue yesterday, to see for myself. I've had a little experience with strange anomalies. He said the day before there were three murdered people—two men, one woman—that somehow the Lieutenant gathered were killed by one Dr. Pritchard. Then next time they look—bam! it's all Nick Milano! That's all I know."

"Ha! They all look like me, eh?" he snickered.

"Yep..."

"I know about Keith. He's always trying to wing me. Why would he bring *you* in on this case?" Milano was going over my wallet and I.D. "It says here you *are* really a private dick. Do you play both sides?"

"If I have to—one's just about as crooked as the other..."

"I think I like you, Denning. So...why *would* Keith bring you in?"

"Because I've had exposure to aliens or as they're getting to be called more and more, *'extra-terrestrials'.*"

"I see...yeah, it makes sense, the cops don't know dipshit about what really goes on left of their brains."

"So...have you experienced them?" I asked, lighting up a cigarette nonchalantly.

"Who?"

"*Extra-ordinary people*—like Keith's talkin' about?"

"Nope. Don't hope to and I'm not sure these 'people' you talk about aren't some scientific experiment gone nuts."

"Okay...and that's it? You can help yourself, ya know, if you tell me all you know about this case. I'm sure you don't wanna bunch of you runnin ' around doin' just about anything and gettin' you blamed for it."

"That's it, Denning...now, I'm a busy man—and as you go out...go out with this in mind. Leave Miss Charity alone—ghetto rat or not—understand?"

"Yeah, Milano, you're loud and clear." I got up and put my hat on. He followed me to the door.

"I—I guess there's one—one *other* thing..."

I looked up into pain-ridden eyes. "I've got a son. He's *different*—I brought him to that son-of-a-bitch Pritchard—that so-called *Doctor*—and the bastard proceeds to fuck him up even more!"

"What's your son's anomaly?"

"*Anomaly*? There's that word again! What the fuck does it mean?"

"Condition, disease, illness, oddness—you name it, Milano."

"Oh. That's just it, nobody knows. He's what Pritchard called an *albino*—hell, the only albino I know of is a horse...ya know, white skin, red eyes, no hair and all. But goddamn it, Denning, my *son's* got it! So I take him in to see Pritchard who's some kind of specialist—you know how those nuts work, tryin' to find something that ain't there?"

"Yeah, go on..."

"So Pritchard says he needs to examine the kid in laboratory conditions for a few days and can I leave him? So I say yeah and drop off Davy the next day, suitcase and all. He didn't wanna go, but I told him it was to cure him. He told me there was nothing wrong with him—son-of-a-bitch, can you imagine? Nothing wrong with the frickin' kid, my ass! Telling me there's nothing odd about my son the freak?!"

"How old is he?"

"He's just twelve Saturday." I was thinking of Cable, Jr. who I would have to confront in a very short while.

"Who's the mother?".

"Hell if I know. You know me, Denning, I've got ten girls on a string at a time—how the hell would I know which broad caught? But suddenly this kid in a basket and a typed out note shows up at my place. So what do I do? Everyone thought the kid was a freak to begin with—even me—you know, the no hair, red eyes, completely white skin—hell, he's even red under his finger nails! But my Aunt Elvira says to keep the kid and help him. So I did."

"So how did you know he was yours?"

"Well, there is one thing of mine the kid inherited. If you'll notice, one ear is definitely larger and lower than the other. Davy inherited that from me. That's why I was sure. It was too frickin' scary to be a coincidence, ya know."

"I'm glad you told me, Milano. I think I'll head down to the county clink and talk to this Dr. Pritchard."

"Yeah, you just do that. I went there and talked until I was blue in the face. The tight-lipped bastard wouldn't say a goddamn word to me!"

"So where's Davy now?"

"Aw, he's out on some funny farm called Sunny Acres up north in a place called San Luis Obispo. But shit, Denning, it's a reformatory for boys—*expensive* boys, I might add."

I knew of San Luis Obispo, but hadn't heard about this Sunny Acres, much less what kind of place it might be. I left the churning world of Nick Milano with the thought that all people are thrown a curve ball at least once in their lives, a surprise package with the letters "*Unexpected*" written on it. Sometimes it sticks, like a kid from out of the blue from some babe who couldn't have cared less—and maybe giving birth to an albino baby might've freaked her out pretty bad. So pass the kid on to Dad. Except that Milano, like me, wasn't exactly the gentle, paternal kind of guy.

The next day was Thursday. Lester Keith was not hesitant about letting me see the infamous Dr. Pritchard at the city jail because he thought I might get some clues to the baffling situation at the morgue. Pritchard was probably about forty-five or so, dark hair and horn-rimmed glasses, a thin nose and crooked teeth. When he saw me standing in front of his cell he didn't get up, but sat on his bunk reading a newspaper. "How much truth do you think the newspaper prints?" he asked stoically.

"About as much as Congress and the War Department combined," I answered, looking down at the sitting man. "You got a minute?"

"What for—so you can tell them what I have allegedly done?" Then he glanced up at me. "By the looks of you, you must be some kind of policeman?"

"Well, close, but no cigar," I chided him. "I'm a private eye. Denning...Cable Denning. I saw the three corpses that were all Nick Milano look-alikes. I understand that the day before, there were two men and one woman. Now all of sudden the three have changed into things that look just like him. Any explanation on that, buddy?"

Finally he got up and came close to the cell bars. "Creeps...like Milano—interior creeps. That's why I didn't talk to him. Handsome on the outside, shit on the inside."

"What about Davy?"

"Davy? So...what about him?"

"How does *he* figure into this thing? I can only suppose you're a *replicant maker* of some sort. And you have *their* help."

He studied my face for a minute. "So by *'their'* you mean beings not of this earth-plane existence, right?"

"Right. So how does what you do tie in with *one*—the corpses at the morgue and *two*—Milano's extraordinary son?"

He wandered away from me, muttering scientific specifics. I was impressed. "He's the most superb example of advanced earthman I've ever experienced. He's tens of thousands of years ahead, in fact."

"And he's not an alien?"

"No, that's just it, Denning. He's not. In fact, his *Oculotaneous Albinism* is a rare genetic disorder found in humans. What sets Davy apart from them is the *Nystagmus Oculari*—rapid eye movement coupled with his *photophobia*—somehow ties in with an intellectual superman ability akin to the gods of old. Unless, of course, the so-named 'gods' were advanced beings such as Davy and he's a throwback—or *throw-forward*...as it were. I thought these kinds of humanoid species just died out in time. But I was wrong. Denning, we're talking about the ability to heal, maybe even resurrect life, charge people he touches with calculated energies from his electrically generating body." He turned and approached me again. "You got a cigarette? I'm out and the damned guards have already drawn and quartered me."

I took out a cigarette, handed it to him and lit it up through the bars. "Beings like Davy continue to 'super-charge', if you will, and then one day they will spin so fast, generating their own electric current that they will dissipate into atoms of consciousness! They won't die, Denning, but they'll leave this earth as frequency so fast that they simply cannot remain in a physical body!" He was excited, as if his quintessential moment had arrived...the reason he was born. "That's why I've made the replicants, that's what I've been doing these years, making experimental people who look, act and respond as other humans. Only now they'll be better. The three people who some stupid cop insisted that I murdered were killed in a freak lightning storm four days ago. I heard the report on the news and rushed to a place north of Trancas Beach to find what I could. When I found them, still in the meat wagon, I stole the three bodies for new replicating material. I didn't know it then, but the cops had a tail on me. By the time they stormed my laboratory, the three corpses had already been injected with my new serum to duplicate the first person they saw. That's one of the results of the *Nystagmus* of this particular variety, the brain records what it sees at hundreds of thousands of miles an hour and duplicates itself into what it has seen. It's a kind of symbiosis I haven't figured out yet. But it's there."

"So how did they get Milano's mug?"

"Milano was clipping his fingernails in my outer office the day he brought in his son. I took some of those clippings out of the wastebasket because the dna is essential to the success of the project. Then I show them a photo of his. I did some research on the gangster Nick

Milano and who the mother might be. No luck on Mom. Anyway, his face was the first my newly formed replicants saw. So they morphed into Nick Milano, crook at large, with dna from his fingernail clippings in the serum I injected them with."

"I see. Well, that solves that, Pritchard. I thank you for your candidness. I'll see what I can do to get you a *get-outta-jail-free card*. I do have one more question, though. What about saving Davy and giving him a chance to be himself without being in a nuthouse of some kind? Maybe he can contribute in some meaningful way."

"I'm all for that. But I'm dangerous to the status quo world, Denning—I'm on the cutting edge of new breakthrough technologies that do not disclude humanitarian considerations. Humanitarianism must outweigh high technology. Otherwise, humans will be numbed out robots, controlled by a moneyed ruling political and hidden class."

"You're wasting your time, Pritchard. I know who rules the world. Besides that, humans have a genetic warring trait in them—a hard-wired mind-set about competition, sex and violence. It would take millions of generations to change that."

"I'm aware of your premise, but I don't agree with the time span. Get Davy's blood into the human blood stream, let it spread like a plague across the globe—and soon a new species will emerge from the old one. Nature does wondrous things given half a chance, Denning."

"I hope you're right, Pritchard. Well, I'm goin' downstairs to talk to Lt. Keith of Homicide. I think since he's

302

seen the replicants as such, he might cite you for some stupid thing, but not murder. And...tell me, once you're out, what's the first thing you're gonna do?"

"See if I can extricate Davy from that hell hole in San Luis Obispo. Maybe I can convince his Dad from a different angle that not only is Davy exceptional, but he could change the world. Maybe you can help. Otherwise, I'll be forced to kidnap the boy and go underground with him...indefinitely."

"I see your point, but kidnapping is a major offense. I'm concerned about a missing woman who just got kidnapped. Okay if I come along to see Davy when you go to San Luis Obispo? I *might* be able to help."

"Yes, thanks, Denning, that would be fine. Let's go together. You're the first non-scientist to support me. I really think I've got something."

"But ya gotta take murder out of your programming equation, doc. Artificial babes like Abbey Allison can't go around being henchmen and bumping people off, German spies or not. Plus I think she had some alien blood in her as well. How else could she just disappear like she did unless she was a form of extra-terrestrial life?"

"Well, Abbey was a clone of an alien male and of some beautiful but not so savory female I dredged up," he laughed to himself.

"That's what I mean—you need to be more selective about who you pick to replicate. Like a thousand Nick Milanos floating around town ain't gonna help the syndicated crime rate!"

"Yes, you're right, I do need to check—uh, more intensively. It is true that the replicants pick up all the traits of the persona they are transforming into...good and bad. Yes, I will heed that henceforth. This duplicating thing is rather new to me."

"Well, it better become old *fast*, Pritchard. Between you, Lichter Grabstätte and the Oculus—and Lord knows who else—the world is filling up with mixes of different beings. How're we gonna know who's who from who?" I barked.

"Yes, I know of the German organization. I don't know the latter. The *Oculus*, you say? What is its purpose?"

"To rule the world, plain and simple. If you think Yale with Skull and Bones was fancy stuff, wait 'til you see *these* guys!"

"Oh, my—I have been very secluded in my work for years, you know."

"Yeah, maybe too secluded, buddy boy." I handed him my card. "When you get out and situated, give me a call. See ya around, doc!" I walked down the corridor toward the guarded door.

"Hey, buddy, I'm an alien, too!" cried a voice from the dark of a cell. "Can you get me out? I heard what you guys were saying."

I chuckled. "Well, if you're an alien, you can get *yourself* out!" I quipped back and left.

Lester Keith wasn't all that accommodating about releasing Dr. Pritchard. But the jail was crowded during these war years with everyone coming to California, particularly Los Angeles, a haven for jobs, mobs, babes and a place to get drunk and raise hell. Military police handled the soldiers, sailors and marines who got into trouble, so at least Keith was relieved of that unpleasant task. The war years had not been kind to Los Angeles folk and everything from petty theft to murder rained down on the city like a long storm that didn't wanna quit.

I also gave Lt. Keith a cock-'n-bull story about if Pritchard was out—and he *was* guilty by association with the aliens—I'd keep an eye on him and report back to headquarters. He grunted that he'd see what he could do to release Dr. Pritchard. It didn't sit too well with him when I told him I thought I even liked the guy. Poor Lester, he still wasn't sure that extra-terrestrials existed, let alone made replicas of people. For him and millions like him, happiness was doing your job and coming home to a house somewhere on a quiet street with a woman waiting to tell you what had to be done around the house. Then, the newspaper, a peaceful evening spent listening to the radio for a while and then off to bed with Mrs. Keith. Not my brand of poison.

The House on San Gabriel Avenue

I got home late. I was exhausted. I think I was slowing down. Or maybe it was the booze and cigarettes—not to mention all the other things wrong with how I lived. I stripped to my tank top and boxers and sat in my comfy chair nursing a gin. I wanted a smoke real bad, but I managed to avoid putting a Lucky Strike in my mouth. Just then the phone rang. "Yeah, I hope you know it's 2:30 in the morning and—"

"—Cable!" a desperate out-of-breath female voice cried. "It's me—Nadia—I'm—I'm—"

"—Jesus—Nadia! I've been so goddamn useless trying to find you! Where are you? Are you okay—I mean, not wounded or anything?"

"No—no—I—I got away and I'm at some kind people's house—I—I got them out of bed and they let me use—let me use their phone. Can you come pick me up?"

"Damn, of course, babe, right away! Where are you?"

"I'm—I'm east of Pasadena in the foothills..." She put her hand over the receiver and I heard her talking. "It's 1127 N. San Gabriel Ave. in Azusa, Cable. It's a small brick house with tiled roof and a big truck out in front. The man says it's just a few blocks above Azusa between 11th and 12th streets on State Route 39. Can you find me?"

"I got a map here, babe, I'll be there just as soon as I can throw my clothes on and grab the map. Hang on, babe, I'm on my way!"

I hung up, dressed, flew down to my car and sped east beyond Pasadena until I reached Azusa about 40 minutes later. It was pitch black with no street lamps, so I had to get out to check out every house that had an address. Fortunately there weren't too many. I found the truck and the little brick house. I jumped out of my car and went running up to the door and banged on it hard. My beautiful Nadia Skorkowsky fell into my arms and held me like there wasn't gonna be any tomorrow! We both wept. The folks invited us back in, but we thanked them and I took Nadia by the hand and we hightailed it back toward Los Angeles.

Nadia confirmed my worst fears, that 'Watty' Watson had kidnapped her and hid her in a secret place somewhere in those foothills. Then he'd have his way with her and kill her. But the best news was yet to come as she sat next to me, glued to my body and trembling. She looked disheveled. Her simple dark blue polka dot dress was torn, she had only sandals on her feet and her hair was mussed. She told me Watty didn't allow her to wear any underwear, so that was also absent. In fact, she looked like a mad woman with no makeup and her countenance reflected strain and exhaustion. "Cable...*I killed him*...I killed my attacker—there was no other way!"

"You what?!!" I exclaimed.

"He was about to accost me sexually. He was a weird doctor of some kind—really crazy man! He told me his name was 'Watty' or something. He had me tied to a bed in his basement—and—and it—it was horrible—like the most diabolical nightmare! All of it!" she let go with the tears and buried her face in her hands. "Then when he untied me to go to the bathroom—I—I did it—I must've acted out of an instinct—because—because— my *Kikku*—the kick-boxing—was so full of fear and power I almost kicked his head off...oh, God!" she whimpered.

"It's okay—it's over now, babe...I'm here with you...you don't have to say anything more until you've rested. We'll go to your place?"

"No, not tonight—please, your office? That way I'd know I'm safe!"

We got back about 4:30 in the morning and I took her into my bathroom and ran her a bath. I let her soak with just an old candle on the sink and sat on the toilet seat talking to her. "Cable—I—I still want to perform

Tosca—I know the part! I've got to call them first thing in the morning! No one told them I had been kidnapped. I just disappeared. They must think I'm like this irresponsible flake or something!"

"Naw, soon as you explain, I'm sure the management and the understudy will understand and take you back in a wink, you beautiful doll! Besides...it *was* all over the papers that kidnapping was suspected."

She grimaced a half-smile. "I—I don't feel so beautiful...at least just now. And I don't want to talk about it anymore, but someone has to go up to that shack of his and get his body. He's—he's been dead for several hours, at least."

"Yeah? Well, I'll call Lester Keith in the morning. Don't you worry about any of it, okay? Most important thing is you're okay—gees, babe, I thought I'd lost you. I suspected it was Theodore 'Watty' Watson. He'd disappeared about the same time you did. But where to look—"

"—it's alright, darling, we're here now...back together...oh, Cable, hold me!" She reached for me from the tub and I clamped my arms around her and comforted her.

"I—I wish we could hold back the time, Cable—I wish we could have gone a different direction! I know you'll blame yourself for my getting stolen right out from under you—and I realize had I not known you, this horror would never have happened...but why can't we?"

"Why can't we what?"

"Hold back the time, my love?"

"No more talk about this thing tonight...okay? We'll get you dried off and I'll hold you all night, babe—and tomorrow you'll begin to forget all this ever happened."

"Easy for you to say, Cable...I'm afraid it's scarred me for life. I don't think I'll ever feel safe alone again in my house."

"Then we'll live there together, Nadia—that is, if you'll have me."

She gave the first glint of a real smile. "You would do that for me?"

"You bet, kid, I happen to like you an awful lot." I helped her out of the bathtub and remembered how wonderful her body looked naked.

I telephoned and awakened Ida Latney to tell her the good news and not to come in tomorrow since Nadia was with me. Ida was happy that Nadia was okay but I could feel the ice when she knew in her heart Nadia would be sleeping with me.

The next day I got a hold of Lt. Lester Keith and told him the latest. He told me it wasn't in his jurisdiction even though it was in Los Angeles County and would refer it to the locals in Pasadena.

Nadia and I made plans to go out to her place and get it fixed up the way she liked it. I'd move in with her and that would be that.

The Eyes of Youth

It was Thursday, June 22, 1945. Sometimes I wish I could see from the eyes of a young person, especially a woman. Ida held her ground through all of this transition without much complaint. I got the feeling she numbed her frustration with alcohol at night, not excessively, just enough to put her to sleep, to stop her from thinking about the man she loves and his many liaisons. And now he was living with a woman she knew he really loved. That must've been tough. But maybe that was the school of hard knocks Ida had to go through. I don't know. Life is full of twists and turns and who knows who ends up with who when all is said and done? Only after ya die, ya really can't change anything, can you? Ah, but for the eyes of youth!

For the most part, Nadia Skorkowsky was doing well. A good sign was that our sex life had upped the ante recently and she was almost as hungry as she had been before the kidnapping. She told me Watty, her would-be killer, would stand there at night as Nadia lay tied to her bed and smell the lingerie he'd stolen from her house. What makes a man do that eccentric thing? Then he told her not to wipe after she went to the toilet, that he'd do it and use her under things to do it with! He'd tell her he was eventually and regrettably going to kill her because he had no choice. Can you imagine sleeping with that thought in your head at night, never knowing what minute it might be that a nut job like Dr. Theodore Watson would peel off another layer of his sanity and do the dirty deed? It was things like that which wore on Nadia. No doubt, it had taken a toll and she wasn't quite the same self-assured woman I knew prior to the abduction.

On the positive side of the coin, Nadia had resecured her job after the newspapers leaked out about her ordeal and the management of the opera association thought it would bring in more people—to actually see the singer who was kidnapped and almost killed by a ferocious and wanted mad doctor named 'Watty'! In fact, opening night would be in just two weeks and I couldn't wait to see and hear my woman up there do her thing among the bright lights and musical sounds of Puccini.

But not all things were rosy for me. Sophia and I had been seeing each other on the side because I needed her to become pregnant to fulfill my part of the bargain with Oscar Brandt and his "scientific" studies. I told the redoubtable Miss Legende about my commitment to Nadia and living with her. She didn't think it would last very long, but that *maybe* it could. Life is strange, she told me in her own inimitable way and added that she wished it were her who shared a home with me. And it *was* a home. Nadia was a superb homemaker and made sure I didn't smoke inside the joint, was moderate about my drinking and made love to her at least once every other day or she'd kill me herself! Ha! I thought to myself—what a deal—even her cooking was excellent! I was allowed two days a week to stay at the office when her girlfriend Natalie would come over and stay with her. At those times Sophia Legende and I got together. What a dame!

"O' Dolci Mani"

Before I knew it, it was Friday, July the 6th and opening night for the truly grand opera, *Tosca* with my Nadia in the title role. The theatre chosen was the marvelous *Philharmonic Auditorium* at 5th and Olive. In a way, it was like a Hollywood Bowl encased by walls. It was large inside and sweeping lighted arches over the front of the stage area extended well out into the audience to a magnificent dome ceiling...also lighted. This made for perfect acoustics, I was told. But then again, what did I know? I rarely frequented the posh and classical music world. I do remember that it was dear Mandy who had introduced me to great classical music in a live setting. And that wasn't all that long ago.

I was recalling my daily visits with my son and Adeline that had taken place a couple of weeks ago. Cable Denning Jr. was now twelve years-old and resembled me at that age. He was growing tall and "weedy" as I was at that age, his Adam's apple protruding a little more than it would when he was finally an adult and filled out some. Most of the visits were perfunctory on my part, but there was one afternoon of complete frankness that did both of our hearts good. While I was telling him what a lousy Dad I'd been and how lucky we were to have Mandy and Adeline, he said something that stopped me in my tracks. "It doesn't matter if you've been a bad father, Dad, or that maybe you haven't always been around—*I didn't need you.* But you're still my Dad." That floored me. I guess I never needed either of my Dads as I grew up. The first one worked or drank most of the time and the second I knew only for a very short time. But my son was right—just like I didn't need *them.* Adeline had exposed the boy to much great music and literature. Maybe some of that rubbed off on him. I don't know. I could tell he had a sharp, observant brain. Hell, his speaking voice even sounded a little like mine! I wondered what he inherited from his lovely, bright mother. When I asked him what he wanted to do in life, he said he wasn't sure, but he thought either a world traveler, adventurer or something might be interesting.

Anyway, my response to Junior's statement was an honest realization that maybe we don't need our Dads as much as we do our Moms when we're growing up, but just to know you have one and he's there if worse comes to worse was comforting, nonetheless. Our best moments were walking in Bronson Park and despite all the shit that was going on in my life at the moment, I managed to focus and remind him that I was indeed there for him if he ever did need me. All in all it was an okay visit, but when I saw them off on the train, I could tell it had been too long for us to bond, I mean really bond. The same thing happened between the original Cable Sr. and myself. My sire had been out of the scene and even though my mother was in love with him until her dying breath, at best we were two men cemented by blood and destiny. Cable Jr. would suffer the same fate, I was afraid. Such is life.

Yep, the night of July 6th was a fateful night in my life. Sophie had told me that afternoon she thought she was pregnant. She wasn't sure she wanted to keep the child, if she was, she told me. Too much responsibility—and of course, there was her career to consider, such as it was. On the other hand, she said, the child would be part of "us" and she thought she might love me, after all is said and done. And so she teetered on the edge. If it were true, then Oscar Brandt would be happy and the laboratories at Lichter Grabstätte would begin the processing of Sophia's ovum to create "a better human being", as Brandt had put it to me earlier. How would *I* handle it? I didn't know.

But the operatic performance was first-rate and I enjoyed Nadia a hell of a lot. When she first came on stage in Act I, she looked elegant and sexy at the same time. She pleaded with the painter, Mario Cavaradossi, to love her and her only and they did an exciting duet. By Act II, when Tosca is confronted by a dark, lascivious villain named Scarpia, Nadia sang like an angel in *Vissi d'arte, Vissi d'amore* and brought down the house. The translation of the song was as Nadia had said... '*I lived for art, I lived for love...*' and that fit Nadia to a tee. In love with the tenor Cavaradossi who faces the firing squad, and resisting Scarpia's sexual demands, Tosca kills him with a knife. But not before she falsely promises herself to Scarpia, and in turn the bad guy promises to have the soldiers use blanks instead of real bullets and set Cavaradossi free. Tosca goes down to the dungeon to tell the lamenting tenor. He is overjoyed and she does not tell him she killed Scarpia, but rather they'll go away together forever. But the bullets *are* real, and Cavaradossi dies. Tosca, now unable to tolerate life any longer without him and hearing voices in the background that the soldiers have found Scarpia's murdered body and they know that Tosca did it—she plunges over the tower parapet to her death.

The packed audience went wild with curtain call after curtain call coming like waves and filled the stage with bravos and flowers. But Nadia was nowhere to be seen. All of a sudden I got this bad feeling in my gut. Maybe she hurt herself jumping off the precipice onto the mattress that awaited her three feet below. I started

314

fighting my way toward the stage, but two roustabouts told me I couldn't go backstage. So I fought through the crowds toward the main exit. Twenty minutes later I finally made it around to the alley and found the back entrance. But there were two men guarding *that* entrance! I told them Nadia Skorkowsky was my girlfriend and they chided me. "Yeah, buddy, every other man in the audience wishes that!" one man declared in a loud, demeaning voice. By now, dozens of other well-wishers were behind me.

"I gotta get in there—Miss Skorkowsky didn't show up for her curtain call—and she's the star!" I yelled.

"So? Maybe she's tired, indisposed or sick o' the likes of you blokes showing up! Scram, buddy, before I sic the cops on you!"

An urge overcame me to bust through the guys, but they were tough and held me at bay. Then I heard sirens and an ambulance came screaming through the night and entered the alley. Now I knew something was wrong! This time I did break through the guys along with several other people behind me, until fifteen or twenty of us were in the backstage area, seeking Nadia. The medics pushed by us with a stretcher, followed by two cops with their guns drawn. I followed. Then I saw her. She was face down on the mattress that was supposed to save her life! Her lovely costume was soaked with blood! I ran, passed the cops and the ambulance people and fell onto my knees beside her body. My senses went into slow motion, like I was living a melodrama within a melodrama—one staged, the other real. A doctor in his tuxedo had been summoned from the audience and he bent opposite me, not saying a word, but feeling Nadia's pulse. I could tell. There was none. The older man with the nice thin white moustache and blue eyes looked at me. "You know her, son?"

"Yeah, she's my girl—we—we've lived together for...for a time..."

"I'm afraid she's gone. You'll have to make room for the ambulance personnel, mister. I'm sorry. Darned good singer, too..."

"How—how'd she die?" I asked, tears filling my eyes.

"It looks like she was pierced by something in the mattress. I can't say more. It's in the hands of the police now. We'll have to move out of the way. I'm sorry." He got up and left. The two ambulance attendants picked me up off the floor and gently moved me aside. As they picked her body up to place on the stretcher, I saw that the mattress had been jimmied with about seven sharp blades coming up out of it. Someone had murdered Nadia!

"Out of the way, please!" one of the attendants shouted as they put a blanket around Nadia's bloodied body and started to move away. People stared at me as I stood there in the middle of the floor, feeling useless, helpless and sad far beyond comprehension. What was I to do? Who had killed this beautiful woman who loved me? In that minute, I knew only one thing—I had to get out of this goddamned joint and head for some fresh air to regain my breath and sanity! I could still hear Nadia's voice whisper to me as we made love a few nights before. "Hold back the time, my love!" she cried there in the darkness. Now maybe it was truly dark for her, maybe we imagined everything and death is the winking out of an iffy life terribly lived. But I couldn't know. You see, I was kinda dead myself right now...

Fools Rush In

How many times in my life had I grieved for a woman who was lost to me by an act of somebody's revengeful violence? I didn't even wanna count. But here I was, alone and walking, glancing at a streetcar filled with strange faces, a flower vendor smiling as I passed, the shoeshine boy at Hollywood and Cahuenga, the cop who didn't know me, patrolling his beat and checking me out, the tall thin taxi driver with the slicked down black hair who always hung out around the curb of the NBC studio down on Sunset...for a customer, or Janie the streetwalker whose age and makeup made her look more like a clown than an appealing woman. Dreams get broken pretty easy, I've learned. So do people. I felt like Jesus on the cross, with thorns stuck through my head and every nail was a living, breathing woman not all that long ago—but each one came to me, came to death, unknowing, despite my warnings, despite that I told them the possible price tag for knowing and loving me. Yet they entered the danger zone. And then they died. It began with Honey Combes in 1929 and just ended with Nadia Skorkowsky, dead on the floor of the back stage of the Philharmonic Auditorium, July 6, 1945. Or *has* it ended? Yeah, I was on the right street alright, the true *Boulevard of Broken Dreams*, the place to go when there *is* no place to go, when nothing makes sense anymore because that man up there in my head has been beating my brain silly until all I can do is laugh at the dead-serious expression on my face as I saw my-self in a shop window and there lookin' back at me was a broken, desolate man.

Ever have a time in your life when everything went wrong? Well, this was it! I had only one desire at the moment, and that was to get so stinking drunk I wouldn't know my name if someone asked me. So I went into a new small club down on Sunset and La Brea called *Cocktails For Two*. Catchy name, I thought. The place was filled with noisy people and some striking redhead had just begun singing the Bloom and Mercer tune *Fools Rush In.* Boy, was that hand-picked for me! It was what I'd been thinking about as I walked the streets. '*Romance is a game for fools, a game I'd never play...*' the lyrics went. Yeah, who can stick to that? We all get burned. Even with Nadia's death I was thinking at the moment of Tara Shiran, that little spark of a Jewish girl who adventured with me and gave me such an in-tense rush with her sexual energy. Tara was *always* ready! Ah, but then again she was an alien and had to go back home, up there, you know, beyond the blue hori-zon. But I thought of her often, especially in lonely mo-ments. There was a certain *something* Tara had with me, as if *all* of her was with me and she'd have gone an-ywhere in the world with me. Maybe it was because I was her first love and she felt she belonged with me. Some women are like that. They bond with you when you mate with them, as if that were the consummating moment of their lives. I don't know. But what *is* crazy is that I'm thinking about someone else when Nadia's body lies still cooling down at the county morgue. Why

318

was I not with her? What could I do if I was? What does one do when none of the pieces fit anymore?

I bellied up to the bar and ordered a bottle of Canadian whiskey. The bartender said he couldn't do that. I asked him why. He told me it was house policy and I could only get a drink at a time. After all, this was a respectable place and the management didn't want any drunks littering up the joint! So I ordered six drinks and I found an empty table way in the back. When a waitress brought the drinks on a tray and placed them in front of me, she looked at me strangely. "Lose your girl, mister?" she asked quietly.

"Yeah, something like that. Or maybe it's life—you know, the helpless, endless bite of it—dealing with criminals, the police, aliens, extra-dimensionals, clients and women." I thought that might give her something to chew on!

She gave me a half-smile and didn't seem too fazed. "All that, huh? Six shots of whiskey? That's a lot to drink at one sitting. Are you sure?"

"Oh, yeah, lady, this is only the first round. I plan to sip away here at least until closing time."

"Please remember, mister, if you get rowdy, the management will kick you out! Just a fair warning—I've seen Marvin do it a lot of times."

"Well, thanks, and I'll try and drink quietly here in the corner and keep my eye on Marvin." As soon as she left I downed the first three drinks in three separate gulps and the alcohol set my gut on fire. It felt good to burn out my ulcer and my pain at the same time. In one hour's time I was good and drunk—mind you, not dead drunk yet, but getting there. My little redheaded chan-

319

teuse was torturing me from my past as she launched into *"I Miss You So"*, a 1939 tune that brought floods of memories back to me, not to mention how it reminded me of Nadia. Why in the hell did I come in here!? Oh, yeah, to get good and drunk. I finished all six drinks and went back up to the bar for more. I was a little unsteady and I leaned into a young man standing next to me. "Oh, pardon me, mister. I'm going for my seventh—where are you?" I asked, my mouth not working so good.

The young man was nicely dressed with a grey suit, his tie hanging loose from the collar, his hair dark and combed nicely. He was also drunk. "I—I just started. That—that's okay, buddy—tonight—tonight you can do anything to me...and—and I won't feel a thing!"

I glanced at him. "Not feel a thing, eh? Sounds like you just lost someone or something. Did he or she go away?"

"Did she go away!? To—to the worst possible place—her mother's! Ya see, her mother hates me...she thinks Doreen deserves better than me. You know, mister, the kinda woman I'm talkin' about?"

"Oh, yeah, buddy, I've met a few in my time." I ordered my drinks and went back to my little table to await them. But some good lookin' babe dressed in black was sitting at my table. "Pardon me, miss, but this—this is my table of—of repose tonight...at least until the joint closes up....okay?"

She looked me up and down and then at the six empty glasses. "Oh, I'm sorry, may I sit here just until my date comes in? The place is so crowded tonight."

"Yeah...okay," I said and sat down. The lady was probably in her late thirties, early forties, but very attractive. Her face and body looked familiar. "Don't I know you—I mean like the movies or somethin'?"

"Oh, I don't know," she replied. "They say I look a lot like Ginger Rogers—but Hollywood is Hollywood. People like to make stuff up."

I took a deep breath. "Yeah, you're right, Hollywood is full of the beautiful people? Ain't that right—Miss—Mrs...?"

"Kitty—they call me Kitty," she answered.

I extended my hand. She took it. "I'm Cable, lady, just plain Cable. I don't even have a last name tonight—how about that?"

She chuckled demurely. "I have nights like that," she answered. "Nice to meet you, Cable-with-no-last-name."

"Well, I'd tell you, but you'd be in trouble if I told you my last name. You—you see, Kitty, I'm trouble with a capital 'T' and that's that. No—no way around it, I'm afraid."

"Then I won't pry."

"Can I buy you a drink?"

"No thanks, it's not good for my skin."

"Oh."

Just then the young fellow who was at the bar stood above us. "Do—do you think I might join you two? I'm Clay Frickinhouse, Jr., second-generation North Carolina. But I was raised here in sunny ol' California. There are no—no more tables to be had tonight—at—at least not right now."

I looked at the lovely blue-eyed woman sitting next to me. "Do—do you mind if this gentlemen joins us, Frieda?"

"It's Kitty, Cable. Remember?"

321

'Oh, yeah...sorry..." I looked up at the young man with two glasses in hand. "I guess it's okay. Even though I wanted to tell you two I'm here to get dastardly drunk and bury my sorrows in rye whiskey."

"At least we're in the same boat—I mean, we two men," the young man said. Then he studied the lovely woman's face. "Don't I know you from somewhere? Do you dance with some, skinny fellow in...in the movies?"

"Oh, you must be talking about Fred. No, I think I resemble what's-her-name—uh...trying to think of her name now..." she said knitting her eyebrows.

"—anyway, okay if I join you? I don't want to impose..."

"Of course you do," I maintained. "All people—all people like to im...impose on others—didn't you know that? Tonight's your night...to impose on—on me, Clay. So go right ahead and sit down." I looked at Kitty. "You see, poor Clay is living a *delusional unreality*—believing his wife is the real thing. She's really a manikin dressed up like a human woman," I spoke out. "Cosmetics—that's the society we live in...cosmetic drug store trap—trappings. Do you wanna know what—what life's really all about, Clay?"

"Why, sure...you mean *your* definition of it."

"Fuck...for you, for me, forever more—it doesn't goddamn *matter*! It's *theee* definition, buddy boy!" I glanced at the surprised Kitty. "You can go if this—this gets too—too in...intense for you, Kitty."

"I would, but I have to wait for my date. He's always late."

"What's your date's name?"

"Jack—Jack 's my husband. But he's always late."

"You already said that." I looked at the young man sitting opposite us. "So...you wanna know what life is really all about, eh?"

"As you—*you* see it, okay, yeah, tell me..."

I glanced again at the lady. "Are you sure you wanna stay?"

"As I said, I've nowhere else to go until Jack gets here."

"Okay, Kitty cat." Then I took Clay's wrist firmly. "You see, Clay, the whole thing is—is a farce. It's simple—for you and me it's tits and pussy, for a woman it's nesting, sometimes with a house and kids and a—a mortgage and bills and relatives and all kinds of shit piling up through the years...*nothing is stronger...than a man's desire to wanna breed with an attractive female.* Period. His life is obsessed with it until he—he be—hic!—becomes too old to dream. Most humans are worthless once the breeding years are over—did—did you know that, Kitty?" I asked, looking over at the very attractive, attentive woman.

She had a kind of gentle smirk on her face. "Oh, yes, I think I've seen much of what you say is true, Cable, yes...I agree with some of it."

I looked back at Clay. "You see? There's a smart woman. You know why she knows? Cause she's very attractive and prob—probably every guy she meets wants to take her panties down and screw her, eh? But they can't—can't help it. They just wanna breed with her. Nature has packed him with desire to per-pu...perpulate...ah shit...uh...keep the species going—and—and that was bad enough. Then along comes a spider—only these spiders are from outer space—and they upped the ante—yeah, upped the ante...they increased the female's breeding season to once—once a month fertility to entice the man to reproduce himself over and over and—hic!—over again." I took one of my drinks and gulped it down. Both of my guests looked on in wonder. "And that...is where the lust for *power* came from—to—to replicate yourself into *everything*, dominate until all that's left is *you*. You'd like—like that, wouldn't you, me boy? And that—that's it, Clay, my boy...everything else...is just his balls being cha—channeled into survival to copulate, *everything!*" I postulated out loud, waving my arms around in meaningless gestures of assertion. "Music, art, politics, religion, science—you name it. Go ahead...*name* it—it's man's frustrated, irrational, berserk balls...that have created the mess we're in. This war is shit—hey, wait a minute—how come you're not in the war, plowboy?"

He smiled at me. "I have flat feet. My Dad used that phrase 'plowboy' when the farmers and ranchers went to the last war—only my Dad never made it back."

"Yeah, what the hell did he die for?" I asserted.

"Nothing. He...he died for nothing. We weren't threatened here at home, the war was among the Europeans. I hate...hate that about war," he quavered, his eyes misting a little as he sipped on his drink.

Just then a slim, dark-haired man approached Kitty. "You...you ready? Who are these people?" I could tell he was insecure and jealous of Clay and me.

"Yes, Jack, I'm ready," she said with a little acid in her voice. "This is Cable, and this is Clay. If you didn't come soon I was about to take off with them for the night. Why are you so late?"

"C'mon, let's go," the man named Jack said. The lady got up, then turned to look at me.

"I'm sorry you're so distorted in your mind, Cable, not to mention drunk. Life is God and God is life and He has his reasons for everything. Where's your belief, or your faith?"

"Wanna know where, sister? It's at the local cemeteries around town—those beautiful young women who died because of me—they—they got worms for breakfast! I—I have faith in *death*, Kitty..."

"You're nuts, mister," Jack entered. "Let's get outta here. Did you reserve a table?"

"Yes, but we lost it because you were an hour and twenty minutes late. Let's just go somewhere else, okay?"

He said no more, grabbed the pretty blonde's arm and off they went. "Damn, I couldn't live like that," Clay commented, watching the couple disappear.

"How do ya live *now*, Clay? Don't you have a millstone around your neck and mortgage payment and a woman who nags and tells you what to do and what not to do?"

"Yeah, in some part, I...I guess I do. But that's what happens when people get married. It's just different, ya know..."

I drew quiet and finished off one more drink. "Yeah, I know."

Eventually my drunk young friend left and the place thinned out. I learned the singer's name was Rhoda Collier—not exactly a singer's name, but her Latin version of *Yours...Quiéreme Mucho...*a little number that promised commitment and steadiness in the human sea of restlessness was excellent. But I was too drunk to really take it in. And for a minute or two I felt lonely, as if someone had walked over my grave and I was alone in a dark place.

I left the place with Rhoda Collier's rendition of *Stardust* still echoing through my brain. That's all it ever was, wasn't it? Stardust...a fine powder of debris cast off by stars burning themselves to oblivion. And even that ya couldn't hold in your hand very long. I could barely stand up let alone drive or walk home. I decided to take a taxi and come back for my car tomorrow. What the hell was I saying—it was already tomorrow. I found a cab that had no fare and he took me to my dingy little block on Franklin, to my dingy little building that contained my dingy little office on the second floor, with the dingy little bedroom in the back. When I got home I saw my reflection in the mirror and I thought I'd beat Ray Milland in *Lost Weekend*, because I looked more lost, more wasted and frazzled than he did in the goddamn movie! Yep, this was gonna be a weekend spent in remorse, booze, guilt and cigarettes. And...no phone calls.

Pictures of Present, Past and Future

Whatever I drank brought on a series of dreams over the next twelve to fourteen hours or so. I was seeing a very distinct face on the planet Mars, as if what someone had told me long ago came back to haunt me. It happened like this: Mars was our *original* home, but millions of years ago we abused the planet until it could no longer support life, so we emigrated to Earth. But the dream was nuts, and could be...so was what I was told. Nevertheless, there it was in the red sands of Mars, a huge eroding face looking up at me.

Just as quickly, I was taken to a quiet, warm planet somewhere. It reminded me of how I had imagined Mount Olympus might've looked. Only Zeus wasn't very pleasant and kept trying to protect his beautiful consort from me. I didn't know gods had sex, but maybe they have their own rendition of it. I don't know. But he was a lot bigger than I was and he picked me up and threw me off the edge of his kingdom and I went sailing into space, down, down, down... My beautiful mother caught me. Somehow I knew it was she. She walked with a grace in the earth life and now she glided underneath me to catch me and next thing I knew we were by the Los Angeles River long, long ago when it really *was* a river. She let me down beside her and began washing her long, flowing hair in the streaming waters. I never desired my mother before, but now suddenly I did! Her diaphanous, sheer gown showed her wonderful woman's body and as I dreamed, I understood why my sire had wanted her so much he was willing to take his brother's wife and in turn, she fell in love with him and conceived me.

Now I was an infant, and she was bathing me in the waters of the river and I was cooing and smiling up at her. Then some creature came up out of the water and snatched me and suddenly I was being gobbled up by a water thing I'd never seen before! It was huge and threatening, but my mother allowed it to happen and smiled as the creature took me beneath the river. It kept going, and soon disgorged me and there I stood on the edge of Eternity, looking at a universe so vast and beautiful, with nebulae and colors, that I thought I'd go nuts just seeing it! Yet, at the same time...it was tranquil. Crazy, huh?

But now my dreams took me *into new* territory, not past nor future, but a marvelous present in which I felt completely at home. I felt myself falling apart, disseminating like a snake loses scales or changes skin. I was losing all of my form and soon I was just a molecule, then an atom and then just a spark of some wonderful kind of *light-presence* and consciousness. The old Cable Denning ceased to exist and all went dark inside of him as I watched my old body dissipate. Then I got it. My whole frickin' human life had been but a dream! Everything I thought was real was just playacting for a day on a stage at school—everything and everyone I ever thought I'd known or experienced was an illusion. Now I figured it. That's why death. That's why it can all disappear into nothingness because it was a classroom experience, a magician's trick, and whatever we were supposed to get from it we got, I guess.

Then I was being pulled back up out of that wonderful serenity and suddenly I was in Nadia Skorkowsky's bloodstream! I was a pinpoint of light traveling in her veins. I could feel her talk to me, a whispered voice I didn't recognize as Nadia's, yet I knew it was. She was telling me not to feel guilty, not to miss her because she was right there with me, inside me, beside me, outside me, away from me. There was no distance between, yet light-years separated us! Then I was being buried with her and I didn't want to go there, didn't want to go into that deep, dark earth hole! No, no! It wasn't my time yet! So I woke up, dripping wet with perspiration and yelling to myself.

The Drizzle in My Eyes

It was Friday the 13th...July...1945. They say that Friday the 13ths aren't too lucky for folks. They sure weren't lucky for Nadia Skorkowsky as she went to her final resting place. She was far too young to die, and none of it made any sense. Bless her...Ida accompanied me to Nadia's funeral. She held my hand and guided me with her softness. It was a closed coffin affair on account of my poor Nadia's face and body had been so bloodied and marred, the mortician could do little with it. The day was glum and a slight rain set in now and then. I was surprised to see dozens of people who came to pay their last respects. Her performance that opening night must have touched a lotta folks, because there they were, dressed and sad, staring and silent as the coffin was lowered forever into the cold damp earth. I remembered my first experience with this sort of thing when Honey Combes was lowered in the same way. I shuddered when Adora Moreno was buried just as I shuddered now among the strangers who came to say good-bye. They didn't know who I was. They didn't know Nadia and I shared a bed and I kept her from harm's way at night and soothed her nightmares when she recalled her kidnapping and having to kill her assailant. Nobody would know, except maybe Ida and Sophie—oh, yeah, and Lt. Lester Keith, who I was overdue to see this very afternoon.

Ida and I were leaving the cemetery when an older couple approached us. "Mr. Denning," a lady's voice called after me. We stopped and the two of them approached us. The lady had a heavy accent. "I am Natalie Skorkowsky, and this is my husband, Gregory. We are Nadia's parents. Since you neglected to do so, Nadia's sister informed us of the—the horrible incident." Their faces were reddened from tears and they looked helpless standing there in the rain. I felt for them.

"I—I didn't know she had a sister and I didn't know how to get a hold of you. Nadia only spoke of you once that I recall...and she didn't say enough for me to know how to locate you." I extended my hand, but instead, Mrs. Skorkowsky took her hand and slapped me hard across the face.

"That—that is for killing my Nushka! Before you came into her life, she was chaste and proud! You ruined her! How *dare* you! You brought on this curse—you—you are a *czernobog*—a devil with a black soul! Now she—she is dead!" she cried. Her husband comforted her and apologized for his wife in some foreign language. It sounded like Russian, but I wasn't sure. Ida took my hand and led me away. Everyone was crying except me. My left cheek stung like hell!

I took Ida home and drove down Sunset Boulevard. The closer I got to the station downtown, the more anger overcame me. *Who did it? Who would perpetrate such a diabolical deed?!* Who would murder a lovely young woman just coming into her operatic prime? I had shoved that anger down for several days, but now it was erupting and I knew Lester Keith wouldn't appreciate me foaming at the mouth about it. For a change, he was quite subdued that Friday afternoon.

"This is the one homicide I can say—*I think*—you had nothing to do with—tell me I'm right, Denning. *Did you?*"

I looked at the inspector. "Whatta *you* think?"

"Forget it, I'm sorry—I'm—I'm just overworked. Too goddamned many murders this month—it's like people are goin' nuts or somethin'. You know what I mean? Too frickin' many idiots out killing—like some phobia has gotten hold of 'em and—"

"—whatta ya want me for, Lester?" I interrupted. "It's been a rather rough day."

"Your left cheek's red—who hit you *now*, your secretary?"

"No, the dead woman's mother. Thought I was responsible for her daughter's death—it's the European way, I guess, to make it known to the offender."

"Well, are you partly responsible? Whatta ya know, Denning? Ya better come clean or else I'll scrub it outta you!"

"You know Watson's dead—and he worked alone—who else could it be? Don't you think I've been tortured tryin' to figure it? I feel guilty as hell, because I keep thinkin' if it weren't for me, Nadia would still be livin' and breathin' and up there on that stage singing her little heart out."

There was a rare look of sympathy on the lieutenant's face. "Yeah, I guess. Who can figure humans? I had some nut in here the other day sayin' he kills people because we were native *Martians* a million and a half years ago, and we ruined that planet. So now we're here to ruin this one! Screw it, I don't know...some people are just insane, that's all there's to it."

I registered what Lester had said. I'd heard that story before. What if we *had* come from another planet like Mars and whatever species we were, we somehow got mixed with the bloodline of the primitive ones that existed here? As if we weren't a mess before, now we're not only what we were...but added to that, the primal scream inside us cries out for identity because we're torn between being 'gods' and men. "Who knows, Lester?"

"Yeah, Denning, who knows? Regardless of that shit, I got things to do, like leave the case open until we find Skorkowsky's killer. All we know is that it was murder in the first degree. That's it. Maybe your lady had enemies we don't know about, maybe a jealous boyfriend or singing competitor in the opera removed her 'cause she was in the way of *her* career."

"I have a hunch we may never know. I wouldn't even know where to begin. Nadia and I were kind of a new item, ya know. I hadn't met any people she actually knew well. I was staying with her because she was scared to death of being at home alone—especially at night."

"So she dies on the stage...ironic, ain't it?" He looked at the file in front of him. "Well, either way, I've gotta keep lookin' for a while. I'm sure you know about forty percent of murderers are still out there on the streets. Crimes of passion, gangs, insanity—temporary or otherwise--alcohol, drugs, the release of frozen rage—you name it. Sometimes I wonder why I chose this profession. It's a hell of a way to make a livin'."

"Oh...c'mon, Lester—you were designed for it. You love the chase, like me. Otherwise you'd waste away in some bureaucratic office or do blue collar work in a factory from eight to five."

"You think so, eh, Denning? Try my shoes for about a week. Maybe it was exciting when I was younger. Now...it just makes me feel old."

"I guess I feel that way sometimes, too." We talked a little more, but I'd left Lester in my head about five minutes before. Next Tuesday I had an appointment to sleep with Sophie. Only the next morning she'd wake up without the forming baby in her womb. I had to make that call to Oscar Brandt. What I really wanted to do was tell Sophie to run and don't look over her shoulder, run until she was in a different land and safe from the butchers of Buchenhorst!

"By the way, I took your advice on this Dr. Pritchard and released him. I really didn't have anything solid, anyway. But...if he shows up on another blotter one day, you'll have some accountin' to do—to me!"

"Thanks, Lester. He's a scientist. Scientists kill for science, mostly. I'm not sure what category you'd put him into—but not out and out murder."

"I hope you're right, Denning. I went out on a limb on this one."

The Death Lurker

It was Saturday, July 14th, and things would be slow for Sophie at the Greystone Mansion. I called her and she had agreed to come over to spend a night with me soon. She didn't have her old zip and that bothered me.

It was now or never and so I called Oscar Brandt's contact number and he *did* call me right back. He said one of his men would drop off a potion that I should put in Sophie's drink and they would come about two in the morning when she was asleep to remove the fetus growing inside Sophie's very female body. I just needed to name the night. God, I felt awful. What was I doing? How fickle could I be? Just days ago I wanted Sophia Legende so much I couldn't do without her. Weeks before that I desired Nadia Skorkowsky the same way! What part was missing in me, I began to wonder? Or was there too much candy available for a good looking gumshoe who has an over-active sex drive and after a while women are a common place experience? So you become inured to taking what you want how and when you want it. Where was my heart?

Ida Latney called me, wanting to know if I wished to come over and take a walk with her. I told her, yeah, that would be fine. So about two that afternoon I found myself walking in Griffith Park with my comely secretary. It was a bit warm but tolerable and Ida wore a very thin polka dot blouse with a nice skirt. She probably didn't know it, but she could dress very sexy in a wholesome sort of way. Her smallish nipples peaked out through her thin slip and blouse and her blondish hair shone in the afternoon light. That flushed clean complexion of hers, her white skin with the slight reddish tone and those blue eyes contrasted with the dirt road and sagebrush as we trudged along. "I've missed you, Cable," Ida intoned quietly as we walked.

"Missed me? I see you four or five days a week."

"You know what I mean. It's been—it's been a long time since we—we—" She flushed and turned her head away. "Well, since we've been intimate. I am human, you know. I miss being held by you—even if I am a little drunk at the time. Maybe that's what I need to uninhibit me."

"I'm sorry, Ida. Half of me feels guilty for flaunting all those other babes in your face—and half of me doesn't know what to do about you. I'm still in that frame where boss and secretary—"

"—shouldn't consort together on an intimate basis, yes, I know. But it's too late for that, Cable. Does it ever occur to you I might desire you and want to make love without admitting to myself how much I want you?"

"Yeah, I suppose, from time to time it does occur to me. But what am I gonna do about it, Ida? I'm not a stud-for-hire, ya know."

I knew I shouldn't have said that. Ida walked ahead of me, pouting. When finally she paused on the road to take a breath, I saw the tears in her eyes. "Gees, Ida, I'm sorry," I told her. "Sometimes that's how I feel, though. But I truly realize you're neat and clean and lovely and efficient and besides—you're really good in bed!" I took her in my arms and she wept.

"I never ask for much, Cable...never...have I? Just a little honest love now and then..."

"At the same time, Ida, I gotta desire you—I mean *really* desire you, not just give you a mercy fuck now and then."

"That's horrible! Is that what it's been for you? No, Cable, I can feel things—you're wrong...I know how lost you are inside yourself when it comes to women. Some-

335

thing went odd along the way, like you can never have enough. But the few times we've made love, I can feel someone who feels and cares and wants what he doesn't even know he wants!"

I raised my eyebrows. I smiled at her. "Ya know, kid, you're okay. Sometimes I forget how okay you really are. And in this insane world, Ida, you're one of the sane ones. Yeah, maybe I am nuts and fouled up in there somewhere. I'll tell ya what. Let's have a wonderful dinner and dancing night very soon, okay?"

She brightened a bit. "Really? You mean it? I hope it isn't a 'mercy date'." We both laughed.

"No, Ida, it ain't that. It's trying to make up for what I can never make up for. But it's an attempt to tell you how much I appreciate you."

"I guess that'll have to do—for now. Maybe someday you'll feel differently about me. I don't know. Once you told me it had to be there in the beginning. Well, it was for me, but obviously not for you."

"I wish I knew what I wanted, Ida. But you of all people know how risky it is to be in my life. Only my secretaries haven't met with the bad ending, so many dames have. And I know that's a major stumbling block—it's always in the back of my head—that I'd endanger a woman who's in my life. And I *have*, even if I don't plan it that way. Bad guys get back by hurting the people that are close to me. Like Oscar Brandt and his cut-throat bastards. I wouldn't want you or anyone else exposed to them if they knew I was sleeping with you. Only Lester Keith thinks we should be together." I was thinking of Sophie.

"He does?"

"Yep. He thinks you're American home and apple pie, the kind of woman a guy could hook up with and have a nice house, a few kids, a white picket fence and a twenty-year mortgage with a large lawn to mow on Saturdays!"

Ida chuckled. It was good to see her wonderful smile pop out from under those naturally sensuous lips of hers. "So...? What's so bad about that?"

"For some guys, nothin'. But I'm a different breed, Ida—the kinda man who's a lone wolf in the night and who sees things from a slightly different angle. I used to pride myself on being a truth man but I've lied so I wouldn't hurt others, including you. I've got so little to hold on to inside myself, like sometimes I feel like I'm caving in and I'm up there somewhere in the universe screaming the primal scream because somehow I don't know where I am anymore!"

She took my arm. "Maybe that's why I want you so much, Cable. You bring out my mothering instincts. I want to care for you, cook for you, have your babies, clean our house and wash your clothes. And on cold winter nights snuggle with you in bed and feel you inside me like a dream come true. That's what I think about, Cable. I just wanted you to know."

"Then it's just a dream, Ida. I can't be those things or that mold you'd like me to fit into. I realize it's a stereotype that's born and bred into us as children. But it can be a trap, too. Ya just gotta be cut out for it, that's all. And I ain't."

She sighed heavily. "So it's dinner and dancing, then...and maybe a kiss in the dark when no bad guys are looking?"

337

We laughed again. "Ya know, babe, if I were some-one else, you'd be the best bet on the block."

"Don't give up on it, Cable, I'm still here..."

"Yeah, Ida, and I'm thankful for that. You're the best!"

We walked in silence for a while and I took Ida Lat-ney's hand. She squeezed my hand tight. "I'm—I'm a lit-tle concerned about Sophie, Cable."

"Yeah? What's goin' on?"

"Oh, she's kind of out-of-sorts lately, you know, down-in-the-mouth. I don't think she enjoys her work anymore. If I didn't know better, I'd think she's preg-nant or something. She turns pale sometimes in the morning and goes to the bathroom. I'm wondering if she throws up. I don't know...she isn't the same ol' So-phie I remember when you first introduced us. But I guess she can't be pregnant because she's always main-tained no man has ever entered her—right?"

"Yeah...well, we all get job burnout," I said, thinking how close Ida was coming to the truth. "She'll get over it."

"Maybe, Cable, maybe, but she's awful depressed..."

Boom!

It was early Monday morning, July 16, 1945. Around five in the morning I felt some kind of shaking going on. Yep, another Los Angeles minor rocker. Earthquakes were more or less common in these parts. The San An-dreas fault was nearby. One of these days it would go, taking parts of the Pacific Coastline with it.

But there was something about this particular 'quake' that didn't feel like a jolt from the depths of the planet. No, instead, it felt like an explosion far away that was so foreboding and monstrously large that the earth shook all way from Alamogordo to here! Was this the day, then? Was this the day the bomb went off and with it all the hopes for nature and humanity in one big bag of man's tricks on himself? I leaned up and turned the radio on. Only two stations were on the air and the sweet music from the dame singing her song across the airwaves gave me a feeling of peace and I fell back to sleep, dreaming of a beautiful babe in red sequins singing to me and then revealing more and more as the dream went on. Yep, pretty sweet!

By 9:30 a.m. the phone was ringing just as Ida came in the door. I was still in my tee shirt and boxers. "Yeah, Cable Denning here..."

"Denning, it's Dr. Pritchard. Thanks for springing me. How would you like to come up north and see Davy on Thursday the 26th?"

"Oh, yeah, hello Pritchard." I'd been thinking about this extra-ordinary boy of Milano's. Or was the kid really his? One never knows for sure. "Yeah, I think I can manage that—but hell, it's ten days away. Anything can happen between now and then."

"Well, make sure it doesn't...I'll pick you up about eight Thursday morning. It's a long trip. But I promise you, it'll be worth it."

"Oh, Pritchard, by the way, I think they finally did it."

"Did what?"

"Exploded the damn atomic bomb." Ida looked up from her desk.

"How do you know?"

"Dollars to donuts I'm right—I got a feelin' for things like that. About five or so this morning. I just felt it, that's all."

"You could be wrong, you know."

"Yeah, could be, but not too likely."

"If it's true, Denning, then no telling what's next."

"Yeah, I've been kinda thinkin' that myself."

"I hope you're wrong. Maybe Thursdays will come and go and nothing's changed."

"Things take time, Pritchard. I'll see ya Thursday morning."

"Yes, sure..."

"I'll meet you down below on the street. Do you know where I live?"

"Who doesn't know where Cable Denning lives?" he jested.

"Oh? I didn't know I was so famous."

"One book can do miracles—what was the author's name?"

"Nancy Gibbons—not her real name. That was Maria Voldt. She's dead, so it doesn't really matter now, does it?"

"No, I guess not. So, then, Denning, Thursday the 26th at eight." I was staring into space, thinking about Maria Voldt.

"How do I get a hold of you if something comes up?"

"You can't. Just make it—providing you're still breathing." He hung up before I could reply.

Then I looked over at my pretty secretary. "Good morning, Miss Latney," I said, half smiling at her in my underwear.

"Good morning, Cable. I see you dressed for the day," she said with a hint of playful sarcasm in her voice and expression.

"Very funny. I was up early and then went back to sleep..."

"Do you really think it was the bomb?"

"I'm not sure...just a hunch. Oppenheimer believed in it. Maybe it was a way to destroy all the waste, the countless pitiful hours humans count out before they're pushing daisies."

"Isn't that a bit morbid?" Ida commented, looking at my underwear as I stood up. "You need to wash that." I dismissed the subject completely much to Ida's chagrin .

"I even memorized that passage of the *Bhagavad Gita*. *'Do not yield to unmanliness, O Son of Pritha. It does not become you. Shake off this base dis-heartedness, and arise, O scorcher of enemies—for I am become as death, destroyer of worlds!'* Pretty good, huh?" I asked as I looked over for Ida's response.

She smiled at me with that refreshing morning smile that lit up my day whenever I was feeling down. "Yes, well recited, gallant one!" Then she sat down and played with her pencil. "So, if it's true, what about the bomb? How come we don't know about it?"

"Oh, you will, when they want you to. The government won't release it right away anyway. But I'll go even further out on a limb. These idiots are gonna blow up Hitler or Japan with the goddamned thing. Forget Italy. They killed Mussolini almost three months ago."

"Yes, I remember reading about it." She cleared her throat. "Really? What would that prove—I mean, if they did that—kill a bunch of other people with some stupid bomb?"

"Nothing. Maybe end the war a month early or so. I don't know."

I continued thinking about Maria Voldt, so I took out her old folder. "Wanna hear a Maria Voldt poem?" I asked Ida.

"Yes, of course, you know how I love her writing. Maybe it's because she loved you so much. Sometimes I...I think about—"

"—Ida...not now...I'll just read, okay?"

"Okay..." I felt bad about stopping Ida's attempts to find my heart and live there. But maybe she wasn't the right girl or something, or maybe I liked her best when she was drunk with me and we whored around in her bed all night. I didn't like either of us sober.

I picked a poem at random:

'All of a life is a game, a short stay in which we pay
With pain and pleasure, work and strain
But when the mountain comes to meet me
I'll look for you and you won't have crossed over
You'll still be the rover you are today
With staying power until the real thing
Comes along. Have a safe journey, love!'
mv

Maria Voldt always brought tears to my eyes. There was something so poignantly beautiful about *her*, as well as her writing. She was a delicate but strong bird who had flown in for the season and then migrated back to where she'd come from. Ida was crying, too. "She loved you so much, but you never saw it, did you?" she half-whimpered, mirroring her own feelings toward me. "And you're still a rover. Maybe will be for the rest of your life."

"Maybe...maybe not...I'm sorry Ida I'm not what you're lookin' for in a man. I would like to be, but I don't seem to keep my fingers out of the wonderful pies in the confectionary shop. You know how that feels?"

"No, but I know that's how *you* are. If Sophie Legende wasn't a prostitute and unavailable, I'm sure you'd try her out, too. And that reminds me, I'm still concerned about her. She seems despondent."

"Despondent?"

"Yes, as if the life has been drained out of her."

I was thinking about the abortion Sophie had yet to undergo while being unconscious.

I shut down and let Ida continue for a few minutes until she realized I wasn't responding and went quiet. Then she returned to her office duties. By four o'clock she was preparing to leave for the day. "You do remember our walk—and what you said—dinner and dancing?"

I sat there trying to decide if I should have my first gin or cigarette for the day. I had abstained the whole of it and I was aching in my lungs and gut. "Yeah, Ida, I do remember. How about next weekend—the one after this?"

"That'd be swell, Cable. Friday or Saturday?"

343

"Oh, how about Saturday night?" I glanced at my wall calendar. "The 28th? That way, in case we—we, uh, become entangled during the evening, we can sleep in."

I knew she'd like that. "I'll be just getting over my period—so I'll be—uh...well, you know. I'll be safe...if—if you want me—I know I'll want you, Cable. It's been so long." Speaking that frankly embarrassed Ida and her face flushed. But she was a woman with an agenda.

I smiled and took her hand. "Yeah, I know, Ida. As I told you on our walk, I'm sorry about that. I just have to feel it, too, ya know."

"Yes..." she answered. Then Ida Latney leaned down and kissed my forehead. Then she put on her hat and coat and left for the day without another word. How can ya figure a dame?!

Hell, after that, I decided to have both a cigarette *and* some gin. Why not? I was puffing and sipping away when I heard a familiar voice in my ear. ""You're a mess, Cable Denning. And after I revitalized you. Your heart...it's—it's been damaged. Smoking, drinking, lack of sleep, too many women—even though that part—"

"—hello to you, too, Erond!" I crackled. "Oh, no, don't tell me you've come to collect part two of my debt to you..."

"No, actually I've given up on that."

"Oh? Thank goodness for small favors. I was beginning to worry."

"My race leaders don't think it'll work long term. So you're 'off the hook', as you earth folk might say. We'll just have to get along without having fun making love or the like. I think I need to heal you up, though. So…go to your back room and lay down."

"I think they set the goddamn bomb off today, Erond."

"Humans will always be experimenting, playing like children at ruining their lovely garden. It's in their mixed up nature, you know."

"Yeah, so I've discovered." I laid down on my bed and soon I could feel the invisible creature's healing rays of warmth penetrate my body. He was silent other than his humming. He always did that. They were pure long tones of varying frequencies and I could tell they were tuned to the organs in my body that he was working on.

"This will heal your heart and give you some energy juice. But watch it, boy, you'll have some extra sexual energy with my overhauling your glandular system. Your lungs, too." Soon he finished my "overhaul" and I felt sleepy. "Now rest, Denning, and if perchance we should meet again, I will find you as a young man of thirty or less! Don't dissipate your health and energies. Now that your girlfriend is dead—whatever will you do?"

Suddenly it occurred to me Erond might know. "Who killed Nadia, Erond? Do you know?"

"How should I know? I wasn't in your consciousness realms when the plan was laid and the woman's body destroyed. We love your planet, but we say 'nix' to your species. So we're not settling here."

"I kinda feel the same way. I don't wanna settle here, either! Shit, only I have no place else to go."

"Don't you?" he returned.

345

"No! Where? At least you have planets to go to."

"I must leave you now, Cable. I'm sorry I mussed up your relationship that night. I didn't have all that much fun, either. And now your Nadia is gone, too. I am sorry for that."

"It's okay, Erond, I guess it was just in the cards."

"Yes, well, perhaps next incarnation I'll be an Axonnian god or the like. That, they say, *is* a lot of fun." I felt a warmth on my inner wrist. "Good-bye, Cable. Stay in touch."

"How can I do that?"

"Just...think of me..." And then I knew he had gone.

Chapter 8

THE DARK AT THE END OF THE WORLD

Broken Places in the Heart

It was Saturday night, July 21st. About 8:45 I heard a light knock on my door. When I answered, a beautiful but sullen Sophia Legende greeted me. She glided into my arms and kissed me on the shoulder as she buried her head in my shirt. "I'm broken, Cable, and I'm pregnant," she murmured. "Quite a combination. Oh, and also depressed, I think."

Oscar Brandt's messenger boys had left off the potion I was to use on Sophie this night. "You need a good stiff drink, kid," I said.

"I've—I've been drinking—can't you tell? But I guess one more won't hurt. Some of your fine English gin?"

"Yup," I said as I went behind my desk and poured the amount of dope into her glass. It was colorless, odorless and I assumed more or less fast acting. "So...why did you say you're broken, Sophie. You look great to me."

"That's because I let you screw me, mister. I always look great to men who can have me—whatever which way that is."

"I thought I was the first—"

"—you are...you were. But I'm...I'm full of shattered pieces inside, Cable." She wasn't quite herself, so I figured she'd been tossing down the booze quite a bit before she got here. "And now—now that I've had you, I want you even more. I need to quit what I'm doing and just do *you.*" She laughed.

"That's hardly a living, Sophie," I said, bringing her glass to her.   She took it, but put it down on my desk. Then she put her arms around my waist and put her cheek to my chest. "I have *money*, Cable... lots of it. I've scrimped and saved—for years. I didn't even know what for. But now I do. Come away with me, you—you darling man, come away to all points north, south, east—west, who gives a fuck?!! As long as you fuck me, that is. I need it now. You've sexualized me as a woman. Me—Sophia Legende—I hadn't happened before, I hadn't happened to the world or myself until you. Now I'm needy. I hate being needy. But here I am. Will you take me to bed right now and then I'll have this drink to celebrate how much I care about us—you and me—us?"

I needed to be on schedule. "How—how about taking the drink first, feeling those warming effects—and *then* screwing me?"

She smiled. "Sure...why—why not?" She was wearing a lovely light pink spaghetti strap gown and silver slipper-like shoes. Her wonderful blonde hair hung like a painting of Veronica Lake before the world got a hold of her. There was an innocence about Sophia Legende that I loved. It was pure and no man could ever have that. It was something she saved for herself. She took my hand and led me to my bedroom and I pulled down the shade, but the damned neon sign across the street still beamed and blinked through it. I watched as the professional Sophia Legende quietly, gently pulled her straps down. Then she turned her back toward me.

"Please...?" she asked me as I unzipped the back of her gown. It fell to the floor and she was wearing nothing under it. "You like me this way, don't you? You like the raw, sensual, sexual woman who throws caution to the wind and shoves your man into my woman—don't you?"

I stood there, searching for a polite way to deal with her drunkenness. "Well, yeah, that's part of it, Sophie. The other part is I really care about you. Maybe at first it was the chemistry thing we have for each other. But now...I don't know...it seems more to me."

She walked over to me, unzipped my fly and put her hand into my pants. "More? Because I'm such a pro that I turn you on at the sight of me? Or is it my voice, my use of the language? Or my pussy? Which is it, Cable?" She was deriding herself.

"You're drunk, Sophie. And I'm not. It's hard for me to take a drunk when I'm not drunk."

"Then get drunk!" she commanded. "Sorry—sorry about that, mister. But tonight, this blonde babe is smashed, thoroughly and sordidly intoxicated. Am I objectionable to you?"

"I'll tell ya what, Sophie. I need to catch up a little," I lied. "I'll go get you your drink, and I'll start guzzling to boot, okay?"

"Okay..."

"Then we can lie in bed together and do anything we want." I went into the other room and came back with both glasses. We toasted and she gulped her drink down. "Whoa, there, girl! That's kind of brisk, don't ya think?"

"Sometimes...I like it brisk...what about you?"

I got her under the covers and soon joined her. I laid on my back and she glided into my arms. I locked her there and it felt good. "I like you, kid." I was thinking what a chump I turned out to be. For ten thousand lousy bucks—well, there *is* the matter of saving my life—I sold our child-to-be to be scientifically experimented on! And all because I was half-alien. Poor Sophie. What would she feel afterward? Would she know right away? And if and when I tell her—will she walk away, disillusioned? Finally I couldn't take it anymore. "Sophie—I feel terrible about something. I—I did a terrible thing, but you gotta know about it now—before they get here."

She was still somewhat inebriated. "Here? Where here—and who?"

"Here...in this room...I—I gave you a drugged drink, babe. Your baby is gonna be taken from you while you're asleep and doped up— later tonight. I made a deal with the *Lichter Grabstätte* to save my ass and get paid ten grand for getting you pregnant."

She sat up and shook her head as if she hadn't heard me right. "Cable...I—I don't think I'm—I'm understanding you..."

"They knew I was half-alien, a specialized human-looking race of beings called the *Sens Parafactors.* My father was one. I'm half of one, my mother being all human—and Irish. They said they'd spare my life if I got you pregnant. I don't know why *you*, Sophie. What do they know about you that I don't? I'm so sorry!" I said with a lump in my throat.

Sophia Legende drew quiet. Then she sobered herself somewhat. Finally she spoke, measuring her words

350

slowly. "I see...so you never...never even knocked on the door of...of loving me?"

"Sophie, I did and I do. But why didn't they choose Nadia or Ida or someone else—why you?"

"Ida's more in love with you...than...I could ever be, Cable. I was just—ha! playing you for a good lay, detective. Or didn't you know? Remember, I'm a whore—slut, hooker, professional prostitute! I look good on the outside of the package, but I'm rotten inside, buddy boy! And the baby? Hell, I was cons...considering an abortion anyhow. Me, Sophia Legende with a brat to drag around? Just think, you'll get a free hack job without using the coat hanger!" she laughed. But it was a phony, forced laugh. I didn't buy it. I think Sophia Legende was hurting inside. "How much money for me, Cable—ten thousand smackers? Ha! What—what a hell of a price for a free bitch-in-heat!" Then her words began to slur more and more. "That—that's what I was, you—you know. I was in-heat for you, mister private, well-hung dick." She paused and changed the expression on her face and her eyes grew wide with apprehension. "I'm—I'm afraid, Cable. Who are these people who—who've come to take my—my baby away from me?"

"His name is Oscar—Oscar Brandt. I'm—I'm sure he'll bring some very trained people to do the operation safely. They don't wanna risk anything, either, ya know. And I won't let you outta my sight, I promise."

"Prom—promise?" She looked up into my face pathetically. "Why...why, Cable, did you have to do this? After all, it was me—here—this me, the Sophie me who really loves you." She turned her head away. "But I know you don't love me. Not really. Do you—do you

351

have aliens go around breeding with pretty white blonde women all the time?"

"No, Sophie, I wouldn't do that. I feel lousy enough. Please, let's not talk about it anymore. You think I have no feelings?"

"Do you? I'm not sure. Maybe you don't. I—I thought I knew—you know that song I do—*Let's Face the Music and Dance*? That—that's what we're doing right now, isn't it? '*There may be trouble ahead, but while there's moonlight and music and love and romance, let's face the music and dance...*' Looks like the romance part is over, doesn't it, Cable?"

"Yeah, Sophie, maybe. You might not want to be anywhere near me after tonight."

"You're not—not getting off that ea...easy mi- ster. I...I might be back...for...for...a good free fuck now and then." She was losing ground and soon she fell into my arms out cold. Personally? I was feeling lower than dirt right about then, but those damn Germans sure knew their science!

While Sophie slept in my arms I was awake and vigilant. I also went into thought I hadn't explored for some time. It was about time for Zelda to make herself known, wasn't it? And what about Nan? And my diamonds, glistening somewhere in a vault on another plane of existence. I must collect them one day. But what the hell would I do with a million bucks? I'd become a simple man with simple tastes. I was also a part-time drunk and a chain smoker. I also thought about two of my favorite people in the world and how I missed them. Bernie and Auina, who had come together and made a wonderful life for each other. But they lived on the East Coast.

At 1:30 in the morning the phone rang. I carefully unwrapped Sophie, got up out of bed and walked to my office desk. I was wondering if the Lichter Grabstätte had changed its mind. "Yeah, Cable Denning here…"

"Cable, it's Ida. Have you heard from Sophie? She told me she was going to work and it would be a slow tonight—and she'd be back early."

"Uh…no, Ida," I fibbed. "Maybe she picked up another 'John' for the night. Ya never know with call girls— they're *on call!* What are you doing up so late?"

"Oh, I was lying in bed thinking about you—and *next* Saturday night. What would you like me to wear?"

I took a deep breath. I was gonna say '*nothing*' but that would excite her with anticipation too much in case I changed my mind. "Well, it's summer time, ya know. How about something light—and maybe just a little bit revealing?"

She giggled. "Yes…that…I'll do it and surprise you, Cable. Sorry to wake you up."

"Well, let me know when Sophie comes home, will ya?"

"Yes…good night, Cable."

"Good night, Ida…"

Punctually at 2:00 I admitted Oscar Brandt and two other people. One was a clean-cut middle-aged man with wire-rimmed glasses and the other a young German woman who really wasn't bad looking—and blonde. "Ve assume ze patient is ready, Herr Denning?" Brandt inquired.

"Yeah, she's—she's in there, sleeping peacefully on my bed."

"*Gut...das ist gut!*" He looked around the room. "Ve vill have to operate on your bed. Zer vill not be much blood, but ve must have an extra sheet, just in case zer is—is ze 'unforeseeable', as your American mystery movies say so often—ya, ze unexpected, you know."

"Yeah." I went and got an old sheet from my closet as the female assistant stripped Sophie of all her clothing. She was so knocked out that she seemed dead to me. That was a shuddering thought. The doctor and his assistant worked quiet and fast. They had an advanced looking machine that resembled a delicate vacuum cleaner. That was inserted into Sophie's vagina and a clear test tube was at the other end. Soon it filled with blood and whatever developed part of Sophie's embryo they wanted. Immediately that went into a warmly insulated mitten-like thing and the two assistants left. Within an hour's time it was done. "Ya...goodt! Ve are finished here—for now. Ze doctor tells me she vill bleed. You must clean her. Give her a morning bath. If za embryo proves to be non-viable, zen you vill have to repeat your performance vis za young fräulein here. Vhen she vakes up she vill remember nozzing. Zo..." He took out an envelope from his breast pocket and handed it to me. "You vant to count it, Herr Denning—or do you trust me?"

"No, I don't wanna count it and I *don't* trust you, Brandt. It's blood money, literally and otherwise. You can slither out under the door you came in. Good night..."

354

He clicked his heels and left. It had been a hell of a night!

I spent the night next to Sophie Legende, listening to her voice singing *Let's Face the Music and Dance* in my head. I washed her regularly and by morning when she began to stir, I felt tired as hell. Finally she awakened and smiled up at me. "Mr.—Mr. Denning...is it?..."

"Yeah, it's me, kid. How are you feeling?" I asked, kissing her forehead gently .

"Okay, I guess. I—I don't remember much. But I like...waking up... with you here..."

"If you can move, I'm gonna get you into the bathtub to soak for a while. I also would like you to call Ida and tell her you're still out at the mansion—you—you had a late night customer or something and you're sorry you didn't call earlier and not to worry."

"All that, huh? You love her...don't you?"

"She called late, wondering about you. You shoulda told her you'd be out all night."

"I—I thought I'd be back after you—after you and I hung around together...for a few hours."

She was sore, but I got her into my tattered by comfy robe, to the phone to talk to Ida and finally into the bathtub. I forgot how beautiful her white body was in the semi-daylight. It was near flawless and perfectly proportioned. Her breasts were perfectly shaped, her nipples were light pink, and her stomach sensuous and flat. "How are ya feelin', babe?"

She looked up at me with those large wonderful eyes of hers. "Okay, I guess. What happened, Cable? I feel different."

"Well, you were half-drunk or better when you got here last night. I helped you out with more booze, gave you a potion that knocked you out. About 2:00 a.m., these three people come in, one a doc and his assistant, the other Brandt. They did what they did and left. That's it."

She stared down at her stomach. "They took my baby...it's a strange feeling, Cable. Somehow I can tell— besides my being sore as hell and out of sorts in my head. I also have a hangover."

"Yeah, quite a night, Sophie, quite a night..."

The Soul Thieves

It was Thursday, July 26th. Sunny Acres was tucked back in the hilly area just southeast of the main town. The place was an all brick building with a flight of stairs leading up to the main entrance in the middle, and building extensions out on both sides. It had a dark feeling about it. The door was opened by an older man with a black moustache and white hair, thick glasses and holding a yardstick firmly in his hand. He seemed fidgety, nervous. "It's the boys—one never knows when they'll turn on you. Mr. Gross and I keep a handy eye on the boys, I must say." He checked both of us out. Pritchard looked like a madman with his hair askew and I looked like some gumshoe who stepped out of a Phillip Marlowe dime novel. He was looking at Pritchard's I.D. He carried a movie actor's British accent. "By the way, I am Salisbury Connert, the director-in-residence here." Then he took a monocle and studied Pritchard's face. "I say, are you Mr. Milano's personal physician?" he inquired.

"Something like that. I've come to take Davy back to his father."

"Oh, I could not—no, sir, I could not do that in a million years! You see, first there is no advance written permission from the father, then the courts—and Monica, our sweet and beloved bookkeeper."

"Well, could we at least just walk about the grounds with him, you know, have an old fashioned talk with the boy. We are close, after all."

"Highly extraordinary, but acceptable, I suppose." Then he turned to me. "And you are Dr. Pritchard's friend—bodyguard?"

"Me? No, just a curious acquaintance. I wanna take a look at the boy."

"Yes, well...quite curious, you know. Poor chap must feel quite alone. For the most part, the other boys shun him. After all is said and done, Mr.—Mr.—"

"—Denning, Cable Denning..."

"Mr. Denning...we have an oddly constructed individual. Personally I would not have him here except that our most efficient mistress of the account books, Miss Monica Blepp by name, insists that receiving double the usual charges for attendance here at Sunny Acres allows us to pursue a few—uh...a few 'extras' on the premises."

I figured these guys were con artists of a sort, real 'sea thieves'. Connert asked us to wait while he fetched Davy Milano. Neither Pritchard nor I were prepared for the condition in which Davy was presented to us. Literally, he was in a leather waistcoat that had leather straps that restricted his arms. He also was confined at his ankles with common county jail shackles. "Lord, man, undo this young person immediately!" Pritchard demanded.

Connert thought it over. I could feel his wheels turning. "Well, I suppose for the walk. Yes."

"I have a few gifts for Davy in my trunk." Pritchard turned to Davy. "Would you like to see what I have for you?"

"Yes, you three go along. I hope you don't mind my having our dear ward followed by Mr. Gross...liability, don't you know..." Connert commented with a slight sneer in his voice.

But the seemingly reticent young man did not reply. As Pritchard freed him up he simply stood and stared, as if there were no emotion in him or on his face. "You do remember me, do you not, Davy?"

The boy slowly nodded his head. Maybe he was mentally impaired by now. I've heard of extraordinary cases where geniuses just burn out real quick in life. And that's it.

So, with the rotund Mr. Gross following behind, we ventured outdoors with Davy in the middle between Pritchard and myself. There was a grove of cypress trees just before the parking lot. Pritchard led us toward it. There were flowers in a bed just before the trees. The doc took one and showed it to Mr. Gross. "Now...this is a wonderful wild daisy family, you know..." The man bent over to smell and almost instantly fainted away. Pritchard showed me a small vile of something hidden in the flower. "Works every time." We dragged him into the trees and Pritchard then led us toward his automobile. Quickly he opened the trunk and I could have fainted myself when I saw what I saw.

There, curled up in a fetal position lay the *exact dupli-cate of Davy Milano!* "Davy, we're taking you back to Los Angeles with us. Please remove your clothing—all of it." The boy began to disrobe as Pritchard peeled a tur-quoise jump suit off the dummy's body. Soon they had reversed positions and Davy lay in the trunk space of the car. "As soon as I revive Gross and take your dupli-cate back, Davy, we'll go. But first I need to awaken this replicated humanoid. Now remember, the first thing he sees is what he will duplicate. So, guess what—it's going to be you, Davy." With that, Pritchard leaned the boy over to peer at the dummy's face. Then he did some-thing to the inner wrist and the eyes of the twin opened and took in all of Davy Milano. We helped the synthetic 'Davy' out and put the real one into the trunk. "There...see you soon...there's air enough for you to breathe until we get back." He shut the trunk and off we went with the rather awkward replicant Davy in tow. But all I can say is that he was learning fast. Pritchard revived Gross and the man had no clue or memory of what had happened. We headed back to the main build-ing and there to greet us stood a suspicious Mr. Connert.

"Well, back so soon? The lad had nothing much to say, did he? He's always that way. If it weren't for the funds trickling our way—"

"—oh, on the contrary, he told us a lot," Pritchard responded.

"Indeed? How curious! He never—I mean never—speaks to us."

"Thanks, Mr. Connert, but I am afraid my friend Mr. Denning was not able to enjoy Davy all that much...didn't seem to want to speak with him much.

But...compliments to your Mr. Gross—a fine watchman as ever you'll find, sir—he couldn't have done it better if he were sleeping on the job!" Dr. Pritchard caroled with his tongue-in-cheek.

Connert looked at me. "Tough go, chap. One simply cannot tell about our boys here. Some are more like little women and talk incessantly. While...others...just seem to...well, seem to hide themselves away. Pity. But we try our very best for them here at Sunny Acres. Good day, gentlemen."

Son of the Stars

As soon as we were humming along the highway toward Los Angeles, Davy's face relaxed and I could hear the wheels turn in his head. After we'd been driving for about ten minutes, Pritchard asked Davy, "*Faber est suae quisque fortunae?*". He nodded to me. "I asked him if indeed he was the architect of his own fortune."

"*Veritas libertas*," the boy responded. I look-ed for an explanation and Pritchard complied.

"He enjoys speaking in Latin as a first language," he told me.

"Does he speak any good ol' American English?" I asked. "What the hell does that mean?"

"*'Truth is Freedom.'* Go ahead, try him...if he likes you, he'll respond. And if he doesn't, tough luck."

"So, Davy, if you don't mind, who are you, why are you, where are you? Your Dad seems to think you're—well, frankly, a misfit."

"We are surrounded by air, yet it does not ask who, why or where it is, Mr. Denning. Nor do I."

360

"I guess I never thought of things that way."

"You should…"

"What does your answer mean—the '*veritas*' something or other?"

"It means what you started out in this world to become—a man of truth. But the world of men has corrupted you, and like rusty metal, you are flaking off the fragments of virtue and, in turn, well-being. You are not even a half-truth man." This from a twelve year-old boy?!!

"Whoa, there! You're pretty brutal, young Davy!" I said, taking exception to his comment to me.

"Slowly…you have not realized how it seeps in, like a canker disease, leaking the purulence of its own deceit. First it's little white lies, then it's bigger ones, attempting to shuffle from one woman to another without the other discovering your so-called 'truth'. Worst of all is lying to yourself, the thing those creatures out there cannot bear to accept—suffering their own frailties. Humans as you know them are not true human beings, but only half-human."

"So…what happened to the other half? And by the way, how did you get that vocabulary and master—"

"—I told you he was far advanced of us. Just hear him out, Cable." Pritchard admonished me.

"It was placed into dormancy by your ancestry long ago. They came to equalize the situation they found here on earth. Their population numbers were dwindling. They knew they had to reproduce with the existing earth humanoids. So they modified your genes in order that children would be born, half of their genes and half of yours. But it didn't work. Millions of the

361

earth-years separated the two species. The earth beings thought they were part gods—and the takeover humanoids felt they were trapped in savage bodies with brutal instincts. So an internal conflict ensued. Now the earth is filling with confused remnants. I feel sorry for you."

"You do? So how do you fit in, then?"

"I don't." He adjusted the baseball cap on his head.

"Genius is always rejected by the layperson at some point. So Davy does not fit and lives in his own universe. Tell me, Denning, who can he share his life with? Surely not you or me," Pritchard observed, pounding the steering wheel of his car.

"So whatta ya gonna do with him?" I asked.

"Find out as much as I can about who he is, how he came to be this way and if indeed I can use his genetic material for reproducing his own kind."

"That's a pretty big order, and ain't ya kinda usin' the kid as a guinea pig?" I said. "Then I turned my head to Davy, who sat in the middle of the back seat." What do you think about that, Davy?"

"I don't know. But I do know I do not want to mix with your society. I've had enough of that with my sire. I don't even think he knows how to love me. It's his sister who made him take me in and give me room and shelter and food. I think she felt sorry for me. That's about it, though."

"I'm sorry, Davy. At least I had parents, a particularly loving mother."

"What about your father?"

"Oh, you mean my sire. He was an adventurer and I met him just before he died. Who was he?" I chuckled.

"He was an alien cross, part *Sens Parafactor*, part earth human."

Davy's eyes grew wide and suddenly he was just twelve years old again. "Really? What a gas! Maybe that's what I sense about you. You're—you're different, aren't you? I really believe in that stuff."

"Different? Yeah, I guess you could say that. Had my share of extra-terrestrial experiences in my time. I thought the way the doc described you before I met you was that you might be an alien yourself. But he assures me you're not, you're just a *Son of the Stars*—an anomaly that happens now and then in this crazy universe of ours."

Davy looked at my eyes and studied me for a minute. "Yes...now and then I guess it does happen. But then again, we're all aliens—it just depends where we show up, that's all."

I laughed. "Yeah, you know—you're right! We're all frickin' aliens!"

I never saw Davy Milano again. Nor Dr. Pritchard. Where they went and what they accomplished will remain a mystery to me.

A Dragon in the Night

Since February 1942 Japanese persons in the United States were placed into internment camps. I assumed most of the 120,000 plus people were U.S. citizens President Roosevelt had placed into compounds by signing order #9066 on February 19th. But there were lies under the table about that, too. West Coast agriculture big shots thought the Japanese-Americans were undercutting and competing with them on produce and distribution. So it was that under the pretext was another pretext. There was a lot of bitterness on the part of the Japanese, most of whom were decent, law-abiding citizens trying to live out their lives in the United States of America.

But there were still lots of Japs in the spy underground, hidden in the fabric of Los Angeles and its environs. I was to learn this the hard way. On Saturday morning, July 28th, I was sitting at my desk, minding my own business, thinking about Davy Milano, Dr. Pritchard, Sophie Legende...who might've killed Nadia and the courses of action I should take—when I received a mysterious phone call. The man's name was really Toshio Miyazaki, but he went under the name of 'Mr. Tanni'. He told me he was a "Japanese person in hiding" here in California. He said he was forced to hide out because of the war. But something terrible and horrible was happening to the Japanese associates around him. Someone or some*thing* had begun mutilating members of a branch of an organization called the *Black Dragon Society* to which he belonged. He felt it might be some white guys who got a handle on the remaining free Japanese in the Los Angeles area and began to eliminate them. His English was good. He told me I came highly recommended and this was a job for a special investigator who had adequate experience dealing with the paranormal. Now *that* intrigued me. Most of the Japanese population was either Shinto or Buddhist and he spoke strangely about some creature being seen near the downtown temple. Of course he was joking about that. Or was he? He pleaded with me to meet with him and promised me gold bullion if I met with him at an undisclosed location and solved the mystery of the gruesome murders. I agreed.

By two in the afternoon I was in what used to be called *Little Tokyo*, or *Japan town*. Now it was called *Bronzeville* because many negro people had moved into the area when the Japs were "relocated". Hatred for the Japanese was very powerful during these war years and even I wasn't crazy about dealing with these "slant-eyed bastards", as many a white man called them. As far as I was concerned, they were entitled to a fair shake, because after all, it's all in the individual.

The Japanese area ran along a few blocks, mostly on 1st Street downtown. One could see the city hall towering in the distance. But the Japanese underground, mostly sect members of the *Black Dragon* and spies who served their Emperor in the real Tokyo, Japan, remained in the area and I was to learn a whole subterranean world existed beneath the streets and in secret basement.

I was led into a dimly lit room with three Japanese men present. Mr. Tanni—Toshio Miyazaki—was a stout official looking man with silvering hair. He had attended Stanford University in Northern California and was an officer in the Japanese Navy. That much he told me. The rest he explained to me was a hell of a lot more conjectural in nature. "Five principal members of the Black Dragon have been brutally murdered, Mr. Denning," he told me. "It would have to be a very large person or creature to do such a thing. And we do not know how he does it. It is like he has a big garden soil scraper and rips the flesh from his victims. It is a terrible thing to see such a corpse."

"Yeah, so it sounds, Mr. Miyazaki...so it sounds..." I looked around at the other two gentlemen. They stood still and were obviously just off the boat because they didn't speak any English, I was told. "So just exactly where do these murders take place?"

"Oh—many places. Most here, in Japan Town. But one was discovered by the *umi*, the ocean, near Pacific Palisades."

"Then that's where I must begin the investigation."

He looked puzzled. "Why not here in Japan Town?"

"Because somehow that murder was displaced, as if the victim were on to something. And that's why I begin there," I answered. "And perchance, was he the last one killed"?"

His eyes, already narrow, became slits and he smiled oddly. "Oh...yes...very wise...to look for an extraordinary circumstance."

"Yeah, something like that. Now, what I want from you is a list of the dead guys, when and where they were discovered, especially the last guy in Pacific Palisades."

"But I did not say the last victim was in Pacific Palisades, sir."

"But he was, wasn't he?"

"As matter of fact, yes. But how did you know?"

"Just chalk it up to experience. I'll need some operating expenses. I get fifty dollars a day plus expenses, like food and gasoline."

"Fifty dollars a day? Very expensive, do you not say?"

"Ration cards on the black market are getting harder to come by. This war your race helped cause is a pain in my ass, Miyazaki."

"So sorry. Yes...if you wait ten minutes I will prepare your information. Would you wait outside, please?"

Pacific Palisades had been founded by a bunch of religionist people back in 1911. It had since grown to quite a fancy neighborhood, bordering the Pacific Ocean over bluffs from which a magnificent view of the sea was possible. The Black Dragon victim, one Tashiro Kirawani, was found on the street in front of 1076 Corsica Drive. It was a pretty classy corner house but didn't resonate for me. But two doors down I thought I found a clue on the street. Hanging on a yellow string near a gutter drain was a little five-sided pendant with what looked like Oriental lettering on it. I ripped the string off, cleaned up the small golden pendant and put it in my pocket. Just then a car pulled up and a nice looking non-Japanese man got out. "Sir, may I help you?" he asked with a discernible Italian accent.

I smelled a rat. "What makes you think I need help?" I said.

"I saw you—saw you pick something up from the gutter. Was it valuable?"

"It was trash, so I ripped the string off and tossed it," I lied.

"Oh. Well, my name is Amletto Vespa. I am leaving your country soon and I am tying up loose ends."

"And what's that got to do with me?"

"You know that a murder happened here a few nights ago?"

367

"No—you don't say…"

He checked out my fedora and trench coat. "You look to me like maybe you are looking for something?"

"Naw, just trying to find an old girlfriend."

"Oh, I see. Well, I'm kind of looking up some folks who lives down the street—and I'm gonna say good-bye to them."

"Yeah, well, good luck Mr. Vespa. I—I don't suppose you'd know if any Oriental people live around here?"

Now he was very interested in me. "Si…yes, I do know that. Are you a policeman?"

"Nope, just a private dick."

"Che cosa? I don't know—"

"—a private investigator."

"E vero! I knew you was looking for someone more than a losta girlfriend."

"Just following through on a case, that's all."

"You know the Giapponese man who was killed here?"

"Nope. Just checkin' things out, that's all."

Then he drew a gun on me. "I'ma sorry to have to do this, private polizia. But I think you picked up something from the gutter. So…just cause I'ma nice-a guy, I'm gonna take you to some Giapponese people."

"Should I put my hands up?"

He snickered. "No, as long as you do not take outta your pistola."

He led me three doors to the north. It was a fancy joint with large thick eves and white and light grey paint, very 'American' looking. He knocked on the door. A little old Japanese lady opened it. Her eyes widened when she saw both of us, particularly Signor Vespa. She said something in Japanese and I was surprised when he answered in her language. "Sorry, signore, but I have to ask you to enter." He kept his gun trained on me. Once inside he relaxed and asked for someone named Ima Soshi. Soon a middle-aged woman appeared and bowed before us. The lady was short but had a determined, proud face. Again, they conversed in Japanese and soon I suspected that Vespa was a goddamned Jap agent. Then Vespa looked at me. "I have to leave you here. Miss Soshi will tell you what she can about the murder. But first suppose you show us what you find outaside, eh?"

"Nothing, I told you."

"How come I do not believe you, signore?"

"That's your problem. Just get me the interpreter so I can get outta here and back home." Vespa put his gun away and waved in disgust at me and left. Miss Soshi gestured for me to sit on a sofa in the large living room. Soon she re-entered, only this time with Madame Butterfly, a real babe with a tallish lithe body and those marvelous sunken in cheeks some women possess. Her eyes were dark brown. I rose as Miss Soshi disappeared, leaving the two of us alone.

She was very polite and her voice was like light honey. "Sir, you wish to know about the terrible killing in this neighborhood." Right away I knew this gal had an inside line on the case. "I cannot help much, but I shall tell you what I know." Her English was perfect.

"Yeah, that'd be swell, lady. I'm Cable Denning—I'm a private detective and I don't have to tell you I'm investigating these apparently brutal murders that have occurred lately within the Black Dragon society—or do I?"

369

"Or that Mr. Miyazaki hired you. I have known for some time. My name is Kimiko Toyama. My brother is head person of the Black Dragons here in America." Now I was getting somewhere. "What do you wish to know, Mr. Denning?"

"Well, a lotta things, but first...this..." I reached into my pocket and took out the pendant I'd found in the gutter outside. "Does this mean anything to you?"

She went white and her eyes widened. "Where did you find that? It is something—something I have lost."

"Now ain't that odd? It was over by the murder scene, three houses down. How do I know it's yours?"

She reached for it, but I kept it from her. "It is five-sided. It represents five symbols of human conduct and their opposites. First symbol is *Desire*, its opposite *Lust*. The second side means *Serenity* while its opposite is *Anger*. The third is *Truth* opposed by *Delusion*. The fourth represents *Natural Abundance* opposite *Greed* and the last means *Self-fulfillment* versus *Envy*. It is pure gold and very ancient." She smiled nervously at me. "Please?" She reached out her hand..

"Well, I guess that's enough for me, lady. Here..." I gave it to her. The second she received it, I could swear her eyes glowed up like little coals that contrasted with her lovely creamy skin. "So I suppose you're an underground person?" She tucked the pendant down her blouse.

"No. I am visiting only. I—I will return soon to the Land of the Emperor."

"How is ol' Hirohito these days? He must be feeling the pinch of all those young men lost in the South Pacific."

370

She walked away a few paces. "His name is *Showa* and he is a spoiled brat who has destroyed the Japanese people."

I raised my eyebrows. "Oh...I see you're not a fan of his."

"No...he is a selfish male pig." Her anger rose and I could feel her energy in the room. "The Japanese people must take a different course after the war. We are defeated only for now."

"Yeah, well, I could've told you that. But I'm sure he'll send every last young boy to his death, given the chance."

Then she warmed up to me. "You seem quite intelligent—and handsome, if you pardon my saying so, Mr. Denning."

"Thank you, Miss Toyama. I think you're a charming and beautiful young woman myself, if you don't mind *my* saying so."

"You may call me *Kim*—"

"—and you may call me Cable, Kim. So, now, if you don't mind, what else can you tell me about the murders?"

"Perhaps I regard them differently than most. Are you of an open mind, Cable?"

"I guess you could say I reserve the right to my opinion, but I'll hear you out with an open mind if it comes to it. How's that?"

She smiled and took a deep breath. Suddenly she was filled with warmth and beauty. "As much as can be expected, I suppose."

"Yeah, so shoot, lady...uh...so let's hear what you know."

She went to a hearth and lit some incense and then a candle. The dusk was upon us and she did not put on the lights. So there we were in the semi-dark with a candle on the mantle of the fireplace. "Suppose I told you the men who were murdered deserved to die...and what if I spoke of extraordinary events and means that brought about their deaths—those that have been and those about to be?"

"Well, okay...I'll listen to anything reasonable."

"What if it is not reasonable to your mind, Cable?"

"Then, Ginger Snaps, I'll just have to listen up, won't I?" I said with a slight smirk on my face. "And you'll have to bear my response."

She didn't answer but began pacing around the room like a caged animal. "Suppose these men had offended the—the honor of a woman and taken advantage of her? Suppose they took her to the place where she lost her virtue and her mind? And then she became something...something else, so terrible that even the Emperor would shake in his golden slippers if he would but behold her?"

"And you, you're the agent of justice for this deflowered and abused woman—seeking revenge by murder?"

"I did not say that. I, personally, cannot kill even a bug. But I know of someone else who can. I beg you to leave this case. Give Mr. Miyazaki his money back."

"He hasn't paid me yet."

"Then do not accept it if and when he offers it to you."

"A couple of pieces don't fit here, Kim. Do you know who killed Kirawani just three doors from here...and the other four men? Doesn't something sound a little fishy to you—a little odd that four men are killed at the Black Dragon headquarters and all of a sudden the fifth victim happens to end up in your neighborhood, Kim?"

She stopped pacing and lowered her head. "Yes."

"Then...*who is it?*"

"I cannot say." Just then I began to feel woozy. The incense—it...it was putting me to sleep! I tried to hide it, but it was a losing battle.

"So...just what...*can* you say?" I asked her.

She came close to me, tip-toed up and gently kissed my lips. "This...calms me...I have always wished to kiss a handsome white American man. It was pleasant. Thank you." But her lips were like ice.

"You're—you're welcome—I think. Did you drug me with the incense, Kim? And if so, why aren't *you* affected?"

"I am very sorry, Cable. We cannot have Americans or Japanese or Italians know what I know. Your death will be calm and filled with peace and visions of a better world than this one."

I had to sit down on the sofa. "But...but...what if I.... I...don't wanna...die...yet...Oh Kim...no...no..." And off I went into the land of nod.

The Pleasure Garden of Emperor Keiko

I was in a magnificent garden under a silken roof by a stream. I was naked with this beautiful young woman who looked an awful lot like Kim. In fact the only thing she *was* wearing was the pendant I had just given her. She was wrapped around me feeding me figs and kissing each fig as it went into my mouth. Her small breasts

373

were painted red and her hair done up in a wondrous black braid. I looked out toward the direction of the lake and the landscape was almost surrealistic. "What next do you wish from your concubine, my Emperor? I am yours to command, my love." She kissed me and it felt good. I kissed her back and then I knew we were not just consorting master and mistress, but that we truly loved each other. I sank my body deep into hers and she sighed as the afternoon sunlight began to fade bringing on the night. "Will you allow me to sleep by your side this night?" she asked me.

I felt my face. It had a beard and moustache and I was wearing a funny little hat atop my long, shiny black hair. I was a goddamn Oriental! "You may sleep on my breast until the first crow of the cock, then you must leave me, for my duties will call heavily to me on the morrow," I found myself saying.

"I will obey you until the end of the world, my love," she answered me. Her beauty shone from her face and her lovely white body was filled with youth and desire. "Will you make love with me before the sun sets into the Great Western Well?"

"No, I shall enjoy you before the torchlight in my chambers before I fall off to sleep. That is when I enjoy you best—when you are warm and close and your lovely woman is seeping my manhood onto the silken tapestry that is our bed."

"As you desire me," she said.

As dusk settled across the small lake, I smiled. "It is here I am happiest. Away from the affairs of state, away from busy mouths and those who wish something from me. Alone here, Hashiota Mandami...when I am with you, I am at the same time, alone...*and* with you."

"Here within the Garden of the Thousand Golden Pheasants, we find our true joy...do we not? It is closer to *Tengoku* than all other things of our knowing, my Emperor, is it not? Put a dagger through my heart if it is not so."

"I cannot, for you speak true, Hashiota. You must never leave me. Ever. Will you live for me?"

"Yes...yes, oh my Emperor—I will live for you!"

"Will you die for me, if necessary?"

"Oh, yes, my Emperor Keishi—only gladly!"

We got up and walked as if we had done this thing a thousand days and nights previous. We washed our hands, ate and I drank lotus juice. Soon we entered the royal Emperor's bedchambers. Hashiota disrobed and lay on her back, summoning me into her arms.

Suddenly I heard a terrible groan and I woke up. It was dark except for a candle across the room on top of a desk. "Wha...?" I asked. "Who—who's there?" I was still woozy, but I knew I wasn't dead yet.

Then the candle moved off of the dresser with Kim's hand attached to it. She bent to her knees and showed me a dead body on the floor next to the bed. "She wish to kill you...but...but I could not let her...I do not know why..." Then her gorgeous dark eyes looked at me through the candlelight. "Why, Cable? Why did I prevent this? You must die—she was commanded to kill you and I was supposed to—"

"—I...I'll tell you why! I had this nutso dream about us, somewhere in Japanese antiquity—and you were my consort—and—"

Her eyes grew bright. "—and? We were in the Garden of a Thousand Golden Pheasants, the garden of pleasure and about to sleep for the evening...we were going to make love...in your bedchambers..."

My eyes widened. "Yeah, how—how did you know?"

"Because I dreamed the same dream in a vision while you slept...it was in the year 74 and we were in love. I know that much...now... I was sitting here on the floor holding your hand as Soshi entered. She carried a knife and told me since I did not kill you—and only put you to dream—and I protected you, *she* must kill you! I could not have that happen, Cable. As I said...I do not know why, exactly, but suddenly I took the knife out of her hand and thrust it into *her*!" She began to cry. "I am ashamed! My ancestors will not forgive me!"

I leaned over and grabbed her and started shaking her body. "Why aren't I dead, Kim!!? And why weren't you put to sleep by the shit that was in that incense?! What happened and where are we?"

She looked at me and her eyes began to glow up like green and orange and red and then back to black. I was astonished. "I could not...give you...the full measure of death potion in your drink...for I love you. Love is the only thing that prevents—prevents me from—from—"

"—prevents you from what, Kim? From murdering me, too? And how could you have loved me when you hardly knew me?! And who *are* you? Tough questions, but you'd better answer 'em and quick!"

She plunged her face into her hands and began sobbing, hard. "I could not hurt you, my love! I am born to obey your every wish!"

I was touched and puzzled and spoke softly. "Yeah, I remember what you said. *'I will obey you unto the end of the world, my love'*, you said that in the dream...remember? I told you I was happiest when I was with you and your name was Hashiota. Do you really believe stuff like that?"

"Yes! Yes! It is true," she whimpered. She put her fingers to her temples. "But I am constrained...you must go now before I become angry—not at you—but at me. You cannot be here when I am angry—please—leave now!"

"Constrained? Angry at yourself for bumping off someone who was gonna bump me off?"

"Please! Go now, my Keishi! I beg you...go!"

"Hey, you just called me what you called me in my dream—Emperor Keishi—yeah, that was my name. Now, if I were you—"

Before I could finish my sentence, Kim darted out of the room into the darkness and disappeared. I composed myself, found my hat and grabbed the candle that Kim had left by my bedside. I called out to her but she was nowhere to be found. I got this spine-tingling feeling I should get out of that house and fast. I walked briskly to my car and off I went into the night, still trying to figure out what had happened.

Chapter 9

DISSONANT CHORDS

I rushed back to my office because I knew this was the night I was supposed to take Ida out on the town. I got back around seven and called her to confirm what time I'd told her I'd pick her up. She said around nine and had I made reservations yet? I hadn't even selected a joint to spend the evening in! I told her I had and I'd pick her up. I said goodbye and ruffled through the newspaper on top of my disheveled desk. I'd heard of a new Italian nightclub in West Hollywood I thought we could try. I called and they had a 9:30 booth-for-two open. I took it.

At ten after nine I was at Ida's. I asked about Sophie, but was told it was a busy work night for her and she was out at the ranch. As I stood at the threshold looking at Ida Latney, once more I was knocked over by how lovely she looked. She was wearing a pale yellow, tight-fitting gown with silver high heels. Her hair was up in an attractive bun and her perfect neck made me wanna take a chunk out of it and spend the rest of the night in bed with her! "Wow! You look great, babe!" I exclaimed. "Where'd you get that outfit?"

"Thanks, Cable...oh, this? Actually, it was my mother's and I fancied it up a bit—puffed out the short sleeves and plunged the neckline lower—that's about it. I could never afford to buy it."

"Yeah, especially on what I pay you. Your mother's, eh?"

"She can't wear it anymore. Too fat, I guess." She spun a 360. "You like it—I mean, really?"

"It fits like a glove—and if your mother wore this when she was courting your Dad, I can see why he married her!" I flattered my date.

"You always say those wonderful things just before we go out. It makes me feel good, Cable, just so you know…"

"Yeah, and it makes me feel good to say 'em—and to spend the time with you."

The club was on Beverly Boulevard near Wetherly Drive. Italians weren't that popular during the war but since Mussolini's death, maybe things changed because the joint was packed with noisy patrons and a medium sized big band. I had ditched my trench coat and fedora and wore my only other brown pin-stripe suit with a more conventional hat. I guess I looked okay except I had on black shoes. But Ida was as happy as a flea on a new dog. We didn't have to wait very long to be seated and not too far from the seven piece band and some pretty babe in a shiny red dress with long-flowing black hair. She looked classy and I could tell by the way she carried herself, she knew her business.

"Hungry, Ida?" I half-shouted over the din to Ida.

"No…not yet—can we dance for a while—maybe order a drink first?"

"Yeah, sure…" I hailed down a waiter and we ordered and went out for our first dance. The band was playing an old Glenn Miller favorite, *I Know Why and So Do You.* I took Ida into my arms. She clasped me tight right away as if she didn't wanna let me get away. Not tonight!

"I want you all to myself tonight, Cable—hope you don't mind..."

I whispered in her ear. "That's how I want it too, tonight, Ida."

"I'm glad...it's—it's been so long, Cable. Sometimes I think you've forgotten I'm also a woman—and still a young woman..."

We danced and the band played and the singer sang. "Do you remember that song, Ida?"

"Yes, more than you know...I went to see the movie back when I first met you, I think. I sang that song over and over, feeling that maybe someday you'd understand that's how I felt about you." She broke away from me and looked up at me. "But you never did. Now here we are, you, tall, dark and handsome...me, pretty, blonde and blue-eyed wondering still why we're not together." She put her finger to my lips. "But don't answer, Cable, I know...I know why...so tonight, I'm going to be with you—all of you—and maybe even get a little drunk."

"Good, Ida, it's good for you to let your hair down once in a while."

"I don't have much hair like *she* does—the singer you keep looking at up there on the stage—but my hair's real blonde and fine-stranded."

"So is the rest of you," I commented, bringing her back into my arms. Just then my eye caught a familiar face standing at the bar, watching us. It was *Amleto Vespa!* He looked uncomfortable, restless. He kept looking around in the crowd of dancing and sitting people for someone. But I knew he'd seen me. When the music ended and the applause settled down, Ida and I made our way back to our table. I kept my eye on Vespa. But he held his ground. Our drinks were ready and I toasted Ida. "Here's to the best secretary a boss ever had, Ida," I said, smiling at her. We were in one of those cozy little half-booths and she scooted over until our hips were touching.

"Cable...?" her voice was quiet as she leaned toward me.

"Yeah?"

"Would...would you ever marry me?"

I didn't know what to say or do at first. I knew all along what Ida had in the back of her little head. But she also knew the rest of the story, the treacherous existence I led and all the buried people I left behind me. "I don't know, Ida—I suppose when I'm old and grey—yeah—I'd consider being hitched to someone like you. But then again, you'd be kinda old and grey yourself," I laughed.

"No, I mean it, Cable. I want a baby...from you. I've been thinking about it a lot lately and—"

"—Ida—how many times do we have to discuss this thing!? I'm gonna tell you something right now that might cool your blood a little. See that dark-haired guy over there, standing and pretending to look at the bandstand? Well, that's an Italian who's a spy for the Japanese underground here in the states. He and everybody else is watching me, Ida, day and night, what I do, where I go, who I'm with—and you'd wanna be married to a guy who's chances for survival past fifty are almost nil?"

She took her hand and squeezed my upper leg sensually. "That would give us five years, Cable. You just turned forty-five, you know."

"I give up, Ida. I can't figure you dames."

Ida ordered us three more drinks before I needed to go to the men's room. But there was another reason I needed to excuse myself. I had this gut feeling Vespa wanted to talk to me but had the courtesy to not include Ida. I walked to the back of the joint, down a dimly lit hallway through the door marked *uomini*. I hoped it was the men's since the other door was marked *donne*. It was eerily quiet. I could feel another presence near me but I couldn't see anything. "Someone there?" I spoke out. Nothing. I finished at the urinal and began to wash my hands when Vespa walked in. "Well, I was wondering when you'd make yourself known, Vespa—whatta ya want? This is supposed to be an evening of relaxation for me."

"I am sorry, signore. But you must know it is following me—and I am frightened. It is also following you because somehow it saw you earlier today at *Shashuki Temple.*"

"Saw *what*, Vespa? *Shashuki Temple?* What the hell is that?" I dried my hands.

"That house you were in...the basement is...is a temple and sanctuary for—for something so terrible I cannot describa to you, signore. I know you were not telling the truth to me. You gave it the pendant—and now it is free to destroy once more."

"Well, you'd better start describing, buster, because when I walked in here I felt a presence of something—well, something *unearthly*—let's put it that way. And you're saying that beautiful young woman I gave the neckpiece to is some—some—"

"—*mostro!* The *Black Dragon* people believes that someone has been offended and is killing the men who did the dirty deed."

"What dirty deed? And by the way, what did Kirawani know that I don't...and got killed for it? What was he on to and what was he doing three doors down from your so-called 'Shashuki Temple?" I grabbed the Italian and pinned him against the wall. "Speak up, buddy, I'm gettin' kinda tired of this runaround shit!"

There was fear in his eyes. "He...he could feel it...he knew it was after him—and once it is after you, you are doomed—both of us—we are going to be pursued by it until it punishes us for—for—" He stopped and then looked down at the floor. "Oh! It has been here, Denning. Look—here on the floor!" I let go of him.

I took a gander at the floor. I saw nothing unusual. But Vespa bent down and picked something up and showed it to me. "This...is from its body—I must go now, Signor Denning." He placed a scale-like thing in my palm. "I would advise you to leave—immediately or you will die this very night, signore!"

"You were saying something—*punishes* you, Vespa, for what? What did we do that offended 'it' so much that it's willing to kill us over it?"

"I must leave now, please—allow me to leave. I am going back to Italia soon—it cannot find me there."

"Don't be so sure, buster—if it's your own fear, it'll follow you wherever you go. So you didn't tell me what 'it' is and why the vendetta against you and the five other men who got it?"

"We—we were drunk one night—on saké—at the Black Dragon hall. A beautiful young woman who was new, fresh from Japan, came in looking for her brother. We did not ask who the brother might be, but it turned out it was a guy named *Toyama*, the head of the Black Dragons! We did not know this at that moment, who it was she was seeking. One very dark, evil and murderous member closed and locked the door of the Black Dragon hall. Then he turned toward this lovely young creature and began to taunt her, to molest her. He told her he was going to have her, and commit *wakame saké* upon her, and drink it from her female organs! She screamed, shouted and said many things in Japanese— but still failed to say it was her brother—as I said, the very head of the Black Dragons—that she had come to this country looking for! We six continued to drink and were very drunk and so...presto! we were all molesting her, like some animal instinct we possessed, and we ripped the young woman's clothing off and seduced her, each of us taking our turn with her, each of us pouring our sake drink into her vagina and then drinking from it in a frenzy of madness! She had fainted sometime during these terrible moments, but we did not stop accosting her. We raped her over and over again until we were spent! I was the last to have my way with her. I was lying on her body when I realized her heart had stopped and she was dead!"

I stood there looking at the now-trembling and ashamed Amleto Vespa. I had never heard of this 'wakame sake' before and it was disturbing to hear about it. "So you gang-raped a pretty little Japanese woman and killed her?"

He put his hands to hide his face. "Si...I was never before drunk...on saké...pure rice alcohol. *Wakame saké* was...was also new to me. I feel terrible."

"So what'd you do with the body?"

"We bring it to Madame Soshi because we learned that the house on Corsica Drive—was where the temple is. We were told to do this."

"By who?"

"Mr. Ushito—the only man outside the six of us we could trust among the Black Dragon Society. He said we had committed a horrible thing and we would be punished. But the young woman had to be *consecrated*, he said, at the temple."

"How long ago was this, Vespa?"

"Weeks...I don't know...I have to go—go now...! Run, Denning!"

With that he darted out of the building into the back alley. I re-composed myself and went back out to join Ida. My secretary eyed me curiously as I sat down beside her. "Are you all right? I saw that man follow you toward the rest rooms. Now I have to go."

I stood up and let Ida slide out on my side. The girl singer was doing her rendition of *Green Eyes* and was she sexy at it! I noticed there was a line down the hall at the entrance to the Lady's room, so I thought I'd take the opportunity to slip the singer a few bucks for her singing—as well as for her costume. As soon as she finished I walked up and stood beneath the stage looking up at her. Her more than ample breasts puffed up through her fine red dress and her hair shone in the spotlight. "Thanks, lady," I said as I put three bucks into her crystal jar by the stage. "I think your singing is swell."

She smiled a sexy smile at me. "Hello, handsome, I do have a name, you know, It's out at the entrance to the club."

"Oh. I—I didn't see it." I knew she was a fun kind of dame, one of those you could enjoy for a night or two and then maybe forget because if you didn't, she'd forget you.

"Joy—Joy Cheryl—in case you're interested," she responded.

I thought it was a nice contrived name and she kinda looked like a *'Joy Cheryl'*. "Oh, but I *am* interested. Pleased to meet you, Joy, my name is—" Just then a blood-curdling scream came from the back of the nightclub and I ran as fast as I could, thinking only of Ida Latney! She was still standing in line and told me she was okay, but a bit shaken. She gave me a peculiar look as if she thought I knew something about what was going on. I told her I'd be right back and I darted out to the back alley of the club. Some of the male help were gathered around a horribly mutilated body and I figured without looking that it was probably Amleto Vespa's. Soon I heard police sirens in the distance. Someone brought a blanket and covered the corpse and I walked around to the side of the joint. There was a large clump of banana trees on the other side of a short fence. I thought I saw someone on the other side. I jumped the fence and went into the thicket. Then suddenly everything seemed to go dead silent except for the siren in the background coming closer. I heard a deep, low growl. Whatever it was, had to be bigger than a dog. Nothing I knew of growled like that. I drew my gun. "C'mon out and show yourself! I think I know the score, and whoever or whatever you are—it's over." I listened. Another deep growl seemed to come from the bowels of the earth itself. "If it's revenge for the dead girl—then she's been avenged—so you can go back home to Japan now. Do you understand me?" Suddenly something lunged at me and I fired as I went down onto the ground. I thought I hit whatever it was, but it kept running. I finally made it to my feet, but it was gone. What the hell *was* it!!

As the police car and finally an ambulance came, I meandered back into the nightclub and I re-joined Ida. After about an hour or so, things settled down and we were able to order some dinner. But my mind was thinking a thousand things. I had seen too much in my time to dismiss the possibility that whatever it was I encountered out there in the banana tree grove could have been a shape-changer of some kind.

Ida and I drank and danced for the rest of the night. By 1:30 in the morning we were pretty smashed. Joy Cheryl was still singing. This time a warm, intimate version of a brand new song...*There Must Be a Way* with a few members of the band. That was it for her this night and she closed up shop and left the stage. About twenty minutes later I had to go to the john again and so as I made my way back down the hallway I met up face-to-face with Joy Cheryl. Her dark eyes were sexy as hell up close and she had a smirk on her lips that could only mean one thing to a guy like me—she was interested. "Too bad about the dead person. But...as it happens, you were about to tell me your name—or is that secret? Or is your wife or sweetheart gonna object if I ask?"

I chuckled. "No...my name's Cable Denning...and that very attractive—yep, I mean *very* attractive young woman I've been dancing and dining with is...is my secretary. I'm—I'm, uh, a private dick, you see."

"A private what?"

I knew I had her and started to laugh. "Dick...private dick...you know what that...that means, Miss Cheryl?"

"Yeah, I know what it means to me—but—"

"—no, no, no—it ain't what ya think, lady. It really means *private detective*—and that's what I am—or do—depending on—depending on how—ya look at it." The booze was hitting me pretty hard.

"I see." She looked deep into my eyes. "I read men, ya know."

I shook my head. "You—you what? Oh—big mistake!"

"*I read men*...you know, I can tell what they have in mind right up front. Most of 'em just want my tits and you-know-what—some of 'em like you maybe...like my singing along with my—my other assets. Tell me how I'm doing, Mr. Cable Denning private detective."

"Okay...okay...read me..."

"Tits and pussy...that's it for you, buster...how's that?"

"O—okay, I guess. Tits and pussy—yep—that's—that's what it's all about, ain't it?" I prattled. "Is there—there anything else men—men are—are good for?"

She smiled at me. "Yeah, maybe a good time and some left over stardust once in a while. But I'm twenty nine and don't think about that stuff so much anymore. Twenty-nine is old, you know."

"Wha—what stuff?"

"Oh, you know, romance, love, kids, a cute little cottage with a nice big mortgage—that kind of thing..."

"Oh...well, I gotta take a pee and get—get back to my—my—"

"—yeah, I know, your secretary. If you ever get free of her, come see me alone some night. I'm here Wednesdays through Saturdays, nine to two."

"Yeah...I—I might just—just do that, Miss Cheryl..."

"I'd prefer you call me Joy—that's what I do best—give joy."

"Okay...okay, Joy..." I staggered down the hall toward that door marked *uomini.*

The Rub in the Eye of the Beholder

It was about 2:30 when Ida and I walked into her house. Ida was almost as drunk as I was. But she could recover a lot faster. "I—I kinda forgot about...about Sophie staying here with you."

"So what, Cable! I do have a...a private life, you know. So what if I sleep in with you tomorrow—it's nobody else's business!" Ida replied.

"Who—who said I'm stayin'—stayin' the night?"

"I did..." She came up to me and moved her open hand up my leg until she was encompassing my crotch. "Please...? I need—I need to feel you Cable..." She took my hand and shoved it hard into her own crotch. "Here...in here...where I know it's safe—from—from the world out there. And—and it makes me feel safe...safe and sound..." She dragged me down the hall into her bedroom. "Now..." she whispered to me as she undid my belt. "Now let me undress you, Cable.

389

Then…you can undress me—and have me. Do you want me?"

At the moment I didn't know what I wanted. Way back in my mind I was still thinking about the events of earlier on and I couldn't shake the questions nagging at me about what I'd experienced. I was too much of a detective to just dismiss all that. "I—I need a—a rain check, Ida. I can't get this particular case outta my head—you—you know, the Japanese Miyazaki thing." Ida stopped what she was doing and sat down hard on the bed.

"I suppose I should thank you for tonight, Cable. And I do." Then she hit the bed hard with her hands. "But, damn, that's what I get for expecting things with you! You do know you're a workaholic, an alcoholic, a tobacco-holic and womanholic! I'm stupid, aren't I? Just tell me that, Cable—I'm just plain *stupid*!"

"Okay…you're stupid, Ida…now are—are you happy?"

"No!" she pouted. "I only wanted…wanted some love, Cable. Is that too much to ask?"

"Not if it's a mercy fuck, lady. That—that ain't good for either of us. How—how many times do I need to tell you that?"

"Not enough, apparently." She buried her face in her hands. "I know, I know, I know…just because I want it doesn't mean you want it—and on and on and on…!"

Just then Sophie poked her head in the darkened door. We both turned. "I—I thought I heard voices in here. Are you alright, Ida?"

"Oh! Sophie! Yes, I'm—I'm fine. Cable and I were having a discussion about some—some things…"

"Yes, I could tell. I'm sorry to barge in on you."

"I thought you'd be gone until tomorrow," Ida asked.

"My last two clients—uh, cancelled. So my midnight drove me home. And here I am."

"Well...anyway, that's my cue to—to leave you two ladies for the night," I muttered. Ida looked crestfallen. I said goodnight to Sophie and made it for the door. Ida followed.

"I don't know what to say, Cable. I don't know how long I can continue to—to do this. I set myself up for a fall most every time, don't I?"

"Yeah, I—I guess you do, Ida. I'm sorry. I wish I were that young man who would make you happy...but I ain't, as you can see..."

"But you make me deliriously happy when we make love!" she whispered loudly so Sophie wouldn't over-hear. "But I can't do it alone now, can I?"

"No, Ida, ya can't. Tell ya what—let's have breakfast in the afternoon and take a walk tomorrow, okay?"

"Yeah, sure...what time?"

"How in the hell should I know? I'll call you."

"Okay..."

Legend of Kiyohime

I made my way up to the second floor. I got my key out, but as I looked down to put it into the lock, I noticed a few drops of blood on the floor. I looked around quickly, but I was still too drunk to have a quick reaction time. I looked down the dark hall. Then I heard that terrible low growl again. Whatever it was, I had hit it earlier and it had followed me here. Now it had come

391

for me. Was this gonna be the end of Cable Denning, then? I drew my gun and fired blindly into the hallway. One...two...three shots rang out from my .38 and two of 'em hit something big and solid! The growling stopped and I had this feeling I'd killed whatever horrid thing it was. But then my horror turned to pity and I felt a gentleness overcome me.

Then from out of the darkness, crawling toward me came two arms and two lovely hands attached to none other than Kimiko Toyama! She was bleeding badly and I got down on my knees and I took her up into my arms. "Gees...Kim—*you!* I didn't dare to think it—"

"—it is okay, Cable..." she spoke in a feeble voice. "It is over now. My family is cursed—cursed with—with the *Hidaka Kiyohime*—she who, when enraged, turns into a—a terrible dragon—to—to exact her vengeance—on—on those who have—who have wronged her." She spit up some blood and I took my handkerchief and wiped her mouth and kissed her sweating forehead. Her beautiful dark eyes looked up at me with so much love I could barely look back into hers. "But you...you, my love, my Emperor Keishi—I—I have loved you...for eternity...and shall...until we...we...meet..." She drew her last breath and lay in my arms broken and bleeding. I glanced at her unfolding right hand. It was clutching the five-sided pendant that she had ripped from her neck in order to make herself vulnerable and so as not to kill the thing she loved most. She *had* died for her Emperor after all.

Masques From an Opposite Stage

Lieutenant Inspector Lester Keith was not very happy about my explanation for what had happened the previous night. He guffawed over the possibility that Kim could have been anything but a beautiful young woman I had killed with four bullets. He dragged me downtown and booked me for murder. "I told you one day I'd get you, shoot-'em-up man! You're a goddamned cowboy, Denning—shooting at the dark because you think you hear something go bump in the night! Shame on you! Good thing we're at war with the Empire of Japan and she was a Jap, mister. Otherwise, I'd nail your ass but real good!"

I said nothing in response but asked Lester to call Ida and tell her I couldn't take that walk with her because I was in jail. But I was tired and it so happened I was in a cell alone. So I dozed off. Three hours later I woke up to Lester Keith's voice blabbing at me. "Up, Denning..."

"I was just beginning to enjoy it in here. Nice and peaceful like with no telephone to answer."

Behind Keith stood a wonderful sight for sore eyes. It was Bernie Hershfeld, a man who went from being a gopher for some Oriental bad guy to a bona fide comedian. He had married Auina, my dead father's girlfriend who had traveled so far to meet me years ago. She was from some minor South Sea island. She had borne my Dad a son, Amosa, who was now about the same age as my son, Cable, Jr. "Ya know, we never really grow up, we merely learn how to act in public," he quipped. "That man over there? If I agreed with you about him, we'd both be wrong. Politicians and diapers have one thing in common, they should both be changed regularly, for the same reason." I jumped up and embraced my old friend as soon as Lester opened the jail cell door.

"Damn! Bernie! Am I glad to see you!" I looked behind Lester Keith. "Auina, Amosa? Are they...are they—"

"—Auina is at the Roosevelt Hotel stealing the towels while Amosa remained back east to attend school. The kid actually thinks he thinks. I'm not sure. Plus he hasn't gotten my bill yet for raising him."

"You can go home, Denning," Lester Keith growled. "Some Jap called me on the phone and bailed you out until your hearing. His name was Miyazaki or the like. He put up ten grand, detective. Americans should be so nice. You're lucky. Me? I would've let you rot here until we discovered the truth."

"Yeah? Well, let me tell you something, Lester. Sometimes we never know the truth...sometimes it gets hidden away in the shit bad policemen and politicians choose to show the public. And, frankly, some truth is best left unknown."

"Suit yourself, Denning. But one of these days I'll get you for murder—you can count on that." Lt. Lester Keith led us down to his office and signed the release papers. I was free!

Bernie and I caught a streetcar back to my office. I cleaned up a bit while Bernie read the paper. "Having troubles, Cable? The early bird may get the worm, but the second mouse gets the cheese. Are you up to your knees in shit?—maybe it's like the news on the radio—

394

they start by sayin' 'good evening' and spend the next fifteen minutes telling you why it ain't."

"Nothing I can't handle, Bernie. We'll get my car, pick up Auina and the three of us will go for dinner—how's that??"

"Sounds good, but she may have taken the silver-ware by then—she may be a bit heavier!" he joked about his beautiful wife. And indeed, when we picked her up in the lobby of the hotel, Auina looked more beautiful than ever. She looked like an American Poly-nesian with black thick hair and dark brown eyes. Her body was still lithe and well proportioned. I saw a little girl standing beside her. I had forgotten she and Bernie had had a kid together too.

We walked along Hollywood Boulevard for an hour or two for old times' sake. Later that night the four of us went back to the club Ida and I had just visited in West Hollywood. Down deep I wanted to check out that sing-er again...Joy Cheryl. We found a nice table and sat about half-way back from the bandstand. I was happy to see Auina again and she held my hand with the same affection she'd always shown me. It wasn't the romantic kind, just a real good loving friend who showed her feel-ings and never got her wires crossed.

"I am so happy to see you again, Cable. You look young and dashing. You must be doing something right. But don't tell me. I think I know what keeps you young, mister lover man!" she teased me.

"And I'm happy to see you—both of you—a lot! I sure hope you decide to move back. What brought you out?"

"We *are* going to stay here in Los Angeles, Cable. We will be neighbors again. Bernie signed a nice contract with the *Tracadero* Club for two years—at four times the salary he used to get," Auina explained. "We are so happy we will have you close by once more."

"Yeah, you watch and see one year at the Tracadero and they'll tear it down for indecency!" Bernie cracked. "But we are glad we'll be close to you again, Cable..."

"Yeah, so am I! It's hard to believe. I never thought I'd see you guys again." My eyes misted as I toasted them. "Ya know, I missed you two—we go back a ways and we have a happy history together—"

"—and we're still alive! That's saying a lot around you!" Bernie quipped. "You know, my mother never saw the irony in calling me a son-of-a-bitch?" We all laughed. "If God is watching us, the least we can do is be entertaining, huh?" The waitress placed a huge New York steak in front of Bernie. Auina and I looked at him and lifted our eyebrows. "What! I didn't fight my way to the top of the food chain to be a vegetarian! But I don't have a clear conscience either, Cable. A clear conscience is usually the sign of a bad memory." Then Bernie looked up at the sexy singer on the stage. "Now, that's sex appeal—you know good girls are bad girls who never get caught!" He laughed to himself. "Oh, by the way, did you know crowded elevators smell different to midgets?" We all laughed heartily. I wanted to say hello to Joy Cheryl but she was too busy. I decided I'd make it another time. But as we left, my memory was shaken when Joy sang a moving version of Honey Combes' old song, *I Can't Give You Anything But Love.* Funny thing about getting older... more memories seem to be waiting around every corner.

I drove them to the Roosevelt Hotel and walked in with them. Bernie and I would have one last drink while I said goodnight to Auina and her sleepy little girl who was a tintype of her mother. "How do ya do it all these years, Bernie, one-liners, I mean, one after the other?"

"Two sides of the same masque, Cable—or was it two masques on the same face?" he answered. "I could go for comedy or tragedy in my life. But when I met Auina, my life changed forever, thanks to your introducing us. Now I can joke about life and not suffer the consequences. We all ride parachutes, buddy. I saw an advertisement the other day. It said, *'Used Parachute for sale, used once, never opened.'* You see? For me, a day without a joke is a like a day without sunshine. A judge says to a prostitute, 'when did you realize you were raped?' 'When the check bounced, she replied.'"

"But life's got a lotta bumps, too, buddy," I said.

"When everything's coming your way, you're in the wrong lane. I say if ya can't convince them, confuse 'em. You know, Cable, I just let my mind wander one day—and it never came back!"

We hugged and parted that night with me agreeing to help Bernie and Auina find a place not too far from me off of Franklin somewhere. We would be together and now in a very definite way I felt I would have a family again. I loved those two people maybe more than I loved myself. They were pure and good in their individual ways. I think that's part of what made the marriage work so well. I don't think they invaded each other's territory. I wish more couples could be like that. Hell, I wish *I* could be like that!

"3-25-45"

It was Sunday, August 5, 1945. I'd promised a still-miffed Ida that I'd take her out for an ice cream and then a walk in Bronson Park later that day. I knew that isn't exactly what she wanted from me, but it'd have to do for now. I enjoyed Ida, a lot. She was lovely to look at, intelligent, well-spoken and was in love with me. What else would a guy want? I felt like a heel on the bottom of a dirty shoe the way I'd been treating her as a woman lately. But who knows what brings on desire besides alcohol and the atmosphere? What chemistry is there inside us that makes one babe like an electric shock to your body and others just a nice warm lay?

As the hours and days ticked on, I knew they were gonna use that bomb on someone. And soon. I was thinking of my old friend Dr. Albert Einstein back in Princeton. I understood he was inured with a group of scientists...called themselves, *The Institute for Advanced Study*, but Einstein had complained that these so-called thinkers never think and never get anything done. He told me the last time we met, that they hang around a big endowment and so little is accomplished. Since the Oppenheimer's little baby exploded in Alamogordo, I knew from newspapers and radio that Einstein was as-sociated with the public as 'the father of the atom bomb.' He must have resented that. He had worked on the physics of splitting the atom, but he had a change of heart when he saw the destructive potential of nuclear devastation.

I thought I'd give him a call. Only through a teacher who had heard him speak of me, was I able to access his phone number when I called the institute on the Princeton University campus. The phone rang at the other end and I got some older gal. She refused to bring Albert to the phone until I made her promise to tell the napping 65 year-old physicist, who it was that was calling him. There was a rustling and soon I heard a loving, familiar voice. "Oh, mein Gott! I vas just thinking of you, Cable! Ya, you must come to see me—can you get avay for a couple of days. I have something most significant to tell you. Ve vill go sailing—and you must meet Johanna."

"Johanna—are you still seeing dames, you dog, you?" I joked.

He laughed. "Oh, ya! Johanna Fantova goes sailing mit me on mein *'Tinef'* vhen I am not noting in mein book. She is my second mate. Most of de time I talk to my parrot und pretend to be sick so no vahn can find me. Und I play Bach and Schubert on my violin."

"That's great, Albert. So...I'll try to get some time off here in a few days and let you know. I don't wanna drive. Can someone pick me up at the nearest airport if I fly?"

"Ya ! Der ist vun not too far. Dat's wunderbar, Cable! Please come...only you vould understand vhat I have to say...and you vill comprehend its consequences."

"Yeah, okay, buddy boy—I'll get back to you in a few days."

"Ya, Cable, good-bye und vill see you soon!" We hung up.

I checked out a U.S. map and found that Princeton was almost a direct shot from Los Angeles, one coast to the other. Probably about four days or so driving. Naw, I'd fly it.

Making Love With Your Pants On

I picked up Ida and I took her to C.C. Brown's ice cream parlor at 7007 Hollywood Boulevard. She was cool at first, but then warmed up when I kept touching her and telling her how "spring-like" she looked. Her blondish hair hung in wisps and her immaculate skin enhanced those very blue eyes of hers. She was wearing a simple light-blue polka dot dress and walking shoes. "So...that Japanese girl that got killed out in front of your office—were you two involved?"

"Now, wait a minute, kid! The answer to your question is no, but you do probe a little too much, Ida. If I were, remember we're not a steady item here or married—so what I do in my private time is just that—*private!*"

"Okay, okay...just curious. Did you kill her?"

"I killed something. But whatever it was, it wasn't human. She was some kind of shape-changer. I've run into them before. But I felt sorry for the dame. She was cursed with some family thing and I guess when she was sexually violated, an anger got stirred up inside her and she lashed out by killing the six men who assaulted her. They were all part of a Japanese underground called the *Black Dragon.*"

"Oh, dear. How horrible! Ugh! I hate stories like that. Sophie told me about her getting raped—only on a regular basis—by her Dad. She told me one night when she'd been drinking. She drinks a lot, you know..."

"No, I didn't know."

"I also think she loves you, Cable. Just exactly how I'm not sure. But something happened to her after you met her."

"Oh? Like what?"

"Well, for one thing, I don't think she likes what she does anymore. I think she'd like to be settled in with—with someone...maybe you. I don't know. But I don't think you two would be a good match. She's too...uh...too unsettled inside, I think. She doesn't know what she wants."

I smiled at Ida. "And you? Do you know what you want?"

"Yes. I'm very clear on that subject, and you know it."

We walked up the trail that led to the little spring north of the parking lot. They had taken the streetcar away, the one that went all the way up Canyon Dr. and turned around at the gate. Those days streetcars had two sets of trolleys and the conductor or motorman got out, pulled one trolley down and the put the other up. Then the motorman went to the opposite end of the car and used the controls from there.

Ida was humming *Long Ago and Far Away* and it sounded good. "That song reminds me of us, Cable. Some man I dreamed about all of my life, namely you, tucked away together in a little cabin with me, maybe up there among the oak trees in that little dell. A couple of children and a cozy fireplace. I always wanted a fireplace." Her eyes were aglow as she described her heart's desire to me. "That isn't too much, is it, Cable? Life is really so short. I'm going into my thirties pretty soon and I haven't much to show for it. Not even a husband or family."

We continued to walk. "Is that it, Ida—is that all for you? Obeying instincts of nesting? I mean, it's okay for most people, I guess. But it ain't my cup of tea. I hope you understand that. Maybe when I grow too old to do what I'm doing I'd think of something like that. But I don't wanna be a fifty-five year old father, either."

"Why not? The Bible is full of old men whose wives conceived late. There's nothing wrong in being an older, more settled man, Cable."

"Yeah, I guess not." I stopped us because the breeze was blowing the trees above us and wafting a shadow across Ida's face and all of a sudden she looked ethereal, glowing like an angel. "Just as you are, Ida...right now...I wish I had a camera. You look beautiful." I took a deep breath and reached for her body. Without another word I took her into my arms and slowly, gently kissed her. She melted. Before we knew it I'd led her deep into the oak forest and we lay on the leaves under a large oak tree. I put my hand up her dress and found her warm, moist mound. I slid her panties down and she pulled her dress up and then and there I unbuttoned my pants and found my schlonger to be quite erect. Ida spread her legs and I entered her. She gasped and cried out as I penetrated that warm, wet womanhood of hers. Maybe it was being outdoors in the fresh air, but it had a different, more exciting sensation to it as we became deeply passionate and sensual with one another. When she reached orgasm I came with her and as soon as my member had gone down to half-mast, Ida turned me on-to my back and licked me off. I had never seen her quite so sexy!

"Oh...Cable...Cable Denning...you make me do things... I would never even have thought of."

"Well, I'll tell ya right now, Ida, that was *somethin'!*" I exclaimed.

"I'm glad. Did it please you?"

"Oh, yeah, and then some."

"So why don't we do it more often? Do you have any idea how pent up I was for you? The other night when you deserted me at my place, I could've killed you! I even tried my hand that night. But it's not the same. At best it gets the edge off," she said, flushing a little.

I reached in my coat pocket for a Lucky Strike. "I don't know, Ida. I guess for one thing, you could get pregnant again. The other thing you already know about, too. The more I'm with you, the more risk I put you in. I wish it were different, but it ain't."

"I told you if I get pregnant this time, I'm having the baby, Cable. Maybe you can help out, but I'll take care of it."

Ida Latney and I talked the things adults talk about when they're making love but not quite settled in with one another. I told her I was gonna fly back east to see Einstein and she was surprised but when I told her it was something of a very confidential manner, she didn't question me further. I drove her home and she invited me in for a drink. I accepted and we ended up in bed, making love for a second time that day. She was wet and wonderful and I was once again enamored with the charms of my lovely secretary, Ida Latney.

A Rain of Ruin

It was Tuesday, August 7, 1945. "Perhaps you shouldn't read the paper this morning, Cable," Ida commented. I greeted her as she came in the office carrying the local newspaper. She looked radiant but she wasn't smiling.

"Oh? And why not, little missy?" I caroled back.

"They did it. Just as you said they would—they dropped the atomic bomb on a Japanese island. *Hiroshima*, I think it was called."

At first I didn't say a word. I slowly took the newspaper from her hand and went to my comfy chair, sat down and opened the paper. **ATOMIC BOMB HITS JAPAN!** was the headline. President Harry S. Truman was quoted as saying, "The Japanese may expect a rain of ruin, the like of which has never been seen on this earth." The subheading read, *"Man's most destructive force, equal to 2,000 B-29 loads, blasts Nips."* Right away I was thinking how Einstein must've felt. After all, the world regarded him "the father of the bomb" and one could live a thousand lifetimes and never live that down. Public opinion has a momentum about it, and whether it's wrong or right—people get it set in their craws and that's that.

"Well, Ida, what can we do? Now there'll be an international arms race and sooner or later some irresponsible asshole will pull the lever and we'll do it all over again."

"Cable! That's such a hopeless picture of it! Maybe it'll end this war and our boys will come home and the world can rebuild again."

"Yeah, peace ever after, Ida? Think again, Toots. Do you think world leaders teaming up with private contractors to make a lotta money are gonna stop wars—if there are little skirmishes here and there to keep the big boys making profit? War is always about real estate, ethnic thinking and money. What's gonna change even if the Japs surrender?"

"There's always hope, Cable. But let's get to work and let's not talk about it anymore today, alright?"

"Yeah, swell. I've gotta go down to my safe deposit box. I wanna get something." I got up and went looking for my keys. I couldn't find them. I thought I'd put them in my black shoes in the tiny closet. I came back into the office. "I don't know where the hell my keys are, Ida..."

"Oh, gees, the extra keys are in my other purse—at home. It's the little shiny one. Here. You do remember you gave me an extra key?" She handed me her house keys. "Try not to wake Sophie, she came home late this morning."

"Yeah, okay." I drove over to Ida's and quietly made my way into the house. I found the purse and took out the keys and started down the hallway toward the front door.

"Cable..." I looked around and Sophie was peaking her head around the corner of her bedroom. "Wha---what are you doing here this time of day? I thought it was a burglar or something."

"Hiya, Sophie, nope...just me. I misplaced my safe deposit box keys and Ida had an extra—"

405

"—please...come here, Cable..." I went back down the hall. "Will you come in for a minute? I have something to ask you."

I gawked at the lady because she was wearing this diaphanous white gown with nothing underneath. Her solid breasts and pink nipples stood out against the fabric. "I—I can't stay long, Sophie. I've gotta a lot to do today and I'm getting ready to go to Princeton, New Jersey to see an old Jew I know."

Of all people, Sophie knew my sense of humor and caught on to things quick. "Old Jew? That's a long way to travel just to visit an old Jew, Cable."

"Well, his name happens to be Albert Einstein. We met some years ago when—when we encountered a strange phenomenon."

Sophie checked out my eyes. "I see...when are you leaving?"

"In a couple of days."

"Oh." Then she patted the bed next to her so I'd sit there. "I've been thinking...about you, about me...maybe even about us..." She held onto my arm. "One never knows exactly what to say sometimes. Plus I'm groggy from lack of sleep."

"We can talk another time, Sophie, that might be better—"

"—no, Cable, I need to get this off my chest." And what a chest it was! I guess some women in this life make it on their looks and other physical assets. I think Sophia Legende was one of 'em. "Here it is, point blank. If I quit what I'm doing to set up house with you, would you do it? I'd even get a legitimate job."

I was taken by surprise...but maybe it wasn't such a surprise, really. I sensed it was coming. A month or two ago I might've jumped at it. But now......That's how unreliable I can be in matters of the heart. "I don't know, Sophie. Even though I laud you for wanting to give up what you do, why? You're good at it and it pays a hell of a lot better than anything you can get in some 9 to 5 sweatshop."

"I'm tired, Cable. And I'm in love with you. How else can I spell it out to you, *I want you, mister!*" she affirmed. But her voice was never loud, but wispy and sexy. "It's true I get sexualized at work because all they do is whet my appetite for you. But I want to be sexualized by you. I want us to become a regular breath in each other's lives."

I put my arm around her and kissed her on the cheek. But her mouth moved around quickly to mine and all of a sudden we were kissing. She moved in on me like a vampire in kill-mode and her teeth were biting my neck. My excited nerves sent messages downward and my back shivered, my penis began to swell. "It's the middle of the day, Sophie, and I gotta get back—"

"—for what, darling?" she sighed as she pulled up her nighty and climbed into her little bed. "Isn't this more fun?"

Being a red-blooded American male still charged my batteries. I quickly stripped and before you could say "lickety-split" I was in bed with Sophia Legende. It felt strange in a way. I'd just had Ida across the hall three nights ago and now I was making love to her roommate! But Sophie had a look on her face I hadn't seen before. It was like a plea from deep inside her somewhere, like 'if you don't love me now I won't make it' kind of thing. There was almost no foreplay as she spread her legs and pulled me onto her. Her pussy was swollen and wet and my extra-hard cock entered her like the Southern Pacific express train along a straightaway. Our eyes locked in together as I rocked her slowly back and forth. She moaned and sighed, then closed her eyes as my thrusts became harder and deeper. "Yes! Yes! Cable! I want this with you and only you!" she whispered out of breath.

I said nothing but did my share of moaning with the extreme pleasure Sophia Legende brought to me. She came two or three times before I let go inside of her with everything I had. For some reason I had to do it that way this particular day. I had to give her the best I could be and do as a man, but there was also an ingredient of real love for Sophie. We both finally reached that place when desire is calmed by that something that catches you afterward. I rolled off of her and we lay there for a while, our fingers entwined in each other's. Then out of nowhere, Sophie began to recite a poem:

"None enter here except through passion's thrust
We are filled with the thrills of orgasmic dust
Deep flawed we are until sign we are sent
Our spirits stretch as far as they were meant."

I was touched. "Wow, that's pretty. Where did it come from?" I asked, lighting up a cigarette.

"From me—or my muse," she answered, squeezing my hand. "I wrote that years ago when I knew there would have to a spiritual component to love making one day for me." She turned her head to look at me. "And I found that, Cable...I found it in you. I am bound to you by spirit as well as desire of my body."

I chuckled...to myself, mainly. "It goes to show, we never know who someone is deep inside, do we? I think you're a hell of a poet, lady. How can I do justice to that, doll? I'm that flawed character you wrote about. What do I have to offer you?"

"You...that's all I want...just you, Cable Denning. For years I separated sex from love because I had never loved. Now I do and I don't want one without the other."

"Sophie, I'm not sure I know how to love anymore— if I ever did. I think 'in love' can be 'in lust' with a man. You know, tits and pussy—and that's it. Some men are like that."

"Yes...*most* men. I think that's one reason I'm tired of the same routine at Greystone. In fact, I'm sick of it. I want to have a life...or I don't want to be around at all. I told you I have money, honey—we could go wherever we wanted and I'd take care of you—I'm even a fair cook."

"I wish it could be that way, kid, for both of our sakes. But I'd only hurt you in the end...or you'd hurt me."

"I remember the first day I met you in your office. When you told me you were happy with Nadia, my heart dropped inside. I know I never told you, but I was attracted to you from the start. You're an unusual man, Cable, in many ways. I love your passionate, animal-like bedside manner," she smiled putting her hand on my wet private parts. "Yet you have a sensitive, tender—

even loving side a girl like me loves to be around. Are you sure you won't reconsider?"

"Yep. At least for now. I told you as I've told Ida and everyone I've ever been involved with. I'm a dangerous guy to be around. Someday I'll have to pay up to the piper, and I don't wanna drag someone else into it. I think I told you that before. Don't you believe it?"

"Yes...but...but what am I going to do, Cable? I think about you all the time. Funny, isn't it?"

I put my cigarette out. "What's funny?"

"A million guys would pay a fortune to have me all the way, or use me as a kewpie doll, an ornament...a good looking woman at their side. And the one guy I give it to willingly doesn't want me."

I got up out of bed and started to dress. "It ain't that, Sophie—please, let's not discuss it anymore today. I gotta get to the bank."

Eliminating Time

It was Wednesday, August 15, 1945. New Jersey was pretty so far and the Princeton University area seemed like a little Hollywood set all of its own. I had begun keeping a journal. I guess you could call it a diary of sorts. Why? Because my life was so unique, so filled with the unusual, I knew if I didn't write it down now, it would be lost forever to fading memories of a life strangely lived.

Since 1936, Dr. Albert Einstein lived at 112 Mercer Street, Princeton, New Jersey. It was a small, unpretentious two-story house in a middle-class neighborhood. We were sitting at his breakfast table the next morning after my arrival. "Now ve are cornered by our own smartness, Cable," the good doctor was telling me. "Ve vill be haunted until za end of za human race. I am afraid long-term atomic radiation vill vun day become a rampant disease, a scourge upon mankind."

"That bad, eh?" I countered. "I was hoping nations might someday see the ridiculous suicide of their ways and come to some sort of agreement."

"Ha! I am sixty-five und I have found people only get vorse mit time!" he explained to me. "But today ve vill go sailing! It is a very varm August day und das ist good. The *Tinef* vill be vaiting for us."

"What's 'Tinef' mean, by the way?"

"Yiddish for *Junk*! ha! ha! Ya, it is like the Frankenstein monster, made from many different parts of many boats throughout the years. But she is lake-worthy at the very least! Ha! I hope you can svim."

Soon we were out on Lake Carnegie sailing with the early afternoon breezes. Albert looked old and pensive. His white hair was straggled about his head, his moustache thick and barely kempt. But he still had a great smile. He was looking out onto the water, far away. "Ve have morally corrupted vorld leaders, Cable, and mit new technologies, dey vill use dem for destructive und manipulative purposes, I am afraid. But zat is not vhat I asked you to come see me about. Tonight, vhen novun is around, ve vill go to my laboratory und I vill show you a big surprise!"

We sailed and talked together like the old friends we were. He told me the world was changing now too fast for most people to catch up. New generations of children would be brainwashed with electronic devices and truth would be withheld more and more from the majority populace of the world. He said Oppenheimer was the new head of the Institute for Advanced Study at Princeton and he told me the tall, slim doctor had told him he was having second thoughts about the bomb and its far-reaching consequences. But it wasn't the role of science, he maintained, that would determine who would use the bomb and why and where it would be employed. The only sure thing was that it was meant to destroy life on planet earth.

That evening Alfred Einstein took me to a quaint little café on Nassau Street, the main drag in this smallish town. We sat at a little table facing the small counter. There was a very attractive young woman at the counter talking to a gum-chewing waitress. "That's Annie," Einstein said. "She serves me." He folded his hands in front of him. "You don't know it perhaps, but I vas quite a 'gay blade' in my time mit zah ladies. Ya, Germany, Stockholm, Austria—zey vere filled mit pretty young things! Ya...it is good to reminisce, no?"

"Not in my case so much, Albert. I've had a lot of my girlfriends come to bad endings. I tend not to look back. However, there are a few I think about now and then. One was a Jewish girl named Tara Shiran. She was cute and sexy as hell—and sang to boot! I think I miss her now and then when I think of her."

"Vhat happened to her?"

"You'll laugh if I tell you."

"I vill? You never know, try me..."

"Well, she was a goddamn alien, Albert, and needed to go home."

He smiled at me with such an odd look that I'll never forget it. "Alien, eh? How appropriate, Cable…"

"Appropriate?"

"Ya…vhat I have to share mit you is—is, vell, along dose lines."

"Oh, I see. Well, then, I can hardly wait to be back in old familiar territory."

Finally the waitress came. "Hello Dr. Einstein— who's the handsome bloke next to ya?" she said in a New Jersey accent while chewing her gum.

"Oh, Annie, dis is Cable Denning, a dear friend from California."

"California, eh? How do ya do…" Annie said.

"Yeah, that's in the U.S. too. And how do *you* do?" I asked.

"I'm okay, I guess. Sometimes I wish I could do something else, but I enjoy folks. Have you guys decided? We're kinda busy tonight."

We ordered a local fish dish each and soon the gal at the counter who had been looking at us from the mirror facing the counter smiled at me through it. I more or less smiled back. Albert caught it. "Vhat? You know her? I have not zeen her before, Cable…"

"Nor have I, but I like what I zee—errr—see. Now ya got me talkin' like you with that damn accent!"

We both laughed. We enjoyed our evening with excellent conversation. Einstein was saying how he regretted that Roosevelt had died before reading his letter inspired by an atomic compatriot, Leo Szilard. Einstein had sent that letter to Roosevelt on March 25, 1945. Roosevelt died April 12th. "Ya, it vas Szilard who thought up chain reaction, so zat nuclear fission vould

413

be possible in a bomb. He and Fermi. But like Oppen-heimer, now he has second thoughts. It is ein Pandora's box, ya?"

I was looking at the attractive woman sitting at the counter. "I wouldn't mind *her* box," I said, a little dis-tracted. I was feeling a bit horny and restless for some reason.

Einstein chuckled. "Vell, perhaps you should meet her and get it off your chest—or out of your pants," the professor suggested.

But I didn't have to. The lady got up, went over to the jukebox and put a quarter in the slot. She was of medium height, darkish hair and wore a tight grey skirt with an off-white blouse. Her figure was just right for my taste...nice butt, flat stomach and stand-out tits. The first song she played was a Harry James up tempo ver-sion of *Out of Nowhere*. She looked at me with eyes that could only have meant she wanted me to know she ex-isted in this world. Then strangely, she smiled as she passed our table and left the café. Now didn't that beat all!

Albert and I looked at each other and shrugged our shoulders. When the waitress came over with our check, however, she took something out of her pocket and handed it to me. "Here's something that peculiar gal wanted ya to have, mister," she said matter-of-fact. "I swear, some people...they're just—just so weird. But she gave me a buck for the effort. I guess it was worth it. Oh! I forgot." Then she handed me a note the young woman had also left with the Annie. "Good luck with her. A dish like that can get ya into big trouble, ya know..."

I smiled. "Yeah...I know..."

Albert's curiosity was piqued. "Zo...? Vhat did she leave you?"

I looked in the palm of my hand and there was a little silver pussycat, the kind that belonged on a good-luck charm bracelet or the like. "I don't know, just a little pussycat." Then I opened the small note. *'Prospect Garden midnight'.* That was all it said. I read it to Albert and he raised his eyebrows. "Zat's za magnificent Garden of Eden surrounding Prospect House, part of za expanded Princeton campus," he observed.

"Don't you think that's a bit forward for a girl?" I asked, checking on the neat penmanship.

"Obviously the young lady, she is—is smitten. I'd go if I vere you, Herr Denning!"

"Please don't say that, Albert..."

"Vhat?"

"*Herr Denning*—it reminds me too much of the German bad guys I'm dealing with right now, one in particular, Oscar Brandt. You remember the *death whistlers*, right?" He nodded in the affirmative. "Well, it's the same organization that sort of co-sponsors the German cause here in America, the *Oculus.* Only not everybody knows that little fact...including some of its leaders."

"Ya...I zee...vell, let's get on to za laboratory. After all, zat's vhy you came, ya?"

A Kaleidoscope of Dimensions

By 9:30 p.m. Albert Einstein and I were inside the building that housed the Institute for Advanced Study. There was a huge basement and we descended some

415

stairs until we stood before a room simply marked "Private". Einstein used his key and suddenly we were somewhere else, in a room filled with stars and a chillingly beautiful universe on the ceiling. "Dis is my private observatory, Cable. Now...look, vat do you zee...?"

"My God—it—it looks so real!" I half-whispered.

"Ya...that is because it *is* real. Somevun has helped me to 'crack za code' of *eliminating time*. Here, in zis room, there is no time. Look at your vatch." I glanced at my watch. It had stopped. "No time, no time keeping, no aging, nothing to do viz time can exist in here. Zere is no history, no future—maybe not even a 'now'!"

"I'll be a son-of-a-bitch! Albert, how did you do it?"

"I wish I could say I did it. But as I said, somevun else did. Zey showed me how za *truly fundamental meaning*—$E=Mc^2$—my formula must never get into the hands of humans. I vas wrong, Cable, I t'ot I could help zem. But no...humans vould abuse it."

"So how did all of this happen? Who's behind it?"

"I don't know. Zey just appear. Large angels...or ze like. Beings...shapes, forms—vhatever you vant! You zee, *each dimension retrofits into every other dimension*, like a long endless chain of dimensions. Zey showed me how za cosmos changes every minute, yet it has no time—only tim*ing*—zey came to me because I had stumbled upon za formula for doubling light to explain vhat I t'ot might be za true relationship betveen time, mass und energy. But I vas only part right, Cable. Light does not bend except in za illusion of reflection. All zat ve see is not pure, but reflected in our eyes. But...zey showed me how laws und rules mazematically extend to zeir nth degrees. Here, let me show you..." He waved

416

his hand at an orange-green orb in the center of the ceiling. Suddenly everything changed. Suddenly there were things I couldn't explain if you gave me a thousand years to do it! Planets, suns, shiny metals, shapes and sizes of things I could not recognize. "Never mind the space travel, Cable. Space as ve know it is za baby germination ground, like an *embryonic kindergarten*. You know, za solar system is simple debris except for za earth. Planets zat have been, vill be or vere. Ve need to achieve dimensions at least to za fifth power to be anyvere near a familiar place—und it is done only srough dimensional travel via za *mind*. Ya, but even my brain ist too small to go zere easily. *Za mind must be trained along mit za brain*, zey have told me." Then he stopped and waved his hand again at the baseball sized orb. Whizzing small objects, mostly circular or oblong, were floating in a plasma-like substance. "Zis is za *inner dimensional universe*, like za body. Zere is no beginning nor ending to it. *'As above so below'* vas za modicum I grew up viz. It is true. Here is proof. Vat you zee up zer is inside my body und everysing traveling. Even our bodies are illusions zat our five senses comprehend as real. But it is okay, because ve must land und rest somevere. At least for a vile."

I was awe-struck. "Who else has seen this?" I inquired.

"No vun. I invite no vun here. Except you tonight. You und I have shared many t'ings, from zis und other dimensions."

"Yeah, I can vouch for that. So whatta ya do with all this knowledge?"

417

"Zere is nothing I can do. First, I entered za vorld viz a partial knowing of tings. Zen I uncovered za incomplete formula. After zat, I provided Fermi and Szilard mit za tools to make a bomb to destroy. Now...zey vill not permit any of vat ve see here tonight to leave zis room. Human beings must, each on his own, discover vat you have seen tonight. If I showed you any more, Cable, you vould lose your reason—I mean, really crazy!"

"I'm already nuts, Albert, so I guess it really doesn't matter."

We both laughed. "Vell, so it is. Ve must step out to see vat za time is. You have an important date tonight mit some young frauline, you know."

"Yeah, so I do." Einstein used his key to open the door from the inside and suddenly we were back to a darkened hallway. We made our way out of the building. A small clock tower said the time was 11:20 p.m. I asked him if he wanted to come, but he said he was tired and would walk home. Did I know the way home? I said no and he explained it to me. We hugged and I walked the three blocks or so to Prospect House. Einstein hadn't told me there was a huge fence around the place, so at the advanced age of 45 I scaled the damn thing and crashed to the ground on the other side of the garden. And what a garden it was! Little lamps lit up a pathway through it and ponds and pools and frogs and night birds could be heard as I trudged towards its center. I found a bench and lit a cigarette. It was cool but pleasant. My watch hadn't started back up so I just waited and assumed my mysterious lady friend would appear when she was supposed to.

About thirty minutes later I heard a voice call out my first name. "Cable...it's me..." I rose to my feet and looked around. There in a semi-lighted shadow stood the unmistakable face and body of Tara Shiran!

"Tara! What—what the hell is going on here?"

She walked toward me briskly. "See? It's me, Cable."

It *was* my little adventurer! "I don't get any of this, lady! First you're some mysterious babe at a café leaving me a pussycat charm and an appointment time—now you're Tara Shiran, one of my girlfriends from long ago. So...you won't blame me if I ask you who you are now, will you?" Everything about her was the same as I remembered Tara: yellow hair, blue eyes, nice mouth, smile, teeth—she was even wearing the light-yellow dress with the flowers all over it she was wearing the day I met her! But there was one thing *not* as I recalled it. Her bust line had grown considerably. Tara never had large breasts, but this gal was more or less bustin' out all over!

"I'm sorry...I thought you would be glad to see Tara again."

"Yeah, I am—but do you know how I knew it wasn't her?"

"No...tell me..."

"Her breasts—Tara never had large breasts."

"Oh, that. Well, I was taking from your deep sexual fantasy-self, perhaps a memory. You must have imagined it at some point."

"I don't know. I don't remember. So...who are *you?*"

"Nothing...everything...no one, everybody. Who would you like me to be?"

"I don't know. Why did you summon me here? So you're not even the gal Albert and I saw at the café on Nassau Street, are you?"

"No, I just made her up. Did you like her?"

"Yeah, she was alright. Look, lady, I've got to go back to L.A. day after tomorrow and I wanna spend as much time with Albert as I can."

"He was admonished, you know. But I think now he understands. He will grow old and perish, just as you will—but you will not grow old."

"So tell me something new. Are you gonna tell me what you wanted me here for or do I climb back over that fence and leave?"

"You don't have to be cross with me, Cable," the voice said that resembled Tara so much it was uncanny. In fact, it gave me the shivers. "This—this body's female sexual self truly liked you...a lot—in fact, she wants you even still—like now—I can feel it..."

"Skip that, would ya, and get on with it. For the last time, who are you and what do you want?"

"I—I am one of Dr. Einstein's guides. I am designated to watch him for a while, to make certain he stays on the straight and narrow and does not further violate laws that are significant to the running of the dimensional cosmos. A little knowing is a dangerous thing. Dr. Einstein scratched the surface, but anything incomplete like that can still be used to create—well, you know, something like the atomic bomb you humans have contrived to make in order to destroy each other."

"Yeah...I guess you're right.

"Everything goes up forever and down forever and around forever and is all things, yet just one thing. For humans that is impossible to understand, I realize. Same goes for sexual orientation. You see a human female before you. But I am in truth neither male nor female. I am a *dimensional being*. I appear like this to be attractive to you, because your psyche appears to be fixated with sexual objectivity."

"So I have a fixated sexual objectivity complex, do I?"

"If that's what you wish to call it."

"It's what *you* just called it." I took out a Lucky Strike and lit it. She watched with curiosity. "So what you're tellin' me is that we're all one, da, da, da, and happiness ever after, eh?"

"You should not inhale those tobacco leaf shreddings."

"I hate to be impolite, but my body is my body, sister. Now, again I repeat, unless there's something else to tell me, I'm outta here. And just for the record, I resent you impersonating someone I cared for—sounding like her, looking like her. To some humans that might be considered cruel. Have you ever been lonely, Miss—Miss...?"

"Complete spirits are never lonely. If I offended you, I apologize—I regret not being able to say to you what I fully intended to say."

"Oh, yeah? And what prevented you?"

"Frankly, you, Mr. Denning. You are crude, rude, probably selfish and have become cynical and pugnacious."

I smiled to myself. Maybe she was right. "All that, huh? Well, it goes to show, hanging out on earth too long can spoil a nice person."

Before I could say another word I felt this whoosh of sound, my eyes were forced shut and I found myself standing in front of Albert Einstein's little casa at 112 Mercer. Nothing had changed except my cigarette had burned a little. The lady must have teleported me. I don't blame her. I guess I was kinda of irritable around her for some reason. Albert had gone to bed and so I sat up for a while in his comfy chair out on the front porch. Yep, it'd been one hell of a day!

Wounded Birds

I got back to California knowing full well it would be the last time I'd ever see Albert Einstein. Either he or I—or both—would die before we met again. But what adventures we had shared! I will always embrace his brave and fun-loving spirit. I suppose I could do without his pipe smoking and violin playing, but hell, they were part of him, too!

Sophie called me and asked me to come see her sing at *Bar of Music* that Saturday night. She said it'd be her last time there and that she was quitting. That bothered me. I told her I'd come in to see her but I thought she oughtta continue singing. But unhappy birds don't sing. I knew Sophia Legende was unhappy. It was about 11:30 p.m. when I finally saw my way clear to drive over to the nightclub. I wish I hadn't. A very inebriated Sophia Legende was up on the stage singing a broken song in a broken voice. I'd never heard the tune before, but she was hanging onto the microphone, barely able to stand—or sing. The band had stopped backing her and only her piano player, Kenny Sutter, was left to do the dirty work of trying to keep her in tune. It wasn't a great song, in fact it hurt me to hear her trying to sing it. The audience seemed to like it and maybe they thought it was part of the act. I don't know. But the *words* said a lot to me. '*I thought I was myself, but I'm every woman who ever loved you...and so I shoved you away, as if I never had to pay the price...now it's harder to remember you were strong when you touched me...*' The song ended with a poignant reminder of how toxic a bad relationship can be: '*...I was every woman on parade, I was afraid, I could have stayed with you, when time was out of the equation...I needed no persuasion to love you so...but time returned last night...*" I think the song was a jazz ballad and the chords from the piano seemed odd and dissonant, just like Sophie was sounding.

She finished the song and staggered away from the microphone. Some youngish tall and handsome guy helped her down and led her down the hall into her dressing room. I followed. I knocked on the door. The man opened it. "Yes?"

"I'm—I'm a friend of Sophie's. I came to see her...she...she...uh, called me earlier today, wanted me to catch her act."

"There wasn't much to the act now, was there, Mr.—Mr.—"

"—Denning, Cable Denning's the name..."

He looked up at me from staring at the floor. "Oh...I see. I think you're why she's crying in her beer, Denning—"

"—who—who's there, Tony?" Sophie muttered in her drunken voice.

423

"The ex-object of your affections...did you ask him to come tonight?"

"Let—let him in, you fool!" The man opened the door wider and I entered. Sophie was draped across a small wooden chair. Her dress was disheveled, clear past her thigh on one leg. Her hair was straggly, her makeup smudged, especially her lipstick. 'Tony' was wearing the other half of it. I got the picture pretty quick. "So you came to see the legend, eh?" Sophie cracked in a dry voice. "How'd I do? You like that song, Cable? It was about you...you know..." Her voice trailed off.

"My name's Tony Lama, Denning. I own the Owl Drug Company Store at Wilshire Blvd. and Western Ave. I—I've been helping Sophia keep her nerves calm. She's kind of lost it lately, and I'm not sure—"

"—*I heard you*!" Sophie snapped. I had never seen this side of her before. "You can—you can talk about me when I'm gone—but tonight *I* have the floor—*and* the bandstand—get it?" She snickered to herself. Then she pointed at Tony Lama. "See, Cable? You taught me how—how to fuck—you know, right in the pussy—and Tony's been getting into that luscious cream pie you liked so much!" She couldn't look me in the eye. "Tough—hic!—tough break, huh? But what's a girl to do, private dick? You didn't want me anymore—"

I was aghast. All this must've happened in the few days I was out of town. "—Sophie—look, I don't think this is the time or place—"

"—let me frickin' finish, Mr. But-in-ski!" She pulled her dress down past her knees. "A girl has to—has to look decent, ya know...even if she *is* a whore. That's what I am, ya know. I've never told you the whole story, have I? But I...I guess that doesn't...doesn't matter now, does it?" She smiled at Tony Lama. "Say...have you met my newest private lay? Tony Lama...Cable Denning—"

He extended his hand. I didn't take it. "Sophie, look, I don't wanna—"

"—stay put and shut up!" she shouted at me in that drunken tone. I've often said, a sober person can't stand a drunk—and vice versa. Then she quieted down, but I knew something was crumbling inside of her. "You're a *man*, and men always take the floor when they wanna— just as they take women when they wanna—only this young lady has—has suddenly become a smart business woman. You see, Tony owns an Owl Drug Store. I fuck him, he provides me with drugs...ha! Drugs to wake up, drugs to make me sleep, drugs to get horny with, hang- over drugs, digest—digestion drugs—you name it, To- ny's my—my man, Cable." Then she got this pitiful look on her strained face. She waved a drunken finger in my direction. "But...but you—*you* were my man...seems like—like only yesterday, doesn't it? Do you remember what you told...told me the last time I—I needed to talk to you and some honest—honest affection? You simp- ly—simply *dismissed me*—'I don't wanna talk about it now—I gotta get to the bank...' That—that's what you said, Cable Denning...I wasn't that important. I was just dispensable tits and pussy in your life—wasn't I?" She paused and her voice dropped to a near-whisper. "I—I guess I rang the wrong number when I called *you*, eh?" she mumbled half to herself.

"Yeah, maybe, Sophie. It ain't always clear." This train wreck of a woman was unbearable to watch. "I—I have to go now, kid. Call me when you're sober and in a better frame of mind," I said in a low, tired voice. I looked over to Tony Lama. "I hope you didn't mix the alcohol with your pharmacopeia, Lama. It could kill her, ya know."

"I have already been careful about telling her that. But she does it anyway. She's just a little nuts tonight. I'll get to the bottom of this," Lama said, measuring his words.

"Yeah, you just do that, mister. Where's she staying tonight?"

"Out at her place of business."

"Oh, the ranch, eh?" I glanced once more at the wasted Sophia Legende. "Sophie...promise. Promise you'll call me when you're feeling better."

She sneered at me. "Why? I was through with you a week or so ago. Why aren't you through with me?"

"Because I care about you, Sophie—I care what happens to you—"

"—what a crock of shit—in—in a way, you're just like Demaine and those bastards—ya want me to suck you off and then slam your cock into me like—like my dear old Daddy used to do! Well, I'm through! That's it, I'm finished with you men—all you men." Then she looked at Tony Lama. "That—hic!—that goes for you, too, my little Lama boy. As soon as I don't need your drugs any more, you're out the door!" She put her hand to her lips. "Oooo! that rhymes." Then she looked at me. "I'm a poet, aren't I, Cable? *Deep flawed we are, until sign we are sent...our spirits stretch...as far as they are meant...*' And my spirit, Cable, is stretched as far—as far as—hic!—it'll go. Good-bye, my old lover man." She smiled and snickered. "You know, that's a song I never sang but—but—I should've, huh? Only I should have called it Lover *Men*, eh? Ha!" she laughed and I opened the door and left.

It was a bright September Monday morning...the 10th. World War II ended September 2nd, and my birthday was on the 13th. The streets were filled with celebrants for days. Soldiers and sailors began to empty out the downtown streets of Los Angeles. It was time to go home now. Somehow we'd all seen enough death, both abroad and at home to last a lifetime. Since I'd returned, my work had kept my nose to the grindstone and Ida and I had accomplished quite a bit, including six old cases, four news ones and a few walks in the park. Like the little boy I sometimes am, I went running to Ida over this last weekend. I had to forget what I'd seen and heard from the lips of Sophia Legende. She'd moved out of Ida's place and now lived back at Greystone Manor. I guess business was good. Still I worried about her.

Ida was a wonderful lover. She was very compliant, young and always ready for me. Yep, she had a lot goin' for her. I told her she could take this Monday off and go shopping. She delighted in my generosity and she asked if I could be with her tonight. I nixed that one because I didn't want us to become a habit. Boss and secretary, you know. I was still a bit uncomfortable about it. But desire overcomes a lotta things when you're horny. She even promised to take me somewhere special for my birthday. That sounded tantalizing!

This day would prove to be unlike the days that had passed since I'd returned from visiting Albert Einstein in Princeton. The phone rang. "Yeah, Cable Denning here..."

"And what's the busy beaver private detective doin' this morning, beaver hunting?" Lt. Lester Keith's voice crackled as he derided me at the other end of the telephone.

"No, Lester, just plain hard work—trying to identify my job description, that's all. Sometimes it's a bit foggy."

"I'm glad you said that, Denning. Because my call's about identification. I wanna talk to you about it this sunny September morning."

"Yeah, so what's up, doc?"

"I'm—I'm holding a suicide note here in my hand. It just so happens to be addressed to...let me see...to...yeah, one *Cable Denning*, done up in real nice script, kinda like a poet might've done it."

A sinking feeling went through my gut. "Anybody we know?"

"Somebody *you* knew, apparently, Mr. Detective. Would you mind coming out here before I remove the body?"

"Where's here?"

"A kinda classy joint, *Greystone Manor*, I think the lady called it. Ring a bell? I want you to see a couple of things. Maybe you can help me find the killer. If for some reason it turns out it wasn't suicide. It might even be you, Denning. It's too bad...she was a wonderful female specimen, you know, blonde, blue-green eyed, great body, made good money out here, too, I hear. Except the body happens to be dead right now."

A pang went through my heart. "Did her name happen to be Sophia Legende?"

"Bingo! You're gettin' smarter every day, wise guy. You saved the name for last, as if you didn't know. Oh, and I'm holding one of her Johns right now. His name is Tony Lama—says he knows you."

"Yeah, we met once." I was shocked and surprised. Yet I wasn't somehow. "How'd she die? I don't think it was murder—not with a suicide note—or do you think I faked that, too?"

"You never know, Denning, what killers will do—*if* you're a killer, that is. I'm not sayin' you are, I'm not saying you aren't...at least for now."

Now Sophia Legende's war had ended, the one she kept waging within herself about who she was and what she was becoming—not to mention who she loved—if, like me, she could really love. With a sense of forlornness and anger I made my way to Beverly Hills and Greystone Manor. I saw Tony Lama standing near a policeman with handcuffs on his wrists. We nodded. Slowly, I walked upstairs, bracing myself for what I might see. Lester Keith greeted me at the top of the stairs. "You had some dealings with this gal at some point, didn't you, Denning?" the lieutenant asked, putting his hand on my shoulder as he led me to Sophie's bedroom. "If she was screwin' that guy Lama downstairs, why did she leave you the suicide note? When did you meet her and what was your business besides the obvious?"

"Yeah, downtown at Zoot Mimby's, a negro club where Sophie got involved with a scumbag named Demaine. She hired me to get him off her back while at the same time, she suspected Zoot Mimby's was headquarters for a white slavery ring that was stealing women from here. Someone was exporting pretty young white things to the island of Martinique. Remember, Lieutenant, I told you about it, but you just scoffed at it and told me you were too busy."

"Which I was and still am. Do you have any idea how many women are taken off our streets every day here in this city?"

"Oh, maybe three or four, I'd guess."

"More like eight to ten during these war years with so many people of unknown origin showin' up all over. We've had as much as sixty missing young girls' reports in one week."

"That many, huh?" We reached Sophie's room. We entered.

"Check out the body, tell me if it's the gal you said she is."

Sophia Legend lay naked on her stomach on the bed. Her body was extra purple-white and stone-cold as I felt her arm. Slowly I turned her body over and her once lovely breasts were squeezed flat against her chest, her blue-green eyes partially open, staring into eternity. The only thing that wasn't stiff as a board was her lovely, flowing blonde hair. I gently rolled her back over. "Yep, that's her." I couldn't take anymore, so I left. Lt. Keith followed. "There's one other thing you should know, Lester. Demaine and his boys killed a gal named Greta Bardini in this room. There was a mad doctor here who took care of the women's health issues. He insisted that I help him load the body into his station wagon and dispose of it. No one would ever know, least of all the police. That's how they did things under Dr. Ephron Rueben. "

"And you went along with it?" Lt. Keith asked, widening his eyes.

"It's a little more complicated. I needed a beard that night to go into the front of Zoot Mimby's while I checked out the basement in the back. The doc agreed to do it if I helped him bury Greta Bardini's body."

"Oh, swell, now you're a gravedigger! Shit, Denning, what else aren't you telling me?"

"I'll bet you'd like to know, Lieutenant! You're gonna have to guess the rest."

"You can write it down and mail it to me every day you're in the slammer, smart ass."

We walked down the stairs and out of the main house. Lester Keith handed me Sophie's suicide note. "One of the gals I questioned told me Miss Legende was in love with you. Who in the fuck ain't? Poor choice, if you ask me. But here...maybe this belongs more to you than me right now. Just bring it down to the station when you're through with it—like tomorrow."

"Thanks, Lester. Can I go home now?"

"Yeah, get outta here." The coroner's boys were bringing down Sophia Legende's body in a stretcher. It was covered with a sheet. "Too bad...I get the feeling she was a nice person—even if she was a whore." He took off his hat and smoothed his thin hair back. "The oldest goddamn profession in the world besides cheating your neighbor."

"She was, Lester...that she was..." I glanced over as Tony Lama was being put into a cop car. "What about him?"

"I don't know. I'll probably scare him a little and release him. I don't think anybody killed Sophia Legende except her own legend."

"Like you said—a good person...she just got lost."

"Oh, by the way, she left a note that wasn't yours."

"Oh?"

"Yeah, it's instructions and money to cremate the remains. She even designated the funeral home. She doesn't wanna get buried, so it seems."

"Which funeral home?"

"Bramble—on Toberman Street."

"Yeah, I know where it is." I was glad she decided to get cremated. That way I would never have to visit Sophie Legende's remains in some cemetery like I had in years past with other women who now lay moldering in the cold, dark, damp earth. How did I *really* feel about her? Did it sink in yet—that she was gone forever? I don't know.

The Boy and the Mountain

One time when we were together I remember Sophie saying she'd remembered a story a friend once told her. Once upon a time there was a boy who loved a beautiful young girl very much. But she wanted nothing to do with him. That was because she was very rich and the boy was poor as a church mouse. A terrible storm arose in their little village by the mountains and the town was buried in snow. Many people died. Finally, the two were forced together in a makeshift hut at the foot of the great mountain that had caused all the trouble. But still she refused his affections. So when spring came

432

and the snow melted and things returned more less to normal, the boy went to the top of the mountain. It was very high and craggy, and dropped precipitously several thousand feet straight down. The mountain was a little reclusive, spending most of its days in the clouds above the little village. But the boy climbed the treacherous peak and when he got to the very top, he spoke to it. *"Oh, Great Mountain, why did you let your snows fall and allow so many people to perish?* The mountain thought for a minute *'Because it's what I am, what I do. I cannot be what I am not. I must do what I am.'* The boy thought on this and the girl he loved came to mind. *'Oh, mountain, how may the girl I love with all my heart accept me for who I truly am? She wants me not, O lofty mountain.'*

The mountain was silent for a while. The boy was tired from the climb and he slept atop the mountain. Finally, just before dusk, the mountain awakened him. *'It is having faith, believing that you can. If you will to jump from my highest peak down into the valley, and land without a scratch, then she will love you.'*

The boy was ecstatic. *'Truly! But darkness settles soon and if I jump, I will be unable to see anything below me.'*

'Darkness has its own kind of light. You must jump now. Trust...'

So the boy climbed a few feet higher until he was balanced on the precipice of the southwest ledge of the mountain that fell away into seeming eternity, down, down, down... He spread his arms and thanked the mountain and jumped out into the air to the village far, far below.

I asked her if the boy ever made it safe to the bottom. Sophie looked at me and smiled. "Maybe we'll never know. We all make plunges into the unknown, don't we?" she'd said. Sophia Legende had just made that plunge, I think. I knew she'd used some kind of painless medication. I also realized Sophie hated pain of any kind. By giving to others through the years, she assuaged her own pain, the kind that gnaws at you all your life. In that case, maybe it was best to go away—forever.

I sat at my desk and lit up a Lucky Strike and gulped a big English gin down my gullet. I took out Sophie's note and began to read:

'My Darling Cable, You made me realize how truly painful it is to love in this human life...and feel and care for someone. Life is bittersweet. Knowing what is ahead for me and knowing also that I cannot have you as I would wish, then there is only emptiness in the quest to find you again among the myriad of men whom I have known or perhaps would ever know. I beg you, don't blame yourself. I have thought of this for years. I'm frightened, Cable, but only now do I have the courage to act on taking the great journey out of this world. You helped me understand so many things. With the simple act of knowing you and with your love in my heart, my spirit will never be lonely. With all my love, Sophia Legende.'

I began whimpering like a child, looking around the room for someone to answer the painful questions—

434

why? Why the journey of this terrible life, the grief I was feeling was all but unbearable. But there was one thing that kept me from taking a bottle of pills and putting myself to sleep. I had learned there's always an opposite for every force in our lives. I realized I made Sophie's dying a sad thing. Maybe to her, maybe to the angels, maybe to the universe there was a joy in sloughing off the old flesh. The ancient Chinese said that anything you can touch can't be permanent. Stay at the root of all things, stay at the spirit level in your consciousness. What is it I would miss about Sophia Legende anyway? Her great blonde hair, her boobs, her wounded self-striving to create balances in this world? Yeah, I was good at that, selecting out wounded birds and gathering them around me until it was time to leave. Trouble is, so many of them died in the process of knowing me. Now that I think of it, maybe it *should've* been me to take those pills and stop my heart. *'Deep flawed we are, until sign we are sent...our spirits stretch as far as they were meant...'* Good night, Sophia Legende...may you sleep and dream the dream that lovers dream...

Epilogue

I couldn't sleep that night. I rolled around in bed until I had to get up and get dressed and decided to walk the Boulevard of Broken Dreams. Ida Latney had taken the news of Sophie's death pretty hard, but she said she felt somehow it was to come. Attribute it to a woman's intuition, she told me. She also sensed that Sophie may have secretly loved me. I said nothing.

435

Monday nights on Hollywood Boulevard are slower and now that the blackout was lifted, a lot brighter. But things felt different. Streetcars prowled the streets like red-orange locusts with a central eye penetrating the dark, and prostitutes looking like would-be young starlets hung around bars where sailors could ogle them. The shoe-shine boy at Cahuenga and Hollywood Boulevard was shining his own shoes and *Lost Weekend* was playing at the RKO Pantages. I heard via Oscar Brandt that the Oculus had destroyed their leader Zxyphon, when things went wrong at headquarters. People were saying that World War II was almost over now, that Hiroshima and Nagasaki had been given the atomic bomb treatment and well over 200,000 people were dead to prove it. Bankers and Wall Street were getting richer and had profited greatly from the war and Los Angeles would grow into a giant metropolis, so some folks were saying. I wondered if President Harry S. Truman was in someone's pocket...could be things might not settle down all that much after the war was over. Someone was still pulling the strings behind the curtain. A war economy was what America would now thrive on. That and big corporations taking an increasingly large slice of the pie, leaving the independent business man a smaller and smaller space to be successful in the world of commerce.

I'd had enough of my neighborhood, so I took a streetcar downtown. I remembered that the *Rhythm Room* down in the basement of the Hotel Hayward on 6th and Spring was a hot spot. Usually a jazz band, but I thought I'd drop by. Maybe there'd be a babe singing there tonight. As I approached the joint, large groups of military men were out in front laughing, drinking and smoking. The cops pretty much left them alone. Some Midwesterner-type came up to me and looked me over...he asked me if I was Phillip Marlowe, the Raymond Chandler character played so ably by Humphrey Bogart on that big silver screen. I told him no, but I was his apprentice. I think the dope believed me!

The entrance was on 6th street and as I descended the marble staircase to the basement I could see the place was filled with people, even on a Monday night. High class prostitutes and well-dressed men and women, the expected military presence lined up at the two bars, and young couples flung each other about on the dance floor or sat quietly in little corners at a table for two. I'd sure like to have entered the head of a great lookin' auburn-haired beauty I saw talking to a sailor. He wasn't getting anywhere and soon he left. I thought I'd try my luck. "Do you think I'd have better luck with you then he did?" I asked her right out as I approached her with a wry smile on my lips.

She stood about five-six or so and had on a tight black dress with a string of pearls. Her eyes were medium blue and her lips very red with a shiny new coat of lipstick. She was slim but measured about a 36" bust, I guessed. She looked me over. "I doubt it, but I don't know, depends what you're selling, mister. I—I'm not what you think. *I* personally have nothing to sell. It's 12:15 in the morning and my roommate and I are preparing to go home. I'm sure you saw how I handled the sailor."

"Yeah, I was impressed, too. You know how to brush 'em off, eh? Why do you think that is?"

"Because I know what I want and what I don't want. And I don't think I want *you*...nothing personal."

"Sounds pretty personal to me...but I don't blame you there. I'm sorry for bein' a tad fresh. I'm kinda disoriented today—I—I, uh...I lost a friend this morning."

"Old age?"

"No, suicide."

Her eyes widened. "Oh...God, death is just too prevalent during these war years, don't you think? It seems everyone's either dying—or grieving."

"Yeah, and we're not far behind." I tipped my hat and started to walk away. "I'm sorry to have bothered you, miss."

She called after me. "You—you didn't even want to know my name?"

"What's in a name? Especially if we ain't goin' anywhere." I saw the band start up and some dish announced this was the last set of the night, so everyone get up and dance. "Unless...unless you wanna dance..."

"I can't...my...my roommate...I need to wait for her..."

"So long, ma'am." I walked away but she was persistent. She followed me. "Are—are you a policeman? You look like one..."

"Naw, I'm a lowly private dick." Her face blushed and I knew she was a good girl at heart. "That means private eye, detective or the like, you know—I do everyone else's dirty work."

"Oh, I see...I—I wasn't sure how you meant that."

"I ain't in the mood for anything else. See ya..." I walked off and this time she didn't pursue me. But she sure was cute as hell—no, she was *elegant*...yeah, that was it, kind of the Eleanor Winston type of elegant. Damn, I hadn't thought of Eleanor for quite a while. I guess when she got shot and killed at the top of Glacier Point in Yosemite three years ago, I kinda shoved it all under the rug so I could get on with my life. I bet myself the dish's first name started with an 'E'—she just seemed the type. I had to know. I turned around and re-approached her. "I—I have a strange question to ask you..."

"Yes?" she said with those large blue eyes of hers smiling at me.

"Does your name begin with an 'E' by any chance?"

"Why, yes, how did you know? My name's *Elena*—Elena Sommers. You also have a name, I assume?"

"I knew it!," I said, smiling. "Denning—Cable Denning..." I extended my hand and she shook it. Her hand felt warm and soft.

"So how did you know my name began with an 'E'?"

"You just look like it, Elena. I was in love with a classy lady once upon a time whose name was *Eleanor*."

"I—I see. Where is she now?"

"Dead. Three years ago."

"I'm very sorry. Didn't you say you just lost someone to suicide today? Is it *you*—or is it—"

"—the nature of my profession, Elena. I'm dangerous to be around."

For some reason that seemed to entice her. "Really...? That's terrible." She glanced out on the dance floor. "I see my roommate has found someone she's enjoying. I'm glad she didn't choose a soldier. I guess we could have that dance, after all. Would you like to?"

I didn't say anything but took her hand and we walked out onto the crowded dance floor. She fit in my arms nicely. One good thing about somebody new: you have a chance to cover up your old mistakes and maybe make the right move at the right time with the right person. The singer up on the stage was singing a medium tempo version of *My Blue Heaven*. "You're a good dancer, Elena...I'm—I'm glad that we met."

"So are you, thank you." She glanced up to the stage. "Do you believe in that—I mean, what she's singing about?"

"Maybe for some folks, probably not for me. What about you?"

"I don't know. I like the dream-like scene she's painting, but I'm too worldly to want to settle down with just one man."

"Wow! Funny, that's exactly the way I feel. I suppose if the ideal woman came along it'd be okay. I think this increasingly fast-moving society kind of ruins peoples' chances to be really happy—I mean, deeply happy. Plus love is a big investment, don't you think?"

She pulled her head back to look at me. "Well! I doubt I've ever heard a *man* say that. Yes, I do think that's true. Maybe you're a little different, Cable. Maybe we can be friends."

"Yeah, maybe..." We drew silent and danced to the last three songs of the evening. The final slow dance was a favorite of mine. It was a tune introduced in a Glenn Miller movie called *Sun Valley Serenade* and was dubbed by a gal named Pat Friday. The name of the song was *I Know Why and So Do You* and couples danced close as the big band singer up there on the stage gave it her best spit and polish. I was thinking how strange it felt that Glenn Miller wasn't making new hits on the radio. He had become an American musical institution. Yeah, there was Benny Goodman, Artie Shaw, the Dorsey Brothers, Louie Armstrong and all—but there was something special about Glenn Miller, his sound and the atmosphere he created when he played a dance, made a recording with his boys or was heard on the radio. After Miller enlisted and was leading the Army Air Force band, his plane disappeared during a routine flight from England to Paris...last December I think it was. No one has found him yet. Maybe he's okay and lost or imprisoned somewhere we don't know about. I'd sure like to hear him again when the world is free—maybe tomorrow on this side of the *White Cliffs of Dover.*

Elena Sommers' roommate turned out to be a famous Norwegian ice skater named Edi Ellsberg, I was told. She did stand-in and performed in professional ice skating shows for a skating star the movies had embraced in 1936. Her name was Sonja Henie. It was very odd, too, because the motion picture, *Sun Valley Serenade,* happened to feature Sonja Henie as the female lead! Serendipity, eh?

I walked the two women to Edi's automobile. It was a fancy 1940 DeSoto...black convertible with a light canvas top. There was money in the family, I thought. Edi, who was a little slip of a thing with dirty blonde hair and cold blue eyes, got in and started the engine. Elena lingered with me. "I take back what I said earlier, Cable," she pronounced in a soft voice.

"What'd you say?"

"That maybe you wouldn't make out better than the sailor I had to shake when we first met this evening. I hope..." She looked down at the ground bashfully. "I hope you may find a way not to be too scarce. Does that frighten you—a woman being so bold?"

"No, but stay away from me, Elena. I'm really sorry I approached you tonight. I was being selfish and was attracted to you...not just because of Sophie's death, but I thought then and still think you're a knockout dish with class and quality."

"Am I not able to make that decision?"

"No, I apologize for being rough on you. But it's best this way, believe me."

"At least give me a business card, would you?"

I took out a card and handed it to her. "I'm trouble, lady. The capital 'T' type. Please...I realize you don't understand the implications. You're gonna have to trust me on this one."

She looked disappointed. "Okay...if you insist—before the spark turns into a flame sort of thing—is that it?"

"That part would be easy, doll. It's the other stuff I'm talkin' about, the stuff that hides out in the dark, the stuff that grabs you when you least expect it, that takes over your life and before ya know it you're grappling in hidden corners with it—with them—with everything that goes bump in the night. It's part of what makes bums like me look like heroes to other people, because I *do* step into those shadows, because some stupid part of me cares about innocent people who get hurt in this world. And as far as you and I are concerned? Look at me, lady, this Hollywood image of a private investigator—ha! one trench coat, a fedora and a .38. That's about all I own in this world, lady, that and some lousy memories about people I've lost because I dared to love 'em, because my crotch got in the way of my reason, and my heart got snuffed out along the way. I eat with this body, I talk with it, walk with it, have sex with it, breath, eat and drink and smoke with it—but love?" I stopped ranting and quieted my voice. I needed a drink. She stood there, frozen, her eyes glued to my face. "I'm not even sure I know *how* to love, Elena, I'm not even sure who that face is in the mirror anymore, the one I see in the morning when I get up and have to confront another divorce case, take Kodak pictures like a damn voyeur through a bedroom window at two lovers escaping into each other's arms who the law says aren't supposed to, or another runaway, or a murdered husband or wife, or a sinister bad guy that belongs in hell, but somehow escaped to haunt my life. I'm forty-five and stupid, lady, I wouldn't make you happy because I can't even make myself happy. Anyone who would wanna love me would have to pick the train up off the side of the tracks and put it back on the mainline, because it's wrecked and shattered inside, thrown to the four winds like autumn leaves that shred into a million pieces and are soon forgotten. Yeah...in the end, we...we all get forgotten..."

Elena had tears in her eyes. "I—I never heard a man talk like that in my life, Cable Denning." She took a deep breath, then came up to me and lightly kissed my cheek. "But I'm pretty good at righting wrecked trains, you know..." She said nothing more, but got into the idling car and away she went into oblivion. Or...so I thought.

I walked out of the parking lot of the *International Club* feeling like someone had just loved me somehow, and I felt something in my heart for Elena Sommers. I wasn't sure what it was, but it was forming inside me like a beautiful lily unfolding from a huge green leaf in the morning sunlight. And that lily would be pure white and glow in me like someone in love, maybe for the first time.

The Long Afterglow

I passed a newsstand in the shadow of the Los Angeles Times Building at 1st and Spring Streets and glanced at the headline. "SECOND DANCE HALL MURDER" the headline read. A week or so ago the first murder happened near the same dance hall, a place called *The Rendezvous Ballroom* on the peninsula of a tiny island called *Balboa* near Newport Beach. The killer had selected pretty women, somehow lured them into the ladies' room, knocked 'em loony, took off their skirt and choked them to death with it! Hmmm...talk about originality! Then my mind started thinking like a detective. First the killer wanted the victim to suspect that "he" was a "she" by luring them into a toilet booth and doing the dirty deed in the women's lounge. But why? What grudge did he have against dancers having fun out there to the sounds of the big bands? I'd have to keep my private dick's eye on this one. I loved the challenge of pitting my mind against a murderer's. One of us was bound to win—preferably me.

It might've been the last streetcar to Hollywood for the night. I boarded it and watched out the window as we passed by the deserted streets and busy garbage trucks. How are we forgiven our sins? What makes us who we become and if we're unhappy about it, what can we do to change it? I looked down the aisles. Three men on their way to work were reading the newspaper, two women clucked on about gossip and a lovely painted Asian lady-of-the-night sat quietly by herself. What was she thinking? Where was she headed? For home after a successful night with a few soldiers or sailors? One wonders.

This year, 1945, perhaps would one day be recognized as the most infamous year in human history. But maybe nobody cared. Life, such as it is, goes on. One thing for certain, there'd be a long afterglow to the detonation of the atomic bomb and its long-term consequences of nuclear radiation gone amuck. And no doubt some frickin' idiot would become insane with power and drop the damn thing on other populations sooner or later. Why can't man use atomic energy for peaceful and positive purposes? And even if he does one day, why did he begin with the destructive force of war? Ah, but then again, it's in his nature. Like chickens, there is an instinctive pecking order in humans, and who gets to play 'king-of-the-mountain' this year?

But maybe after all, Oppenheimer was right in his first belief, that he had arrived as a harbinger of chaos and destruction: *I am become Death, Destroyer of Worlds!* rang a bell inside me. Hell, someone's gotta do it, right? Maybe it was the instrument to eliminate excessive world populations. But as I said, the afterglow of the atomic radiation might wipe us all off the planet— and everything else organic with it except maybe turnips!

This year of 1945 had been a momentous one for me, too. It started with an old lady who had held out on some remote Pacific island, forgotten by humanity until she was found, brought to the mainland and died of white peoples' diseases within weeks. The year ended with Sophia Legende's suicide and a note that told me not to feel guilty, because she had been contemplating it for a long time.

In between those two events, I'm not exactly proud of all that happened. There was murder aboard the S.S. America caused by a female alien named Abbey Allison. That's how I met Nadia Skorkowsky. What a wonderful woman...intelligent, sophisticated, loving, great in bed and sang like a bird! But life is filled with strange twists and a real nut case who had escaped from an even nuttier joint appropriately called *Walnut House* eventually kidnapped Nadia. To escape, Nadia ended up killing the would-be assassin. But as life's ironies would have it, maybe a copycat murdered her at the end of the opera *Tosca* when Nadia jumped from the castle precipice onto a mattress of dagger-like spikes. I get the shivers when I think of it. To this day, no one knows who killed my little songbird. But I haven't stopped wondering. In the back of my head I suspected Abbey Allison, aka "Zitzy", a weird killer-type of extra-terrestrial. Nadia had punched out Abbey in my office one terrible night. We tossed her body in a garbage heap near the docks in Santa Monica. I knew she was indestructible. Now that I think about it, maybe I shoulda killed 'er. But that's not my style and I'm not sure Abbey was incapable of forgiveness—in any dimension. But she'd disappeared, too.

Time would tell. Things have a way of regurgitating, bubbling up from the past like painful memories.

Yeah, and I saw the so-called "Death Tower" in the middle of the desert near Alamogordo, New Mexico. I was hired to stop the development of the bomb. But once Roosevelt signed on, even Einstein couldn't stop him. Oppenheimer's henchmen had sentenced me and two women to death atop a wooden platform stacked with dynamite about to go off. We were rescued by an invisible dimension-changer, one *Erond Mantis Spiricus*, who said he preferred not to manifest into a physical being because to us humans he resembled a cross between a praying mantis and a potato bug! But there was a price he wanted to extract from me. In the end, it was more expensive than anyone dreamed it would be.

And then there was the strange "detour" adventure in Martinique in the Caribbean that began at a negro bar called *Zoot Mimby's* downtown and ended up as a ritual in a fiery volcano, sacrificing pretty white virgins to some unseen god called *Maybouya*. I had a brief but happy love affair with a good-looking schoolteacher there. Her name was *Letichia Moreau* and she was not only beautiful, but gutsy. I told her some day in the future I would want to settle in the quiet of an island paradise with one good woman by my side. But, hell, I thought, who am I kiddin'? I'm a city rat, born and bred.

During this time, I first met Sophia Legende. After the Martinique incidents came to a close, Sophia began to come into my life increasingly, and despite the fact that she had lived with my wonderful secretary—and occasional bed partner—Ida Latney, we found a getaway time and it was truly amazing and maybe I fell in love with Sophie a little. But Oscar Brandt and the German underground known as *Lichter Grabstätte* threatened my life unless I got Sophie pregnant so they could have the embryo of a half-alien—that was me—and a beautiful blonde, human woman. So it happened that way. Now I'm sorry, because I thought it changed everything between Sophie and me. But more than anything else, I think it changed her and started her on the course she took.

Added to the mix of a nutso year was the entrance of a beautiful Japanese woman who turned out to be a terrible murderous dragon woman, known to Japanese legend as *Kiyohime*. Unlike the murders of war where many innocents are killed, this creature-woman killed those who had gang-raped her and therefore to some, the victims got what they had comin' to them. I don't know. Murder is murder. Maybe sometimes you can't stop, you can't help it because the rage is so great.

So I'd lost a lot this year. Nadia and Sophie topped the list because each time I came close to love I lost it. But death has a way of changing the odds. But what did I *gain* through it all? Maybe after all, love is the whole thing. Even if you don't know how at first, one foot in front of the other and sooner or later you can love, maybe. I'm not sure. Whatever this life holds for someone looking over the rainbow, maybe it was like Judy Garland sang, maybe there was a hope that the stupidity and misery of everyday existence could be transcended: *"Someday I'll wish upon a star and wake up where the clouds are far behind me, where troubles melt like lemon drops away above the chimney tops—that's where you'll find me...!"* Yeah, me too, Judy, me too... **The End**

Acknowledgements

Cover images:

Atomic explosion: ©Can Stock Photo/solarseven
Vintage Woman w/cigarette: ©Can Stock Photo/prometeus
Cable Denning: Kenneth Cox Photography.

Original Cover Designs: Frances Walker-Moss
Editing and Research Consultant: Frances Walker-Moss